Highland Wolf

By Lynsay Sands

HIGHLAND WOLF
HIGHLAND TREASURE
HUNTING FOR A HIGHLANDER
THE WRONG HIGHLANDER
THE HIGHLANDER'S PROMISE
SURRENDER TO THE HIGHLANDER
FALLING FOR THE HIGHLANDER
THE HIGHLANDER TAKES A BRIDE
TO MARRY A SCOTTISH LAIRD
AN ENGLISH BRIDE IN SCOTLAND
THE HUSBAND HUNT
THE HEIRESS
THE COUNTESS
THE HELLION AND THE HIGHLANDER
TAMING THE HIGHLAND BRIDE
DEVIL OF THE HIGHLANDS

WHAT SHE WANTS
LOVE IS BLIND
MY FAVORITE THINGS
A LADY IN DISGUISE
BLISS
LADY PIRATE
ALWAYS
SWEET REVENGE
THE SWITCH
THE KEY
THE DEED

THE LOVING DAYLIGHTS

Lynsay Sands

Highland Wolf

AVONBOOKS

An Imprint of HarperCollinsPublishers

Excerpt from *Immortal Rising* copyright © 2022 by Lynsay Sands.

First Avon Books mass market printing: January 2022
First Avon Books hardcover printing: January 2022

Print Edition ISBN: 978-0-06-321242-8
Digital Edition ISBN: 978-0-06-285544-2

FIRST EDITION

22 23 24 25 26   LSC   10 9 8 7 6 5 4 3 2 1

Highland Wolf

Chapter 1

CLARAY WAS STANDING AT THE WINDOW, DEBATING THE MERITS of leaping to her death rather than marry Maldouen MacNaughton, when knocking at the door made her stiffen. The loud banging sounded like a death knell. It meant her time was up. They'd come to take her to the chapel.

Claray's fingers tightened briefly on the stone edging of the window, her body tensing in preparation of climbing up and casting herself out. But she could not do it. Father Cameron said that self-killing was a sin certain to land you in hell, and she was quite sure that ten or twenty years of hell on earth as MacNaughton's wife were better than an eternity in the true hell as one of Satan's handmaidens.

Shoulders sagging, Claray pressed her cheek to the cold stone and closed her eyes, silently sending up one last prayer. "Please God, if you can no' see yer way clear to saving me from this . . . at least make me death quick."

Another knock sounded, this one a much louder, more insistent pounding. Claray forced herself to straighten and walk to the door, brushing down the skirt of the pretty pale-blue gown she wore as she went. She wasn't surprised when she opened it to see her uncle Gilchrist framed by the two men he'd had guarding her door for the last three days since her arrival. She *was* a little surprised by the guilt that briefly flashed on his face though. It gave her a moment's hope, but even as she opened her mouth to plea that he not do this, Gilchrist Kerr raised a hand to silence her.

"'Tis sorry I am, niece. But I'm tired o' being looked down on as a lowlander and MacNaughton has promised MacFarlane to me do I see this through. Ye're marrying him and that's that."

Claray closed her mouth and gave a resigned nod, but couldn't resist saying, "Let us hope, then, that ye live a long time to enjoy it, uncle. For I fear yer decision will surely see ye in hell for eternity afterward."

Fear crossed his face at her words. It was closely followed by anger, and his hand clamped on her arm in a bruising grip. Dragging her out into the hall, he snapped, "Ye'll want to be watchin' that tongue o' yers with the MacNaughton, girl. Else ye'll be in hell ere me."

Claray raised her chin, staring straight ahead as he urged her up the hall toward the stairs. "Not I. Me conscience is clear. I may die first, but 'tis heaven where I'll land. Unlike you."

She'd known her words would anger him further, and wasn't surprised when his fingers tightened around her arm to the point she feared her bone would snap. But words were her only weapon now, and if what she'd said gave him more than a sleepless night or two between now and when he met his maker, it was something at least.

Claray tried to concentrate on that rather than the trials ahead as her uncle forced her down the stairs and out of the keep. The man was taller than her, his legs longer, but her uncle didn't make allowances for that as he pulled her across the bailey. He was moving at a fast clip that had her running to keep pace with him. Claray was concentrating so hard on keeping up that when he suddenly halted halfway to the church, she stumbled and would have fallen if not for that punishing grip on her arm.

For one moment hope rose within her that his conscience had pricked him and he'd had a change of heart. But when she glanced to his face, she saw that he was frowning toward the gate where a clatter and commotion had apparently caught his attention.

Hope dying in her chest, Claray turned her uninterested gaze that way to see three men on horseback crossing the drawbridge.

Guests arriving late to the wedding, she supposed unhappily, and shifted her attention toward the chapel where a large crowd of people awaited them. The witnesses to her doom were made up mostly of MacNaughton soldiers and a very few members of the Kerr clan. It seemed most did not wish to be a part of their laird's betrayal of his own niece.

"The Wolf," her uncle muttered with what sounded like confusion.

Claray glanced sharply back at her uncle to see the perplexed expression on his face and then surveyed the three men again. They were in the bailey now and riding straight for them at a canter rather than a walk, she noted, some of her disinterest falling away. They were all large, muscular warriors with long hair. But while the man in the lead had black hair, the one behind him had dark brown, and the last was fair. All three were good looking, if not outright handsome, she decided as they drew nearer.

Claray didn't have to ask who the Wolf was, or even which of the three men he might be. The warrior who went by the moniker "the Wolf" was a favorite subject of the troubadours of late. Every other song they sang was about him, praising his courage and prowess in battle as well as his handsome face and hair that was "black as sin." According to those songs, the Wolf was a warrior considered as intelligent and deadly as the wolf he was named for. But he was actually a lone wolf in those songs, because he spoke little and aligned himself with no particular clan, instead offering his sword arm for a price. He was a mercenary, but an honorable one. It was said he served only those with a just cause.

"What the devil is the Wolf doing here?" her uncle muttered now.

Claray suspected it was a rhetorical question so didn't bother to respond. Besides, she had no idea why the man was here, but she was grateful for it. Any delay to this forced wedding was appreciated, so she simply stood at her uncle's side, waiting for the men to reach them.

"Laird Kerr," the Wolf said in greeting as he reined in before them. He then reached into his plaid to retrieve a scroll. Holding it in hand with the seal covered, he let his gaze slide briefly over

Claray before turning his attention back to her uncle. "I understand your niece, Claray MacFarlane, is visiting. Is this her?"

"Aye," her uncle muttered distractedly, his gaze on the scroll.

Nodding, the Wolf leaned down, offering him the sealed message. Claray resisted the urge to rub the spot where her uncle's hand had gripped her so tightly when he released her to take the missive. Her upper arm was throbbing, but pride made her ignore it as she watched him break the seal and start to unroll the scroll.

Claray was actually holding her breath as she waited. Hope had reared in her again, this time that the missive might be from her cousin Aulay Buchanan. Perhaps this was his response to her cousin Mairin's plea for help on her behalf. She might yet be saved from the fate the MacNaughton would force on her. Distracted as she was, Claray was completely caught off guard when the Wolf suddenly scooped her up off her feet as he straightened in the saddle.

She heard her uncle's shout of protest over her own startled gasp, and then she was in the man's lap and he was turning his mount sharply and urging it into a run toward the gates.

Claray was so stunned by this turn of events she didn't even think to struggle. She did look back as she was carried out of the bailey though. She saw the two men who had arrived with the Wolf following hard on their heels, and beyond that, her uncle's red face as he began to bellow orders for the gate to be closed and the drawbridge raised. A quick look forward showed the men on the wall scrambling to follow his orders, but the gate was released one moment too late. The spiked bottom slammed into the ground behind the last horse rather than before them, and while the bridge started to rise as they rode across it, it was a slow process and had only risen perhaps two or three feet off the ground by the time they'd crossed it.

The Wolf's horse leapt off the tip without hesitation, and Claray instinctively closed her mouth to keep from biting off her tongue on landing. She was glad she had when they hit the hardpacked dirt with a bone-jarring jolt she felt in every inch of her body. Teeth grinding against the pain that shuddered through her on impact, Claray glanced back again to watch the other two men follow them off the bridge. She was more than a little surprised when the fair-haired warrior caught her eye and gave her a reassuring grin followed by a wink.

Flushing, Claray turned forward once more and tried to sort out what was happening and how she should feel about it. However, her thought processes weren't very clear just now. She'd had little to eat these last three days but what Mairin had managed to sneak to her that morning, and she hadn't slept at all. Instead, she'd spent that time alternately pacing as she tried to come up with a solution to her situation, or on her knees, praying to God for His intervention. She was exhausted, bewildered and, frankly, all her mind seemed capable of grasping at that moment was that this did seem to be an answer to her prayer. She would not be marrying Maldouen MacNaughton today.

Relief oozing through her, Claray let out the breath she'd been holding and allowed herself to relax in her captor's arms.

"She's sleeping."

Conall lifted his gaze from the lass cuddled against his chest and glanced to Roderick Sinclair, who had urged his horse up on his right. The man looked both surprised and amused at the woman's reaction to the situation she found herself in. Conall merely nodded and shifted his gaze back to the lass, but he was a little surprised himself.

Lady Claray MacFarlane had been asleep before they'd got a hundred feet from the drawbridge of Kerr's castle. Conall had been a bit befuddled by that at the time, and still was. He'd basically just kidnapped her. She had no idea who he was, yet hadn't struggled or even protested. Instead, the lass had curled up like a kitten in his lap and gone to sleep. He wasn't quite sure what to make of that and had fretted over it as they'd met up with his men and then galloped through the morning and afternoon, riding north at a hard pace that he'd only just slowed to a trot because the sun was starting to set.

Aside from the fact that the horses couldn't keep up that speed indefinitely, Conall wouldn't risk one of their mounts or men being injured by traveling at such a pace in the dark. They'd have to travel more slowly and with a great deal of care through the night. But they wouldn't stop. Despite the information in the scroll he'd given her uncle, Conall had no doubt Kerr would have sent men after them. Even if he didn't, certainly MacNaughton would. From all accounts the man was determined to marry the lass no matter that her father wouldn't agree to the match.

Conall didn't really understand the man's tenacity on this issue. The lass was bonnie enough, he acknowledged as his gaze slid over the waves of strawberry blond hair that framed her heart-shaped face. But she wasn't so bonnie it was worth going to war with your neighbors over.

"So ye told her who ye are while we were riding?" Payton asked with a surprise that Conall knew was born of the fact that it was hard to talk at the speed they'd been moving. The pounding hooves of so many horses and the rush of wind would have meant having to yell, not to mention taking the risk of biting your own tongue while you did it.

Conall hesitated, but then admitted, "I've told her naught."

A moment of silence followed his announcement as both men turned stunned gazes to Claray sleeping peacefully in his lap.

"But—" Payton began, and then paused and simply shook his head, apparently not having the words to express his amazement.

"She's slept quite a while," Roderick said suddenly, a touch of concern in his voice. "Is she ailing?"

Conall stiffened at the suggestion, his gaze moving over her face. She looked pale to him, with dark bruising under her eyes that suggested exhaustion. Concern now slithering through him, he shifted his mount's reins to the hand he'd wrapped around her to keep her on his horse, then used the back of his now free hand to feel her forehead. Much to his relief, she didn't feel overly warm. But his touch apparently stirred her from sleep. Her lids lifted slowly, long lashes sweeping upward to reveal eyes the blue of a spring morning, and then she blinked at him before abruptly sitting up to glance around.

"Are we stopping?" Her voice was soft and still husky with sleep as she took in their surroundings.

Conall opened his mouth, intending to say, "Nay," but what came out was, "Do ye need to, lass?" as he realized she might wish to relieve herself after so long in the saddle. Actually, he could do with a stop for the same reason.

Claray turned a shy smile to him, and nodded with obvious embarrassment. "'Tis the truth, Laird Wolf, I do."

Conall blinked at the name he'd battled under for the last twelve years, surprised that she knew even that much about who he was, but then shifted his gaze to survey the landscape around them. He'd come this way often and knew exactly where he was and what lay ahead. Lowering his eyes to her once more, he said, "There's a river no' far ahead if ye can wait just a few moments. But if yer need is urgent, we can just stop here."

Claray considered the trees bordering either side of the path they were on, and then peered over his shoulder and stiffened, her eyes widening.

It made Conall glance over his shoulder as well. He had no idea what had startled her so. The only thing behind them were his men. But then perhaps that was what had overset her. There had only been the three of them and her when they'd ridden out of Kerr. She'd been asleep by the time they'd met up with his warriors who had been waiting in the woods around Kerr while he, Payton and Roderick had ridden in to get a lay of the situation. In the end, they hadn't needed the men, so it was good he'd left them behind. He suspected an entire army riding up to the keep would have got an entirely different welcome than just he and his two friends had received.

Turning back to Claray, he raised his eyebrows in question. "Here or the river?"

"I can wait 'til we reach the river," she assured him quickly, and then managed a smile. "I'd like to splash some water on me face to help wake meself up ere I tend to other business."

Nodding, Conall tightened his arm around her and urged his horse to a gallop, leaving the others behind. Moments later he was reining in next to a river that was really just one step up from a babbling brook. Claray seemed pleased, however, and flashed him a smile before sliding under his arm to drop from his mount. She did it so quickly that Conall didn't get the chance to even attempt to help her down, and then he dismounted himself and headed into the woods on the other side of the clearing to water the dragon.

When he returned a couple moments later it was to find that the others had caught up. Roderick, Payton and Conall's first, Hamish, were waiting in the small clearing by his mount, while the rest of the men were gathering on the path beside it, some dismounting to wander into the woods on the opposite side of the trail to take care of their own business, others watching the horses.

"Where's Lady Claray?" Payton asked as Conall walked to his horse.

Conall nodded toward the trees she'd disappeared into as he mounted.

Payton's eyebrows rose slightly. "Ye let her go off into the woods by herself?"

Settling in the saddle, Conall glanced to him with surprise. "O' course I did. She's tending personal needs and would no' want an escort for that. Besides, 'tis no' as if she's like to get lost."

"Aye, but . . ." Payton grimaced, and then asked, "What if she tries to escape?"

The suggestion amazed him. "Why would she try to escape? We came to save her."

It was Roderick who said, "Mayhap. But ye said ye'd had no chance to explain, so she does no' ken that. She may flee out o' fear o' what ye plan to do with her."

Conall frowned at those words in Roderick's deep rumble. The man was not much for talking. Which was why when he did speak Conall, and anyone else who knew him, listened.

"She did no' seem afraid," Conall muttered, his eyes scouring the woods Claray had disappeared into. He was now worrying over the fact that she hadn't yet returned, and fretting over whether she hadn't burst into a run the moment she'd got out of sight and was even now trying to fight her way through the forest.

"Nay, she did no' seem afraid," Payton agreed, but sounded more troubled by the knowledge than relieved before asking worriedly, "Does that seem right to ye? I mean, ye did just scoop her up away from her uncle and ride off with her moments ere she was to marry another."

"She was to marry Maldouen MacNaughton," Conall reminded him grimly, still disgusted by the very idea. "The man's a lying, conniving, murdering bastard."

"But does she ken that?" Roderick asked.

"Probably no'," Payton answered for him. "All she probably kens is that he's handsome, wealthy and would marry her. And no doubt he's taken the trouble to be charming to her in the wooing." The warrior shook his head. "Meanwhile, ye carried her off with no explanation at all. Even were she no' taken in by his good looks and sweet lies, surely she must still be concerned about being kidnapped?"

"I did no' kidnap her," Conall growled. "Her own father sent me to rescue her."

"But she does no' ken that," Roderick reminded him.

A knot forming in his chest now, Conall turned to peer toward the woods again. He debated the issue in his head, and then cursed and dismounted. He had no desire to embarrass the lass by intruding on her privacy while she was relieving herself, but now he was concerned she might just be making a run for it. He wouldn't have explained that he was her betrothed—that had to remain a secret—but he could have explained that her father had sent him to fetch her back. That should have soothed her, he knew, and he berated himself for not doing so. Especially before letting her rush off.

Silently calling himself an idiot, he strode into the woods.

Chapter 2

CONALL HAD HOPED TO FIND CLARAY EITHER ON HER WAY back, or five or ten feet inside the tree line, squatting behind a large tree to tend her business. However, she wasn't five or ten feet in . . . or even twenty, and Conall was just about to shout for his men to come help him search when he spotted a splash of pale blue among the brown and green of the trees ahead.

Breath leaving him on a sigh of relief as he recognized the material of her gown, Conall moved slowly forward, just wanting to get close enough to assure himself it was her. Then he would turn his back and afford her the privacy she deserved, he told himself.

Several steps later, Conall was quite sure it was her, but now was a bit confused as to what she was doing. She wasn't squatting, though she was low to the ground. However, it looked to him as if she was on her knees and hunched slightly as if her stomach pained her. Forgetting his desire to allow her privacy, Conall hurried forward and found the trees suddenly disappearing on either side of him as he stepped out of the woods onto a six-foot strip of grassy verge that ran along the river. Turning his head to the right, he could see where the clearing started some twenty feet away. They weren't very far from it, he noted.

"There, there now. 'Tis over."

Conall shifted his gaze back to Claray at those murmured words. All he could see was her back, but there didn't appear to be anyone in front of her that she could be speaking to. In fact, she was kneeling at the river's edge. Was she comforting herself? Perhaps she'd been sick and was telling herself it was over?

"What is over?" he asked brusquely.

Claray glanced sharply over her shoulder, her eyes widening when she saw him behind her. "Oh, heaven's, m'laird, ye startled me."

As Conall mumbled an apology for giving her a fright, she stood and whirled to face him with a bunny in her hands. Its fur was wet, it wasn't moving and there were three long wounds on its side. Conall eyed it briefly, wondering how she'd killed it. She had no bow and arrow, so he supposed she'd used her sgian dubh to end the wee beastie's life. It was impressive, and he wasn't surprised if she was hungry after riding all day, but—

"Lass, I'm sure MacNaughton has sent his men chasing after us," he said solemnly. "We've no time to skin and cook a rabbit."

Claray's eyes widened with horror at his words, and she cuddled the bunny protectively to her chest. "Ye're no' skinning this bunny!"

Conall eyed her with uncertainty. "Then why did ye kill it, lass? 'Tis just wrong to kill a wee beastie ye do no' plan to eat."

"I did no' kill it!" she exclaimed, peering down at the furry creature with concern. "I washed the blood away . . . and 'tis no' dead, just wounded. I think a hawk or falcon must have tried to carry it away and dropped it or something o' the like. It has scratches on its side that could have been from talons."

Conall dropped his gaze back to the rabbit, grimacing slightly when he saw one of its long ears twitch. It was alive, and he had a bad feeling that she planned to—

"I'm going to take it with me. It will no' survive out here wounded as 'tis. It would be easy prey for the first fox or hawk that came along."

Conall had to clamp his lips together to keep in his instinctive protest. They were on the run. He had to get her back to the safety of MacFarlane and her father before MacNaughton's—and possibly even her uncle's—men caught up to them and tried to steal her back despite the scroll he'd handed to Gilchrist Kerr. It had been from her father, claiming something unexpected had occurred and he needed her back home, and the Wolf and his comrades were to escort her back at once.

The message had been MacFarlane's idea. For some reason the man had hoped it would save his daughter. Conall had thought it a foolish hope himself. After all, Kerr and MacNaughton had planned to force the lass into marriage without his approval or her agreement—why would they care that he wanted her home? However, the missive had come in handy for distracting Kerr long enough for him to snatch up the lass and ride off with her.

In truth, luck had been with them today. He'd been concerned that he was too late when he'd ridden in to see the gathering around the chapel. But then he'd spotted Kerr dragging a lass from the keep toward the church and he'd realized that the timing of his arrival had been perfect.

Now he could hardly believe how easy it had been and was worried his luck wouldn't hold. Conall wasn't really concerned about taking on MacNaughton's and Kerr's men. His warriors were some of the best sword arms in all of Scotland and even England, but he didn't like the idea of a battle erupting with the lass there. She could get hurt or even killed by a stray arrow or sword strike. He'd rather get her safely away without battle.

"We should get moving, Laird Wolf," Claray said suddenly. "As ye said, MacNaughton and me uncle may ha'e sent men after us. We've no time to dawdle."

Blinking his thoughts away, Conall glanced to Claray, amazed to see that she was already heading back into the woods the way he'd come, leaving him behind. The rabbit was still cradled to her chest.

Muttering under his breath, he followed quickly, catching up to her just a few feet inside the cover of the trees. He eyed her sideways for a moment, watching her fuss and coo at the rabbit, and then cleared his throat and said, "Lass, I ken ye've no idea who I am, or why I took ye with me, but—"

"O' course I do."

He eyed her sharply. "Ye do?"

"Aye." She didn't bother looking up from her bunny. "Ye're the Wolf, a brave and honorable warrior who fights only in battles whose cause ye believe in."

Conall grimaced at the description, recognizing it from those fool songs the troubadours had taken to singing about him.

"And God sent ye to save me," she added, and Conall nearly tripped over his own feet at the words.

"God?" he choked out.

"Aye. I prayed fer three days and nights fer Him to save me from MacNaughton, and He sent me you," she announced, and then asked, "Do ye have any scraps o' linen ye could spare, m'laird?"

"Linen?" he echoed, befuddled by the change in topic. "Nay. Why?"

"I really think 'twould be better to bind Brodie's wounds," she explained.

"Who is Brodie?" he asked, even more confused.

"The rabbit," she explained.

"Ye've named it?" he squawked with disbelief.

"Well, I can no' keep calling it bunny," she pointed out, and then muttered, "Mayhap one o' yer men have something I could use to bind him," and rushed ahead of him as they stepped out of the woods.

Conall followed more slowly, watching as she rushed to Roderick, Payton and Hamish. He wasn't terribly surprised by the men's reactions to her rescuing a wounded rabbit. All three looked taken aback at first, and then vaguely amused. But then Hamish reached into one of his saddlebags and retrieved a strip of linen big enough for the job. He even got down from his horse to help her with the task of binding the wounded rabbit.

Conall just shook his head. Hamish was always prepared. It was the reason he was his first. No matter what came up, the man usually had whatever was needed in any given situation: strips of linen for bandages, herbs for remedies and tinctures, spare strips of leather to mend damaged boots, a small whetstone to sharpen your sgian dubh, a sack of oats to make oatcakes on a hot rock around the fire . . . The man seemed to think of everything. He was also quick about his work and the pair were finished with their fussing over the rabbit by the time Conall reached his horse.

As he mounted, Conall listened to her ask Hamish his name, and then thank him for his aid. The man's gruff, slightly embarrassed response made him smile with amusement. None of them were used to the presence of ladies and his first was obviously uncomfortable with her appreciation. Or perhaps he was embarrassed at helping to mend a rabbit, Conall thought as he studiously avoided the questioning glances Roderick and Payton were giving him. They wanted to know if he'd explained who they were. But he hadn't, and was now more than a little annoyed that she hadn't given him the chance to.

"M'laird?"

Conall glanced down blankly to see that Claray had returned to his side and was now eyeing him with uncertainty.

"Do I ride with you again? Or did ye bring a mare fer me to—Oh!" she gasped with surprise when he leaned down to catch her under the arms and lift her up before him, rabbit and all.

Settling her in his lap again, he urged his mount to return to the trail before asking, "Can ye ride, then?"

"O' course. Horses like me," she assured him.

Conall dropped his gaze, trying to see her expression to determine whether she was teasing him or not. It seemed a nonsensical answer to him. But he could only see the top of her head, not her expression. Shrugging, he let the matter go and concentrated on the path ahead as they continued their journey.

The sun was barely peeking over the horizon now, daylight waning. If they traveled through the night at a slow but steady pace, and sped up to a trot during the day, they should reach MacFarlane in two or three more days. Once there, he would hand Claray over to her father and let him explain everything to the lass. He'd also recommend MacFarlane keep her at home until he was ready to come claim her. Conall had no desire to be rushing off to save her from the likes of MacNaughton at every turn, and it was her father's responsibility to keep her safe until they wed.

Conall was distracted from his thoughts by Claray fidgeting before him on the saddle. The lass was wriggling about like she had a squirrel up her skirts. She was also sighing over and over again, he noted.

"Lass," he began with concern.

"I got distracted by little Brodie and forgot to . . . er . . . tend to the business we stopped for," she blurted, interrupting him before he could ask what was wrong.

For some reason Conall's lips were sent twitching at the babbled confession. He had no idea why. He should be bloody annoyed. Instead, he was amused. But he flattened his lips out to hide his laughter when she glanced back anxiously.

"I realize ye must be angry, but—"

"I'm no' angry," he assured her solemnly, ending whatever else she would have said, and then he urged his horse quickly forward around the next bend and another to leave the men back a ways, before steering his mount to the edge of the trees. Conall had barely brought the animal to a halt before dismounting. He then lifted Claray to the ground and stepped back.

She turned and had hurried several steps away before suddenly stopping. Whirling, she rushed back to shove the rabbit at him. "Could you—? I can no' hold him and—"

Claray didn't finish. Conall had automatically taken the rabbit when she shoved it at him. The moment his hands closed around it, she broke off her explanation and hurried off into the woods.

Sighing, Conall stared down at the furry creature and then turned toward Roderick, Payton and Hamish as they caught up to him, the other men close behind.

"She got distracted with the rabbit at our last stop and did no' take care o' business," he growled when they raised their eyebrows in question.

The three men exchanged glances, and then Payton commented, "Well, let us hope she's no' distracted by another rabbit this time, then."

"Aye," Hamish agreed, looking sorely put upon at the thought.

Alarmed at the suggestion, Conall turned to glance to where Claray had disappeared into the woods.

"Have ye told her that her father sent us to fetch her?" Payton asked after several minutes had passed.

"Nay," Conall snapped, his gaze sliding from the woods to the bunny he held. He felt foolish and awkward standing there holding the damned thing. It wasn't full grown, too small to make a meal of, really, but it was soft and warm and trembling something fierce. Rabbits were not known to take stress well, and this one was obviously distressed. It would probably drop dead ere they reached MacFarlane, he thought, and hoped she didn't blame him for it.

"Ye do no' think she might be fleeing, then?" Payton asked after several more minutes had passed. When Conall glared at him for the suggestion, the younger man shrugged and pointed out, "She seems to be taking an inordinate amount o' time."

"Mayhap she's got herself lost," Hamish suggested.

"Here, take this and I'll go find her," Conall said with exasperation, crossing to Hamish to pass him the rabbit when the man reluctantly held out his hands. Turning on his heel then, he strode into the woods in search of his errant betrothed. It took him several minutes to find her. Or at least her blue-covered bottom sticking up into the air. The lass was on her knees in the grass, her head down near the ground as she poked a hand into the hollow of a tree, feeling about.

Conall halted abruptly at the sight and then gave his head a shake and strode forward. "What the devil are ye doing, lass? Ye'll ruin yer gown like that. Get up."

Claray's behind dropped at once to rest on her feet as her upper body rose and she glanced over her shoulder. She then turned to scoop up something and twisted to hold out her cupped hands and show him what she held. "Look what I found, Laird Wolf. Is he no' the sweetest thing?"

Conall paused next to her and peered down at the small ball of fine pale silver down in her hands. Recognizing what she was holding, he immediately closed his eyes and prayed for patience.

"He's so small I near to stepped on him ere I spotted him," Claray said now. "There was some red brown fur and a patch of blood near him. His poor mother must have been moving him to a new nest when she was attacked and carried off. I was just trying to find her nest to see if he had any little brothers and sisters left behind too. There appears to be a nest of grass and leaves in this hollow, but 'tis empty. It must be the old nest. I considered looking for the new one, but fear 'twould be impossible to find. It could be anywhere and we really do no' have the time to search properly, so I suppose we'll ha'e to leave them," she said sadly.

"And that one too," Conall growled.

"What?" she asked with surprise, raising a frown his way.

"'Tis vermin, lass," Conall said shortly. "Just drop it there and let us go."

"'Tis a stoat kit," Claray said, scowling right back.

"Aye. Vermin," he repeated with irritation.

"But 'tis just a babe, m'laird. It's only got one eye open yet, so 'tis no more than five weeks old. 'Twill die if left on its own," she protested.

"'Tis vermin," Conall said for the third time with exasperation. "Besides, stoats as young as that one can no' stay warm on their own. 'Twill probably die anyway."

"Oh, aye," she murmured, peering down at it with concern, and then much to his amazement, she tugged the top of her gown away from her chest and eased the small creature inside to nestle between her breasts. "That should help to keep him warm."

Conall gaped at her, so stunned he didn't even think to help her to rise when she then struggled back to her feet.

"We should probably go, m'laird. The MacNaughton's men could be on our trail," she reminded him as she headed away.

Conall stared after her briefly, and then gave his head a shake and hurried to follow.

"Wait. Lass, ye can no' . . ." His words died out when she paused and turned to smile at him, her head tilted in question. He had been going to insist she leave the stoat behind, but she looked so damned sweet . . . Giving in with a resigned sigh, he asked instead, "Did ye tend yer business ere ye found the wee beast, or do ye need another minute?"

"Oh." She flushed, but shook her head. "Nay. I'm fine, m'laird. I found the stoat after . . ." Rather than finish the statement, she waved vaguely back the way they'd come, but it was enough.

Conall could only be grateful. With the way things were going, had she not already accomplished the deed and yet needed to relieve herself, she'd probably stumble upon the nest with the rest of the orphaned stoats and insist on bringing them along too. The lass seemed to have a soft heart when it came to wee creatures. It was something he'd have to work on with her once he claimed her to bride, he supposed. But for now, Conall merely nodded solemnly, and took her arm to escort her out of the woods and straight to his horse.

He noted the questioning looks Payton, Roderick and Hamish were giving him, but ignored them as he mounted and then leaned down to lift Claray up before him. The moment he had her settled, Hamish moved up next to them to hand Claray her rabbit.

"Oh, thank you." She gave the man a beaming smile as she accepted the wee bunny and immediately cuddled it to her chest.

Conall considered mentioning the stoat inside her gown and to be careful not to crush it, but caught himself at the last moment and shook his head. Both critters would probably be dead ere they reached MacFarlane anyway, he thought, and urged his horse to move.

Chapter 3

CONALL EXPECTED CLARAY TO LEAN BACK INTO HIM AGAIN and go to sleep as she had for the first part of the journey, but she didn't. Instead, she sat up a bit, her head swinging one way and then the other in response to every sound in the woods they traveled through. He didn't know why she bothered—there was little to see. The sun was fully gone now, and night had blanketed the land, making the woods on either side of them nothing more than dark masses they were passing by. But her tension was making him tense in response and he finally pressed her head to his chest in a silent order to sleep.

She rested there for all of a heartbeat before popping back up to sit upright again.

Conall was about to verbally order her to sleep when she asked, "From whom was the message ye gave me uncle?"

Conall scowled down at the top of her head, but since she couldn't see it, in the end he just answered, "Yer da."

"Oh." She seemed to consider that briefly and then asked, "What did it say?"

"That ye were needed at home," Payton responded when Conall didn't.

"So, me da sent ye to save me?" she asked, her head turning to his fair-haired friend rather than Conall.

"Aye," Payton said, and then commented, "Ye seem surprised."

"I am," she admitted. "I thought ye'd come to fetch me in response to Mairin's message to our cousin Aulay Buchanan."

"Who's Mairin, lass?" Roderick asked.

"Lady Mairin Kerr, me cousin," she explained. "'Tis she I'd gone to Kerr to visit. Her mother, me mother's sister, passed this last month and Mairin is now the lady o' the castle. She wrote that she was a bit overwhelmed and would appreciate me advice and assistance for a bit as she settled into her new role. O' course I could no' refuse. I ken how hard 'tis to step into such a position at first. Especially while still grieving."

Conall frowned slightly as he recalled his uncle mentioning some four years ago that Claray's mother, Lady MacFarlane, had passed. He now supposed Claray had taken over her responsibilities as Lady of MacFarlane at the time just as her cousin was presently doing at Kerr.

"So ye'd gone to visit yer uncle Gilchrist and cousin Lady Mairin, and then the MacNaughton showed up to force yer uncle into allowing a wedding?" Hamish reasoned out. The three men were riding as close as they could to them to hear this conversation.

"Nay. Me uncle was conspiring with MacNaughton," she told them with some vexation. "'Twas all a grand plan. Me uncle was the one to suggest Mairin invite me down to assist her, and while she was, at first, grateful for the suggestion and rushed to invite me, once she thought about it, she realized how out o' character it was fer her father to even consider her troubles. Me uncle is a most selfish man as a rule," she explained, "and this just seemed too thoughtful and considerate to her. That was the first thing to trouble her."

"What was the second?" Payton asked with interest.

"She began to realize that there had been a lot o' messages arriving and being sent out of a sudden. Messages her father was most secretive about. That all made her suspicious enough that she decided she should get a look at them and she started searchin' her father's room while he was out and about his day."

Pausing her petting of the bunny, she turned her head to the right where Payton and Hamish were side by side, and told them, "That was very brave o' her. Me uncle is free with his fists when angry and would have been most irate to discover her riflin' through his personal papers."

"I see," Payton murmured, and Conall thought he spotted concern for the cousin crossing the man's face.

Apparently satisfied that he understood that her cousin's efforts were no small thing, Claray turned her attention back down to her bunny and continued, "Fortunately, Mairin found the messages he'd received quite quickly and managed to read them all, return them to where they belonged and slip out o' me uncle's room without bein' discovered."

"The messages were from MacNaughton?" Payton asked, although it wasn't really a question. They all knew they must be.

"Aye." The word came out on a long gust of air, and Conall saw her shake her head. "That man is evil," she informed them solemnly. "He had heard o' me aunt's passin', and 'twas he who suggested me uncle have Mairin invite me to help her in their time o' travail. He kenned I'd no' refuse."

"How did he ken that?" Payton asked with a frown. "Do ye know the man?"

Claray nodded with displeasure. "He's our neighbor, and used to be considered a friend of sorts. He kens the whole family."

"Oh," Payton murmured with a frown.

"Anyway," Claray continued, "once I reached Kerr, me uncle was to send fer him and he would come, bringin' his own priest. They would force me to marry him, and then the MacNaughton would see me whole family dead and me uncle could inherit MacFarlane and double his riches."

"What?"

Conall actually felt Claray give a start when all four of them bellowed that shocked word as one. She recovered quickly, however, and nodded to assure them what she said was true.

"Kill yer whole family?" Payton asked with dismay. "And yer uncle agreed to this?"

"O' course he did. He's a greedy fool," she said with irritation. "And stupid enough to believe MacNaughton would let him have MacFarlane."

"Ye do no' think he would?" Conall asked quietly. He was quite positive that would not have been the case had their plans not been disrupted by his stealing Claray away before MacNaughton could marry her, but was curious to hear her opinions on the matter.

"Oh, do be logical," she said, sounding exasperated. "I am no' some ravin' beauty a man would kill to gain."

Conall frowned at her words, not liking them, though he wasn't sure why. He'd thought the same thing on first seeing her. Before he could consider why her thinking so upset him though, she continued.

"Besides, once he'd forced the wedding, murderin' me family would ha'e been unnecessary if havin' me to wife was all he wanted," she pointed out, and then assured them, "MacNaughton wants MacFarlane fer himself and were the rest o' me family dead, I would certainly inherit, no' me uncle. He's no' a MacFarlane. He's only a relation through marriage to me aunt, who was me mother's sister and a Buchanan like her."

"But," Payton said, "as yer husband, MacNaughton could sign it over to yer uncle to keep him silent about—"

"About forcin' me to marry him and killin' me family, which would no' be necessary to gain me to wife if the forced wedding were already over?" she suggested dryly, cutting Payton off. "A forced wedding that me uncle helped to engineer so could hardly go cryin' to the king about?"

"Oh," Payton said with realization.

"Aye. Oh," Claray said unhappily, and shook her head. "MacNaughton does no' truly want me at all. 'Tis MacFarlane he wants, and had I thrown meself out o' the window o' the room they locked me in for three days, or simply refused to marry him, he would have forced one o' me sisters to marry him and killed the rest o' us anyway to get MacFarlane."

Conall was frowning over her words. He was wondering if she'd actually considered self-killing to avoid marriage to the MacNaughton when Hamish asked, "Why does he want MacFarlane so badly?"

"MacNaughton land is bordered by Loch Awe on one side, MacFarlane land on the other and Campbell land both above and below," she pointed out. "'Tis no doubt verra uncomfortable havin' the Campbells above and below like that. I suspect MacNaughton fears they may one day just wipe out MacNaughton altogether to make it one grand sweep o' Campbell land. No doubt he hopes that gainin' MacFarlane's land, soldiers and wealth would prevent that ever happening."

Conall bit back a smile at her words. She'd spoken his own thoughts aloud, and he was oddly proud of her for seeing the strategy in MacNaughton's plan. It was actually quite a good one.

"So ye think he planned to marry ye, kill yer father and siblings—and what? Just leave yer uncle to fester in his outrage at no' getting' MacFarlane as promised?" Payton asked, and then pointed out, "Surely he'd have to give MacFarlane to yer uncle to keep him from tellin' one and all that MacNaughton had killed yer family."

"No' if he killed him too," she pointed out, and told them, "Part o' the plan was fer me uncle to take me back to me father once the wedding was consummated, and tell him it was done and I was married to MacNaughton. Apparently, me uncle was then supposed to claim that the MacNaughton wished to come to some sort of conciliatory agreement for me sake. Once he'd eased me da's temper and got him to agree to see MacNaughton, Maldouen would come in and kill him and my siblings." She shrugged. "But I suspect he would have killed me uncle too. Or mayhap he would ha'e let me uncle have MacFarlane for a short while, and then kill me and me uncle later and force Mairin to marry him. That way he would add both MacFarlane and Kerr to his holdings, makin' him even stronger."

A moment of silence passed as they all considered that and then Roderick asked, "Did yer cousin say if the messages mentioned how MacNaughton planned to kill everyone?"

"Poison."

The word was almost a whisper, but it cut through Conall's soul like a knife, sharp and breathtakingly painful.

"MacNaughton thought 'twould be fittin' since 'tis how me betrothed was murdered some twenty-two years ago," Claray said quietly. "Then everyone in me life would have been taken from me the same way."

"Yer betrothed?" Payton asked sharply, his gaze shooting to Conall.

Claray nodded, her voice sad when she admitted, "Me betrothed, Bryson MacDonald, his parents, Bean and Giorsal MacDonald, and most o' their clan were all murdered by poison when I was but a couple o' months old. It was just the day after me parents left from a visit with them where they arranged and signed our betrothal." Sighing, she shook her head. "Apparently, me parents were only a day into their journey home to MacFarlane when a messenger caught them up with the news. They turned back and rode straight to MacKay." Breaking off from her story, she explained, "Ross MacKay was Giorsal's brother, Bryson's uncle, Bean's best friend and their nearest neighbor. The messenger had come from him."

"Why return?" Conall asked. He knew the real reason, but wondered what she'd been told.

"Me parents were friends with Giorsal and Bean as well as the MacKays. 'Tis why the betrothal was contracted. So, o' course, me father wished to help bury the bodies and find out who had murdered them. But they never did manage to sort it out." She sank back against his chest as if suddenly exhausted. "I ken me father still frets o'er it to this day and tries to sort out in his mind who may ha'e done it. He says Bean and Giorsal were wonderful people and deserve justice. Even now, all these years later, he can no' seem to let it go." She fell silent for a minute, and then added in a sad, husky voice, "I think 'tis why he's never arranged another betrothal for me. It would mean admittin' they are dead, and I think 'twould break his heart to do that."

Conall knew that Payton was glaring at him. His cousin, Payton MacKay, wanted him to tell her that he was Bryson

MacDonald, son of Bean and Giorsal MacDonald, nephew of Ross and Annabel MacKay, and her betrothed. But he wasn't going to do that. Few knew his true identity and she was not among that few for a reason. A reason that hadn't changed. Besides, she'd done enough talking. Her voice had grown husky and rough as she spoke. She needed rest and appeared to be doing that now, he noted as she shifted against his chest with a small sigh. The lass was sleeping and the realization made him smile. He liked that she trusted him so much. He also liked the way she cuddled into him as she did. He liked the heat of her body against his own too. And he liked her smell. Every time her hair whipped into his face, he got a whiff of wildflowers and spring rain. It made him want to duck his head and inhale her scent more fully, and when she sighed and shifted against him again, Conall did.

He lowered his head until his nose brushed against her hair, inhaled deeply and closed his eyes as her aroma overwhelmed him, sweet and fresh despite the hours of travel. He wanted to run his hands through her glorious hair and bury his face in the soft tresses while continually inhaling. However, the presence of the other men made that impossible and he reluctantly lifted his head and turned his gaze and attention to the path ahead as he tried to ignore the soft, sighing woman in his lap.

CLARAY DIDN'T REMEMBER FALLING ASLEEP, BUT IT WAS HER stomach that woke her up. Moaning at the ache in her belly, she opened weary eyes and blinked, then turned her face into the bed linens to hide from the sunlight assaulting her. Only it wasn't bed linens, she realized as what she'd thought was a bed bounced against her cheek and a chuckle struck her ears.

"Ye've done little but sleep since leavin' Kerr, yet do no' appear to much like the morning, lass," the Wolf said with gentle amusement.

Claray scowled at his teasing and pushed herself upright to glower at the man. Her voice husky, she assured him, "Actually, I do like the mornin' as a rule, but I did no' sleep or eat the entire time I was at Kerr. Apparently, it makes me tired and cranky."

Her words brought an immediate frown of concern to the man's face. "Ye've no' eaten fer four days?"

"Is that all it's been?" she asked wearily, her voice barely more than a whisper. Her throat was sore and dry and speaking actually hurt.

"Nay, I guess this may be the start o' the fifth day," he muttered, suddenly lifting his head to look around.

Claray grimaced at the claim, and then admitted, "Mairin managed to sneak me a small crust o' bread and a bit o' cheese while she was helping prepare me for the wedding the last mornin', so I have no' been completely without fer that long."

The words made her glance down at the dress she wore. It had actually been quite pretty when they'd presented it to her and made her put it on, but now it was wrinkled and dust covered from their journey. She supposed she shouldn't really care. After all, this was the dress she'd been meant to marry MacNaughton in. As such, she should probably wish to remove it and burn it at the first opportunity. But it seemed unfair to blame the dress for MacNaughton's intentions, she thought, and then shifted away from the Wolf with irritation when he began to dig about in his bag.

"Here."

An oatcake appeared before her face, and Claray's eyes widened with wonder. She was so hungry she simply leaned forward the few inches necessary and bit into it. Realizing what she was doing, she glanced up to the Wolf's startled face and took it from his hand as she began to chew the first bite.

Unfortunately, she hadn't had much to drink in the last four days either. A pitcher of watered-down mead had been brought to her room the first and third day, but that was it. Although several had been brought up on the fourth morning, the day of the wedding. It hadn't been watered down though. Claray suspected her uncle had hoped that the combination of strong mead and lack of food would make her more compliant. That suspicion had been enough to keep her from drinking more than one glass despite how parched she'd been. Now her mouth was so arid she couldn't even work up saliva. Not a good combination with hard, dry oatcakes, Claray realized as she tried to swallow and started to choke.

The next few minutes consisted of choking, coughing and desperately trying to catch her breath while the Wolf pounded her repeatedly on the back and tried to force liquid down her throat that she merely spewed everywhere as she coughed some more. When it finally ended, she was sagging against the poor man's wet plaid, her stomach still aching with hunger, her breath coming in raspy gasps and too weak to do more than moan when he asked if she was all right. It should have come as no surprise to anyone when her reaction to the Wolf draping a plaid over her and urging his horse to move again was to lapse back into a deep sleep that took her away from all her discomforts.

"How is she?"

Conall tucked his plaid back around Claray and met Roderick's concerned gaze with a grim one of his own. "Sleeping. She needs food and drink. I should ha'e thought o' that sooner."

"Ye could no' ken she had no' been fed or watered properly while at Kerr," Roderick said solemnly.

"Watered?" he asked with faint amusement. It was like the man was talking about a horse or dog.

Roderick just shrugged and said, "There's a clearing west o' here. We could set up camp for a bit. Let the horses rest while we hunt up some food for her."

"Or we could just cook the rabbit we have," he said dryly.

"I somehow do no' think she'd be happy with that," Roderick said with amusement.

Conall grunted in agreement, but found himself lifting the plaid again to check on her as he realized she hadn't even noticed that the bunny, Brodie, was missing. He'd removed it from her lap and passed it to Hamish when she'd fallen asleep the first time. The man had placed the creature in his saddlebag and assured him it would be perfectly happy there. Conall didn't really care other than he, for some reason, didn't want Claray upset. He definitely didn't want her choking again either. That little episode had scared ten years off his life, he was sure. Her face had gone past red to purple and she hadn't been able to catch her breath. It had been quite alarming. The way she had gone limp against him afterward hadn't done much to reassure him either. He couldn't tell if she'd fallen back to sleep or was in a faint, but despite the amount of sleeping she'd been doing since they'd ridden away from Kerr, she was still very pale and still had those black pouches under her eyes.

"So?"

Conall let the plaid drape back over Claray again and glanced to Roderick. "Aye. The clearing in the west. Lead the way," he said, and followed when the man pulled out ahead to do just that.

Chapter 4

CLARAY MURMURED SLEEPILY, SMILED AND CUDDLED INTO the warmth wrapped around her. Only to blink her eyes open with surprise when her shifting brought on a responding movement that saw her suddenly on her back with something heavy thrown across her legs and something else almost equally heavy across her chest just below her breasts. There was also a sleepy grumbling in her ear that blew the hair around her face. It was followed by a smacking of lips and a murmur of unintelligible words.

Despite all of this, it took a full moment for her to realize that the warmth wrapped around her was the Wolf. She'd been resting on top of his chest; however, her squirming around had made the man roll and now he was the one on top. Well, sort of, she acknowledged wryly. Really, he was on his side next to her. But his one arm and leg were cast over her and cuddling her close, while his lips were now . . . well, she wasn't sure what his lips were doing, though it felt like he was chewing lightly on her ear.

And why was that sending little arrows of heat and tingling through her body?

Claray had no idea, but it did seem to her that getting out from under the Wolf might be a good thing. Especially since she had a terrible need to relieve herself. Fortunately, that was the only discomfort she was experiencing at the moment.

This was the third time Claray had woken up since they'd stopped in what was the prettiest glade she'd ever seen. The first time it had been close to noon, and she'd barely opened her eyes before the Wolf was plying her with ale and mead. Enough to near drown her. Once he'd decided she'd had enough liquids, he'd then produced an entire pheasant for her.

Still warm and on the stick used to roast it over the fire, it had been bursting with the scent of fine seasonings and wild spices, and had honestly smelled like heaven. But despite how hungry she was, Claray couldn't eat pheasant. She didn't eat meat and hadn't for some time. Rescuing, mending and befriending a wee bird with a broken wing had made it impossible for her to eat the meat of flying creatures, and helping Edmund, the stable master at MacFarlane, mend a bull with a broken leg and then having it follow her everywhere like a dog had added beef to the list of things she wouldn't eat either. By the time Claray was fifteen years old, there wasn't any meat she could bring herself to consume. She'd explained this quietly to Conall and, much to her relief, while he'd looked surprised, he hadn't raised a fuss, and she'd then gone into the woods to find wild berries, mushrooms, wood sorrel and elderflower to munch on to ease her hunger. When she'd returned with her selection of foraged food, Conall had been waiting with a couple of oatcakes still warm from cooking on a stone by the fire. Thanking him gratefully, Claray had eaten her meal quickly, and then had curled up on the ground to rest while Conall and his men ate their meat.

Instead of just getting the few minutes' rest she'd expected, Conall had let her sleep through the day. Claray had woken again as the sun was setting to find the Wolf pressing another round of oatcakes and drink on her. This time he'd also offered her fish someone had caught in the river. Again, it had been seasoned and cooked over the fire. Fortunately, fish was something Claray had no issue eating. She'd never befriended a fish, so she'd gobbled up the food without hesitation. But much to her embarrassment, once finished eating, she'd again just curled up and fallen asleep.

Now, was the third time she was waking, and it appeared to be the crack of dawn. The sky was just starting to lighten, the darkness overhead turning a deep red that lightened to orange and then a thin streak of yellow as it reached the horizon, but there was no sign of the sun yet.

A glance around showed her that nearly a dozen fires had been built in the large and pretty glade for the men to sleep around. They were now reduced to embers, and the hundred or so men bedded down around them were still sleeping. There were also half a dozen or so men sitting or standing about, obviously standing guard over the others while they slept, but she had no idea where the rest of the men were. She was sure though that there were more somewhere. It had looked to her like at least two hundred men had been following them when she first woke up after leaving Kerr.

Claray turned her gaze to the Wolf again and bit her lip as she looked over his sleeping face. She'd thought that he was handsome the first time she'd seen him, but now, asleep and with the grimness missing from his face, he was more than handsome. He was perfect, with full, pouty lips, high cheekbones and a strong chin. Claray thought she could look at him for hours if she didn't really, really need to get up and relieve herself. The problem was how to slip out from under the Wolf without waking him.

After some consideration, it did seem the only thing for her to do was to slide to the side until his arm and leg were no longer on her. Taking a deep breath and holding it, she began her maneuver. It was a very slow process, and by the time she was free, Claray was in imminent danger of wetting herself, which would be most embarrassing. Desperate to avoid that, she lunged to her feet and made a dash for the woods, hopping and jumping over the bodies stretched out around the glade rather than taking the time to weave around them. She probably woke a man or two in her rush, and she certainly startled the men who had been left to guard the sleeping party, but much to her relief, none of them moved to stop or question her and simply watched wide-eyed as she fled into the woods.

Claray's need was so great that she didn't flee far. She went perhaps ten feet into the trees before stopping and squatting. She barely had time to make sure her skirts were out of the way before her body decided it had waited long enough and began to do what it wished. The reduction of pressure was such a distracting relief that it wasn't until she'd finished and straightened that she noticed the warm squirming going on between her breasts.

Glancing down, Claray stared blankly at the tiny furry face that suddenly poked out of the top of her gown. The baby stoat. Both its eyes were open now, which meant she'd been off a little on the age. It was probably closer to, or a little over, six weeks, she realized, and supposed she should have guessed that by its coloring and size. While its fur was mostly the soft silver down of a newborn stoat, there were hints of the red brown fur it would eventually have. As for the size, it looked to be a good four or five ounces in weight, which was twice what a five-week stoat would be, but perfect for a six-week-old stoat. It would probably double again in size the next week. Stoats did seem to grow quickly at this stage.

When the kit began to squeak in what sounded to her like complaint, Claray smiled faintly. She'd quite forgotten all about the baby stoat, and he could almost have been lecturing her on that. Or perhaps he was complaining that he was hungry, she thought as she realized that while she'd eaten and slept, it hadn't eaten since she'd slipped it into her gown the night before last. Not a good thing for such a young baby. The problem was, she had nothing to give it. At this age it might be able to eat meat, though they usually ate it raw, and it would still need milk at this stage, but she had none to give it.

Biting her lip, Claray petted the soft head of the small creature, and then gently pinched the loose fur at its neck. Much to her surprise, it immediately sprung back into place when she released it. That suggested it was well hydrated despite not having been fed for more than a day. Claray should have been relieved by that, but instead was just confused. She was also worried, for while she could give it bits of cooked meat when they next ate, she had no way to get it milk.

"Claray?"

Spinning on her heel, she watched the Wolf approach and was surprised to see concern on his face.

"Are ye all right?" he asked as he drew near. "Allistair said ye raced off in a hurry. He thought ye might be sick."

"Oh." Claray flushed and shook her head. Guessing that Allistair was one of the men who had been standing guard, she said, "Nay. I am fine. I just needed . . . a moment," she finished with embarrassment rather than describe what she'd been doing.

Much to her relief, the Wolf understood and nodded. His gaze then dropped to the stoat kit now climbing out of the top of her gown and scaling the material to reach her shoulder nearest to the Wolf. Once there, it sat up and squeaked at him most demandingly.

"He's probably hungry," Claray murmured, scooping up the small fellow. "But we have nothing for him."

"Aye, we ha'e milk." The Wolf turned on his heel and strode back the way he'd come, leaving her staring after him with surprise.

"Milk?" she asked finally, tripping after him before he got too far away.

He stopped to allow her to catch up. "We are on Dougall land, and there's a farm or two no' far from the glade. Yester morn after we stopped here, Hamish rode out to the nearer o' them and traded for some goat's milk fer little Squeak there."

"Squeak," Claray murmured, a smile tugging at her lips. "Ye named him?"

"Aye, well . . ." He grimaced, looking embarrassed, and then turned away to continue forward, growling, "I could hardly keep calling him vermin. That seemed to upset ye, so—" He shrugged as if it was of no consequence. "Ye can change the name do ye like."

"Oh, nay. Squeak is perfect," she assured him, beaming at his back as she hurried to catch up to him. "He does seem to squeak a lot. And it seems directed at you," she added as she noticed that Squeak had squirmed about in her hand until he could see the Wolf and was continuing to squeak at him in a most outraged manner.

The man slowed and glanced toward the wee kit to see that it was indeed squeaking in his direction, and she thought she saw his lips twitch, but his voice was gruff when he said, "Aye, well, he's probably demanding his breakfast, and since I was the one feeding him every few hours yesterday, he most like thinks 'tis me job now."

"Ye fed him?" Claray asked with amazement. It was just something she wouldn't have expected. In fact, she couldn't even picture the huge man feeding the wee creature. Squeak wasn't even as big around as his thumb. Though he did look like he would be longer than it.

"Ye were sleeping and there was no one else to do it," the Wolf muttered, and then as if he thought she might not believe that, he added, "Me men were busy setting up camp, gathering wood fer fires, hunting and cleaning their kill to cook food fer ye."

"Aye. I'm sure they were most busy," she said, lowering her head so that he wouldn't see the happy smile on her face. He'd fed Squeak. Purely for her, she knew, because he'd wanted nothing to do with what he considered vermin when she'd first found him, and it was just so sweet and kind and she didn't know what to say except, "Thank ye."

The Wolf grunted and then muttered, "Ye're welcome," and then took her arm to escort her back to camp.

Everyone was awake now and bustling around getting ready to leave. Claray knew the Wolf must be impatient with the delay that this whole day and night of rest had caused, so fully expected to be hustled to the horses and pulled up before the Wolf again so that they could set off. It was something of a surprise, therefore, when instead he settled her on a log and moved off to speak to Hamish before disappearing into the woods. She was even more surprised when Hamish then approached to present her with more cooked fish, a skin of ale and a much smaller skin of goat's milk for Squeak.

Thanking him, Claray set the square of linen holding the cooked fish on the log next to her, let Squeak climb back up her arm to her shoulder and then opened the skin of ale to drink from. She almost spat it all out on a laugh though when Squeak rushed along her

shoulder to her neck and then stretched to try to reach the skin
of ale at her lips, his little paws digging at her face. Deciding she
would wait until she fed Squeak, she closed the watered-down
ale and set it aside to turn her attention to the skin of goat's milk
instead. The problem was she had no clue how she was supposed
to feed it to Squeak.

Claray tried opening it and tipping it into Squeak's mouth, but
just ended up drenching the poor creature. She was considering
tearing a bit of cloth off of her gown and making some kind of
nipple with that for the wee beast when the Wolf returned. He
seemed to recognize her problem at once, and simply settled
down next to her, plucked the skin of milk and Squeak from her
hands and said, "Eat."

She did as instructed and picked up the fish, but rather than
eat, she watched with curiosity as the Wolf poured some milk
into his palm, and then set Squeak on his fingers. The wee kit
immediately crawled to the base of his fingers and began to lap
up the milk puddle.

"So simple," Claray muttered with self-disgust, and took her
first bite of fish, only to blink in surprise when she realized that it
was still warm, as if fresh from the fire. It was also still moist and
fresh tasting, not day-old meat. Blinking, she glanced at the Wolf
with confusion. "When did they—?"

"I set half the men to get up early to hunt and cook more meat
and fish so we could eat ere we left," he said, his attention on
pouring some more milk into his palm without knocking Squeak
off his perch.

"Oh." That explained where "the rest of the men" had been
when she'd got up that morning, and she wondered where they'd
gone to hunt and fish.

"There's another clearing no' far from here," the Wolf said as if
reading her mind. "I had them camp there so they'd no' disturb
everyone when they rose early, and so we'd no' disturb them
when they went to sleep early."

"Oh," Claray repeated, and then realizing she was just sitting
there staring at him, she gave herself a shake and quickly started

to eat. After a bite or two, she asked with curiosity, "How were ye able to get to Kerr so quickly?"

"We rode fast," he said, sounding distracted.

"I'm sure ye did, but I meant . . ." Claray hesitated, aligning her thoughts, and then said, "Mairin told me she sent her message to Buchanan because it was closer. How did me father and you both end up getting the news so quickly?"

"We were both at Buchanan when the messenger arrived," he said simply, easing his hand closer to his chest. It looked to her like a protective move. It placed his hand over his legs, giving Squeak a softer landing and shorter fall if he tumbled off his hand, Claray noted, but was more interested in what he'd said.

"Da was at Buchanan?" she asked, and couldn't hide her surprise. Her father hadn't mentioned making such a trip before she'd left for Kerr. "Why?"

"Because he kenned I was there," the Wolf answered, and then scowled as if just realizing what he'd said.

"Did he wish to hire ye fer something ere all this came up?" Claray asked, trying to understand.

The Wolf was silent for a minute, and then shrugged uncomfortably. "Who can say. The messenger arrived ere he'd more than dismounted, and then all was forgotten but getting ye away from yer uncle and MacNaughton."

It sounded perfectly reasonable, yet Claray got the feeling he wasn't being entirely truthful. Troubled over that, she glanced down to Squeak to see that he'd finished off the milk that had been poured for him. Claray started to offer a bit of her cooked fish to the kit, but the Wolf pulled the hand holding Squeak away from her and removed a small wrapped linen from his sporran with his free hand.

"Open it," he said, offering the linen to her.

Eyebrows rising, Claray set the fish aside and opened the linen to see little strips of cut up raw meat inside. The feel of something on her shoulder drew her head around and she nearly chuckled when she saw that the Wolf had set Squeak on her shoulder and he was now scrambling down her arm to reach the meat.

"Thank you," she said solemnly as she watched the wee kit throw itself at the food and begin gobbling it up. It looked like rabbit meat to her, and the thought made her suddenly sit up straight and turn to the Wolf with wide eyes as she realized she'd forgotten all about the bunny. "Brodie."

"With Allistair," he said soothingly. "He tends the horses when we travel and offered to look after the bunny fer ye while ye were under the weather. But I'll go get her fer ye now if ye wish."

"Her?" she asked uncertainly.

"Brodie is a she," he told her with amusement. "At least Allistair says she is, and since he kens more about animals than I ken about war, I'm believing him."

"Oh," Claray murmured.

He stood and moved off to speak to a tall, redheaded warrior who immediately unslid some sort of long sling of plaid cloth from around his neck and shoulder and offered it to the Wolf. She watched with curiosity as he carried it back to her, her gaze sliding over the contraption with interest.

"Allistair says Brodie likes to rest in the sling," the Wolf announced as he stopped before her. "He says 'tis warm and dark and makes her feel safe."

"Mayhap Squeak would like it in there too, then," Claray said, scooping Squeak up to hold him in her hands as she stood to allow the Wolf to settle the sling around her neck and one shoulder as Allistair had been wearing it. Unfortunately, she was much smaller than Allistair and while the bottom of the sling had rested just above the waist on him, it landed at the top of her thighs. She stood patiently as the Wolf began to fiddle with it.

"Or mayhap Squeak would eat Brodie," he said as he untied and then retied the sling to shorten it for her. "Stoats eat rabbits, ye ken."

"Aye, I ken that," she assured him. "But Squeak is just a bairn, and Brodie is so big."

"I once saw a stoat attack and kill a rabbit a good ten times its size, lass. They're fearsome hunters, and 'tis instinct with them. Ye may want to keep them out where ye can see them both when ye introduce them, rather than sticking them in a bag where Squeak might leap on Brodie and bite the back o' her neck, or Brodie might kick Squeak in the head out o' fear," he suggested, finishing with the knots and then stepping back.

"Thank ye," Claray murmured, and then eased Squeak back down the front of her dress to nestle between her breasts so that her hands were free for her to open the sling a bit and look in at Brodie. The rabbit seemed fine. Allistair had obviously taken good care of her and she seemed happy in the sling, so Claray let go of the sides and then glanced around. The Wolf had moved off to talk to Hamish, Roderick and Payton while she'd checked Brodie. She watched the men talk briefly, and then he returned to her.

"Have ye had enough to eat and drink?" he asked, and when she nodded, he raised his eyebrows. "Would ye like to make a quick trip into the woods ere we set out again?"

Claray opened her mouth to say no, and then snapped it closed as she had second thoughts. Both they and the horses had all had a very long rest and he'd most like want to travel at speed without stopping to make up for the delay she had cost them. It seemed smart to her to take this opportunity to relieve herself now rather than risk annoying him later, so she nodded solemnly and headed off into the woods.

Chapter 5

"*H*OW MANY MORE DAYS DO YE THINK IT'LL BE ERE WE REACH MacFarlane?"

Conall glanced around with surprise at that question from Roderick. They'd ridden hard through the day, but it was night again. They were back to traveling at a walk, and the man had urged his mount up beside his.

He considered the question, sorting out how far they had to go and the speed they could reasonably expect to manage to cover it. Had they continued to travel at a walk day and night as he'd originally planned after their first day traveling at speed, it would have been another couple of days to reach MacFarlane at least. But after letting the horses rest a day and night, and getting that rest themselves, they'd been able to travel at a gallop again through the day. They'd also taken a shortcut he hadn't originally planned to take because it had been available during daylight due to their delay. Had it been night, he never would have risked the track of land through the woods. But during daylight it had been no problem and they'd actually made up time so that they were a little closer than he'd expected to be at this point.

Realizing that Payton and Hamish had moved up to hear the answer to Roderick's question, and that they were all waiting, Conall finally shrugged. "Another day or day and a half, mayhap. With luck we'll arrive late tomorrow night or early the morning after," he answered, and then asked, "Why?"

"Well, we seem to ha'e collected a new animal for every day o' travel," he said, and then counted off, "The bunny, the stoat kit and the fox pup she found this morn." He raised his eyebrows, and pointed out, "That's three animals in three days."

Conall's mouth flattened out with displeasure at the accounting and he glanced down at the baby fox cradled in a sleeping Claray's arms. He was definitely regretting asking her if she'd needed to relieve herself again that morning before they'd left the glade where they'd rested. He had been ever since she'd returned from her trip to the woods carrying the new beastie—an abandoned fox pup whose mother, or some other creature, had chewed off both of its ears for some reason.

Conall had groaned aloud the moment he saw her step out of the woods carrying the furry little animal. One look at her charmed face as she'd cooed and cuddled the creature had told him he'd have a fight on his hands if he tried to make her leave it behind. Not wanting to upset her by making even an attempt to convince her, he'd simply mounted and waited silently as Hamish had supplied the salve and linens she'd needed to treat and bandage the injured pup's ears, as well as a strip of plaid that she'd wanted to swaddle it in.

Once satisfied that she'd done all she could for now, Claray had made her way to his side, smiling at him widely. Conall had silently lifted her up before him—bunny, stoat, fox and all—and set out without a word. Now he scowled at Roderick for reminding him that he was traveling with a growing menagerie of animals and growled, "So?"

"So, I was just wondering how many more animals we'll have with us ere the end o' this journey," he drawled, making Payton and Hamish chuckle.

Conall ignored them until the laughter faded away and Payton said, "I'd guess she'll add at least one more animal ere we arrive." He paused briefly and then said, "What I'm wondering is what it'll be."

It was Hamish who suggested, "I'm thinking mayhap a dormouse or a wounded pine marten."

"Nay," Payton said at once. "She went bunny, stoat, fox. Each one is more predatory than the last. I'm thinking the next'll be a wildcat."

"I'm betting on a wolf," Roderick announced.

Conall closed his eyes briefly, not liking any of the options. He didn't want another damned animal on his horse. He really needed to talk to Claray about this tendency she had to rescue every lame beastie she encountered. He—

His thoughts broke off as Squeak crawled out from the top of Claray's dress, climbed up her body to his and made his way to his shoulder where he sat down to chitter squeakily at him in demand.

Sighing, Conall shifted his reins to his teeth and dug out the linen-wrapped raw meat he'd tucked in his bag for this purpose. Retrieving a good-sized strip of meat, he set it on his shoulder next to Squeak and then rewrapped the linen.

Conall wasn't surprised that the kit had gobbled up the food before he'd finished packing the linen-wrapped meat away and retrieved the reins. He *was* surprised that Squeak didn't immediately return to his little safe spot inside Claray's dress though. Instead, the kit remained where he was on Conall's shoulder, his little head turning this way and that as he surveyed everything around them. For some reason it reminded him of Claray when she'd woken up the first night of this journey and that thought made him smile faintly.

"Ye're going to leave her at MacFarlane."

Conall glanced to Roderick with surprise at that comment. It was not a question, but he responded as if it were. "Aye. 'Tis where she belongs."

"Is it?" Roderick asked quietly.

Conall narrowed his eyes at what sounded almost like a reprimand to his ears. But all he said was, "It is until we marry."

"And when will that be?" Roderick asked with interest. When Conall didn't respond right away, he added, "I only ask because I'm quite sure that's why her da chased to Buchanan to see ye when he got wind Aulay had ye there discussing business. Ye ken the man is growing impatient to see the contract fulfilled and his daughter wed."

When Conall merely scowled at the possibility, he said, "She's two and twenty now, Bryson. Most lassies her age ha'e been married fer six or even eight years and ha'e half a dozen bairns hanging off their skirts."

Conall's mouth tightened. Not just at the mention of Claray's age and the bairns she should have had by now, but at Roderick's use of his true name. He *never* did that, and the fact that he had now made him glance around to see that Hamish had dropped back to talk to one of the soldiers. It didn't ease his tension any. Because while Campbell Sinclair, their friend, Roderick's cousin and a man who was like a brother to Conall himself, often forgot and used his birth name, Roderick never did. Which made Conall suspect he'd used it deliberately to emphasize his point. It didn't please him any more than the rest of what he'd said did.

Conall was very aware that had his life gone as it had been meant to, Claray too would be married already and have that handful of bairns Roderick mentioned. His bairns. For a moment he allowed himself to picture that in his mind. A smiling Claray with a babe in her arms, a toddler at her knee and three or four more playing on the floor around her as he walked into MacDonald keep and strode forward to greet her with a kiss and . . . tripped over the floor stones buckled from the tree trunks growing under them, then grabbed at one of the vines covering the walls to keep from falling.

He ground his teeth together as the true image of MacDonald imposed itself over the cozy scene he'd originally imagined. His childhood home was a shambles, uninhabitable. It had been bad when he'd first seen it at sixteen after ten years away, and would only be more so now. It was why he hadn't gone to claim Claray, his betrothed, and why he'd been working as a mercenary these last twelve years. To earn the coin needed to bring it back to its former glory.

"One more year and I'll ha'e made enough coin to make MacDonald habitable again," he said stiffly.

"Ye ha'e more than enough fer that now," Roderick said solemnly. "We both ken that."

"Aye," Conall admitted through gritted teeth, and then added defensively, "But I also need enough to hire the people to work it, and to feed and clothe everyone fer a year or two until the crops can support us."

"Lady Claray comes with a fine dower that should take care o' that," Roderick pointed out, not backing down.

"I'll no' use that," Conall said stubbornly. "MacDonald was healthy and well when the contract was drawn up. She was no' meant to have to use her dower to make a life."

"She was no' meant to still be unmarried this late in life either," Roderick responded sharply.

When Conall merely scowled and raised his chin belligerently, Roderick sighed and shook his head. After a moment, he asked, "Will ye at least tell her who ye are, then? So she kens her betrothed yet lives and will someday claim her and give her the children all lassies yearn for?"

Conall glowered at the suggestion. Claray hadn't said that she yearned for any of that. But she *had* sounded sad when she'd said she didn't think her father would ever replace her betrothed. She thought it was because Gannon MacFarlane couldn't admit his friends were dead, but the truth was that her father couldn't make a new betrothal because they were all still bound by the first. The betrothal between him and her.

Claray's father was one of a handful of people who knew who he really was and that he'd survived the murder attempt that had taken his parents' lives and nearly taken his own. The other people who knew included his uncle, the king, Artair Sinclair and Artair's son Campbell, as well as Roderick and Payton.

Conall suspected that many of his warriors had surmised who he was too, but not one of them had questioned him openly, and he'd never announced it to them. He wouldn't dare do that until he claimed MacDonald and his title as clan chief. Conall had had it drummed into his head at a young age that it was dangerous to reveal his true name to anyone. The people who were aware of his real identity only knew because they had to.

Artair and his son Campbell Sinclair knew because Conall's uncle, Ross MacKay, had sent him to live at Sinclair the night his parents died. It had been a desperate bid to keep his parents' murderer from knowing they had failed to kill him. His uncle had feared that if they knew he yet lived, they might try to finish what they'd started. Because of that worry, he hadn't dared to take Bryson into his home and raise him as he wanted. Instead, he had sent him to live and train at Sinclair under the name Conall. His uncle had hoped that changing his name would help hide his survival from the rest of the world. He'd told him that he'd chosen that name because it meant "strong as a wolf" and that he feared that was what he would have to be now to survive the loss of his parents and most of his clan as well as everything else life might throw at him in the future.

As for Payton, he knew not just because he was Ross MacKay's son, and Conall's cousin, or even because he was old enough to remember him where Payton's younger sisters weren't and thought they were without close family other than their female cousin, Joan. Payton knew because he had trained with Conall at Sinclair, along with Roderick. His uncle had thought it would be best for the other two boys to know so that they could watch Conall's back, and help guard against any attack should the murderer discover his existence. It was a job they had been given as boys, but willingly continued with as men.

The king knew because he had to be told to avoid the risk of his granting MacDonald to some other laird before Conall was able to claim it. And Gannon MacFarlane knew his true identity because his daughter was betrothed to Conall, and his uncle Ross hadn't wanted to risk the man arranging another betrothal for her thinking the one with his parents was null and void due to his apparent death.

Of course, MacFarlane had wanted to tell his daughter Claray the truth. That she was yet betrothed, but Conall had argued against it. He hadn't wanted her hopes to be raised only to come crashing down if something happened to him. Aside from the threat of the unknown murderer, there was the life he had lived since earning his spurs that had convinced him that was for the best. Being a mercenary was dangerous work. Conall had spent years neck-deep in bloody battle, a hairsbreadth away from his own death. He'd thought it would be kinder to keep the fact that he was alive a secret from Claray until he had made the coin he needed and could quit the deadly business. Just in case he didn't survive to come to claim her. He still believed that. This way, if he survived to collect and marry Claray, it would be a nice surprise. He hoped. If he didn't survive . . . Well, at least she wouldn't be disappointed or left grieving, since she already thought him dead.

"Ye can no' leave the lass untethered like this forever," Roderick said solemnly. "If nothing else, her father'll no' allow it. I suspect do ye no' claim her soon, Laird MacFarlane will go to the king to have the betrothal canceled."

Conall stiffened at those words, his heart skipping a beat. Mostly because he knew them to be true. In fact, he'd half expected MacFarlane to do just that for a couple of years now. The possibility had never bothered him before this. But then he hadn't met Claray yet. Now he had, and the idea of losing her was surprisingly alarming of a sudden.

Swallowing, he peered down at where she nestled against his chest, the swaddled fox pup in her arms. It was easy to imagine that it was a bairn in that swaddling rather than a baby fox. Their bairn. But even as he thought that, his last memory of his parents rose up in his mind. The two of them sitting at table. His father leaning to the side to kiss his mother. Then they pulled back to smile at each other . . . until confusion suddenly replaced his mother's smile. Her hand moved to her stomach and fisted as she cried out in pain. He remembered his father's concern when she'd suddenly slid to the floor. How he'd dropped to his knees to try to help her, and then he'd stiffened, pain filling his own face. In the next moment they'd both been convulsing on the floor . . . along with every other clan member at table that night.

Watching his parents die had been the absolute worst thing Conall had experienced in his life. He would never forget it. And he couldn't forget that the murderer had never been found. That they were still out there somewhere, and that it was just a matter of chance that he hadn't died with his parents. He'd been meant to. His dinner had been poisoned as well, but he hadn't eaten it. What if whoever had killed his parents all those years ago and tried to kill him still wanted him dead? How many would they kill this time to see their chore finished?

Much as he didn't want to lose Claray to her father canceling the betrothal, it would be better than watching her die as his parents had. In fact, perhaps it would be best if he told her father to go ahead and break the betrothal and find her another husband. Someone no one had tried to kill and might try to kill again. Someone she could be safe with.

He'd barely had the thought when a drop of cold water landed on his nose. Stiffening in the saddle, Conall lifted his gaze skyward, surprised to see that while he'd been distracted with his thoughts, clouds had moved in overhead—dark clouds heavy with rain that blocked the moonlight. Even as he made that discovery, the heavens opened up and began to pour water down on them.

Cursing, Conall lowered his head just in time to see Squeak scramble down his chest to Claray and rush back into the safety of her gown. Envying the little kit, Conall glanced toward Hamish. Before he could request the spare plaid he'd covered her with after her choking incident, the man had retrieved it and was handing it over.

Muttering a thank-you, Conall quickly shook it out and then swung it around his shoulders before drawing it around in front to cover both him and Claray. Once he was sure she was protected from the rain, he tugged the plaid up over his head so that only his eyes were left uncovered, and settled in for a miserable night.

"OH, DEAR." CLARAY LIFTED HER SKIRTS A BIT TO GET A LOOK AT her feet. She'd woken up a few moments ago to a beautiful sunny morning, a bunch of grumpy men and a terrible need to relieve herself. The Wolf had not been pleased at the need to stop. He'd not said so, but his grim expression as she'd passed him the fox pup and bunny sling before slipping from his mount, along with the sharp order he'd given her to "make it quick" as she'd rushed off into the woods, had made that clear.

Claray had been so overset by his abrupt attitude she'd been in something of a state and hadn't really paid attention to her surroundings. She'd simply rushed deep enough into the woods that she was sure she couldn't be seen by the men, taken care of business and then hurried back the way she'd come.

Unfortunately, she appeared to have got herself turned around somehow and had gone in the wrong direction. Claray had only realized that when she'd found herself trekking through a patch of boggy ground she was quite sure she hadn't passed through on the way out. However, she'd rushed quite a distance into the waterlogged area before the liquid had soaked through her shoes to tell her that she'd taken a wrong turn somewhere.

Claray had paused to actually take a good look at her surroundings. It was only then she'd realized that it must have rained at some point during the night, and quite heavily too from the looks of things. She was several feet distance into a large puddle that could have passed for a small shallow lake or pond if it weren't for the trees everywhere.

Not wanting to traipse any further into the puddle and find out how deep it might be, she'd started to turn, intending to head back the way she'd come, only to find that she appeared to be stuck. Now she peered down at where her feet had sunk into the mud to her ankles and wondered how it had happened so quickly.

Holding her skirts up to keep them safe from the mud, Claray put all her weight on her left foot and tried to pull her right foot out of the sucking muck. It was ridiculously hard to do, however. Her foot didn't seem to move at all, so she was grateful when she heard what she was quite sure was the Wolf calling her name.

"Here!" Claray shouted, so relieved that help was coming that she didn't even care if that help came in the form of a cranky man.

"Where?" he called, but his voice sounded closer.

Since she had no idea where she was, all Claray could respond with was another, "Here!"

"Aye, but where the hell is—? Oh."

Claray peered over her shoulder to see the Wolf staring at her from some ten feet away. His gaze was fixed on her lower legs with a sort of heated interest that made her look down. It was only then that she realized that she was holding her skirts rather high. They were actually halfway between her knees and her nether region, leaving an indecent amount of leg on view. Groaning, Claray quickly let them drop until they were just an inch above the mud and tried not to blush as she turned back to see him finally drag his gaze up to her face.

"I'd be guessing ye're stuck in the mire," he said after a moment, and started forward again.

"Aye," she murmured, glancing down at her feet to see that they, thankfully, had only sunk a little further into the mud since she'd realized she was stuck. "It appears to have rained while I was sleeping."

"Oh, aye, it rained," he assured her dryly. "Verra hard and for a verra long time. Our plaids kept the worse o' it off o' us, but the horses were no' as lucky. Aside from getting soaked, the storm made some o' them anxious. Unfortunately, there was no cover nearby or I would ha'e brought a halt to our journey until the storm ended."

He stopped next to her, grasped her by the waist and lifted upward, his eyes widening with surprise when nothing happened.

"Aye, ye really are stuck," he muttered, releasing her. The Wolf bent to grasp one ankle in both of his hands and instructed, "Try to lift yer leg as I pull. Hopefully between the two o' us, we can—" His words ended on a grunt of pain as her knee suddenly slammed up into his face. It wasn't deliberate. Claray had felt him start to pull as he spoke, and had followed his instructions by trying to yank her foot upward out of the muck. She'd put all of her effort into the pulling, and this time it had worked. Too well. While her shoe stayed, her foot was yanked out of it so abruptly that her knee slammed up into his nose.

The Wolf immediately jerked upright and a step back, leaving Claray swinging her arms wildly as she tried to balance unexpectedly on one foot.

Hearing her cry out as she lost the battle and started to tumble backward, he made a grab for her, stumbled over the foot that was still stuck in the mud and they both went crashing down into the puddle.

Chapter 6

CLARAY BREATHED OUT SLOWLY AND STARED UP AT THE TREES overhead, mentally checking for pain or injury from her fall, but there didn't appear to be any. The landing hadn't exactly been soft, but it hadn't been as bad as she'd anticipated when she'd realized there was no saving herself either. She hadn't had the wind knocked out of her, or hit her head on a stone or log hidden in the mud and knocked herself out. All in all, her fall hadn't been too bad . . . except for the mud squishing up around her back and sides, cold and wet and incredibly foul smelling.

She was grimacing over that when an irate squeaking caught her ear. Lifting her head out of the muck to look at her chest, Claray found herself nose to nose with Squeak. She'd forgotten that the baby stoat was sleeping, cuddled between her breasts. Apparently, the fall had woken the wee creature, and while he didn't appear to be hurt, he was definitely irate at being disturbed. At least that was what Claray was guessing from the way the little kit was squeaking away and trying to climb her face. On the other hand, she didn't speak stoat, so he could just as easily be exclaiming over her fall and checking to be sure she was all right.

Spitting sounds distracted her from the stoat, and Claray turned her head to look at the Wolf. The warrior had landed next to her, face-first in the mud. Now he'd pushed himself onto his elbows to get his face out of the muck. Claray bit her lip as she took in his mud-covered face and the way he was trying to purge more mud that had apparently gotten into his mouth.

Giving up the effort after a moment, he sighed unhappily and turned to look at her. His gaze traveled over her lying in the mud next to him, and then he said, "Well, that did no' go at all to plan."

When a startled laugh slipped from her lips at his words, Claray instinctively covered her mouth with her hand to silence it for fear of upsetting him. Unfortunately, her hand had landed in the mud and her action had slapped mud across her face and inside her own mouth. It tasted as disgusting as it smelled and Claray stared over her hand, wide-eyed with horror.

"Spit," he said at once, pulling her hand away from her mouth, and tugging on it as he added, "Come, roll on yer side and spit it out, lass. It's fair foul."

Desperate to remove the godawful taste, Claray did as he said and rolled toward him to spit as much of the muck out of her mouth as she could into the small open patch of mud between them. Very aware that ladies did not spit, she blushed as she did it, and ignored the angry tirade of chirps coming from Squeak as he scrambled up onto her side to avoid being dumped in the mud.

Much to her embarrassment, Claray was still spitting when Roderick, Payton and Hamish found them. Groaning at the humiliation of it all, she gave up her spitting and simply waited to see what new embarrassment would be visited on her.

As several more men poured out of the woods around them, Roderick announced, "We heard yer shout and Lady Claray's scream, and came to investigate."

"Aye." Payton's lips twitched, but he managed to keep a mostly solemn expression as he asked mildly, "Is there a reason the two o' ye are rolling about in the muck?"

"Shut it, MacKay, and give me a hand," the Wolf growled. "I swear I do no' ken why I've suffered yer presence fer so many years."

"Because I'm yer cousin and me da makes ye," Payton said with a laugh as he stepped to the edge of the lake of mud and extended his hand out to the Wolf.

Claray stared at the men with silent surprise. She'd heard the other men call the fair-haired man Payton. It was the only reason she'd known his first name. But now she'd been given his clan name and was a bit shocked by it. Payton MacKay.

Laird MacKay was a dear friend to her father and frequent visitor to MacFarlane. But while his wife and youngest daughter, Kenna, occasionally accompanied him on his visits, his older children, a son and married daughter, Annella, didn't. However, now that the name MacKay had been mentioned, she recalled that the son's name was Payton and knew he must be Laird Ross MacKay's son and heir. And the Wolf was apparently a cousin to him. Was he a MacKay, then, too? she wondered. The songs about him claimed he kept his clan name secret, and most assumed it was out of shame. But there was no shame to being a MacKay. They were a fine clan.

"Lass?"

Claray blinked her thoughts away and glanced to the Wolf. He was out of the muck and on his feet now. He was also standing where Payton had been a moment before, bent at the waist and his hand held out toward her.

"Can ye reach me hand?" he asked, leaning a little more forward.

Still on her right side in the mud, Claray extended her left hand toward him. The moment their fingers met, Squeak raced up her arm and across their hands to his arm, then charged up to his shoulder to watch what followed.

Claray grimaced at the stoat's defection and then almost groaned aloud as the Wolf began to pull. At first, her still-stuck foot prevented any movement and she briefly felt like she was on the rack. She was sure he would pull her arm right out of its socket. But then her foot popped free of her shoe and she was dragged forward through the mud. When the sloppy muck built up in front of her right shoulder as she went, she turned her head away to avoid it covering her face, but a moment later she was free and being lifted to her feet to stand barefoot in the grass in the middle of the four men.

"Well," Roderick said after a moment of silence had passed. "I'm thinking ye'll both want a bath ere traveling any further."

The Wolf frowned at the suggestion, and said, "We can bathe when we reach MacFarlane. The mud'll dry and fall off on the way."

"Aye," Payton agreed with a grimace. "But will the stench fall away with it? We still have another day and part o' a night at least ere we reach MacFarlane. I do no' ken about you, but I would no' be able to stand that smell fer an hour, let alone a day or two."

When the Wolf's shoulders sagged with defeat, Roderick said, "There's a river just a half an hour's ride from here. Hopefully, the worst o' the muck will dry and fall away by the time we get there and then the two o' ye can bathe away the rest."

"Aye," the Wolf said with resignation, and then took Claray's arm to escort her back to his horse, but the back of her gown was heavy and wet with mud, and her feet were bare. After half a dozen stumbling steps, he simply scooped her up into his arms. The moment he did, Squeak scrambled down his body to hers and disappeared inside her gown again. She felt him squirm around between her breasts, finding a comfy spot, and then glanced up to see Payton walking beside them, staring wide-eyed at where the stoat had disappeared.

Catching her eye he grinned. "I did wonder where ye kept him hidden all the time. Now I ken."

"Aye, now ye ken," the Wolf growled with irritation. "So ye can stop ogling the lass. She's betrothed to another."

Claray turned to him with surprise. "Nay. I'm no'. Remember? I told ye. I was betrothed to Bryson MacDonald, but he and his parents were murdered while I was still a bairn. I ha'e no betrothed now."

"See. She has no' betrothed now," Payton said cheerfully, and then confided to her, "Fortunately enough, m'lady, neither ha'e I. Mayhap we should get to know each other better and see if we would no' suit each other."

"Oh." Claray's eyes went wide and she could feel herself flushing with embarrassment as she tried to think what to say. Payton MacKay was a handsome man and seemed good-natured, but she hadn't even considered him as a betrothed ere his bringing it up. In truth, she hadn't thought about marrying anyone in years. She'd actually resigned herself to never getting wed and simply taking care of her father, younger siblings and MacFarlane until her dying days.

Fortunately, she didn't have to say anything in the end since the Wolf suddenly started to move much more swiftly, leaving the other man behind. She could have sworn she heard him growl as he did it too. But perhaps she'd imagined that, Claray decided as they reached his mount and he set her down while he climbed into the saddle and then pulled her up before him again. He was urging the mount to move before the other men had even caught up or mounted.

Much to Claray's relief, Roderick had been right and they reached a clearing on the edge of a river some thirty minutes later. She did not think she could have withstood their combined stench much longer. Truly, they both smelled so rank her stomach had heaved a time or two as they rode.

Claray expected the Wolf would dismount in the clearing and escort her to a private spot along the river and then leave her to bathe. He didn't. He reined in briefly in the clearing to bark orders, asked her to retrieve Squeak from her gown and then took him from her and passed the small stoat to Hamish along with the skin of milk and the linen-wrapped meat Squeak ate. The man, already burdened down with the bunny sling and the swaddled fox, accepted everything with a resigned expression, and then the Wolf urged his horse to move and steered him down to the river's edge before following it away from camp.

Claray remained silent and peered around with interest as they rode for another couple of minutes, and then the Wolf brought his mount to a halt again, dropped the reins, scooped up Claray and slid off of his horse with her in his arms. She expected him to set her down then, but instead he carried her to the river's edge and beyond. He was knee-deep in the water before she realized his intentions and began to protest.

"Nay, m'laird. Ye can no'—Ahhh!" she cried out, her arms tightening around his neck as she pulled herself up, curling around his head in an effort to escape the cold water when he dropped to sit down in it.

Laughing, he unlocked her arms from around his neck, and forced her to sit in his lap as the water rushed around them.

"Why?" she gasped with amazement, huddling close to the heat emanating from his chest as she shivered in his arms.

"Our clothes need a good cleaning too," he pointed out. "We may as well get the worst o' the mud off ere we bathe."

Claray merely shook her head at his reasoning, thinking it was madness. He obviously had no idea how heavy and hampering a gown was when wet. She'd be lucky if she did not drown in it. Although 'twas just as likely she would freeze to death first the water was so cold, she thought grimly.

"Whist! 'Twill warm quickly," he assured her, wrapping his arms around her and holding her close as her teeth began to chatter.

Claray just buried her face in his neck and waited for what he promised to happen. She was so distracted with the cold that it took her several minutes to notice that he was running his hands down her back, scraping away the worst of the muck into the water and letting the river carry it away. Unfortunately, while the mud had dried and flaked away from both their faces as they'd traveled here, that was all that had happened. Riding as they had with her muddy back to his muddy chest, it hadn't dried there on either of them, at least not where their bodies had met, and there was a good deal of it still coating her gown.

His chest too, she realized, glancing down between them. The mud was a good inch thick on his shirt and plaid and Claray grimaced as she realized she was getting it all over the front of her gown, pressing against him as she was.

Leaning back a little, she started to do for him what he was doing for her and began sweeping her hands over his shirt and plaid, scraping away great hunks of the smelly mud. They worked silently for several minutes until Claray became aware that the Wolf had gone still, his hands resting at her waist unmoving.

She glanced up with curiosity, and her eyes widened as she took in his expression. Confused by the heat and intensity in his eyes, Claray lowered her gaze to her hands and realized she had worked her way down his chest to his lower abdomen, shifting back in his lap as she went. Her fingers were now brushing perilously close to parts she had no business brushing.

Claray stilled, but then didn't know what to do and simply sat there staring at her immobile fingers. She stayed like that until one of his hands left her back and rose to her neck. When his fingers then glided into her hair to cup her head, Claray had the oddest urge to close her eyes and lean into the caress. Instead she met his gaze and watched as his face lowered toward hers.

Despite seeing it coming, the first brush of his lips across hers was startling. Claray closed her eyes as a frisson of awareness ran through her, and instinctively tipped her head up to make it easier for him as his lips moved over hers again. But she gasped with surprise when he nipped at her lower lip and then sucked it into his mouth briefly. It seemed the oddest thing to do, and yet it felt so nice, she thought faintly just before he let it slip from his mouth and ran his tongue along the seam of her lips.

Unsure what he was doing and if that was part of kissing, she started to pull back and opened her mouth to ask if it was, only to gasp as he followed and took advantage of her attempt to speak by slipping his tongue inside. Claray stilled again in shock as his tongue explored her in a way she'd never anticipated, and then a whole host of feelings she'd never before experienced rose up in her and she melted against him.

Heat and excitement were suddenly coursing through her, setting off little explosions everywhere their bodies met. Feeling off-kilter, Claray slid her hands up his chest to wrap them around his neck, needing something to hold on to. She felt the hand at her back urging her forward in his lap, and went willingly until she was plastered against his chest, but that just seemed to increase what she was experiencing. Her breasts suddenly felt heavy and tender where their chests pressed together, and heat was shivering through her body making her arch against him as his hand tilted her head to the angle he wanted and his mouth devoured hers.

When his free hand suddenly slid between them to cover a breast and knead the excited flesh through the cloth of her gown, she broke their kiss on a gasp, and threw her head back to suck air into suddenly starved lungs. Bereft of her mouth, the Wolf immediately trailed kisses down her throat and Claray shuddered and moaned, her fingers gliding into his hair to cup his head as this set off a whole new round of excitement and need inside of her.

She felt his hands tugging at the top of her gown, felt it loosen, and then he reached up to cup her head again, drawing it back down so that he could cover her mouth with his own once more. This time, Claray kissed back. Unsure what she was doing, she simply emulated his actions, allowing her tongue to tangle with his. It brought a growl from his throat that made her shiver, and then his kiss became hungrier and deeper, almost violent as his hands began moving, caressing her everywhere.

He kneaded her back, urging her flush against him again, then let his fingers slide over her arms, and her sides, before his hands suddenly clasped her waist and he lifted and turned her to straddle him. The moment he'd settled her there, his hands shifted down and around to clasp her bottom. He then squeezed her cheeks through her gown, his fingers meeting in the middle and brushing against her core through the cloth.

Claray gasped into his mouth at the touch and began to suck frantically on his tongue in response. When he released her bottom to tug at the top of her gown, dragging it off her shoulders, she let her hands drop to help him. The moment the wet cloth slid away to pool around her in the water, his hands claimed her breasts through the thin cloth of her shift.

Claray broke their kiss on a cry at the touch, her hands grasping his upper arms and then moving down to his wrists, urging him on. She looked down then to see that the thin linen of her shift had gone almost transparent. She could see the pink of her breasts and the darker rose of her nipples as his fingers squeezed the full globes and his thumbs ran back and forth over her hard, excited nipples.

Watching him touch her so intimately only added to Claray's excitement and she found herself shifting in his lap, mindlessly rubbing herself against the hardness she could feel beneath her. When the Wolf gasped in response and claimed her mouth again, she kissed him frantically back and continued to move against him until he suddenly released her breasts and rolled them in the water. Only his hand under her neck kept her head from being submerged.

Distracting her with kisses, the Wolf dragged her closer to shore until her head was out of the water and then broke their kiss to move upright. Kneeling with his legs on either side of her he then let his eyes slide over her, hot and hungry.

With her wet gown tangled around her waist and hips, Claray knew her upper body was as good as naked, her breasts visible through the thin, damp linen. Rather than being embarrassed, she found herself excited by his expression, and arched invitingly, her arms reaching for him in silent invitation. Claray wanted his kisses again. She wanted him touching and caressing her. She'd never experienced the excitement he was stirring in her ere this and she wanted more.

"Kiss me," she pleaded in a whisper when he continued to stare at her.

Much to her relief, he bent to cover her mouth with his again. This kiss was rough and demanding, increasing her excitement. It had her wrapping her arms around him again. He shifted to lie on her, his body pressing into hers everywhere. Despite that, she found herself digging her nails into his back, wanting him closer still, though she thought that was impossible.

When he ground against her through the bunched-up material of her gown, she cried out into his mouth and drew her knees up on either side of his hips to lift herself into the caress. She was almost mad with need, and didn't protest when she felt him tug her gown over her hips and push it down her legs.

When one hand clasped her behind and held her in place as he ground against her again, she wrapped her legs around him and groaned. The Wolf squeezed the cheek of her bottom almost painfully in response, and slid his hand between them to drag the hem of her shift up to her waist. When his hand then slid between her legs to touch her unimpeded by cloth, Claray froze in shock. Her legs instinctively tried to close, but his hips held them open and then his fingers began to move.

Continuing to kiss her, he rubbed and circled the center of her pleasure, driving the sudden anxiety out of her and replacing it with an excitement and need like none she'd ever known. Soon Claray found her heels digging into the river's sandy bottom, lifting her hips into the caress in a mindless search for something she didn't understand but knew was almost in reach. Her entire body grew taut and began a fine trembling, and she simply couldn't manage to return his kisses anymore. Instead, she simply kept her mouth open, accepting his kiss as her attention focused on what she sensed was coming. And then, just as she was sure she was about to find out what she was climbing toward, the Wolf withdrew his touch and she felt something probing her opening.

For Claray, it was like a bucket of cold water had been poured over her. Fear and dismay immediately pushed every other thought and sensation from her mind. Even as she felt something trying to push into her, she let her hips drop back to the riverbed, turned her head away to break their kiss and gasped an uncertain, "M'laird Wolf?"

He stopped at once and froze above her, his eyes wide with what looked like realization, and then he moaned and let his head drop to rest in the curve of her neck. They stayed like that for a moment, both breathing heavily, and then he pressed a kiss to her neck, pushed himself up off of her and strode out of the water, growling, "I'll leave ye alone to clean up."

Chapter 7

CLARAY LAY STILL FOR A MOMENT AS SHE LISTENED TO THE squelch of the Wolf's wet boots moving away, and then let her breath out slowly and sat up. Drawing her knees up to her chest, she wrapped her arms around her legs and lowered her head to rest on them briefly. Her body was still humming, but her mind was awash with confusion. She was both sorry he'd stopped and immeasurably grateful at the same time. She was also ashamed of herself for acting so wantonly with him. It wasn't how she'd been raised to behave and she'd never been so free with her body before. In fact, he was the first man to even kiss her.

Lifting her head, Claray pressed her fingers over her lips as she recalled those kisses. Just the memory was enough to make her body tingle and her nipples harden again, and she closed her eyes in shame over her body's response. According to Father Cameron, even a husband should not garner a response like that. Only sinners enjoyed such congress. Worse yet, not only had she enjoyed his kisses and caresses, but she had enjoyed them from a man whose name she did not even know, Claray realized with self-disgust. For while he went by the moniker "the Wolf," she knew that could not be his true name.

Groaning, she dug her fingers into her damp hair and grimaced when she felt the clumped-up mud caught in the strands on the back of her head. She definitely had some cleaning up to do.

Sighing, she started to rise, but stopped to grab up her gown where it floated next to her. Taking it with her, Claray then moved out into the river until she was knee-deep again. She wouldn't go any deeper; the water was moving quickly even at this shallow point and she wasn't sure it was safe to go out further. So she knelt in the water, noting as she did that it no longer felt cold to her. That was something at least, she thought as she set to work scrubbing the rest of the mud from her gown. It seemed to be coming out quickly and easily, Claray noted, and only wished she could wash away the memory of what had just happened from her mind as effortlessly.

"WELL, YE'RE HALF-CLEAN."

Conall ignored Payton's amused comment as he led his horse into the clearing and walked past him to take his mount to where Allistair was tending the other horses. He'd walked the beast back rather than ride him to give his body time to calm down. It wouldn't have done to return with his cock making a tent in his plaid. Which is what it had been doing when he'd left Claray. Fortunately, it had calmed down and deflated during the trek back. Unfortunately, his emotions hadn't calmed down along with it.

Conall's thoughts were in utter chaos at the moment. Half of his mind was recalling how sweet Claray had tasted when he kissed her. How her moans and mewls and gasps of pleasure had excited him. How her kisses, though inexpert at first, had quickly become as hungry and demanding as his own. How her nails had dug into the skin of his back and shoulders as she urged him on. And how her body had responded to his touch, her nipples pebbling, her body writhing and rising to meet his caresses. The feel of her warm slick excitement as he'd delved between her legs to caress her had almost driven him mad with the need to plunge into all that wet heat. He still wanted to.

But then her voice rang through his head. *M'laird Wolf?*

It was that name in a voice trembling with fear and uncertainty that had pierced through his eagerness to thrust into her. *M'laird Wolf.*

She didn't even know his damned name, which was bad enough, but the fear and uncertainty he'd heard in her voice had made Conall freeze, then pull back to look down at her. He'd found her staring back, the corner of her lower lip caught between her teeth, her eyes wide and full of trepidation in a pale face. It was then Conall had realized what he was doing and to whom. He'd tossed up her shift and been about to take her innocence there on the shore of the river like some lightskirt, and Claray was definitely no lightskirt.

Sighing, he ran a hand through his damp hair, and shook his head. He'd definitely lost his mind.

"Ye do ken the lower half o' yer plaid is still thick coated with mud, do ye no'?" Payton asked, apparently still following him.

"I'll go clean up properly after Claray finishes," Conall growled, wishing his cousin would leave him alone. He wasn't in the mood for Payton's teasing just now.

"Ye did no' leave her alone in the water, did ye?" Payton asked, sounding surprised and even concerned.

"She'll no' run away," he assured him, weary of the suggestion. "If she was going to do that she'd ha'e already made a run fer it. Besides, she kens her father sent us after her," he pointed out.

"Aye," Payton agreed, but now sounded annoyed rather than soothed. "But ye left her alone in a river where the currents are strong. No one should be left alone to swim here."

Conall stopped walking at once at those words. For one minute he just stood there, alarm coursing through him, and then Payton cursed and muttered, "I'll go keep an eye on the lass."

"The hell ye will!" Conall roared, turning to catch the man's arm and draw him to a halt. "Take me horse to Allistair and ask him to clean me saddle. Then see if Hamish has something fer her to wear while her gown dries. I'll go back and watch her."

Not waiting for a response, Conall then strode quickly back the way he'd come, his speed increasing with every step as he had visions of Claray getting caught in a current and dragged under and spat out downstream, pale and lifeless.

Christ, he'd lost his mind, Conall thought with self-disgust. He knew about the currents here and how dangerous they could be. Yet he'd walked away and left her there in the water on her own when she probably had no idea how dangerous it was to go too far out into the river here.

Conall was running by the time he hurried around the last bend before the spot where he'd left Claray. Spotting her in the water, he slowed and then stopped to simply stare at her. She was kneeling in the river, scrubbing her dress, the water reaching no higher than her waist despite being on her knees.

Sighing his relief, Conall hesitated, unsure what to do. He suspected she'd be uncomfortable if she knew he was there, but he didn't want to leave her alone. All was fine right now, but that could change quickly and he wanted to be near to hand to help if she needed it. After a moment to debate his options, he moved into the trees before continuing forward until he was apace with her. Stopping there, he leaned against a tree and watched silently as she worked.

Claray appeared to be muttering to herself as she scrubbed and he wondered to himself if she was berating herself for what had happened just as he had been doing before Payton had scared him into coming back. Or perhaps she was silently cursing his behavior, he thought unhappily. Now that her passion had waned, Claray no doubt was seeing how sorely he had treated her. A man didn't take advantage of an untried lass like that. Not if he had a lick of honor in him. Conall knew that and he was ashamed of himself. But it didn't stop him from wanting to do it all over again.

Shaking his head, he crossed his arms over his chest and watched as Claray suddenly surged to her feet and carried the dress to shore, wringing it out as she went. Apparently, she was done cleaning it, he decided when she stopped next to a large boulder, finished wringing out the gown and then spread it over the large stone before turning to walk back into the water.

Conall tensed with concern, but she didn't venture far. Claray was only knee-deep again when she stopped and lowered herself to sit in the water. She then reclined on her elbows until she could dip her head back into the river. Leaning on one elbow, she used her other hand to swish her hair around under the water, removing the mud that had caught in it when she'd fallen in the puddle.

It was about the sexiest thing Conall had ever seen. While her gown had hidden most of her as she'd carried it out of the water, and she'd turned away quickly after laying it over the boulder, there was nothing hiding her assets now. Her shift was as good as useless, the nearly transparent material clinging to her curves as her position thrust her breasts into the air. Her nipples were small pebbles peaking the cloth. They looked to be as hard as they had been when he'd caressed her and now he wondered if it had been him or the cold that had brought on that result earlier.

The snap of a branch drew his head around and he straightened as he spotted Payton approaching through the trees. His cousin was walking in his direction, but his eyes were locked on Claray with an interest and admiration Conall didn't care for at all.

"She's a beauty," Payton said in a hushed tone when he reached him, but still hadn't torn his eyes away from Claray.

Teeth grinding, Conall stepped between the other man and the river, blocking his view of Claray. Once Payton focused on him, he asked shortly, "Is that for her?"

Payton glanced down at the material he carried as if he'd forgotten he had it, and then nodded slowly. "Aye," he said, but didn't sound sure and his voice was a tad gruff. Giving his head a shake, he cleared his throat and then nodded again more firmly and held out the cloth. "Aye. Hamish sent a plaid, a shirt and a length o' rope fer her to use as a belt, but only a fresh plaid and no shirt fer you. He apologizes for that, but said 'twas the best he could do."

Conall grunted at the claim, knowing it was true. Hamish always did his best, and truth be told, he was surprised the man had been able to supply the shirt and two plaids. Most men didn't carry much with them on the trail. A sword, some oats and a sgian dubh was all many bothered with. Hamish was the exception, of course, but even he had his limits. Conall hadn't expected him to have a dress or anything.

"I guess I'll head back," Payton said once Conall had taken the items of cloth.

"Aye," he said dryly. "Tell the men to get ready to leave. We should no' be long."

Payton nodded, and turned to head away but then glanced toward Claray and paused to turn back. "If ye're no' going to claim her to wife, ye should break the contract and set her free to find someone who will appreciate her."

"Someone like you?" Conall suggested, his ire rising at the very thought of Payton or anyone else having the right to touch Claray the way he had.

"Mayhap," he said, and then turned to peer at her again. "As I told her, I'm no' betrothed. And it would be no hardship to fill her belly with a bairn or nine . . . Aye, no hardship at all," he said solemnly as Claray finished with her hair, stood up and turned to walk to shore again, her transparent linen shift clinging to her curves.

Her breasts were full and high, her hips curvy, and the triangle of curly strawberry blond hair at the juncture of her thighs was as visible as her dusky rose nipples.

Conall heard Payton move away, but didn't take his eyes off Claray. She was a sight to make a man's mouth water and his cock spring up, ready for action, and he was experiencing both right then. He wanted to taste those dusky nipples rather than just touch them, and he wanted to bury his face between her legs and sample her sweetness.

But he couldn't do either, he reminded himself firmly, and took a couple of deep breaths before heading out of the woods to give her the shirt and one of the plaids.

CLARAY PAUSED AT THE FOOT OF THE BOULDER AND STARED down at her gown with a small frown. She really had no desire to pull it back on. It would be cold and wet, difficult to don and uncomfortable to wear. The very idea was about as appealing as letting the blacksmith pull a tooth. But she didn't really have much choice. It was all she had to wear.

Sighing, she bent to pick it up.

"Ye can no' wear that. Ye'll catch a chill and sicken ere we got ye back to MacFarlane."

Claray gave a little start, and drew the dress to her chest to cover as much of herself as she could as she watched the Wolf approach.

He smiled crookedly at the action, and set the stack of material he held on the boulder where her dress had been a moment ago. "Hamish managed to find me a fresh plaid, and ye a plaid, a shirt and a length o' rope fer ye to fasten it. 'Tis no' perfect, but'll do until our clothes dry."

When she nodded and murmured a quiet, "Thank ye," the Wolf grunted and started to walk past her, but then stopped and swung back.

"Me friends call me Conall," he told her.

"Conall," Claray echoed, but he had turned away again to continue down to the water's edge. She stared after him, her eyes widening when his plaid suddenly dropped to pool around his feet. He then tugged his shirt off over his head, bent to grab up the heavy plaid and strode into the water carrying both.

Claray knew she should turn away, but couldn't seem to manage that as her eyes slid over his wide, muscular back and then down to the round curves of his derriere. They stopped there briefly before moving on to his strong thighs, and shapely calves. Claray had never thought she would call a man beautiful, but Conall was, and she found herself fascinated by the play of muscles in his back, buttocks and legs as he moved.

Claray continued to stare right up until he stopped walking and dropped to sit in the water. When he then slung his shirt over his shoulder and started working on cleaning his plaid, she let out a shaky breath and turned to the clothing on the boulder. The top plaid was a mix of blues, greens and reds, the lower one blues, reds and yellows. Claray took the top one, the shirt and the rope. She then tossed her wet gown over the boulder next to the remaining plaid before hurrying into the trees to dress.

She took a moment to briefly debate the merits of keeping her shift on, but it was wet and clinging to her uncomfortably, so in the end, she whipped it off and pulled the shirt quickly on in its place. Claray had no idea whose shirt it was, but it was huge on her, drooping off one shoulder, and the sleeves hanging well past her hands. Big as it was though, it didn't reach even to her knees. She felt terribly exposed in it and quickly set about pleating and donning the plaid. Once it was on, she adjusted it to be sure it reached past her ankles, and then straightened the pleats the best she could. She then considered herself, and frowned.

The shirt was much too large, of course, falling off her shoulders and threatening to slide off her arms if she let them hang at her sides. Aside from that, she didn't have a pin to finish wearing the great kilt the way the men did. That being the case, she gathered up the extra cloth hanging down the back and drew it over her head and pulled it around her like a shawl. She then caught the ends at the front, tied them together and slid that over her head to rest around the cloth at her neck.

Claray peered down at herself again, and then tugged and fussed at the cloth until she was sure she was covered decently. Deciding that would have to do until her gown dried, she turned to head back out of the trees only to freeze when her gaze landed on the Wolf.

Conall, she corrected herself silently as she stared at the man. He had apparently finished cleaning his clothes and set them on the boulder while she fussed with her plaid. Now he was done bathing too and was coming out of the river, his front as fully on display as his behind had been as he'd gone in.

Claray's eyes ran over his chest and arms, taking in his wide shoulders and bulging pecs, then cascaded down over his rippling stomach to—Gasping, she whirled abruptly away and covered her eyes as if she could erase what she'd just seen. Good heavens, that was really . . . a terribly undignified appendage, she thought with a shake of the head.

It wasn't the first time Claray had seen a male's fiddle. She had a little brother she'd helped bathe and care for as a bairn, so of course had seen his fiddle several times when he was young. She'd thought it funny looking then, but since men seemed so proud of the appendage, she'd assumed it grew some dignity as a male aged. It didn't. Frankly, she had no idea what they were so proud of.

"Are ye ready?"

Claray whirled around at Conall's grim voice, relieved and then confused when she saw that he was wearing the plaid she'd left on the boulder and was carrying her damp gown and shift along with his own wet clothes. It made her wonder how long she'd stood there thinking about his fiddle and fiddles in general, and then her gaze took him in and she frowned slightly. He'd pinned the excess plaid at his shoulders as men usually did, but those men usually had shirts on under it, and he didn't. It left a great expanse of his chest, shoulders and arms naked where the plaid didn't cover it.

For one brief moment, she considered offering him the shirt she wore, but while the plaid covered most of her at the top, the center between the sides gaped quite low, so she bit her lip on the offer and forced an uncomfortable smile and answered his question.

"Aye," she said finally.

He barely looked at her, merely nodded and took her arm to escort her back to where the men were waiting. He was obviously still disgusted with her, she supposed, and could not blame him. Her behavior had been most shaming. Even more shaming was the fact that his light touch on her arm was enough to bring about tingling there, and she wished he'd kiss her and do all those lovely things again that he'd been doing to her in the water.

Obviously, she was shameless, Claray decided. She would have to spend the next two or three weeks on her knees praying for God's forgiveness. And that was only if he didn't kiss or caress her again, for she knew without a doubt that if he did she would respond just as she had the first time and may not stop him then.

In which case, she would need to spend the rest of her life praying for her soul. Or maybe just her desires were enough that she was damning herself to hell by having them. In which case, she should probably just give it up and become a bride of God, because she was quite sure these thoughts would not stop so long as she was around Conall.

The thought made her sigh unhappily. Claray had never before even considered becoming a nun, but if it would save her soul . . . Of course, the fact that it would remove the problem of Maldouen MacNaughton from her life was an added bonus.

Although he could still cause problems for her sisters, she considered, and frowned over that. She would not like her sisters to find themselves in the same spot she had been in. But if she did take vows and become a nun, Claray was quite certain her father would finally agree to allowing her sisters to marry their betrothed would-be husbands. At least she hoped he would. Wanting her, as the oldest, to marry first was the only reason she had been able to come up with for why her father hadn't agreed to her younger sisters marrying already. Certainly Allissaid's would-be husband had requested the marriage take place twice now, but her father had apparently refused both times. And Annis's betrothed had visited just this past year, though Claray didn't know if he too had requested the marriage take place or not. Her father refused to speak of any of it to them. Not that she'd pressured him too much on the subject. The one time she'd asked if he intended to see to a new marriage contract for her since her betrothed was dead, he had reacted so poorly and been so short with her she'd never dared bring up the subject of marriage again. Not hers, and not her sisters'. But surely, if she took vows he would allow Allissaid and Annis to marry?

"Ye're sighing up a storm there, Lady Claray." Payton's teasing voice stirred her from her thoughts. "What are ye thinkin' on so hard?"

"Fleeing to a convent and taking vows," she admitted absently, her attention on the fact that they'd reached the clearing and the waiting men. Conall's fair-haired friend was standing just in front of the rest of the mounted party, holding the reins to both his horse and Conall's. It seemed they would leave right away.

"What?" Payton asked with amazement even as Conall roared it next to her.

Blinking, Claray glanced with confusion from one man to the other, and then realized what she'd said. She supposed her announcement would be a little surprising, but didn't understand this degree of dismay and what seemed to her to be outrage. It was not as if her decision really affected either of them.

Sighing, she waved them both off with a touch of annoyance, and pulled her arm free from Conall to approach Hamish where he sat his mount.

"Thank ye fer watching the wee beasties," she said solemnly.

"Me pleasure," the man responded, which she was quite sure was a polite lie, since he immediately leaned down to pass the swaddled fox pup to her. Even as he did, Squeak, who was sitting on his shoulder, rushed down his arm, across the swaddled fox and leapt onto Claray's shoulder instead.

Ignoring the way the small stoat was chittering at her as if giving her hell for abandoning him for so long, Claray smiled at Hamish, said, "Thank ye," again and then asked, "Do ye think I could ride with you from now on, good sir?"

Hamish froze in the act of unhooking the bunny sling from around his neck, and shifted wide, shocked eyes to her. Sounding almost horrified, the man asked, "Ride with me?" as if he thought he couldn't have heard her right.

"Aye. I—Oh!" Claray gasped when she was caught from behind and found herself lifted and dragged up to sit sideways in Conall's lap. It appeared he had mounted while she was taking the fox from Hamish. It also appeared he'd just given her the answer to her question.

"Keep the bunny with ye," Conall growled the order at Hamish, and then turned his mount and urged him past the others and out of the clearing.

Not given any other choice, Claray settled against Conall's chest with a dissatisfied huff and checked on the fox while Squeak climbed down to make himself comfortable inside her plaid.

"Why did ye ask to ride with Hamish?" Conall growled as she decided the baby fox was fine and let it sleep. "Do ye no' like riding with me?"

Claray debated making up something that would be less embarrassing to her, but felt her earlier behavior had already put her soul in jeopardy. Lying didn't seem the way to help save it. Humiliating as it was, she supposed she'd have to tell him the truth.

"I like riding with ye very much."

"Then why ask to ride with Hamish?"

"Because I like riding with ye very much," she repeated simply, and then her voice going husky, she admitted, "And I liked yer kisses and caresses in the river. I ken I responded most wantonly to them and have given ye a disgust o' me. I apologize fer that, m'laird, but much as I ken these feelings and desires and me own behavior will surely land me in hell, I can no' stop wanting ye, and would no doubt act the very same way did ye touch or kiss me like that again." She paused to take a breath after blurting that all out, and then added, "So it did seem better to ride with Hamish, who seems nice but does no' make me tingle with just a glance and threaten me soul with damnation by his very existence."

Chapter 8

CONALL'S MIND AND BODY WERE IN AN UPROAR. HE'D KNOWN by her responses that she'd enjoyed what they'd done, but hearing her admit it was having a most distressing effect on his body. And her confession that she wanted him and would respond exactly the same way if he were to kiss and caress her again . . . Well, God's teeth! It just made him want to kiss and caress her right then and there.

The thought made him glance down at her. She was sitting slumped in his lap, her head against his chest, leaving him a clear view down her body. Curled up a bit as she was, the front of the plaid had loosened and gaped open, revealing the linen shirt beneath. He could see her nipples pressing against the cloth, forming slight peaks, and his fingers itched to touch and pinch them.

"That is why I've decided to join the convent and take vows."

Conall stiffened as her words pierced his lusty thoughts. "Vows?"

"Aye. I shall become a bride of God. Hopefully, do I commit myself to Him and spend the rest o' me life doin' good works, He'll forgive me this flaw in me character."

"What o' yer betrothed?" he growled, outraged at the thought that she would throw their betrothal contract aside to join a convent.

"He's dead," she pointed out with a small sigh, and then shook her head. "I do wonder now if had he lived and married me . . . mayhap I never would have met you and found me soul in jeopardy. Certainly, no one else has ever made me feel like this."

Conall was just puffing up at those words when she added, "Although no one has ever kissed me before either. Mayhap 'tis a flaw in me and any man who kissed me would have made me feel this way. Perhaps I'm just lucky no one did ere this."

That comment took the wind from his sails and had him glowering down at her.

"I do no' think the MacNaughton would have had this effect though," she added thoughtfully. "The few times he's been to MacFarlane to approach me father about marrying me, I've found me skin crawling in his presence. I was most relieved when father said nay every time."

Conall's expression eased again at those words, and some of his irritation soothed, until she added, "Laird Payton seems nice though."

"Payton's no' a laird yet," he growled with irritation, finding he didn't like that she thought the other man nice.

"And he did mention that he too is no' betrothed and mayhap we should see if we would no' suit," she pointed out, apparently unconcerned that Payton wasn't a lord yet. "And he is handsome too."

Conall's hands tightened on the reins as he was suddenly plagued with the unusual desire to plow his fist into his cousin's "handsome" face.

"Mayhap I should ask him to kiss me."

"What?" Conall snapped.

"Well, mayhap 'tis only you who makes me all hot and bothered," she said, turning her head up to explain earnestly. "Mayhap Laird Payton's kisses would only affect me a little, or no' at all. If that were the case, then I could do two or three weeks o' penance fer me behavior and the way you make me feel. Then I could marry Payton and have bairns and a family like I used to dream about before I realized me da had no intention o' finding a replacement to me betrothed."

Conall felt his anger ease as he realized she was considering marrying Payton because she was hoping he *wouldn't* stir her the way he himself did. He tucked that bit of information away to consider later, but asked, "Ye dreamed o' marrying and having bairns, did ye?"

She smiled crookedly at the question. "Does no' every lass? 'Tis what we're trained fer from birth—to grow up, wed, have a family o' our own and run our own home."

Conall stared down into her face briefly and then couldn't resist claiming that sad smile with a kiss. Much to his pleasure, Claray didn't pull away, but responded at once, opening her mouth when he demanded entrance. The small moan she released into his mouth made him smile, and kiss her more deeply. After several moments he shifted his mount's reins to his left hand to free his right to caress her. His eager fingers went straight to her breast to knead briefly before focusing on her nipple.

Much to his satisfaction, Claray gasped and arched into the caress when he pinched and teased the sensitive tip as he'd wanted to do. Her response to his touch was most gratifying. Her kiss became frantic, and she squirmed in his lap, her bottom unintentionally rubbing against him in a most exciting manner.

Eager for the moans and mewls of pleasure he'd drawn from her in the river, Conall released her nipple and let his hand drift down over the swaddled fox and below to press between her legs through the plaid she wore.

When Claray immediately broke their kiss on a gasp, he pressed more firmly, then claimed her lips again and thrust his tongue into her mouth as he began to rub her through the heavy cloth, eliciting those groans and mewls he'd wanted.

She was so damned responsive to him it made him ache, and if it weren't for the fact that he had Payton, Roderick, Hamish and two hundred warriors at his back, he'd have ridden into the woods, dragged her to the ground, thrown up her skirts and sunk himself into her. As Payton had said, bedding her every night and filling her belly with a bairn or nine would be no hardship at all, and where before Conall had thought he wouldn't care if her father decided to break the betrothal and find her someone else to wed, the idea was now anathema to him. He wanted her for himself. He wanted to sink himself into her wet heat and stay there for a week. The only way to do that though was to claim and marry her. Oddly enough, that suddenly didn't seem a bad idea.

Claray's going stiff, crying out into his mouth and then convulsing slightly in his arms told him she'd found her release. He broke their kiss at once, retrieved his hand and wrapped it around her, pressing her to his chest. As she sagged there weakly, panting, he glanced over his shoulder.

Much to his relief, Roderick, Payton and Hamish were riding a good ten yards back with the rest of the men behind them and hadn't seen anything. Hardly able to believe he hadn't considered that ere this, he turned back to see that Claray was still leaning weakly against his chest, but she appeared to be regaining her breath.

Smiling faintly, he couldn't resist pressing a kiss to her forehead. When she blinked her eyes open and peered up at him solemnly, he found himself announcing, "Ye'll no' be marryin' Payton, or fleeing to a convent, lass."

Her eyes widened slightly. "Nay?"

"Nay. Because I'm goin' to have to marry ye."

She reacted as if he'd stabbed her in the bottom with his sgian dubh. Jerking upright, she gaped at him with wide eyes and gasped, "What?"

"Ye heard me. We're marryin'," he announced arrogantly.

"But ye—I can no' just—Me da—" she stammered, apparently unable to finish a complete thought.

Deciding to save her poor lust-addled mind the effort, he explained away any possible concern he thought she could have by saying, "While I have gone by the name Conall, or the Wolf, these last twenty-two years, I was born Bryson MacDonald. I'm yer betrothed, lass. Yer da kens it, and kens I did no' die. And 'tis time I claimed ye to wife." He then pressed her stunned face to his chest and ordered, "Now sleep. We've a ways to go ere we reach MacFarlane, and ye'll want to be well-rested fer the wedding."

CLARAY LAY STILL AGAINST CONALL'S CHEST FOR THE LONGEST time, his words echoing in her head. He was her betrothed, Bryson MacDonald. Her father knew it and also knew that he hadn't died. And he was claiming her to wife.

Her mind was having trouble accepting that information. She saw no reason for the man to lie. It wasn't like he was trying to run off with her and get her to marry him at some far-off keep amongst strangers. He said they were on the way to MacFarlane and her father knew who he was.

On the other hand, Claray found it hard to believe that her parents would have lied to her all these years either. They'd told her when she was . . . Well, she couldn't recall when she'd been told that a betrothal had been contracted after she was born, but that her betrothed had died shortly afterward and she was without. However, she'd known that for as far back as she could recall, so it must have been young.

She didn't know what to think . . . except that it would be better for her soul if he were lying. Because then her father would clear everything up and send the man on his way as the liar he was. But if he was telling the truth . . . Dear God, at this point, she would be on her knees for a month or more doing penance for the way he made her feel and what she'd let him do both by the river and just now. If she was forced to marry the man and suffer that kind of overwhelming, mind-numbing pleasure every single night . . .

Claray shivered at the thought. Part of her reaction was alarm for her poor soul. But a good portion of it had nothing to do with her soul, and everything to do with her body's response to the man. Just the thought of his kissing and touching her every night sent tingles racing through her body that had her wishing he'd kiss and caress her again.

"I'm going to hell," she muttered sadly.

"What's that, lass?" Conall asked.

Claray blinked her eyes open with dismay as she realized she'd spoken the thought aloud. She was even more dismayed to see Roderick riding beside them. Dear God, she'd forgotten all about the men. Had they been able to tell what was happening between her and Conall? Roderick hadn't been beside them then, had he? Dear God!

"Lass?" Conall nudged her with the arm at her back when she just gaped at Roderick. "What'd ye say?"

Claray finally lifted her gaze to his face, flushed with embarrassment and muttered, "Nothing," before quickly lowering her head again. She then closed her eyes and forced herself to relax against his chest, hoping he'd think she'd fallen asleep. He apparently believed it, because he didn't ask anything else. But it was a long time before her mind stopped wrestling with the problem that was Conall-the-Wolf-Bryson-MacDonald and the possibility that he might be her betrothed who would marry her and surely send her to hell with all the pleasure he would give her.

Eventually though she did drift off to sleep.

"She's asleep."

Conall glanced to Roderick with surprise at that comment, and then shifted his gaze down to Claray in the dying light of day and admitted, "I thought she'd fallen asleep ages ago."

Roderick shook his head. "I think that's what she wanted ye to think, but she was grimacin' and makin' faces fer quite a while. Must ha'e been frettin' on something."

Conall's eyebrows rose slightly at that, and he said, "I do no' ken why she'd be frettin'. I'd think her worries would be over now."

"Oh?" Roderick asked with interest. "And why would that be? MacNaughton is still a threat."

"No' once I marry her, and I told her that would happen once we reach MacFarlane," Conall admitted quietly.

Roderick's eyebrows rose at this news. "Ye told her yer true name, then?"

"Aye."

"And ye've decided to marry her now?" he asked.

Conall nodded.

"And return to MacDonald to rebuild and rule it?"

Conall nodded again, though less enthusiastically.

Roderick considered him briefly and then merely said, "'Tis about time. Hamish and the others'll be glad to hear it."

When Conall glanced at him sharply in question, Roderick shrugged. "They've battled fer ye fer many long years. Those with wives and wee ones yearn to return to MacDonald to live, and those without would build their own homes, and start their own families. The announcement that ye're finally givin' up mercenary work and claimin' yer heritage and theirs'll be a relief to them."

The words made him frown. Conall had started to work as a mercenary the moment he'd earned his spurs at sixteen. By eighteen he'd started gathering men to fight under him and begun contracting them out for jobs himself rather than work for others. They had been small jobs at first, but as the size of the men following him had grown, so had the jobs. Most of the warriors he'd gathered around him were MacDonald men whose families had been struck hard by the loss of their laird and lady, and had been forced to move to MacKay or other lands to find shelter and protection.

Some had struggled to continue on MacDonald land, but found themselves targets of bandits or attacks from other clans who knew they had no protection. With their crops and animals constantly stolen or destroyed, the younger men and even some of those older than Conall had turned to mercenary work to survive. He'd hired on every one he got wind of and added them to his ranks, training and paying them well to work with him.

Conall had never told them that he was Bryson MacDonald, son of their murdered laird and lady, and heir to MacDonald, but he wouldn't be surprised to learn that most knew or at least suspected as much. Campbell's slipping up and calling him Bryson in front of them more than a time or two had helped with that. But Conall knew he looked a lot like his father, and had noted an older soldier or two squinting at him with a certain look of recognition. No one had said anything though. At least not to him.

Aside from that though, Conall had never considered how his men felt about the life they'd all been forced to live—constantly battling for coin, spending months and sometimes longer away in battle with only very short visits with their families and loved ones between. Most of their families were sheltering with in-laws in their homes on lands other than MacDonald, he knew. But Conall's main concern had been earning the coin needed to return MacDonald to its former glory and support everyone for a year or two until the fields were producing and would support his people.

At least, that's what he'd told himself. Although if Conall were to be honest, he had enough for that now. Perhaps even more than enough, yet he'd intended to work another year or two. And the hell of it was, he couldn't say why. Conall had no idea why he was so reluctant to claim his inheritance, and rebuild and rule MacDonald. He would have to do it now though, if he married Claray.

His gaze dropped to where she lay curled in his lap, the fox pup in her arms, and Squeak, who had climbed out from the plaid she wore, now sitting on her chest peering around. When he'd set out for her uncle's to save her from the forced marriage Gilchrist Kerr and Maldouen MacNaughton had planned, she had been nothing more than a stranger. A name he'd heard repeatedly over the years, but not more than that. He hadn't even known what she looked like. All the meetings her father had arranged to try to find out when he would claim her had taken place with his uncle at MacKay and without her present.

Conall had known that his dragging his feet was annoying her father, that Gannon MacFarlane was losing patience and ready to break the contract and find her another husband. He hadn't really cared ere this. But that was before he'd tasted her passion by the river. And the moment she'd said she would join a convent or possibly marry Payton if his cousin's kisses didn't stir in her what his did . . .

Just the memory of her saying that made him grind his teeth. There was no way on God's earth that he would allow her to marry his cousin. It would mean the end of their relationship. Conall wouldn't dare risk being around the lass again after what happened at the river if she married Payton. That little episode had raised a thirst for her in him that was hard to ignore. Her being married to his cousin would not slake that thirst. If she were married to Payton, he'd have to avoid them both to avoid betraying his family and his own code of honor.

As for her going to a convent and becoming a nun, that would be a crime against God himself. Claray had not been made to spend her life on her knees in prayer. The lass had too much passion in her for that. So, he would marry her, reclaim his name, title and home and set to work filling her belly with bairns.

The thought made him smile, and imagining all the ways to accomplish the task of filling her belly, all the positions and places he could do so, helped pass the time as they continued their ride through the long day and the evening that followed.

Chapter 9

$\mathcal{I}$T WAS THE LOUD HOLLOW CLOP OF HORSE HOOVES ON THE drawbridge that woke Claray. Opening sleepy eyes, she peered around with confusion, slow to understand the shapes surrounding her. It was late. She had no idea what time, but the light of several fires lit up the night. Claray recognized the familiar curtain wall of MacFarlane stretching away into the distance, and noted the crowds of soldiers gathered around fires in front of its moat.

Eyes widening, she glanced over Conall's shoulder and saw that while Roderick, Payton and Hamish were following them, the rest of the warriors were now breaking off to join the soldiers already surrounding her home. No doubt they would build their own fires as they set up camp.

"It seems me da has company," she murmured, shifting to face forward as they rode under the barbican.

"The Buchanans," Conall announced even as she got her first glimpse of the bailey and the mass of men there. She'd thought there were a lot of soldiers outside the walls, but there were nearly as many inside. The light was better here, or perhaps her eyes had merely adjusted. Whatever the case, she could see that not everyone was on their feet or even awake. Their arrival had obviously roused the castle from sleep, and while some had risen in case trouble followed them, others were still attempting to get their rest.

MacNaughton would be a fool to try to take on so many warriors, she thought, and glanced toward the keep in time to see three men come out and start down the stairs. They were all tall, but while her father was gray-haired and barrel-chested, the other two men were younger. Both had longer, dark hair and were leaner, with the upper arms and chests of men who spent long hours swinging heavy great swords.

"Aulay and Alick Buchanan," Conall murmured.

"Nay," Claray said with disbelief as she took in the two men with her father. She recognized Aulay, of course—he looked much the same as the last time she'd seen him—but . . . "That can no' be Alick. The last time I saw him he was still mostly a gawky youth, lanky and all feet."

Conall chuckled softly at the description, and then asked, "And when was that, lass?"

Claray had to stop and think before saying, "At the celebration of Aulay's marriage to Jetta. They'd had a quiet wedding with just their sister and the brothers and their spouses, but held a larger celebration fer the rest o' the family a week later."

"That was more than four years ago," he pointed out with amusement.

"Was it?" she asked with surprise, and then nodded slowly. "Aye. I suppose it was. Me mother was still alive then. She was no' feelin' well at the time, but insisted on goin' anyway."

"Yer mother was their father's sister?" Conall asked.

Claray nodded. "Aye. She was the second o' six Buchanan daughters born after me uncle Odart, Aulay and Alick's father. And then there was Uncle Acair, o' course. He was the youngest o' the brood."

She couldn't tell from Conall's grunt whether this was news to him or not, and found herself adding, "Mother said they were all very close while growin' up, but she and Uncle Odart's wife, Aunt Seona, got on very well and became the best o' friends. Fortunately, Da liked Uncle Odart too, and we tended to visit back and forth a lot. MacFarlane is on the northern border o' Buchanan, so close as can be for travelin'," she pointed out, and then added, "'Tis the only reason me da agreed to attend the weddin' celebration. Mother was sick at the time, ye see," she explained, lest he think anything untoward about her father. "She was coughin' and wheezin' a bit with a lung complaint and we were worried about her travelin', but she insisted. Mother was most fond o' me cousins. Aulay especially. She was glad he'd found a love match."

Claray paused briefly, and then added sadly, "It was the last celebration she was able to attend. She grew too sick and weak after that. By the followin' summer the lung complaint had taken her from us."

"I was sorry to hear o' yer mother's passin', lass," Conall said quietly. "From all I've heard, she was a fine woman."

Before Claray could respond, they were stopping at the foot of the keep stairs and she was grasped by the waist and dragged out of Conall's lap.

"Alick!" she squawked on a laugh when she realized who had grabbed her. If she hadn't been holding the fox pup, she'd have smacked her cousin in the chest for his handling of her when he swung her around in a small circle.

"Look at ye, Claray. Ye're all grown," he said, grinning from cheek to cheek.

"Aye, well, so are you, cousin," she replied, and couldn't hold back her own grin. She and Alick were the same age and she'd always had a soft spot for him. But that didn't stop her from kicking him in the shins to stop him when he tried to hug her. "Watch the fox!"

Pausing, he held her away and peered down at the swaddled pup in her arms. "Another beastie ye've rescued?" He set her down and tugged the swaddling aside to get a better look at the baby fox's fuzzy face. A smile tipped his lips as he took in the linen bandages running around his head and tied under his chin. Shaking his head, he warned, "Lovey'll be jealous."

"Aye," Claray acknowledged with a small sigh as she peered down at the now squirming bundle.

"He does no' seem too happy at the moment," Alick commented.

"He's no doubt hungry," Claray said, her eyebrows drawing together with concern. She'd been most negligent of the fox pup and the bunny the last day while sleeping. Babies had to eat regularly. He should be fed.

"I'll tend him, lass."

Claray turned to find her father's stable master behind her and smiled at the older man as she gave up the pup into his capable hands. "Thank ye, Edmund. Be careful o' his ears. Some vile creature chewed them off."

He nodded, but then arched one bushy salt and pepper eyebrow. "Is it only the fox I need fetch?"

"Oh. Nay, there's a bunny too," she admitted. "Hamish has him." She glanced around to see that Hamish was standing in a circle with her father, her cousin Aulay, Conall, Payton and Roderick. They all looked most serious, she noted, and wondered what they were discussing. Probably MacNaughton, she suspected, but couldn't help wondering what they were saying about him.

"I'll fetch the bunny, lass," Edmund said, drawing her gaze back to him. Despite the words, he didn't leave at once, but tilted his head and considered her briefly before asking, "Is that it?"

As if the question were a cue, Squeak climbed out of her plaid and scrambled up to sit on her shoulder.

"A stoat?" Edmund asked with a pained grimace as Alick began to chuckle.

Claray scowled at her cousin, but assured Edmund, "I'll manage Squeak. He's fine with me."

The stable master just shook his head and turned to walk toward Hamish.

"I see yer da has no' reined in yer habit o' rescuing the wee beasties," Alick said, eyeing the stoat on her shoulder with amusement.

Claray turned her head to try to see Squeak, and the small creature immediately scrambled closer, rose up on his back legs and grasped her face with his tiny front paws, then commenced to chitter and squeak most demandingly.

"The fox pup is no' the only one who's hungry," Alick said on a laugh as he scooped Squeak off her shoulder and away from her face to offer him to her.

"Aye. I'd best feed him," Claray murmured as she took the stoat from his hands into her own.

"Him? I meant me," Alick said on a laugh, throwing an arm over her shoulders and turning her toward the keep stairs. "Ye should feed both o' us."

Claray shook her head with amusement, but was thinking that she was quite hungry herself. Probably Conall and the others would be too. As far as she knew none of them had eaten anything other than an oatcake or two in the saddle since their stop in the clearing when they'd captured, cleaned and cooked up the fish for her. That had been a day and a half ago. Maybe even two. Claray had lost track of time on this journey and wasn't even sure what day it was now. Setting aside that worry for the present, she glanced toward her father and the other men, and asked, "Should we ask if they want something to eat too?"

"Nay. Just assume they do and leave them to their planning," Alick suggested, and then said solemnly, "Yer da has no' eaten more than a bite or two this last week since we got news o' what Uncle Gilchrist was up to and the peril he'd put ye in. He was most concerned."

Claray wasn't surprised to hear this. Her father always lost his appetite when trouble was afoot. It had been something of a concern when her mother was ill. He'd lost so much weight that Claray and the rest of her siblings had begun to fear they would lose him too. In fact, if her mother had struggled on living any longer than she had, they might have.

"Then let's go see what we can scrape together," Claray suggested, starting up the stairs with him to the keep doors. "Hopefully, Cook has food left over from the day that we can make a meal of."

"Now?"

Conall tore his gaze from where Claray was slipping into the keep with her cousin Alick Buchanan, and turned to face his outraged soon-to-be father-in-law. "Aye. Now," he responded, and then raised his eyebrows and added. "I thought ye'd be pleased. Ye've been natterin' after me fer years to do me duty and marry yer daughter, and now I am."

"But 'tis near to midnight," Gannon MacFarlane pointed out. "Father Cameron'll be sleepin' and—"

"Wake him up," Conall interrupted reasonably.

Claray's father opened his mouth, closed it and then tried again. "Surely this can wait until the morrow? We could prepare in the mornin', hold the ceremony in the afternoon, have a celebration feast and . . . Stop shakin' yer head, dammit. She is me daughter and I'd see her married proper."

"Then ye'll want to hold it now and see the proof o' consummation in the morn, because we leave at first light fer MacDonald," he informed him, and when MacFarlane looked ready to explode and opened his mouth again to protest, Conall turned to Aulay Buchanan and asked, "Ye're sure MacNaughton is still at Kerr?"

"Aye. After ye headed out to retrieve Claray, I sent men to follow and watch Kerr and MacNaughton. I wanted warning if he, or they both, followed and planned to attack. But he's remained there. I am hopin' he's given up, but . . ."

"But?" Conall prompted.

Aulay shook his head. "But Maldouen MacNaughton is known to be a stubborn, sneaky bastard. I half suspect he's just lettin' us think he's given up and plottin' something else." He raised his eyebrows. "What do you think?"

"I think MacNaughton is determined to get his hands on MacFarlane. He no doubt sees it as his only protection against the Campbells chargin' right o'er him and takin' o'er MacNaughton to make it part o' their own lands. And if Claray is to be believed, he's desperate to the point he's willin' to kill every last one o' us to manage that. I think he's remained at Kerr to lull us into thinkin' he's given up on Claray and she is safe, but that he's probably sent a man, or several, out to try to sneak in here and either poison the food or drink, or pay one o' the people here to do it."

"But that would kill Claray too," Claray's father protested with a frown. "He could no' force her to marry him and claim MacFarlane if she's dead."

Conall had already considered that during the journey here and now pointed out what he'd realized when Claray wouldn't eat the pheasant. "She would no' be harmed if the poison was on the meat. Claray does no' eat meat."

"Nay, she does no'," Gannon agreed with a small frown, and then shook his head and muttered, "She's a soft heart, our Claray. She's forever findin' wounded beasties, from wee birds to big bulls. She mends the damned things and, worse yet, befriends them, and once she's done that, she can no bring herself to eat the flesh o' their kind," Gannon admitted with a sigh. But then rallied and said, "But no' one o' me people would agree to kill everyone here. Especially Cook. He's been with us forever, keeps a close watch on his kitchens, and rubbin' poison in every side of meat here would take forever." He shook his head firmly. "No one could sneak in and rub poison on the meat without being caught."

"They do no' have to," Conall assured him, and then pointed out, "Hemlock can and has been mistaken for fennel a time or two. His man could just switch out the dry fennel in the kitchens with dry hemlock. Cook would unsuspectingly rub it on a roast boar or such and—" He shrugged. "No doubt all or most would eat it and Claray would soon be standin' alone in a castle full o' dead kin, being forced to marry MacNaughton."

When Gannon MacFarlane blanched at the suggestion, or perhaps at the realization that something of the like would probably work, Conall pointed out, "'Tis safer fer Claray, and every other member o' yer family, if we are married and quickly away. If nothing else, MacNaughton will have to come up with another plan. It'll give ye time to figure out how to deal with him." He shook his head. "I'll no' risk Claray endin' up in that man's hands by delayin' by even a day."

Gannon MacFarlane nodded on a sigh, and then turned away. "I'll wake up Father Cameron meself."

Chapter 10

"$\mathcal{I}$ DO NO' THINK COOK WAS PLEASED," ALICK MURMURED near her ear as he followed Claray out of the kitchens.

"Aye," she agreed dryly. "But I can no' blame him. Ye did wake him and everyone else in the kitchens when ye stepped on the sleepin' spit-boy's hand and set him screaming."

"It was an accident," Alick assured her for the fourth time since he'd done it. "The fire was burnin' low and I did no' see the boy lyin' there. 'Sides, I told one and all just to go back to sleep and we would fetch some food ourselves. Cook is the one who insisted he would tend it and shuffled us out o' the kitchens."

"Cook does no' like anyone fussin' about in his kitchens. Once awake there was no chance he would let us handle things."

"Oh, well," Alick said with a shrug. "'Tis his choice. And this way we'll surely get something more substantial than the bruised old apples from last fall and stale bread ye were collectin'."

"Oh, I'll most like still get bruised old apples and stale bread," she assured him. "But he'll most like serve you and the others burnt stew and ale he's spit in. 'Twill be his thank-ye fer yer wakin' him."

"Nay! He would no'. Would he?" Alick asked with horror.

Claray bit back the smile that wanted to claim her lips at his reaction to her teasing. Cook would never do something like that. No matter how annoyed he was. He prided himself on being a fine cook and would never serve anything less than quality food. Before she could say as much though, her attention was drawn by the opening of the keep doors.

"Ah, Claray!" her father said with relief as he spotted her across the great hall. "I was just comin' to look fer ye, but ye've saved me the trouble. Now come here. Quickly, lass. Everyone is waitin'."

"Who is everyone? And waitin' fer . . . ?" Claray began as her father turned and hustled back out of the keep. As the door closed behind him, she finished weakly, "What?'

She glanced to Alick then, hoping he might have some idea what was happening, but he merely shrugged.

"I've no idea what's about. Best we go find out though," he suggested when she just stood there.

"Oh. Aye." Giving herself a shake, she started quickly across the great hall. "Ye do no' think MacNaughton has caught up to us and approaches the castle, do ye?"

"He'd have to be an idiot to approach with all the soldiers here at the moment," Alick assured her, and reached over her head to push one of the keep doors open for her as they arrived at them.

Claray was frowning over that when she slid under her cousin's arm and walked outside. She paused then, confusion running rife through her as she saw that her father was waiting at the bottom of the steps with both her mount and his own. Aulay was already on his own horse and holding the reins of another.

"Hurry, you two. Come mount up. Ye're holdin' everyone up," her father called impatiently, and then turned and mounted his own horse.

"What in heaven's name," Claray breathed, but tripped quickly down the stairs. Alick lifted her into the saddle the moment she reached her mount, then hurried to mount the horse Aulay was holding for him as Claray asked, "Where are we goin'?"

When her father didn't answer, but started his horse moving, pulling her mount behind him, Claray shifted to hook her leg over the pommel of the saddle to keep her balance. She was not at all used to riding sidesaddle, especially on a normal saddle. But she wasn't wearing braies under the plaid and wouldn't ride astride without them. Hoping they weren't riding far, she glanced over her shoulder. Alick and Aulay were following a little behind, her younger cousin leaning toward his older brother and obviously asking him what was happening. When she saw Aulay's lips begin to move, she wished they were closer so she could hear the explanation. She had no idea what was going on.

"I'm sorry, lass."

Claray turned to see that her father had slowed to ride beside her and was frowning almost guiltily. Eyebrows rising, she asked, "For what?"

"For ne'er tellin' ye yer betrothed yet lived," he said solemnly. "I wanted to. But . . . at first ye were too young to trust with the secret."

"Why was it a secret?" she asked when he paused.

"Well, ye ken the boy's parents were murdered," he said, and when she nodded, he continued. "It seems the lad was meant to die too. 'Tis only luck he didn't eat the poisoned food. Ross MacKay, his uncle," he explained, "arranged it so that everyone thought young Bryson had died with his parents and everyone else at dinner that night. He was tryin' to protect him, ye see, make the murderer think he'd succeeded. So he changed his name to Conall and sent him to train at Sinclair to keep him safe while we tried to catch the murderer."

Gannon MacFarlane sighed unhappily. "In our arrogance, we thought we'd solve it right quick, bring the murderer to justice, and the lad's survival could be revealed. He would have then been returned to his uncle's home and raised amongst family as Bryson MacDonald again. But that did no' happen," he pointed out grimly.

"Still, we ne'er gave up," he assured her. "But the years passed without any results in our hunt fer the killer."

Claray nodded solemnly. She already knew that; as she'd told Conall and the other men, her father had seemed to her to be obsessed with the chore. Now she asked, "But why did ye and Mother never tell me that he still lived? Do ye no' think I should have kenned?"

Her father grimaced. "At the time o' the murders ye were but a bairn, and then later as a child we all agreed it was better no' to tell ye fer fear ye might let it slip that young MacDonald still lived without ever meanin' to. Such a slip could ha'e cost the lad his life. His parents' murderer might ha'e got word he yet lived and hunted him down and killed him."

Claray nodded again in understanding when he glanced her way. She supposed it would have been risky telling a young girl something like that. But she hadn't been a young girl for a very long while. Before she could say that, her father continued.

"And then, once ye were older, yer mother and I wanted to tell ye, but the lad insisted we should no'," he said, sounding a bit irritated. "Conall thought it better ye no' ken in case he died in battle ere he could claim ye. That way, he said, I could just arrange another betrothal and ye'd be none the wiser and suffer no upset at his death."

"Oh," Claray murmured, and sort of understood his reasoning. If she had met and got to know him, she very well might have suffered upset and even grief at his passing. Except she'd never even met him ere this, so suspected she wouldn't have felt much more than a bit of disappointment on learning of his death had that happened.

"No' tellin' ye was the only serious bone o' contention between yer mother and I in all the years we were married," he added sadly. "She wanted to tell ye when ye were twelve, so ye'd have something to look forward to. But I'd given me word, and I had to make her give me hers. Ye ken now though," he added, sitting a little straighter in the saddle, "and he's ready to give up his mercenary work and claim ye, so all will be well."

Claray wasn't at all sure that was true. The "all would be well" part. Not when the man made her toes curl and her body tingle with his kisses and caresses. His decision to give up this mercenary work and claim her might see her in hell for heaven's sake. Which was something she planned to talk to Father Cameron about first thing on the morrow. Surely he would know some way to save her soul from the lust her betrothed stirred in her. Perhaps a pilgrimage or something would do it. Those were perilous and painful and took a long while, but she doubted Conall intended to rush her to the chapel of a sudden. He certainly hadn't shown any indication that he was in a hurry to marry her ere this.

Aye, she'd talk to Father Cameron about a pilgrimage first thing on the morrow. Before she even broke her fast, she decided, and then glanced to her father and asked, "If he's the Laird o' MacDonald, why has he been livin' as a mercenary all these years?"

Her father grimaced at the question, and then said, "Right after the murders, most o' the survivin' clan members fled. They had no idea what had happened, and there were superstitious whisperings about God strikin' them down or some such rot. The few that remained behind had it rough with no laird or warriors to protect them. Ross did his best, but he was constantly sendin' men to ask questions and try to sort out who would want Bean and Giorsal dead. And he did no' have the manpower to set a permanent guard on MacDonald that would have been big enough to protect it from rievers and rival clans. He lost a lot o' men to the effort to do so before givin' it up," he added solemnly.

"Anyway," he said after a moment of silence, "Bryson was six when his parents died and he went to Sinclair. By all accounts he was a good quiet lad, and worked hard. He actually earned his spurs at sixteen, which is young as ye ken?"

Claray murmured her agreement. Most were closer to eighteen when they earned their spurs.

"Well, he rode straight to MacDonald when he was done with his trainin'," her father went on. "But ten years had passed. The fields had disappeared under grasses, shrubs and young trees, the wall and roof were crumblin' from lack o' attention and repair and the keep . . ." He shook his head. "A lot o' coin was needed to repair everything . . . and o' course there were no longer MacDonalds there to work the fields either. He had no choice but to try to earn coin with his sword. He's been workin' these last twelve years to earn enough to not only repair MacDonald, but to lure back the survivors o' his clan, and support them all until the fields could be made good again and start supportin' everyone."

"Twelve years," Claray breathed.

"Aye," her father said solemnly. "But now he's made enough to do it. He can marry ye, and return to MacDonald where he'll take up his title o' laird and lead his people once more. As his wife, ye'll assist him with that."

"I will?" Claray asked weakly, but supposed she would. It seemed she would be marrying Conall. Or Bryson. She really wasn't sure what she should call him now. But then there was a lot she wasn't sure of at the moment. She'd spent so long thinking she'd never marry, have bairns or rule her own home, but now it seemed she would. Which was fine. Once she was over the shock of it she was sure she'd be happy about this turn in events. At least she would once she sorted out how to do it without landing herself in hell for enjoying her husband's attentions. She would definitely make sure she sought out Father Cameron first thing on the morrow, before she'd even broken her fast, to broach the subject. Surely, he'd have some helpful advice for her on the matter.

"Here we are," her father interrupted.

Dragged from her thoughts, Claray shifted her attention to her father to note that they'd stopped and he was dismounting. She then glanced around to see that while they'd been talking, her father had led her horse out of the bailey, over the drawbridge and out into the midst of the warriors camping outside the castle's curtain wall. They had actually ridden out past the Buchanan soldiers and were in the middle of Conall's warriors. Though it looked like even more soldiers had arrived and were setting up camp beyond Conall's men.

Her gaze slid over the mass of soldiers crowding around them with now dozens of fires beyond, and then settled on the small circle her horse was stopped on the edge of. Men bearing torches made up the edge of the circle, lighting the area and keeping the others back. Conall, Roderick, Payton, Hamish and Laird and Lady MacKay, along with their daughter, were there as well. Ross MacKay was a big brawny older warrior with salt and pepper hair, while his wife and daughter were both petite women with dark hair. Lady Annabel's was dusted with gray, however, while Kenna MacKay's was lush and glistening in the firelight as it curled around rosy cheeks and a lovely face.

"Why are the MacKays here?" Claray asked when her father moved to her side to help her down.

"They're Conall's uncle and aunt and cousin," her father pointed out as he lifted her off her mount and set her on the ground. "We sent word to them when Conall left to collect ye and they headed out at once. They arrived shortly after you did."

"Oh," Claray murmured, and started to turn toward her father, but paused when Ross MacKay moved aside and she spotted Father Cameron behind him. The priest was dressed in his finest vestments, and for some reason that sent alarm coursing through her. "Why is Father Cameron here?" Turning to her father she caught his arm and asked, "What are we doin' here?"

Her father sighed with resignation, faced her fully and clasped her shoulders as he said, "Ye're getting' married, lass. Ye're finally goin' to marry, rule yer own home and get the bairns ye were meant to have."

"What?" she squawked with amazement. "Now?" And then glancing down at her borrowed clothes and bare feet, she added, "Like this?"

"Claray," her father began soothingly.

"Is there a problem?"

Claray glanced to the side at that solemn question to see that Conall had left the others and come to join them.

"Nay, nay," her father said at once. "'Tis fine. I just—"

"We can no' marry like this," Claray interrupted him to say.

Conall's eyebrows rose, but he asked patiently, "Why?"

Claray stared at him blankly, and then babbled, "I was supposed to give me confession to Father Cameron first. And weddings always take place at the steps o' the chapel, no' in front o' the curtain wall, and me sisters are no' here, and I smell! I ha'e no' bathed properly in more than a week other than a dip in the river. Me hair is most like a mess. I'm wearin' a borrowed great kilt, me feet are bare and—"

Her protests died in her throat as Conall suddenly covered her mouth with his in a searing kiss that made her forget the long list of reasons that were lining up in her head for why they shouldn't marry here and now. That wasn't all she forgot either. She forgot that her father stood beside her, that hundreds of soldiers surrounded them and, worst of all, that Father Cameron stood just feet away, witness to her horrible, sinning ways when she melted against Conall, wrapped her arms around his neck and sighed and moaned as he devoured her mouth.

When Conall's hands slid down her back, pressing her body firmly against his and then curved under her bottom and lifted her off the ground, Claray instinctively wrapped her legs around his hips, then gasped into his mouth as he began to walk, his body rubbing against her core with each step.

When he finally broke the kiss, she opened her eyes on a murmur of protest and flexed her thighs, trying to raise herself up enough to meet his lips again. Claray had even almost managed the feat when a loud throat clearing made her stiffen and glance around. Horror quickly replaced her passion as she found herself almost nose to nose with Father Cameron.

A squeak of alarm slipping from her lips, she unhooked her legs and arms at once. Fortunately, Conall was grasping her waist now so she didn't plummet to the ground like a stone. Instead, he set her down gently on her feet, and even kissed her forehead before whispering by her ear, "All will be well."

Swallowing, Claray took a moment to brush down her wrinkled and borrowed great kilt and shirt, then patted at her no doubt greasy and flyaway hair as if that might straighten it. Once she'd done all she could to look more presentable, she clasped her hands loosely and turned to the priest, her eyes demurely downcast.

A moment of silence passed where Claray was afraid that Father Cameron would address her wanton behavior, but after what was probably only minutes, but felt like hours, he cleared his throat again and began to speak.

Were she asked what the holy man said, the passages he read or what vows she'd made, Claray couldn't have answered. She didn't hear a lick of the droning ceremony and only repeated what she was told to when she was told to. Really, her mind wasn't there at the ceremony at all. It was now recalling all the reasons this marriage shouldn't happen at this specific time to this particular man. She was fretting over her soon-to-be-lost soul . . . or perhaps it was already lost. Claray didn't know, but thought it was terribly sad one way or the other.

Conall's clasping her chin and lifting her face drew her from her thoughts and then he was kissing her again. This time it was just the briefest brushing of his lips over hers though. Even so, it caused a roaring in her ears. At least that's what she thought, until he ended the kiss and the roaring continued.

Peering around with confusion, Claray realized that the sound she was hearing was actually the soldiers surrounding them, shouting their approval of the kiss. A little overwhelmed and unsure how she should be reacting, Claray found herself sidling closer to Conall. When he clasped her hand and gave her a reassuring squeeze, she looked swiftly up and managed a grateful smile.

Conall squeezed her fingers gently again in response, and then turned to raise his free hand and gestured for the crowd to be quiet. Once the silence was so complete you could have heard a pin drop, rather than speak, Conall glanced to his uncle.

Ross MacKay immediately moved up between him and Claray, took their clasped hands in his and raised them into the air as he announced, "I give ye me new niece, Lady Claray MacDonald, and her husband, me nephew, Bryson Conall MacDonald, son o' Beatham and Giorsal MacDonald and long-lost laird o' the MacDonald clan. May his rule bring peace and prosperity to his people, and return Castle Deagh Fhortan to the happy home it once was."

If Claray had thought the shouting when they kissed loud, she learned differently. This time the response was deafening with joy, relief and celebration as the soldiers understood the message that their long years of battling were over and they would be returning home to be a clan once more.

Chapter 11

"$\mathcal{I}$ can no' believe ye never told us Bryson was still alive and that he was Conall, Mother. He's our cousin. We should ha'e been told."

"We were trying to keep Bryson safe, dearling. No one was told," Annabel MacKay said soothingly. The older woman's speech still retained a good deal of her English accent despite living in Scotland since her marriage to Ross MacKay some twenty-eight years ago, Claray noted as she listened to the woman and her daughter, who were following her up the steps to the keep doors.

After his uncle's announcement, Conall's warriors had roared with approval and then had crowded forward to offer congratulations and pledge their fealty to him as laird now that he had been officially acknowledged as Bryson MacDonald. There were so many of them trying to get close to him to do that that Claray had found herself stepping further and further back to keep out of the way. And then Lady MacKay had approached and suggested they make their way back to the keep and await the men there. Recalled to her duties as hostess, Claray had led them to where the horses waited and they'd ridden back across the drawbridge, and through the bailey to the keep stairs.

"You kenned," Kenna pointed out grimly. "So did Father, and Claray and her father, and—"

"I did no' ken," Claray interrupted as she stopped to open the door to usher them inside the keep.

"Ye did no' ken either?" Kenna asked with surprise, stopping before her, and when Claray shook her head, she protested, "But he was yer *betrothed*."

"Aye," Claray agreed, but thought, *And now he's me husband*. She considered that silently as Lady MacKay urged her daughter to start moving again and ushered her into MacFarlane's great hall. Following the women in and toward the trestle tables, Claray pondered that. She was a married lady now. Shouldn't she feel . . . different somehow? She'd expected to. She'd thought if she ever married she'd feel more a woman and less a child. But she felt the same now as she always had.

"Oh, m'lady."

Claray paused as she reached the trestle tables, a smile coming to her face at the sight of Mavis bustling toward them with a tray holding a pitcher and three mugs. The older woman had been the head of the chambermaids for as long as Claray could remember. She was short, round and rosy-cheeked with a smile that could soothe you and warm your heart all at the same time, and she had been a great support and comfort to Claray since her mother's death and even before.

"Cook said to tell ye he's puttin' together a light repast to celebrate the wedding," Mavis announced as she set down the tray and picked up the pitcher to start pouring drinks. "Nothin' huge, mind, it being so late, but somethin' nice. And there's water on the fire, warmin' fer yer bath. It should no' be long at all."

"Thank ye, Mavis," Claray murmured as the maid set the pitcher on the table and quickly passed out the drinks.

"Me pleasure," Mavis assured her, picking up the empty tray. She started to turn toward the kitchens, but then paused and turned back to ask, "Do ye think the men'll be long?"

Claray hesitated, and then grimaced and admitted, "I'm no' sure, Mavis. There were a fair number o' men wanting me husband's attention when we left them."

She nodded thoughtfully, and then smiled and shrugged. "Well, the longer they take, the more time we ha'e to prepare. Sit down and rest a bit, then. I'll let ye ken when the water is ready fer yer bath."

"Thank ye," Claray murmured, and watched the woman go before settling at the table with Lady MacKay and her daughter.

"So," Kenna said once Mavis had disappeared back into the kitchens, "ye really did no' ken that Conall was me cousin Bryson?"

"Nay," Claray assured her.

"When did ye find out who he was?" she asked now. "Surely they told ye ere the wedding at least?"

"Aye. Conall told me on the journey here from me uncle's," she admitted. "Ere that though, I thought me betrothed had died and I would ne'er marry."

"Oh," Kenna breathed. "That was terribly unkind." She turned to scowl at her mother as she said that, obviously holding her partially responsible.

Lady MacKay sighed at the accusation in her expression and said, "We did what we thought was best to keep Bryson safe."

"And is he?" Kenna asked at once.

Claray glanced at her sharply at the question. It was one she should have thought of herself. The man had been in hiding his entire life to keep him safe from whoever had murdered his parents, and that murderer still had not been caught. Was it safe for him to reveal the fact that he lived?

"We are not sure," Lady MacKay said quietly. "We never sorted out a reason for the murders or even got close to finding a suspect. But a lot of years have passed and a lot has happened. The surviving clan members were scattered about after the deaths and had it very hard. A lot died. If one of them was the murderer, it's possible they are dead now, or perhaps just old enough that they are no longer a threat."

"But as ye said, ye're no' sure," Kenna pointed out with a concerned glance toward Claray. "Would it no' ha'e been better had he revealed himself to be Bryson MacDonald, laird o' the MacDonald clan, and then spent a year or so rebuildin' the keep and such before claimin' Claray? That way, were the murderer still around and like to try to kill him again, at least she would no' be at risk."

"Except that it would leave her vulnerable to the MacNaughton's machinations," Lady Annabel pointed out. "He is the reason we are all here right now." Turning to Claray, she explained, "Your father and your cousin Aulay sent us news of what had happened and that Bryson had ridden out to rescue you. He suggested that if he succeeded, the best plan might be for him to wed you to prevent MacNaughton trying again, and he asked Ross to come help him convince Bryson to finally do that." She smiled faintly, and added, "But as it turned out, there was no convincing needed. Instead, we were just in time for the wedding."

"So me cousin Aulay kenned Conall was Bryson MacDonald?" Claray asked with a small frown. It was starting to seem like everyone else *had* known but her. And Kenna, of course.

"He did not know until the messenger reached Buchanan with your letter," she assured her. "I gather your father said a few things that let the cat out of the bag, so to speak. The moment Bryson rode off to Kerr, Aulay and your father sat down and wrote a message for us, then sent it with a courier to us at MacKay."

"Will their bein' married keep Claray safe from MacNaughton now?" Kenna asked with concern.

Lady Annabel hesitated, and then apparently deciding enough lies had been told over the years, admitted honestly, "Perhaps not completely, but it will help. The wedding has at least added a layer of protection against his forcing her to marry him. He'd have to kill Bryson to be able to do that now."

"Or kill both o' us and force me sister Allissaid to marry him," Claray pointed out with a grimace.

"Good Lord," Kenna muttered. "So the marriage has doubled their troubles for both o' them. Claray now has MacNaughton and Aunt Giorsal and Uncle Bean's murderer to worry about, and so does Bryson."

"I am afraid so," Lady MacKay said solemnly.

They were all silent for a minute, and then Kenna stood and moved around behind Claray and bent to wrap her arms around her shoulders in a hug. "Welcome to the family, Claray. I'm happy to have another cousin."

"Thank ye," Claray murmured, clasping the young woman's arms where they crossed over her collarbone.

Lady MacKay watched them with a small smile, and then stood to embrace her too when Kenna released her. "Welcome to the family, dear. I truly hope you and my nephew will be very happy."

"Thank ye, Lady MacKay," Claray said quietly, touched at how welcoming the women were being.

"You cannot call me Lady MacKay!" the woman protested with a laugh as she released her. "We're family now. And I would be most pleased if you called me Aunt Annabel."

"Aunt Annabel, it is, then," Claray said with a smile.

"Oh!" Kenna said, suddenly straightening. "Annella should know."

"Ye remember Annella," Aunt Annabel said now. "My eldest daughter. She used to come with us when we visited before she married the Gunn."

Claray nodded. The MacKays hadn't visited since her mother's death, but she did recall Annella. She'd always like her. She'd liked both of the MacKay daughters.

"Married," Kenna snorted. "Ye can hardly call what poor Annella has a proper marriage."

"Kenna," Annabel said in warning.

"Well, 'tis true," Kenna said with irritation, and told Claray, "After weddin' her six years ago when she turned eighteen, her 'husband' just dumped Annella at Gunn and went off on a pilgrimage leaving her there with his mother and father . . . and they do no' treat her well at all."

Claray noted Lady MacKay's pained expression, but couldn't resist asking, "Surely he is no' still on pilgrimage?" The longest pilgrimage she'd heard of was to Palestine. The trip could take two or even three years. She'd never heard of one that took six years though.

"Aye. Though I suspect he's dead. Killed by bandits on the trail else he'd surely be back by now," Kenna pointed out. "Laird Gunn has been sendin' men out to look fer him the last three years, but there is no word back yet. I hope he's dead."

"Kenna!" Lady MacKay gasped.

"Well, 'tis true," Kenna said defiantly. "Annella is four and twenty now. Married six years without a single bairn, and a husband who basically abandoned her. She deserves better."

"Aye. She does," Lady MacKay admitted on a sigh. "Still, 'tis unkind to wish anyone dead."

Apparently, uncaring if it was unkind or not, Kenna shrugged and moved around her mother to drop back onto the bench, then stifled a yawn. "Goodness, I hope the men return soon. Else I'll be sleepin' on the tabletop ere they do."

"You do not have to wait up for them, dearling. You can retire if you wish," Lady MacKay said, rubbing her daughter's back affectionately. "The men could be quite a while."

Claray blinked at those words, her eyes widening as she realized she had not even considered sleeping arrangements for their guests . . . and that was a problem. MacFarlane only had six bedrooms. Her father occupied the largest, which left five rooms for eight children. As the oldest, Claray had her own room, as did her brother, Eachann, as the only male. The other three rooms were shared by her six sisters, two girls to a room. She was happy to give up her own room, but would have to wake up her siblings to provide rooms for the MacKays as well as Aulay and Alick.

She'd barely had the thought when the kitchen door opened and Mavis rushed out, heading in her direction. Standing, Claray hurried to meet the woman.

"Mavis, we ha'e to make room fer the MacKays and Buchanans. We need to wake—"

"'Tis done," Mavis interrupted soothingly. "We rearranged where everyone would sleep when the Buchanans arrived. Young Eachann has been on a pallet in yer father's room since, and young Islay and Cristane gave up their room too, and shifted to share yer other sisters' rooms fer them as well so each man had his own room. When we got word that the MacKays had reached the border of MacFarlane, the Buchanans said they'd shift to the barracks so Laird and Lady MacKay could take one o' the rooms, and the young Lady Kenna could have the other. I immediately sent maids up to change the bedding and clean the rooms."

"Oh," Claray breathed. "Well, that's fine, then."

"Aye." Mavis smiled faintly. "I came to tell ye that the water is ready fer yer bath. Would ye like it now?"

"Oh. Nay. 'Twould be rude to leave Lady MacKay and Kenna—"

"Do not fret over that, Claray," Annabel MacKay said now, letting her know they'd heard everything. "We had a long journey and are very tired. It's probably best if Kenna and I find our beds now."

Claray felt herself relax at this news and nodded as she turned back to Mavis. "Aye. I'd like me bath now, then."

Once the maid hurried back toward the kitchens, Claray returned to the table, asking, "Would ye like something else to drink or something to eat ere ye retire?"

"Not for me, thank you. I fear I am too tired even to chew," Lady MacKay assured her.

Covering another yawn, Kenna nodded in what Claray could only assume was agreement since both women then stood.

"Well, then, I'll show ye to yer chambers," Claray murmured, and led the way above stairs.

By the time she escorted them to the rooms that had been made up for them, wished them good night and headed along the hall to her own room, Mavis was stepping onto the landing. The older woman carried a tray with food and drink on it, and was followed by a parade of servants bearing a large tub and buckets of steaming water.

Claray hurried the last few feet to her door, quickly opened it and stepped inside to get out of the way for the servants to enter. She then left the door open and moved to sit on the foot of her bed to retrieve a sleepy Squeak from where he was nestling inside the borrowed plaid she wore. Claray petted the wee creature soothingly while she watched her bath being prepared. The servants set down the tub, and then began to dump in the water, each leaving after their task was done, until only Mavis was left.

"There we are, then," Mavis said as she closed the door behind the last servant. "Let's get ye bathed and tucked up in yer bed all nice and comfy. Ye must be tired after yer trip too."

"No' really," Claray said as she set Squeak on the bed and stood to walk to the steaming bath. Once there, she unhooked the plaid from around her neck, and undid the rope she'd used as a belt to let the material slip away as she admitted, "I slept through most o' the trip."

Mavis chuckled as she took the plaid from her. "Ye always did sleep on long journeys. Yer mother, God rest her soul, was the same way, and yer father just used to shake his head in wonder at the pair o' ye, that ye could."

Claray smiled faintly at the claim as she removed the borrowed shirt and handed it to Mavis before stepping into the tub. Her mother had been close with her sisters and brothers, and the family had traveled several times a year to visit them. The closer ones had been easy to get to and allowed for short day trips or overnight stays. But the ones who had married into clans further away had meant much more in-depth journeys that they'd only taken once or twice a year.

Most of her sisters had found those longer trips a boring trial, at least the journeys themselves. They'd complained that they were exhausting and miserable, and that by the time they arrived at their destination, it took days to recover enough to enjoy the visit. But Claray and her mother had been the opposite. They'd pretty much slept through what everyone else considered the hard part of such journeys, and then had lots of energy for the actual visits themselves on arriving.

"Lovey'll be happy to see ye on the morrow," Mavis commented as she folded the plaid and shirt. "Edmund says he's been pining fer ye in yer absence."

Claray frowned at this as she sank into the hot, steamy water and reached for the soap Mavis had set on a chair beside the large tub. She took a moment to dip her head under the water to wet her hair, and then began to soap and wash it as she asked, "Where is Lovey? I'm surprised he's no' shown himself by now."

"Oh, well, yer father thought what with everything going on and all the visitors about, it would be best if Edmund kept him in his rooms in the stables until the morrow."

"Oh," Claray sighed the word, and supposed she couldn't blame her father. Lovey didn't like many people, and she supposed with the bailey full of soldiers it might be less stressful for him to be kept out of the way. She'd make her way down to the stables to see him in the morning, she decided. She'd go right after she approached Father Cameron for advice on her issues with the marriage bed.

"Let's get yer hair rinsed," Mavis suggested, setting the material aside and reaching for a bucket. "Then ye can finish yer bath while I find ye a gown to set out fer the morning."

"Thank ye." Claray sat up in the tub and tipped her head back for Mavis to pour the water over. Once it was done, the maid wrung out her hair and wrapped a smaller linen around it to keep it out of the soapy water while Claray quickly finished her bath. She then brought another, larger linen for her to dry off with when she stood to get out.

Claray dried herself off quickly, and then wrapped the large linen around herself toga style and moved to the fur in front of the fire to brush her hair. That's where she was when the door suddenly opened.

Claray glanced around in surprise, thinking Mavis must be leaving for something, and then blinked when she saw that it was Conall entering. He paused in the doorway when he saw her by the fire and Mavis setting a fresh gown over a chest in the corner, then held the door open expectantly. It was all he had to do. Nodding, Mavis murmured a good night to Claray and then bustled out of the room.

Chapter 12

CLARAY SWALLOWED AS SHE WATCHED CONALL CLOSE THE door, then turned her head quickly toward the fire and continued brushing her hair as she listened to him move around. Her mind was suddenly racing. Ridiculous as it was, she was more than a little taken aback at his presence there in her room. It wasn't that she'd forgotten that they were married now, but she hadn't really been thinking of it and what it meant. Good Lord! She was married! Which meant he would share her room, her bed . . . and her body.

She swallowed thickly again at that thought as Claray heard the soft shushing plop of material dropping to the rush-covered floor and then the sound of water moving, which she assumed meant he was getting in the tub. That put her in a bit of a quandary as she debated whether she should be offering to help him with his bath or not. Her mother, before she fell ill, had often aided her father in the bath, Claray knew. But she wasn't sure if that was expected of a wife or just something her parents had enjoyed. They had been happily married, their love for each other obvious to anyone in their presence for more than a few moments.

Before she could decide the matter, she heard a great deal of splashing that suggested her husband might be done with his bath and getting out. Unable to help herself, Claray glanced quickly over her shoulder to see that, yes, he was getting out. He was presently standing in the tub, drying his long, wet hair vigorously with a linen that Mavis must have left for him.

His face was covered by the cloth as he worked, and knowing he couldn't see her, she found herself drinking in the sight of his body. He was such a well-made man, his body toned and muscled. Even the scars that flecked his body from years as a mercenary couldn't detract from his beauty in her eyes, and there were a lot of scars: a puckered one on his upper chest that looked to be from an arrow, a jagged slice in his side from a sword or knife and several smaller nicks on his arms and legs. But there was a very large one on his hip that had to be from a sword or battle-axe, she thought, and then realized that his body had stopped moving. She lifted her eyes quickly to his face to see that he'd finished drying his hair. Conall now stood, the damp linen crumpled up in his hands as he watched her examine his body.

Blushing, Claray turned back to the fire and started to brush her hair again, but only got two strokes in before she heard him cross the room toward her. When he settled on the fur behind her and took the brush from her hand, she released it without protest and then sat tense and anxious at first as he took over brushing her hair. When that's all he did, her muscles slowly began to ease, soothed by the long slow strokes of the brush. But then he pressed a kiss to her shoulder. Claray blinked open eyes she hadn't realized had closed and turned her head toward him with surprise.

The moment she did, Conall claimed her mouth in a soft, questing kiss that had her turning her upper body instinctively toward him as well. Her lips parted almost at once, and he immediately accepted the invitation and deepened the kiss, his hand reaching up to cup the back of her head as his tongue thrust in to fill her.

Claray moaned at the excitement that began to stir to life in her, and slid her arms around his neck as she kissed him back. She did love his kiss. She loved the tingling it started, and the heat it sent through her body, the way it somehow turned excitement and passion into molten lava that pooled low in her belly until it overflowed to leave her wet and aching.

So consumed by his kisses was she that Claray was only vaguely aware of it when Conall clasped her by the waist and turned her toward him. So, when he suddenly broke their kiss, she was somewhat surprised to find herself on her knees between his. She saw amusement flicker across his face as he took in her startled expression, but that died quickly when he untucked the linen wrapped around her chest and it dropped to pool around her knees, leaving her entirely on display. His gaze grew intense then, and hungry, like a starving man presented with a feast.

Claray's instinct was to cover herself with her hands, but instead she dug her fingers into his shoulders and remained still. She then gasped and stiffened when he lowered his head and leaned forward to latch on to one breast, sucking the nipple into his mouth and flicking it with his tongue. Even as she cried out and arched into the caress, his hand was laying claim to her other breast and kneading the eager flesh, before switching his mouth to claim that nipple now as his fingers plucked at the first.

Hardly aware of the little mewls of need and pleasure slipping from her lips, Claray withstood that as long as she could, and then slid her hands into his damp hair, and pulled his head back so that she could cover his lips with hers. Much to her relief, he gave in to her silent request and kissed her again, his mouth demanding and hungry as he palmed and squeezed her breasts, then alternately tweaked and rolled her nipples until her head was swimming with pleasure and need.

Claray was so caught up in the sensations he was raising in her that she didn't realize he was lowering her to lie on the fur until she felt it press into her back as he came down half on top of her. His knee pressed between her legs then, rubbing against her and making her cry out into his mouth, and he did it again with the same result. Then his leg shifted and his hand replaced it, his fingers gliding through the folds to find her most sensitive spot.

Claray stilled briefly, and then began to suck frantically on his tongue as he began to rub his fingers gently over, then around, the treasure he'd found. Within moments she was panting, and writhing beneath him, some fine string inside her body tightening as taut as a bow. So caught up was she in that feeling that she hardly noticed when he broke their kiss and began sliding down her body, his mouth grazing over one breast and the other and then licking and nipping his way down across her stomach.

She was vaguely aware of him urging her legs to open wider, so that he could settle between them. However, it wasn't until his fingers stopped their caressing and his head dipped down between her spread legs that she took notice. She was glancing down with confusion when he nuzzled his face between her thighs and lashed her most sensitive area with his tongue. When Claray gasped and bucked in shock, Conall grasped her upper thighs to hold her in place and pressed his mouth between her legs again.

For one moment, she was too stunned to feel anything else as he began to caress the sensitive nub with his tongue, and then suckled at the lips around it. But that soon passed as her body responded to his hungry feasting. It was like nothing she'd ever experienced before, nothing she'd even imagined. It was all so raw and carnal and overwhelming and she didn't know what to do. Claray was quite sure this was not something the church would approve of. He could not give her his seed like this. This was—

"Oh God," she gasped, her thoughts scattering on the breeze as he began to suck on the most sensitive part of her. And then it became a mantra, "Oh God, oh God, oh God."

She felt his finger push into her, and struggled against the hands holding her, wanting to move her hips, though she had no idea why, and couldn't with him holding her down. He was still caressing her with his mouth even as he withdrew the finger. He then pushed in again and again until something inside of Claray snapped and she cried out breathlessly, her body suddenly thrashing as pleasure overwhelmed her.

Awash in the aftermath, little waves of pleasure still rippling through her, Claray was barely aware of what was happening when Conall shifted, scooped her up and carried her to the bed. She had a moment's thought of Squeak when he bent to toss the furs aside and set her in it, but then Conall came down on top of her, his mouth claiming hers once more.

Stretching under him as he stirred the embers of her excitement back to life with but a kiss, she wrapped her arms around his shoulders and responded in what was at first a desultory fashion, but soon turned more invested. When he then ground his hardness against her, she murmured excitedly into his mouth and let her legs fall apart so that he settled more comfortably between them and pressed more intimately against that part of her he'd earlier been caressing. The effect was most galvanizing, sending shock waves of need and excitement through her again as he ground against her in rhythm to his tongue thrusting into her mouth.

Claray groaned, arched and thrust into the caress with mounting excitement, and then his tongue withdrew and she felt something pushing into her again. But this time it was not a finger; it was much bigger, and painful as he tore through her maiden's veil.

Conall's mouth on hers muffled Claray's pained cry as she locked around him like a vise. Her arms and legs were suddenly clenched in an effort to hold him in place and keep him from moving as she struggled with the shocking pain. Despite that, she suspected he could have kept going had he wished, but he didn't. Conall remained still briefly, giving her a moment, and then broke their kiss that was no longer really a kiss anyway, and raised his head to peer at her with concern.

"I'm sorry, lass," he got out finally, his voice a husky growl. "The first time is—"

Claray covered his mouth with one hand and shook her head. Ere she'd died, her mother had spoken to her about the first time a woman was with a man. At the time, she'd been bewildered as to why her mother would think she should when Claray was quite sure at that point that she would never marry. In the end, she'd just put it down to the illness affecting her mother's mind.

However, she understood now that it hadn't been the illness. Her mother had known this day would come and had wanted to prepare her. Claray didn't need him to tell her that the pain was to be expected . . . and truthfully, it wasn't as bad as she'd thought it might be from her mother's description. It was just in an area where that kind of pain didn't usually occur. And she supposed that its coming in the midst of such pleasure made it more shocking as well.

Now that he wasn't moving, however, the pain was fading quickly.

"Are ye all right?" Conall asked when she finally let her fingers drop from his mouth.

Claray nodded, too embarrassed to speak or even meet his gaze. "Is the pain better?"

He sounded worried and somewhat strained, she noticed, but still couldn't meet his gaze and merely nodded again.

They were both silent for a moment, and then he cleared his throat and said, "I'm going to move, lass, and I want ye to tell me does it hurt. All right?"

Claray eased her grip on him, and nodded for a third time, and then waited. After the briefest pause, Conall began to ease out of her. Much to her relief the sharp pain did not return. All she felt was a slight twinge. There was no pleasure now either though, and the feel of him then pressing slowly back into her body was just odd now that all of her excitement and need were gone.

Aware that Conall was watching her face, she forced what she hoped was a smile, but suspected might have looked more like a grimace when a little breathless puff of laughter slipped from his lips, and then he stilled fully buried inside of her and began to kiss her again. This time his lips brushed over her closed eyes, then her nose, each cheek and finally found her mouth to nip and suck at her lower lip briefly, before settling into a more proper kiss.

It wasn't the deep, hungry kiss she'd grown used to. Instead, it was a patient, gentle seduction that had her slowly relaxing. It was only once she began responding that he deepened the kiss, nursing her passion back into play. Shifting to rest his weight on one hand, he then let the other trail down her body to caress her breast and Claray moaned and arched her back, pushing herself more fully into his touch as her nipples tingled and hardened. When he then lifted himself slightly so that his hand could drift down between them to caress her above where they were joined, Claray gasped and shifted into that touch too, her hips beginning to move of their own accord, drawing him deeper into her body and then releasing him to slide partway out before drawing him in again.

There was no pain now. Or at least not enough to override the pleasure he was causing, and she was soon moving almost frantically, seeking out the release she'd experienced earlier. Claray was vaguely aware that Conall was holding himself as stiff as a plank, nothing moving but his fingers against her slick skin as he let her use him for her pleasure, but had no idea what it must have cost him until she cried out into his mouth as she found her release and his stillness ended.

Breaking their kiss then, he rose up onto his knees, hands clutching her hips and raising them off the bed as he began to thrust into her almost violently. Claray was at first startled by the ferocity of it, but once that passed, she became aware of the way his body rubbed against hers, the feel of him inside her and her own excitement returning and building once more. In fact, she was quite sure she was about to find that lovely release again when he suddenly stiffened, full deep in her, and roared her name as she felt heat pouring into her. Her eyes widened when he then sank down on top of her, gathered her in his arms and rolled to his back, taking her with him to rest on his chest as she felt him shrinking inside of her.

Claray lay still where he'd settled her and listened to his breathing slow and grow deep. But it wasn't until she heard a slight snuffling snore that she realized that Conall had fallen asleep and it was definitely over. The realization was not a happy one since she was still a bit worked up, her body achy and wanting the release it had expected.

For one minute, she considered nudging him awake again to ask him to please finish what he'd started, but Claray didn't have the nerve to do something like that. Besides, it occurred to her then that while she'd slept the majority of the journey from Kerr, Conall hadn't. He and his men had ridden through all but one of the nights of their trip. Considering that, she supposed it was rather amazing that he'd managed to stay awake as long as he had and given her pleasure twice.

And really, was she truly going to complain that he hadn't given her pleasure for a third time? What of her poor soul? She'd been all-fired worried about that earlier, but was now annoyed that he wasn't continuing to give her pleasure?

Obviously, this pleasure business had her thoughts all twisted up. 'Twas no wonder Father Cameron warned against its evils all the time. Which just reminded her that she had to talk to the priest in the morning.

Sighing unhappily, Claray eased off of Conall's chest and shifted onto her back beside him. The moment she did, Squeak scrambled to her and nestled into the curve of her neck. It was only then she recalled the tiny creature. She reached up to pet him lightly, wondering where he'd been while she and Conall had . . . well, obviously he'd been somewhere safe. Perhaps the corner of the bed or something, because he seemed unharmed. They hadn't squashed the poor little guy.

Leaving her hand cupping his little back, she closed her eyes and tried to sleep. But Claray had done little else but sleep for the last four days and wasn't tired now.

Puffing out a breath between her lips, she opened her eyes again and was considering her options when she recalled the tray of food and drink that Mavis had brought up. It reminded her that Cook had been going to make a light repast for her wedding celebrations and she wondered if any of the men had bothered to eat on returning to the keep. She was pretty sure that Conall couldn't have. She'd barely got out of the bath ere he'd arrived in their room. Although she supposed he might have managed to eat something if he'd returned directly after she'd come above stairs and had eaten quickly.

Either way, she'd have to be sure to thank Cook on the morrow for his efforts. The poor man, along with his workers, had been rousted from sleep and pressed into service, although that hadn't been her intention when she and Alick had gone in search of food. Actually, she supposed she'd have to make sure she thanked everyone else too: Edmund for his assistance with the horses and her latest addition of injured animals, as well as the maids who had prepared the rooms her Buchanan cousins had been using so that the MacKays could use them this night, those servants who had heated the water and prepared her bath, the kitchen staff . . . Even Father Cameron, who had probably been dragged from his bed to perform the ceremony. The people of MacFarlane had all put in extra effort this day, and should be thanked for those efforts.

She'd also probably have to apologize to her brother and sisters for their not being disturbed. As far as she could tell, they were the only inhabitants of MacFarlane who had been allowed to sleep through her return home and her wedding, and she was quite sure they would be upset that they hadn't been there for that.

A faint smile curved her lips at the contrariness of the situation, that the people who had been forced to wake and work would probably have rather slept, while her siblings, who had been left sleeping, would probably resent not being woken. She shook her head at the situation without thinking, and then stilled when Squeak chittered at her unhappily for the movement. But when the stoat kit climbed up her chest to try to burrow between her breasts in the hopes of finding his usual sleeping spot, she scooped him into her hand and sat up on the bed. He began to squeak and chitter at her at once, but Claray ignored that and got up to cross to the table where the food and drink waited.

Much to her surprise she saw that Mavis had brought a bowl of milk for the small creature. The realization made her smile and she set Squeak down next to it. The stoat continued to chitter at her briefly in a most irate manner, which began to sound a bit less vociferous as his nose began to twitch, and then ended altogether as he turned toward the bowl she'd set him next to. Giving up his complaints then he moved to the bowl to begin lapping up the milk. Chuckling softly, Claray left him to it and went to where Mavis had laid out a fresh gown and shift for the morning. She left the gown, but pulled on the shift.

Feeling a little less exposed now that she was no longer nude, Claray then returned to the table and settled in one of the chairs to consider the offerings. Aside from the bowl of milk, there was bread, cheese, fruit, fish poached in wine and herbs and some cold roasted chicken, probably left over from dinner. The chicken was undoubtedly for Conall, she knew. The fish though had probably been freshly cooked for her, which meant she really mustn't forget to thank Cook. While he grumbled and complained about her refusal to eat meat, he still troubled himself to cook special for her. He needn't have bothered. She had not expected him to and would have been happy to make do with just the cheese, bread and fruit, but dear God, the fish smelled good. Tasted good too, she acknowledged moments later as she started gobbling down the food.

Once done eating, Claray scooped up Squeak and walked back to the bed to look down at Conall. He was showing no signs of stirring though, so she considered her options. There didn't appear to be a lot of them. There was really no reason to leave the room. From the sounds of it, or more importantly the lack of sound coming from the castle outside her door, everyone had retired and she didn't want to disturb anyone. As for inside her room, the fire was starting to burn low, and would soon be out, leaving her in darkness. Besides, she had things to do in the morning, several people to thank and talk to, Lovey to check on, etc. So, while she wasn't tired, trying to sleep seemed a good idea.

Moving around to the opposite side of the bed, Claray sat down, set Squeak on the corner where he'd be out of the way and then drew the furs up to cover both herself and Conall as she lay down next to him. Then she lay there, watching the shadows dance across the ceiling as she waited for sleep to claim her. The fire went out long before that happened.

Chapter 13

$\mathcal{I}$T SEEMED TO CLARAY LIKE SHE'D BARELY FINALLY DRIFTED off to sleep when pounding at the door startled her back awake.

Sitting bolt upright in bed, she stared blankly at the wooden panel and then glanced to Conall as he grumbled and rolled toward her, flinging an arm out in her direction that surely would have landed on her chest if she'd still been lying down. Since she wasn't, it didn't, but landed on the empty space behind her instead.

Shaking her head, she slid out of bed and hurried around it to reach the door before whoever was pounding at it could knock again and wake him up. Poor Conall had missed out on a lot of sleep to save her and, in her opinion, deserved his rest. So she was less than pleased to pull the door open and find her father, Ross MacKay, cousin Aulay and Father Cameron in the doorway.

"Me husband is sleeping," she told them with a small frown. Knowing they were there for the bed linens, something else her mother had explained to her, Claray was about to suggest they return at a more decent hour when a heavy plaid was suddenly draped over her shoulders. Even as she glanced down with bewilderment at the heavy cloth, it was wrapped around her body to cover her, and she was scooped off her feet and carried out of the way.

"Mind the stoat," Conall warned, his voice rough with sleep as he carried her to the table and set her down in one of the chairs. He then straightened and turned to watch the proceedings, hands propped on his hips. It left Claray staring at his bare arse. She blinked at it several times as she listened to the men tromp into the room, and then Conall turned slightly and she saw his very large, very erect penis waving about. It had dried blood on it. Hers, she realized with dismay.

Flushing with embarrassment, Claray launched out of the seat, dragging the plaid off as she did, and immediately wrapped it around her husband's waist instead.

"Wife," Conall protested on a laugh as she tried to tuck the material into the waist to keep it in place.

Claray froze at the title. Lifting startled eyes to his face, she breathed with realization, "I am."

"What?" he asked, concern claiming his expression now.

"Yer wife," she said weakly, and had to wonder that she still didn't feel any different. She was married and had been bedded. Her innocence was gone, but she didn't feel any different than she had the day before, or the day before that. When was she supposed to start feeling different?

"Aye, yer me wife," Conall agreed, dragging out the words and looking even more concerned. Truthfully, he was eyeing her a little warily now, as if he thought there may be something wrong with her. "Did ye hit yer head while ye were bathing last night or something, lass?"

Understanding the suggestion that she was addled, Claray narrowed her eyes on the big lummox, and then gave a start and whirled to face the men when her father said, "There 'tis. Are one and all satisfied the marriage was consummated?"

Father Cameron and the others grunted and nodded as they stared at the sheet with the watery-looking bloodstain on it, and then Claray was distracted by Conall wrapping the plaid around her again. She immediately lifted her hands to remove it once more and cover him up instead, but this time he held it in place with his hands in front of her, pressing her back against his front to manage the feat. Since that meant he was presently covered, if only by her, she let her hands drop rather than wrestle with him and forced a smile when the men turned their attention to her and Conall.

"I'll go hang this over the rail," her father announced, his cheeks flushing a bit pink.

Claray wasn't sure if the show of color was because he was holding the proof of her innocence, which was also proof that that innocence was gone, or what was causing it, but he was definitely blushing as he rushed out of the room.

Father Cameron was not blushing, however. In fact, he was giving her a rather dour look as he peered at them. It made Claray think perhaps the plaid was gaping open in front or something, but when she glanced down she found that wasn't the case. She did see though why the prelate was scowling at them. The way Conall was holding the plaid in place made it look like he was cupping her bosoms.

Choking out a sound of embarrassment, Claray reached up to try to pull his hands away, but he wasn't letting go. After a brief tussle, she simply turned in his arms so that his hands were at her back and scowled up at him. For some reason, that made the man's lips twitch with amusement, she noted with an irritation that only increased when she heard that amusement echoed in Ross MacKay's voice as he said, "Annabel and Kenna are up and ready. We'll wait fer ye in the bailey."

Claray glanced over her shoulder at those words, wondering what they would be waiting for, but the man was already ushering Aulay and a still dour-faced Father Cameron out of the room and pulling the door closed behind them. Frowning, she turned back to Conall. "What—?"

The question died there, silenced by Conall's mouth covering hers in a kiss that had her melting against him with a sigh. Her response seemed to please him, and he reached down to clasp her bottom and lift her up until she could feel his erection pressing against her.

Moaning into his mouth, Claray wrapped her legs around his hips and kissed him eagerly back as he now rubbed against her core through the cloth of the plaid and her flimsy shift. The sensation had Claray burning for him, and judging by the groan it elicited from Conall, he was not unaffected either, so she was somewhat startled when he suddenly broke their kiss and dropped her, keeping hold of the plaid as he did.

Claray's squeal of alarm ended on an "oomph" when she landed on the bed.

"Dress," Conall growled, and then knelt on the floor at the foot of the bed and began to pleat his plaid . . . completely ignoring her.

Claray stared at him blankly until Squeak came and scrambled up her hip and chest to get on her shoulder. Reaching up, she patted him absently, and then stood and moved over to the chest to collect her dress. She didn't don it right away, however, but instead moved to the tub and set the gown over the chair beside it. She then set Squeak on top of that while she quickly used the cold water and the now dry strip of linen from the night before to clean herself up.

She washed her face first, and then did a quick standing wash of the rest of her body, paying special attention between her legs to clean up any remaining mess from her breaching. When she finished and turned to rinse out the linen and hang it over the tub, she was embarrassed to see Conall kneeling by his pleated plaid, but watching her rather than donning it.

Blushing with embarrassment, she turned her back to him and set Squeak aside to snatch up the gown to quickly pull it on and do it up. Claray then scooped up the little kit again and set him on her shoulder as she went to find her brush on the fur by the fire. She'd barely started to pull it through her hair when the sound of splashing water made her glance back to the tub.

Conall was now having a quick wash as well, she saw. When he turned the cloth and his attention to the dried blood on his penis, she quickly whirled away and stared at the cold ashes in the fireplace as she finished brushing her hair.

"Claray," Conall said a few moments later.

She turned in question to find he was now dressed and waiting by the door. When he held his hand out and raised his fingers in a come-hither gesture, she stood and set the brush on the table, then crossed to him. Conall took her hand the moment she was within reach, opened the door and tugged her out of her room to hustle her up the hall.

Fortunately, despite his apparent rush, he wasn't making her run to keep up with him as her uncle had done back at Kerr. While her husband was much taller than her and probably could have moved much more quickly, he chose a pace that allowed her to keep up at a swift walk with just the occasional skip to keep from falling behind.

The great hall was just showing the first signs of life as he led her down the stairs. None of her siblings were up yet. In fact, there was no one seated at the trestle tables at all at the moment. But servants were moving around, yawning and stretching as they set about their early morning tasks, their gazes occasionally moving to the linen hanging from the railing.

Claray took one glance at the broad strip of white cloth with her blood on it, and then ducked her head and avoided looking at it again. Honestly, to her mind, it was humiliating to have it up there. Now everyone in the castle knew what they'd got up to last night. Which she supposed they would have known anyway, but still, it was embarrassing, so she was almost relieved when rather than lead her to the table and sit her there on display for everyone to gawk at, Conall led her to the keep doors.

It was only as he pushed through them, tugging her behind him, that Claray recalled his uncle saying something about waiting in the bailey. Even remembering that now, she was startled when she saw the MacKays all mounted next to her horse and Conall's mount, with her father, his stable master, Edmund and her cousins Aulay and Alick Buchanan standing before them.

Her gaze following two MacKay men riding away from the group toward the gate, Claray opened her mouth to ask what was happening. Before she could, Conall started down the stairs, barking, "Where is Claray's horse?"

"This is Claray's mount," her father announced, and she couldn't help noticing his pride as he glanced to the black steed pulling impatiently at the reins Edmund was holding on to to keep the huge beast from charging up the steps to greet her.

"It's a stallion," Conall protested as they reached the bottom of the steps. "Ladies usually ride mares."

"Aye. Well, she rides him well, and the stubborn bastard'll no' let anyone else on his back so I gave him to her two years ago," her father explained as Claray slipped her hand from Conall's to move to the horse and give him a soothing hug. The moment she touched his neck and leaned her head on him, the horse calmed, rested his head on her shoulder and raised his front leg to hook his foreleg around one of her calves in his version of a hug.

"I forgot the stubborn bastard liked to do that," Alick said on a laugh as her horse dropped his foot back to the ground. "It's the only horse I've ever seen hug back."

Claray thought she heard Conall mutter something, but couldn't make it out, and then he was beside her, urging her further along her mount. But when he tried to lift her into the saddle, she resisted and pulled back.

"If we are riding, I'll need to don braies," she protested.

Conall blinked at her and then lifted his head to stare at the saddle. "'Tis no' a sidesaddle."

"Nay. I never ride sidesaddle. 'Tis why I need braies," she explained quietly, and didn't add that that was the only reason she still had her beautiful horse. Her father hadn't wanted her traveling to her cousins riding astride so had made her leave the stallion behind and travel in a cart. It had made for a much longer and uncomfortable journey there, but she was grateful for that now since her horse would have been left behind when Conall had carried her off from Kerr.

"Braies," Conall muttered, looking vexed, but then they all turned toward the keep when the doors opened and Mavis came bustling out.

Waving a bundle of dark cloth overhead, she hurried down the stairs, calling, "Ye'll need these, lass. I saw ye'd forgot them as I was straightening yer room," the maid added as she came to a breathless halt before her. She paused then, however, to take in the situation, and then urged Conall back a couple of steps, and took up position before Claray with the horses on either side of her. "Pull 'em on quick, lass. Ye can no' be riding without 'em."

Claray's mouth opened, and then closed, and then she glanced around. Conall blocked anyone seeing her from behind, and she couldn't even see the MacKays from where she stood between the horses, but her father, Edmund and her cousins were just on the other side of Mavis. When the foursome turned toward each other and away from her, she gave her head a shake and donned the braies, stepping into them and yanking them up under her gown.

"There we are," Mavis said with satisfaction, brushing down her skirts as Claray let them fall back into place over the pants. "Ye're all set." She fussed over her for another moment, and then raised sad eyes to her face, and murmured, "I'll miss ye, child. Come visit as often as ye can."

Much to Claray's horror, the woman then dashed away a tear and turned to hurry back the way she'd come. Whirling on Conall, she asked with growing dread, "What's happening? Where are we going?"

"Home," he said simply.

"What?" she squawked with amazement. "Now?"

For some reason that made his eyebrows quirk and amusement tug at his lips, but he merely nodded and then lifted her into her saddle.

"But—" Claray shook her head with dismay, and protested, "I was goin' to speak to Father Cameron, and I have no' packed, and what about Lovey and me other animals? I can no' just leave them. And I ha'e no' even spoken to me brother and sisters since returnin'. I ha'e to say goodbye."

Claray regretted bringing up Father Cameron the moment the words were out of her mouth and she realized the comment might make him ask why she needed to speak to the prelate. Fortunately, he didn't, but focused on some of her other complaints instead.

"Yer father's havin' yer clothes packed as we speak," Conall said patiently, mounting his horse with her reins still in his hand. "He's sendin' them and yer other things after us in wagons that should arrive at MacDonald a week or so after we do. He'll send yer animals too," he added, sounding a bit testy now. "We'll make do until then."

"What about—?"

"Yer brother and sisters will understand. Yer da will explain," he said before she could ask that question again.

Claray stared at him, consternation, fear and anxiety gripping her. This was all going much too quickly for her. She'd just got home little more than a handful of hours ago. In that time she'd got married, been consummated and now was being taken away from the only home she'd ever known? It was too much, too fast. She was on the verge of giving in to panic when her father touched her knee.

Lowering her head, Claray stared at him blankly, her emotions whirling and probably on her face for him to see. Instead of giving her sympathy and soft words, her father did the thing mostly likely to stiffen her spine.

"MacNaughton," he said quietly. "'Tis safer fer all if yer away so he can no' poison the meat or try some other trick to kill all but you, then force ye to marry him to gain MacFarlane."

Claray closed her eyes briefly at those words, knowing they were true. MacNaughton wouldn't attack outright with Buchanan, MacKay, MacDonald and MacFarlane soldiers filling the castle and surrounding area. But he could try poison or some other trick to get what he wanted. With her away, there was no profit to trying to kill anyone at MacFarlane. If everyone here died, the land would go to her, but be under Conall's care and control.

"Chin up," her father said firmly. "We'll deal with the bastard and make him pay fer his plotting. Meanwhile, Bryson's a good, braw lad. I trust him to keep ye safe. And," he added, his voice dropping to almost a whisper, "I ken ye'll keep him safe too."

Claray opened her eyes and met his gaze, then took a deep breath and raised her shoulders determinedly. "Aye, Da. I'll keep him safe."

Gannon MacFarlane nodded and then squeezed her knee one more time before stepping back with a gruff, "Safe travels, daughter."

Claray nodded, but didn't respond. She couldn't for fear she'd start weeping like a baby. She was already struggling to keep the tears pooling in her eyes from spilling over onto her cheeks. Forcing herself to take deep breaths, she merely listened as her father wished Conall safe travels too, and requested he send a messenger once they'd reached MacDonald.

Her husband assured him he would, and then turned his horse, pulling hers along with him as he headed across the bailey.

Her mount resisted for half a second, but Claray had expected that and leaned down to press along his neck and run a soothing hand down his shoulder. The moment she did, he calmed and let Conall lead him.

They rode across the drawbridge and past the Buchanan camp to where Roderick, Payton and Hamish waited astride their mounts with two older men she didn't recognize. A good three hundred horses fanned away on either side of the small group, each holding a MacKay or MacDonald warrior.

Claray's eyes went wide as she took in the size of their escort in the dawning light, and decided her father's wishing them safe travels had been completely unnecessary. MacNaughton would be a fool to try anything with an escort this large, she thought as Conall's uncle moved up to ride beside him. The older man spoke briefly and then her husband dropped back to ride beside her as he handed over her reins.

"Stay close to me if there is trouble," he instructed solemnly, and waited for her to nod before urging his mount back up beside his uncle. A moment later, Roderick and Hamish dropped back to take up position on either side of her, while the two older MacKay men dropped back behind them. It left Payton and Ross

MacKay to ride on either side of Conall as they trotted past the mounted warriors.

Once they'd moved beyond the last of the waiting soldiers, Conall urged his horse to a canter. As she urged her own mount to follow suit, Claray glanced over her shoulder. Lady MacKay and her daughter were directly behind her with the two older soldiers on either side of them. The rest of the warriors, both MacKay and MacDonald, were falling in behind their small group in a very long three-man formation. It was a most impressive sight, she decided.

Chapter 14

"*Y*OU SEEM TROUBLED, CLARAY. IS ALL WELL?"

Claray tore herself from her thoughts and glanced around to see that Lady MacKay had moved alongside her, with Kenna on her other side. She grimaced at the concern on their faces as she acknowledged to herself that she'd probably sat slumped in the saddle since leaving MacFarlane more than an hour ago. Certainly, her thoughts had been depressing ones. Aside from silently mourning the fact that she'd just left her home and family behind without even being able to say goodbye, she was fretting over the life she was traveling toward. And the more she fretted on it, the more problems she envisioned ahead.

Of course, the largest problem was her worry over her enjoyment of the marriage bed and what that might mean for her soul. Something she certainly wouldn't discuss with her husband's aunt. But there were other issues as well, and one popped up now when Lady MacKay said, "Is it anything to do with Bryson?"

"You and me father call Conall Bryson," she said with a small frown.

"'Tis the name he was given at birth," Lady MacKay said solemnly.

True enough, Claray supposed, but really the name grated on her nerves every time she heard it and she tried to explain that to Lady MacKay. "I ken 'tis his name by birth, but it sounds odd to me. I ken him as the Wolf, or Conall, and think o' him as that. Should I be calling him Bryson too?"

Lady MacKay smiled wryly and took a moment before admitting,

"I fear after calling him Conall for twenty-two years I find it odd to call him Bryson as well."

"Ye do?" she asked with surprise.

"Oh, aye," she assured her. "It took me a good year to remember to call him Conall after his parents died. He had always been Bryson to me, ere that. But it was important. My husband was hoping to keep him safe with the change in name, and eventually I got used to it." She sighed and shook her head, but then continued. "Now, however, Ross thinks it would be best to address him as Bryson to reassure his people that it is truly him, and I suspect he is right. So, I'm having to call him Bryson again, which feels just as odd to me as calling him Conall did at first."

She smiled at Claray. "So, I do understand what you mean when you say it feels odd to think of him as Bryson. But mayhap you can avoid the issue by simply calling him husband, or some term of affection instead."

Claray thought that might work. At least the calling him husband part. Conall had called her wife already a time or two, so should not protest her calling him husband in return. As for a term of affection, she would have to think about that.

"Might I ask you something?" Lady MacKay asked.

"Aye, o' course," Claray murmured, glancing to the woman.

"Why did you wish to speak to Father Cameron?"

Claray barely kept herself from groaning aloud at Lady MacKay's question. This was the very last one she would wish to answer, and she was searching her mind for something to tell the woman that wouldn't have to do with worrying over her soul because she enjoyed the bedding, when Lady MacKay spoke again.

"I was raised in a convent and was an oblate until my wedding."

The woman couldn't have said anything that Claray would have found more shocking. Nothing could have stopped the gasped "Really?" that burst from her lips at this news.

Lady MacKay nodded. "Aye. I only married Ross because my older sister fell in love and ran off with another. My parents then had to withdraw me from the convent to fulfill the marriage contract she'd forsaken. Otherwise, I would now be a nun."

"I can no' imagine ye as a nun, m'lady," Claray admitted solemnly. The woman just did not strike her as someone who would have been happy shut away in such a place.

"Well, I did not say I would have been a good nun," Lady MacKay said with amusement. "In truth, I do not think I was suited to that life at all, so I was very lucky to marry Ross instead. He has been a wonderful husband. And he's given me three wonderful children," she added, smiling affectionately at her daughter.

It made Claray miss her mother terribly in that moment.

"But the reason I bring it up," Lady MacKay continued, "is that the church's teachings on the marital bed caused some problems when I was first married, and I wondered if that was what you wished to talk to Father Cameron about? If so, I might be able to be of some assistance," she added gently.

Claray hesitated and glanced around. Conall, Payton and Laird MacKay were riding a good ten feet in front of them. A glance back showed that Roderick and Hamish were a little closer behind them with the two older MacKay soldiers behind that, but she didn't think Roderick and Hamish were close enough to hear if she spoke quietly. Deciding it was safe to speak about it, Claray turned toward Lady MacKay.

"Aye, 'tis that I wished to speak to him about," she acknowledged, and then blurted, "Father Cameron was very clear on the matter o' the marital bed and that only sinners bound fer hell enjoyed it, and I do no' want to go to hell, but . . ."

"But ye enjoy Conall's kisses and touch?" Lady MacKay suggested when Claray paused and flushed with embarrassment.

She nodded miserably, and then scowled and added, "God's truth, I do no' ken if 'tis a flaw with me or him, for he does do things I'm sure the church would no' approve o', but either way it puts me soul in peril and I do no' ken what to do."

"I do not think 'tis a flaw in either of you, dear," Lady MacKay said gently, and when Claray looked dubious, added, "Did you not vow to obey your husband during the wedding?"

Claray hesitated, and then grimaced and admitted, "I may ha'e, but I fear I was so overset by everything during the ceremony that I was no' payin' attention to what I agreed to."

"Ah." Her lips twitched with amusement, but she told her solemnly, "Well, I was not overset and I did hear you agree to obey him."

Claray just nodded. She could hardly argue the fact when she'd just admitted she didn't recall.

"And that being the case, if your husband is doing things intended to make you enjoy it, then I assure you he wants you to enjoy. Because it is much easier not to make that effort to please you. So, if he wants you to enjoy it, then it behooves you to obey and enjoy it, does it not? Surely your soul is not in danger if you are simply obeying him as you vowed before man and God to do."

Claray frowned over that. She understood what Lady MacKay was saying, but it was not as if Conall had actually ordered her to enjoy his bedding her. Now, if he were to do that, it would surely salve her conscience, because God would understand that she had to obey her husband. But he hadn't ordered it. She opened her mouth to say as much, only to pause as she heard a wolf's howl from somewhere behind and to the right of them.

"Was that a wolf?" Kenna asked, glancing around with surprise.

"Aye. It sounded like it," Lady MacKay murmured, looking around as well. When a second howl sounded a moment later, seeming closer, she frowned and added, "I have never heard one howl during the day. They are supposed to hunt only at night."

"Perhaps it has the madness," Kenna said nervously when the howl came again, sounding closer still.

Claray frowned at the words, knowing the kind of panic they could instill. The madness was an ailment that drove dogs, foxes, wolves and several other animals to a behavior so rabid and violent they would attack without provocation, and they could pass on that madness to anything and anyone they bit.

It was a most unpleasant ailment to suffer, one of the worst that she knew of. It often started mildly enough in people who had caught it, with some general malaise, an achy head and no desire to eat. But that was followed by a strange sensitivity to sight, sound, smell and even touch. She'd heard tales where the person who had been bitten couldn't bear the feel of their own hair brushing against their skin, or the wind on their cheek. Where even a small candle made their eyes burn and sunlight was blinding to them. Where the slightest sound was like a drumming in their head, loud and unbearable. It was around that point that victims also became seemingly terrified of liquids, and if forced to drink would retch violently, and even vomit until their throat ruptured and they spewed blood. And then the madness would set in. They would be calm one moment, their mind and thoughts seemingly fine, and then would suddenly erupt in a mad fury, becoming wildly agitated and uncontrollable, scratching and biting those around them until they suddenly calmed again. She'd heard that oftentimes toward the end they seemed to be sunk deep in terror, screaming endlessly and carrying on as if suffering hell's torments. It was supposed to be monstrous to see and worse to suffer, and so when they finally fell into a deep sleep and died, all were relieved that their suffering had ended.

Or perhaps all were just relieved that the threat of their getting it was ended. Because even the hint that an animal might have the madness was enough to instill panic. People bitten by animals it was even suggested might have it had killed themselves before knowing for sure if that were true. But then she'd heard stories where people who had been bitten by just stray dogs who didn't even have the ailment were beaten to death, or otherwise killed by those around them, even loved ones, rather than risk getting the ailment.

They called it the madness, or the raging madness, but Claray often thought the title suited the people around the victim of that illness as much as the one who had been bitten. She had no desire to see that madness break out among this large group of armed warriors. Especially when she suspected the wolf howling as it chased after them wasn't suffering the madness, but might just be looking for her.

A warm hand covering hers drew Claray's startled gaze around to see that Conall had dropped back and was taking her reins again to draw her to a halt. His uncle and cousin too had fallen back to take up protective positions next to Lady MacKay and Kenna while Hamish, Roderick and the two MacKay soldiers had moved up to help surround them. Their party had now come to a halt, and a glance back showed that the warriors were all following suit as they warily watched the woods on the right of their traveling party. Several had drawn their weapons, their swords or battle-axes at the ready.

Sighing, Claray turned back to Conall.

"Husband, I think—" she began worriedly, only to be shushed as he watched the woods and listened.

A moment later another long, mournful howl sounded. This one was closer still, and appeared to be coming from the woods almost directly beside them, though at some distance into the woods. Claray's mount whinnied loudly and turned his head, trying to turn his body toward the sound, and that's when she knew for sure that the wolf howling was no threat.

"Husband," she said more firmly, but he ignored her and turned to bark an order at the men. Much to her alarm, Roderick and the two older MacKay soldiers were suddenly away, leading a dozen other men toward the woods, their weapons already raised.

Panic coursing through her, Claray didn't bother to try to explain to Conall again, but tried to pull her reins from him to regain control of her mount instead. When he tightened his grip and scowled at her distractedly, she barked, "Stubborn Bastard!"

It was only when Conall turned a shocked, furious face her way that she realized he thought she was talking to him. She didn't have time though to explain and soothe him; her mount was responding as expected and rearing on the spot, tugging the reins from Conall's startled hands. Claray didn't bother to try to reach them—she wouldn't have been able to anyway—so left them hanging and leaned along the horse's back, ordering, "Go."

The other men's horses were crowded around them, leaving little room to maneuver, but Stubborn Bastard managed to push his way through. The path he chose nearly sent Payton toppling from his horse when he bit the man's mount to make him move and the animal reared.

Claray looked back as they finally broke free of the group and charged for the woods. She was relieved to see that her husband's cousin had maintained his seat. She also saw that Conall was staring after her, looking equal parts horrified and furious, and was shouting her name as he tried to maneuver his own horse around the others and give chase.

Ignoring that, she simply turned forward and scanned the woods ahead, then glanced toward the men she was now racing. They'd got a head start and their horses were strong and well-trained warhorses. But Stubborn Bastard was the finest horse Claray had ever encountered. He was stronger, and faster, and was also only carrying one slim woman while the other horses bore men twice her size, weighted down with broad swords and other weapons. The stallion quickly caught up with—and then outstripped—the warriors, flying past them so swiftly she barely heard the men's alarmed shouts.

Claray considered having Stubborn Bastard stop and turn to block their path so that she could explain and reason with the warriors. But the fear that they might just ride around her without even slowing made her give up that idea almost the moment she had it. Instead, she urged Stubborn Bastard on, hoping to reach the wolf far enough ahead of them to get the excited greeting part over with and calm the beast before the men caught up.

Claray really thought she could do it. But she hadn't expected the wolf to be as close as he ended up being and cursed under her breath when he ran into her path some ten feet ahead and simply sat down to stare at her expectantly. It wasn't the first time he'd done it, and Claray couldn't do anything but what he expected.

She shouted, "Stubborn Bastard!" but this wasn't the first time for her mount either. It was one of the wolf's favorite games. The horse was already reacting to his presence, and slowing. When he was a mere three or four feet in front of the beautiful gray wolf, the stallion started to rear to avoid running him down.

Already lying flat along the stallion's back, Claray grabbed the saddle pommel, and let her legs swing back to trail down the horse's back as he went upright, then dropped lightly to the ground behind him while he was still on his hind feet, his front legs slashing in the air. Once she was off, he crashed back to all fours with a whinny and shake of the head, and then followed when she hurried the few feet to the seated wolf.

The thunder of the other riders loud in her ears, Claray didn't hesitate, but threw herself protectively to her knees in front of the wolf, her arms instinctively going around him, lest any of the men thought to attack the beautiful creature. Of course, the wolf thought this a fine game and promptly started licking the side of her face, her head and shoulder and anything he could reach, making happy little whining sounds of greeting as he did. At which point, Stubborn Bastard decided he wasn't to be left out and started to nibble and lick at the back of her head as well.

"I think she kens the wolf."

Conall stopped gaping at his wife at that comment from Roderick and cast the other man a disgusted glance. "Ye think?"

Much to his amazement, his sarcasm made the usually solemn man laugh.

Shaking his head, Conall turned back to watch his wife being mauled by a great beast of a wolf—he'd never seen one so big— and her stallion, who both seemed determined to give her a bath with their tongues. He didn't move or speak for a moment though. He was still trying to regain his composure. The last couple of minutes had been most stressful to him.

First Claray had called him a stubborn bastard—something he still didn't understand since he didn't think he'd done anything to deserve it. And then her horse had reared, and just as he was about to pull her off the mount to save her from a tumble, the steed was off charging away with her.

Conall was pretty sure his heart had stopped at that point. It had certainly skipped a beat at the very least. He'd known she didn't have the reins and couldn't possibly reach them to regain control of her horse, and his mind had filled with all sorts of horrible endings to this escapade as he'd raced after her: Claray tossed from her mount and landing in a broken heap in the grass or, worse yet, tossed off into a tree that broke her back. Or, if she managed to keep her seat, then Claray and her horse both attacked by the wolf they'd heard howling, an animal he'd been sure was suffering the madness since wolves were night hunters by nature and simply did not run around howling first thing in the morning.

With all those possibilities spurring him on, Conall had forced his horse to dangerous speeds to catch up. He'd just passed the men and was closing in on his wife's mount when he'd seen the wolf appear on the path before her. His heart had stopped again when the stallion reared once more. But rather than being tossed, or tumbling from the saddle, she'd dropped off the beast as if it was her usual method of dismounting. She'd then rushed to embrace the wolf as if he were a long-lost friend. And that's what the horse and wolf were acting like too. Both were licking at her like they were mother cats cleaning a kitten who'd returned after being missing. Conall had reined in at once, and had heard the other men catch up as he dismounted, but had then simply stood staring at his wife and the beasts until Roderick had joined him and spoke.

"I guess I win the bet," Roderick commented now, and when the words brought Conall's blank gaze back to him, he shrugged. "Hamish thought the next animal would be a dormouse or pine marten, Payton thought a wildcat, but I bet on a wolf." He grinned, something else he rarely did, and pointed out, "It's a wolf."

"Aye," Conall growled, his gaze sliding over the rest of the warriors that had followed Roderick to hunt down the howling wolf. All of them had dismounted and now stood with their swords in hand but hanging at their sides, their wide eyes watching his wife and her beasts with uncertainty. He suspected they thought everything was fine and the wolf must not be suffering the madness, but weren't one hundred percent certain since they'd never seen a wolf act like this one. Or a horse, for that matter, he supposed, turning back to the trio on the path as Claray released a small giggle, and put a hand back to push her mount's nose away.

"Give over, Stubborn Bastard," Claray said on a laugh. "Me husband rushed me off so quick I've no' apples to give ye."

"Well, at least I'm no' the only one she calls a stubborn bastard," Conall growled, irritated all over again. He thought he'd been most kind as a husband and surely didn't deserve the title.

"It's his name."

Conall glanced to the soldier who had spoken and recognized him at once as his uncle's first, Gilly. The man was as old as his uncle, his hair more gray than anything else, but he was still one of the finest warriors Conall had ever met, which was why he was still his uncle's first, he supposed.

"'Tis true," Gilly said, putting his sword away. "Her da was talkin' about the beast while we waited in the bailey fer the two o' ye to join us this morn. Yer uncle said as how it looked a fine beast, and MacFarlane said 'twas a stubborn bastard, and in fact its name is Stubborn Bastard because they got so used to calling it that when it would no' let anyone ride it. Claimed he was thinkin' the beast a waste o' horseflesh and was considerin' killin' him when his daughter, yer lady wife, took an interest in him. He said she tamed it with a few soft words and an apple or two, and the next thing he knew it was following her around the bailey like a dog and letting her ride on him."

Gilly's gaze moved back to the horse as he added, "He said the beast still would no' let anyone else ride him though, and tries to bite anyone who gets too close. So, he gave the horse to her. Said she tried to change his name, but stubborn bastard that he was, the beast would no' answer to aught but that, so Stubborn Bastard he is."

"Did he mention the wolf?" Roderick asked as a half squeal and half laugh drew their attention to Claray, who had lost her balance and fallen to the side and was now having her face bathed by the wolf, who was whimpering happily as if it were a game as she tried to block his tongue with her hands. Conall supposed her hysterical laughter was helping to make the wolf think that.

"Aye," Gilly said, amusement in his voice. "MacFarlane mentioned she had a pet wolf too who acted much the same way as the horse. He said the pair o' them had been pinin' after her since she left fer Kerr. He said the horse'd be happy to see her, but mentioned his worry on how to get the wolf to Deagh Fhortan without her help. Then ye came out and Machar and I rode out to be sure the men were ready to leave, so I do no' ken what else was said."

"Looks like the wolf took care o' the problem o' how to get him to Deagh Fhortan," Roderick commented when the man fell silent.

Conall grunted at that, and then asked Gilly, "Did her father mention the wolf's name?"

"Aye." A wide grin claimed the old man's lips. "She calls him Lovey."

"God's teeth," Conall muttered.

"He does no' look like a Lovey," Roderick said, and there was no mistaking his amusement now.

Conall scowled at the words as his gaze took in the animal. Without Claray blocking the view, he could see that the beast was a good six feet long, perhaps four or five inches short of three feet high at the shoulders, and looked like he weighed a good ten stone. He'd never seen a wolf so big. But it had some damned fine coloring. Its fur was a combination of gray and white with black on the tip of the tail and around the face and ears.

"I guess 'tis fitting," Roderick said suddenly.

"The name?" Conall asked with amazement, thinking there was no damned way he was calling the great beast Lovey.

"Nay. That she has a wolf," Roderick explained, and when he didn't comprehend right away added, "She married you, the Wolf, and she has one fer a pet. 'Tis fitting."

Conall just shook his head and started toward his wife.

Chapter 15

$\mathcal{J}$T WAS WHEN LOVEY STIFFENED OVER HER, HIS HAPPY WHIMPERS becoming a growl, that Claray recalled where they were and why. Burying her hands in the fluffy fur on either side of the wolf's face, she turned her head sharply to see that while the men who had been sent out to hunt him were standing back and simply watching, Conall was approaching.

Whispering, "'Tis all right," to Lovey, Claray urged the wolf off of her, pushed Stubborn Bastard's head out of the way and scrambled to her feet between the two animals. The pair immediately closed in on either side of her, Lovey so close his head was against her left hip, while Stubborn Bastard had his head over her right shoulder.

"Hello, husband." Claray managed a nervous smile, and then ran her hand over the wolf's soft head. "This is Lovey. He's me friend. He's no' got the madness. He just must ha'e got out o' Edmund's room in the stables and came to look fer me." She frowned slightly down at the beast with concern and muttered, "Edmund'll be frettin' o'er where he got to."

"I'll send a couple o' men back to let him ken yer wolf is with ye," Conall said solemnly.

Claray beamed at him briefly, and then glanced to Stubborn Bastard when he nudged her shoulder. Recalling Conall's expression when she'd shouted at the horse as she'd rushed off to keep the men from killing Lovey, she reached up to rub her hand down the stallion's nose as she told Conall, "Me horse is named—"

"Stubborn Bastard," he finished for her. "Gilly just told me. It was a relief to ken it was no' me ye were calling that."

"Oh, nay. I'd never call ye that," she assured him quickly, and then grimaced and admitted honestly, "Well, mayhap I would if ye were being one and I was really annoyed. Though I'd be more like to just think it rather than actually say it."

For some reason that admission had his lips twitching, and Conall closed the distance between them.

Lovey immediately straightened next to her, his ears pulling back as he squinted at him, and then going straight up when Conall continued forward. When he then bared his teeth and growled low in his throat, Claray tightened her fingers in the fur at the back of his neck in warning, then turned to bare her teeth and growl at the wolf in return.

Lovey didn't look happy, but he did relax a little. Though she noticed he stood a little taller, puffed out his chest and went back to squinting suspiciously at Conall too.

"Wife?"

Claray turned to him in question. "Aye, husband?"

"Ye just growled at the wolf," he pointed out.

"Aye," she agreed, and smiled at him. "'Tis what he understands."

"I see," he said, but didn't look like he did and then asked, "Where's Squeak?"

Eyes widening as she recalled the baby stoat, Claray glanced down at her top, concerned that he might have been hurt when she was tussling with Lovey. A gasp slid from her lips when she tugged the material of the gray gown she'd donned that morning away from her chest and found the spot where he usually settled empty.

"Oh, no! I—Oh," Claray said as she glanced around wildly and spotted the baby stoat sitting on Stubborn Bastard's saddle. Moving along the horse, she reached up and scooped the small stoat off the saddle, muttering, "He must have climbed out while I was dismountin'."

She turned toward Conall with the stoat, to show him he was all right, but froze when Lovey was suddenly there nudging her hand as he sniffed the wee creature. Squeak had started to chitter and squeak at her the moment she'd picked him up, but froze now to eye the wolf with a decidedly wary air. Knowing her emotions would affect the wolf and his reactions, she forced herself to take a deep calming breath, and simply let him sniff. She relaxed fully though when the wolf's tongue whipped out to lash the wee creature, who immediately commenced to tremble in her hands.

"'Tis all right, Squeak," she murmured with a grin as she tucked him quickly back into the top of her gown. "That was just a welcoming lick."

"That or he was testing to see if he'd taste good," Conall suggested.

Claray shook her head at his teasing, and then gasped when he caught her at the waist and lifted her off the ground to kiss her. She thought she heard Lovey growl again, but ignored it and melted against Conall until he broke the kiss and eased her away, then lifted her onto Stubborn Bastard's back. A small sigh slid from her lips then, and she absently patted a squirming Squeak through her gown to calm him as she watched Conall gather Stubborn Bastard's reins for her.

"Will yer wolf make it to Deagh Fhortan on his own, or should I send him back to be brought out on a wagon in a cage with the other beasts and goods?" he asked as he held the reins up to her.

The dreamy expression that had been softening her face since he'd kissed her was immediately plowed under by a scowl. "Lovey's never been in a cage. I'd no' do that to him. He's a wild creature."

The look Conall gave her then was dubious. "Wild, eh?"

"Aye," she assured him. "A wolf is no' like a dog, husband. Ye can no' tame them. No' really."

He grunted at that, and asked, "But has he the stamina to make it to MacDonald on his own?"

"Oh, aye. Do no' worry. He'll most like run beside Stubborn Bastard most o' the way there. They're friends."

"Friends," he echoed with disbelief, and shook his head before walking back to where his horse waited by the other men.

Claray watched him go and then glanced down at Lovey. The wolf was watching Conall with an expression she couldn't decipher. Sighing, she clucked her tongue to get the wolf's attention, and when he looked her way, she warned, "Ye'd best get used to him, Lovey. He's me husband now." When the wolf just stared at her, she tilted her head and murmured, "We should find you a mate."

"Wife!"

Glancing over, she saw that Conall was mounted and waiting impatiently. Claray urged Stubborn Bastard in his direction, patting at her hip as she did to gesture for Lovey to follow.

"WHERE DID YOU COME ACROSS LOVEY?"

Conall heard the question from Lady MacKay, and found himself slowing his mount a bit in a bid to hear his wife's answer. It was something he'd wondered himself, but with three hundred warriors, the MacKays and Roderick waiting, there hadn't been time for him to ask everything he wanted to know.

"Oh, well, the villagers killed his pack when he was a pup. They were attacking livestock," she explained sadly. "Anyway, the next day, I was out for a ride and heard him cryin', or tryin' to howl, I suppose. It was the sweetest thing. It turned out I was ridin' right past their den. There were five of them altogether, and he was smaller than the rest, the runt of the litter, yet the only one still alive."

"He was the runt?" Lady MacKay sounded shocked, and Conall couldn't blame her. He'd never seen a wolf as big as Claray's Lovey.

"Aye," Claray said on a laugh. "Hard to believe now, is it no'? He's grown quite a bit this last two years. I think 'tis all the good food he gets."

"Hmm," Lady MacKay murmured, and after a moment said, "So ye took him home and raised him?"

"Aye."

"And yer da did no' mind?" Kenna now asked, sounding curious as she joined the conversation.

"Nay. He's used to it. I fear I'm always bringing stray or lame beasties home and nursing 'em back to health. They seem to find me wherever I go, and I've no' the heart to leave them to be prey fer others."

A moment of silence followed, and then Conall heard Kenna say, "Me mother used to work with animals in the stable at the convent she lived at before marrying Da."

"Did ye?" Claray asked with interest.

"Aye," his aunt answered. "Fortunately, I was able to take what I learned there and use it to help tend the injured and ailing animals and people at MacKay, so it worked out to my benefit."

"Oh!" Kenna said with excitement. "Ye'll probably be good at healin' the people o' MacDonald too, then, Claray!"

"She probably will," his uncle said beside him, and Conall missed Claray's response as he turned his attention to the man.

"Aye, but she probably has some trainin' in mendin' people as well," Payton commented. "Most lasses learn things like that durin' their trainin', do they no'?"

Conall waited, curious to hear the answer. He had no idea what lasses learned when they were growing up. He'd always been out in the practice field training in battle before he'd earned his spurs, and then once he'd set out to hire out as a mercenary, the women he'd mostly encountered were camp followers and the occasional lady in passing as he met with lairds who wanted to hire him.

"Probably," Ross MacKay agreed. "Yer mother taught yer sisters that, amongst other things."

Conall wondered what those other things might be, but then decided it didn't matter, since he doubted they would be very useful to Claray at MacDonald. At least, not at first. Deagh Fhortan wasn't your usual castle where a new bride could swan in and begin ordering servants about and discussing menus with the cook, or whatever they normally did. There actually weren't any servants yet, or even clans people other than his warriors.

Although those with wives and families would surely want to bring them to MacDonald now. He also hoped once word spread that he was there, the other surviving members of his clan would return. If there were any. In the meantime, there would be a lot of work needed to even make it livable, let alone a home, and he began to worry now about what Claray was expecting and what he was taking her into. The last time he'd seen the castle, nature had already got a good foothold on it, and that had been twelve years ago. It could only be worse now.

"What are ye going to work on first at Deagh Fhortan?" Payton asked suddenly, as if reading his troubled thoughts.

Conall grimaced at the question as he realized it wasn't something he'd really thought about. Mostly what had concerned him was getting together enough coin to repair it and return it to a working castle. Now he considered all the work that would no doubt need doing, and said slowly, "The castle wall and stables, I suppose."

"Smart," his uncle said with an approving nod. "The two most important matters. A wall for defense and the stables to keep yer horses safe and dry and healthy. A man is naught without his horse."

Payton gave a snort of amusement. "I would no' let Mother hear ye say that, Father. Or ye might find yerself sleeping in the MacKay stables when ye get home."

Ross MacKay scowled at his son. "She'd agree with me. Without a horse, ye can no' go hunting, or travel, or ride into battle."

"And without a wife ye've no one to keep ye warm of a night and give ye bairns," Payton pointed out. "I'm pretty sure keepin' a wife warm and safe and healthy is important too."

"Aye, o' course it is. But Castle Deagh Fhortan still stands and merely needs some cleaning up and such," Conall's uncle said. "The stables, however, fell to wood rot long ago. The lasses can clean the castle while the men shore up the wall and rebuild the stables."

"And what lasses would that be?" Payton asked with interest.

"Yer mother, Kenna and I are staying fer a bit to help," Ross MacKay said with a shrug. "Between the three of them they should have the place tidy in no time."

Recalling the state of the keep when he'd last seen it, Conall suspected his uncle might be a little off with that belief.

"'Tis beautiful."

Claray blinked her eyes open at those words, her gaze immediately finding Kenna. The woman was sitting on her horse directly beside Conall's horse, with her mother on her other side and her father next to her. Meanwhile, Claray was riding with her husband. Although that was a generous description since the horse presently wasn't moving and she wasn't doing anything like riding. The truth was she'd been sleeping in his lap throughout most of the five-day journey.

Claray had started every morning on Stubborn Bastard's back with Lovey trotting along beside them, and if the MacKay ladies were feeling chatty, she could last for hours in the saddle. But once the talking slowed and stopped, she started to nod off and found herself dragged into Conall's lap where she slept for the rest of that day's ride. Which meant that when they stopped for the night, she was incredibly perky and wide awake, while everyone else was dragging themselves around and ready to collapse inside their plaids and sleep.

It had made for a long boring trip with days spent sleeping, and nights spent staring at the stars in the night sky. She'd spent her evenings wondering what her brother and sisters were doing, how her father was and if Edmund was doing all right tending all her creatures by himself. Claray had spent very little time thinking and wondering about her future home and new husband though. That was mostly because he was a cranky bastard when traveling and she was almost afraid to consider what shape Deagh Fhortan might be in.

Deagh Fhortan meant Good Fortune, but from what she could tell the MacDonalds had enjoyed precious little of that, and after twenty-two years of neglect, she suspected the castle would need a lot of what her mother had liked to call "love and attention." Which translated to hard work and a good cleaning.

"Aye. 'Tis quite lovely from here," Lady MacKay said, drawing her from her thoughts.

Claray turned to look at the scene ahead and below them and caught her breath with surprise. They were stopped on a hill, looking down over a large, lush green valley with Deagh Fhortan on a smaller hill at its center. And it could only be Deagh Fhortan since she doubted there were a lot of abandoned castles strewn about Scotland. This one was definitely empty. Nothing was moving and everything was green except where bits of a pale beige stone with a tint of red to it was peeking out. The castle was still there, its shape obvious, but it was covered with greenery, as was everything around it.

Trees, shrubs and grass filled the land where most castles would have a clear space to prevent attackers sneaking up on them. Trees and grass were also growing along what she guessed used to be the moat, but now was a bright green ring around the castle. There were also trees and shrubs and greenery filling the bailey, and some kind of vine seemed to be covering a good portion of the walls of the keep, the towers and most of the curtain wall. But most surprising was the greenery she could see inside the buildings themselves. At least the ones that no longer had roofs to cover them and keep out the sunlight. It was as if the forest had laid siege, and taken over the castle.

But it was beautiful with the sun dappling all that green, Claray acknowledged. It looked like a fairy castle . . . It also looked like she had a lot of work ahead of her to make it a home.

"Well, we'd best head down and see what needs doin'," Ross MacKay said solemnly.

Claray felt Conall's chest move as he expelled a breath and nodded his head. When he then urged his mount forward to lead their party down into the valley, she sat up in his lap so that she could look around. She didn't think she'd ever seen a land so verdant and beautiful. There wasn't even a path down the side of the hill anymore; they were trotting through grasses that grew past the horses' legs and probably tickled their bellies.

For some reason that made her think of Stubborn Bastard and she shifted to look over Conall's shoulder in search of her stallion. She found him right beside Conall's mount a little behind where she sat, his head right next to her own. Shifting further around, she reached toward the horse, and smiled when he turned his head to lick her hand.

"Ye're no' holding his reins," she said with surprise when she noted them looped around Stubborn Bastard's pommel.

"No need," Conall said dryly. "He does no' let ye out o' his sight."

"Oh," Claray said, but wondered how long he had just left the horse to follow like that. She was pretty sure Conall had been holding the reins the first night when she'd woken up in his lap, but wasn't sure about the nights after that. Patting the horse's nose, she dropped her gaze to the ground, asking, "Where is Lovey?"

Conall's eyebrows rose at the question, and he too looked down at the space between his mount and Stubborn Bastard, then frowned. "I'm no' sure. He was there earlier."

"He ran off into the grasses when we stopped on the hill," Hamish announced, and she turned to see the man riding directly behind her husband's horse.

Claray frowned at this news, and then turned forward in Conall's lap and peered around. But the grass was so high she wasn't sure she'd see him if he was standing right in front of them. Concerned, she tipped her head up and called, "Owooooo!" long and loud, doing her best to emulate the sound Lovey always made when looking for her.

"What the devil are ye doin', wife?" Conall asked on a sudden laugh.

"Calling Lovey," she explained, but couldn't help the blush that crept over her face as she noted the startled expressions of the people around them and the soldiers following. This reaction was the reason she hadn't howled back when Lovey had been chasing them and howling for her. Claray supposed the fact that she'd just woken up was the only reason she had done it now. Her thoughts weren't clear enough for her to have considered how the others would react. They probably thought her mad now, she supposed unhappily.

Claray was distracted from that concern when Lovey responded with a long, loud howl of his own.

"Over there," Conall said, pointing through the trees on their left.

Claray twisted in his lap to look, and caught a glimpse of the top of Lovey's head and ears as he bounded through the tall grass toward them.

"He's got a rabbit," Conall said a moment later when the wolf had nearly reached them.

"Aye," Claray murmured, and then leaned down to brush her fingers over the top of the wolf's head as he fell into step beside them, carrying his catch. The wolf suffered it for a moment, and then raced ahead, charging down the path and out of sight with his dinner.

"Where's he goin' now?" Payton asked with curiosity.

"To eat," Claray sighed as she leaned back against Conall. "He'll be waitin' ahead."

Everyone was silent for a minute, and then Payton asked, "Do ye often howl at wolves?"

"Only Lovey," Claray answered. "He's the only wolf I ken."

"Ye ken Conall, and he's the Wolf."

"Aye," Conall agreed aloud, and then leaned down to whisper by her ear, "And ye howled fer me on our weddin' night. Hopefully, this night I can make ye howl again. Finally."

Claray stiffened in surprise and then felt heat suffuse her face as his hand crept up her waist where it was resting, and his thumb brushed over the bottom of one breast.

She hadn't howled on her wedding night. Not like she had when calling Lovey. But Claray had moaned, groaned, cried out and made sounds deep in her throat that she couldn't even think to describe or deliberately repeat and she knew those were the "howls" he was referring to. And he was suggesting he'd like to bring them on again. This night. Finally.

The thought made her quiver and her breathing pick up. It had been four nights and five days since their wedding night, and all that time had been spent in the company of the people now around and behind them. There had been no tent for them to sleep in, and no way to even slip away from the group for privacy since Kenna and Lady MacKay had joined her every time she'd headed out to relieve herself. Even the one time they'd camped by a river on the way here and Conall had asked if she'd like to bathe in it, they hadn't got to go together as she suspected he'd intended. Claray had been so embarrassed at the idea of stripping naked before him she'd blushed bright red and stared at him wide-eyed, incapable of speaking. The next moment, Kenna had announced she thought that a grand idea, and that the three women should go together. She'd then chivvied Claray and her mother out of camp.

All of this meant that Conall hadn't done more than kiss her since they'd left her room at MacFarlane. But it was sounding like he wanted to do that and more now that they'd reached Deagh Fhortan. The very idea sent excitement writhing through her and kept her mind fully occupied as they completed the journey down into the valley and to the castle entrance.

Chapter 16

"I'M THINKIN' THE STABLES AND CURTAIN WALL ARE NO' goin' to be yer first task here after all."

That comment from Payton brought an unexpected huff of laughter from Conall as they stood in front of their horses and surveyed what remained of the castle drawbridge. Which wasn't much. It looked like a giant had taken a bite out of it, leaving a strip perhaps a foot wide on the one side that curved toward the center at the top and bottom. They would not be crossing it, he thought as his uncle squatted to examine it more closely.

"Wood rot," the older man diagnosed, brushing his hands off as he straightened and stepped back beside him. Shaking his head, he muttered, "I should ha'e checked the castle yearly. Had I realized the drawbridge was out, we could ha'e brought—"

"Lovey!"

Claray's alarmed cry distracted them, and Conall started to turn, but stopped when a gray and white flash streaked past him and his uncle and raced across the now much reduced, and rotten, one-foot-wide drawbridge.

"Bad wolf. Ye could ha'e been hurt," Claray said with exasperation, stomping up to the foot of the drawbridge and glaring at the furry beast on the other side. The wolf merely looked back with confusion, and then dropped to the ground on the other side of the ruined bridge to eat his rabbit. It was something he'd been trying to do since reappearing with it when Claray had howled for him. He'd run ahead of the horses, managed a bite before they'd caught up and then picked it up and run ahead again repeatedly until they'd reached the drawbridge. Conall didn't think he'd got more than three or four bites of his meal up to now. But it looked like he would be able to finish this time. They were not going to be catching up to him anytime soon, he thought unhappily and then barked, "Wife!" with alarm when Claray suddenly hurried across the narrow strip of drawbridge right after the wolf.

Rushing to the foot of the bridge, he watched with his heart in his throat until she reached the other side. Once there, she turned and beamed a smile that didn't hide her own relief at reaching land safely.

"Lovey weighs more than me, so I thought mayhap if he crossed safely, I could too," she explained, and then—looking quite pleased with herself—added, "And I did."

"Aye," he said grimly, his gaze dropping to what was left of the drawbridge as he debated whether it might hold his weight as well.

"Nephew?"

Sighing, he turned sideways at his aunt's pleasant enquiry, and then automatically stepped back when he saw how close she was. He only realized what she was up to when his uncle began to shout in alarm.

"Annabel, do no' e'en think about—Ah, damn!" Ross MacKay ended with disgust as his wife traipsed across the drawbridge with their daughter on her heels.

Conall glanced from the drawbridge to his uncle, debating the matter, and then was suddenly bumped to the side. His uncle caught him when he stumbled forward, but the man's eyes were huge in his head and staring past him when Conall regained his feet and straightened. A bad feeling in his gut, he turned at once and was just in time to see Stubborn Bastard trot across the small strip of bridge too. The wood trembled and creaked and Conall swore he heard a cracking sound or two, but the horse made it to the other side and walked straight to Claray to nuzzle her shoulder.

"Well, Gannon did say the horse followed her around like a dog," his uncle muttered, shaking his head.

Conall didn't respond. He was watching his wife, who had turned to caress the stallion's neck, and was crooning, "Who's a brave boy! Aye, you are. Are ye no' clever to test it fer the men? What a brave Stubborn Bastard. Aye, ye're a good boy!"

"She's unmanned the poor beast," Gilly said in a mournful tone as he joined them to watch the powerful horse respond to Claray's coos by licking her cheek and forehead. "She'll be tyin' bows around his neck, or some sech thing next."

Conall shook his head with disgust and started across the drawbridge. If the damned thing could hold a horse that weighed close to two tons, it could surely hold him. At least that's what he told himself as he moved quickly across the narrow strip of bridge. Despite those reassurances to himself, Conall was more than a little relieved when he reached the other side without falling through into the moat below, which, despite how it had looked from the hill, was still a moat. The surface of the water though was covered with some kind of bright green algae that he didn't think he'd like to fall into.

Pausing once he reached solid ground, Conall surveyed the curtain wall. Now that he was close, he could see that it was green from moss and mold growing on it. He surveyed it briefly, considering how he would get rid of it or if he even should. The covering would be slick and make it harder for anyone to scale the wall, he thought, and then glanced over his shoulder, unsurprised to see that his uncle, cousin, Roderick, Hamish and his uncle's men Gilly and Machar were following him over the bridge one after the other. The rest of the men waited on the other side with the horses. Deciding that was a good thing, Conall turned toward the women, but they weren't there.

Eyes wide, he surveyed his surroundings and just glimpsed Stubborn Bastard's tail end disappearing into the forest of trees now filling his bailey. Knowing the beast was following his lady wife, Conall instinctively looked down to where the wolf had been moments ago, not surprised to find the beast was also gone.

"Lovey went with yer wife," Roderick told him with amusement.

"O' course he did," Conall said dryly, but then frowned and added, "Though it may be a good thing. He and Stubborn Bastard'll keep the ladies safe if any wild animals ha'e taken up residence in the bailey or keep."

"Damn," his uncle said with realization, concern crossing his face as he peered to where the women had disappeared. "There *could* be animals in there."

"I'm sure there are lots o' them," Payton said with a shrug. "Stoats, pine martens, birds."

"That's fine, but I'm more concerned with larger more feral animals like wildcats."

"Or boars," Roderick added grimly.

"I had no' thought o' that," Payton said with sudden concern.

"Neither had I 'til this minute," Conall admitted on a sigh, and when his uncle and the other men started into the bailey to chase after the women, he turned quickly to Hamish. "Divide the men into three parts. A hundred are to stay on the other side o' the moat to watch the horses and guard against anyone approaching. Another fifty are to sort out the issue o' a temporary, or e'en a permanent, new bridge if they can find old leftover tools somewhere in the bailey. They can use the trees growing inside fer wood," he added.

Hamish nodded. "And the other half o' the men?"

"Four on each wall to keep a lookout, if the stairs are passable," he instructed. "I want the rest to spread out and search the bailey and buildings fer any man or beast who may ha'e set up residence while the keep was empty. Select them first, and quickly," he added firmly, growing more anxious as he considered the possibility that not just wildcats or boars may have made their home here over the last twenty-two years, but bandits and outcasts too . . . and the women could be heading straight into their midst.

That thought in mind, Conall didn't wait for Hamish to respond, but turned to hurry after his uncle and the others. He caught up to them quickly, but didn't slow. Instead, he rushed past, a little desperate now to get to Claray and make sure she was all right.

"The bailey is beautiful like this," Kenna said on a sigh as they moved through the young forest that had grown up inside the wall. "But I suppose Conall will tear out all the trees and such."

"No doubt," Lady MacKay agreed. "The men would have trouble practicing at battle around all these trees."

"And they'll need room for the stables to be built," Claray pointed out, wondering if she would be able to convince Conall to build a special section in the stables for any wounded beasties she found, like her father had done for her at MacFarlane.

"I can no' imagine how hard it will be to remove all these trees," Kenna said, sounding dismayed now.

"It should no' be that hard," Claray assured her, watching where she was stepping to avoid tripping as she pointed out, "Most o' the trees are only ten to twenty years old by the looks o' it, and ha'e surface roots. Wrap ropes or chain around the trunk and attach it to a couple o' horses and these trees should pull out easily, roots and all," she assured her.

"Really?" Kenna asked with interest.

"Aye. They'd probably all ha'e blown o'er ere this if no' fer the curtain wall blocking any strong winds," she said, unsurprised when Kenna immediately began an interested survey of the roots growing across the ground.

"Why did the roots grow like that instead of making their way into the ground?" Kenna asked, her gaze moving up the oak tree she was now passing.

Claray gave a shrug. "The dirt was probably too hardpacked fer the roots to go deep after a century o' hundreds o' men and servants working and walking in the bailey. Ye ken plants need soft, fresh-turned earth to grow well."

"Hmm," Kenna said, and then laughed. When Claray and Lady MacKay eyed her with curiosity, she explained, "I was just thinkin', Conall was probably cursin' up a storm when he saw all the trees in here, but they're no' only goin' to be easy to pull out, which is surely better than havin' to cut down trees in the surrounding forest, but they do no' have to be dragged from the woods to be used to build the stables or whatnot. They're right here already. 'Twill save him time and trouble in the end."

"Aye," Claray agreed with a faint smile. There was always a silver lining if you looked for it, and it appeared Kenna was one who looked. She liked that.

"Oh, my."

Claray glanced with curiosity to Lady MacKay when she murmured those words and saw that Conall's aunt was a few steps ahead of her, at the edge of the small forest they'd been walking through. Seeing that her mouth was agape, Claray stepped up beside her and followed her gaze. Her eyes widened at once as she stared up at Deagh Fhortan keep, and Claray found herself echoing Lady MacKay's words. "Oh, my."

"Oh," Kenna murmured, joining them now too. "'Tis so lovely."

Vines started where the trees ended. They started at the base of the keep wall and wove their way down to the edge of the woods, as well as up the wall. They were like a large rush mat before them, and covered the walls in a tapestry of greenery that covered the thirty-foot keep wall from top to bottom. Claray couldn't even tell where the windows were, or if it even had any, and the door was nearly fully covered as well, leaving just a hole about a foot high and three feet wide at the bottom of where large double doors had no doubt been.

"Giorsal loved ivy," Lady MacKay said quietly. "She said it represented fidelity and eternal love. Bean knew that she liked it and had some planted on either side of the doors to please her. He then set a servant to the task of cutting it back regularly to make sure it did not go wild."

"He sounds a wonderful husband," Kenna said on a sigh.

"He was," Lady MacKay assured them. "And Giorsal was a wonderful wife to him. They truly loved each other and Bryson. They were a happy family and a joy to be around. I missed them terribly after they died." She sighed, and then confessed, "I still do."

Claray glanced to the woman, noticed that Kenna had reached out to take her hand in a comforting gesture and turned her eyes quickly back to the keep.

"Conall was six when they died," Kenna said after a moment.

"Aye," Lady MacKay said, but there was a question in her voice.

"But they had no other children?" she asked with a small frown.

"Nay. That is the only thing that made her sad during all the years I knew her," Lady MacKay told them solemnly. "She wanted more children, little brothers and sisters for Bryson, but year after year passed with nothing . . . and then it happened."

Claray glanced at her sharply to see her nodding.

"Giorsal was with child when she died. She was only four months along at the time, but so happy."

Claray let her breath out on a sigh, her gaze moving back over the ivy spread out before them. The more she heard, the more tragic it all seemed . . . and so unfair. Conall's family was not the only one destroyed by the poisoning all those years ago. The entire clan had been all but decimated that night. They deserved some happiness and some real good fortune, and Claray determined then and there to do what she could to ensure they got it.

"Well," she said, straightening her shoulders and stepping carefully over the ivy as she moved forward. "I guess I'd best take a look inside and see what needs doing."

"Aye," Lady MacKay agreed, following her. "As Ross likes to say, 'Once done, 'tis over.'"

"And as ye like to say, Mother, 'It can no' get done without starting,'" Kenna added on a laugh.

Claray smiled faintly at the women's words as she reached the steps and started up, careful of where she was placing her feet. The ivy had been around a long while and some of the vines were thick and likely to trip her. She was moving cautiously to avoid that and was halfway up when Stubborn Bastard whinnied with alarm and Lovey started to growl. Pausing, she glanced around with surprise.

Lovey had followed when they'd first started into the trees, but had soon wandered off on his own to explore. Apparently, he was back though, and while Stubborn Bastard was tossing his head and stomping his feet at the base of the stairs, Lovey was creeping up them toward her, his head lowered in what she recognized as a defensive mode.

"What's the matter, Lovey?" Claray asked, and frowned when she noted the wolf was staring past her to the hole in the ivy where the door should be. Turning back, she eyed the hole now herself. At first, she didn't see anything, but then she thought she saw movement in the shadows beyond the hole in the ivy.

"It looks like Deagh Fhortan has inhabitants already," Lady MacKay said with concern. She was half a dozen steps back, and no longer moving, Claray noted, and then turned to look through the hole again, trying to better see what might be inside the keep. She would have expected bats or birds of some variety to have made nests, and tons of mice, of course, but whatever she'd seen had been much larger than a bird or mouse.

"Mayhap we should have the men check inside first," Lady MacKay suggested, retreating down the stairs as Kenna rushed down to grab Stubborn Bastard's reins and soothe him. Much to Claray's surprise, he allowed it.

She started to follow Lady MacKay, but glanced over her shoulder as she did. She was just in time to see a piglet scurry out through the hole on wobbly legs. It was adorable, wee and round with striped fur down its sides . . . and her heart melted.

"Ahhh," she crooned, and stopped to stare at the cute little creature. She had no intention of approaching it. Claray knew better than that. She also knew that she should probably back slowly away in case the mother was around too. Before she could though, she was tugged down a step by her skirt. Whirling around, she scowled when she saw Lovey had grabbed hold of the hem and was backing down the steps, trying to drag her with him.

Pulling back, she said with exasperation, "Let go. I'm coming, Lov—"

That was as far as she got before the wolf suddenly released her skirt and leapt past her, snarling and growling. Having been pulling back against the wolf's tugging, Claray lost her balance the moment she was released and cried out as she staggered back. She tried to twist around as she fell, to get her hands out in front of her to soften the landing, but was only halfway around on impact.

Claray grunted as pain shot through her hip on landing, but otherwise ignored it and twisted her upper body toward the source of snorting and snarling behind her. Getting slapped in the face by Lovey's fluffy tail was more a shock than anything. She hadn't expected him to be that close, but he was right behind her, his jaws clamped on the snout of a huge boar sow that was just a step or two above him. The boar was shaking its head, dragging Lovey from side to side in an effort to make him let go. It had obviously come out through the ivy after its piglet and charged on her while her back was turned.

The beast must have been damned quick to get down the stairs as far as it had before Lovey had lunged past her to stop it, Claray thought grimly. The wolf had probably saved her life. There was nothing more dangerous than a boar. Many a hunter had been killed in a tussle with them. They were unpredictable, with tough hides, and could take what one would think was a killing blow, and get up and charge again. Boars, both male and female, had a tendency to ram the legs out from under you. If they got you on the ground, they were deadly.

Knowing that, Claray scrambled back to her feet, but didn't rush down the stairs as Lady MacKay was doing. Instead, she pulled her sgian dubh and watched anxiously as Lovey struggled with the boar, intending to help if she could. There was no way she could just stand by and let him be killed for trying to help her, and while wolves were a boar's main predator, they usually attacked as a pack, or with at least two or more wolves. One on one, the odds were not in Lovey's favor.

"Claray!"

She didn't even get a chance to look around at that shout before she was picked up and swung around, then set down at the base of the steps next to Lady MacKay.

"Get back," Conall growled, and then was gone.

She watched with concern as Conall rushed up the steps, retrieving his sword as he went to help Lovey. She was more than a little relieved when his uncle, Payton and Roderick rushed past her and started up after him, their own swords already out.

Claray's gaze shifted to Lovey, and she bit her lip anxiously as she saw that though the wolf still had the boar by the snout, he was obviously tiring. On the other hand, the boar seemed just as energetic and frenetic as it had been when she'd first seen them tussling and was emitting furious huffing, screeching and piercing cries that nearly drowned out Lovey's growls.

Just as Conall moved past Lovey to come up on the boar's side, the boar charged forward, forcing Lovey to scramble backward down the steps as he tried to hold on to the sow, who was still shaking her head wildly. Off balance and weary, the wolf wasn't able to keep his hold and his teeth tore from the snout, snapping together with a clack.

Free now, the sow turned on Conall. He immediately drove his sword into the beast. Claray suspected no one was terribly surprised when the animal stumbled, fell, rolled down a step or two onto its back and then back onto its front where it then bounced back up to go after Conall again. Fortunately, the other men had reached and surrounded her by then and added their swords to the chore of stopping the animal.

Even with the four swords in it, the boar didn't drop at once. The men all backed away a step or two and watched warily as the sow staggered a step closer to Conall. It then just stood there panting for a moment, shook its head and then stumbled, fell and rolled down the steps toward them.

Claray glanced around when someone grabbed her arm and dragged her backward. Her wide eyes landed with surprise on Laird MacKay's first, Gilly. She hadn't even known he was there too. But apparently he and Machar had remained behind to guard the women, for the two of them had pulled her, Lady MacKay and Kenna back out of the way.

She flashed him a small smile of appreciation, and then turned, intending to check on the sow, but found herself staring at Conall's chest. He'd followed the pig down the stairs and was taking her arm to usher her away from the scene.

"Is it dead?" she asked, trying to glance over her shoulder.

"Aye. 'Tis dead, ye're no' mending it," Conall said grimly, scooping her up when she tripped over a vine. He carried her some fifty feet to the corner of the keep before setting her down. "Ye're to stay away from the keep until we clear it out."

"But—"

"Ye can go around back and see if aught is left o' the gardens and orchards," he continued over her protest. "But I want the men to check inside first to be sure there are no bandits or other wild animals about." Pausing, he bent to give her a quick, hard kiss, and then straightened and ordered, "Wait here fer the men to tell ye 'tis safe to go in."

Conall started to turn away then, but paused when he saw Lovey had followed and was sitting beside her. Nodding at the animal, he gave it a pat, and said gruffly, "Good wolf."

Then he was gone, rushing back past Lady MacKay and Kenna as they approached with Laird MacKay escorting them. Claray could tell the man was talking, but it was only when they got closer that she could hear enough to know that he was giving his wife and daughter much the same lecture as Conall had given her. It seemed they would be looking at the gardens next.

Chapter 17

"With a little pruning, I think the orchard should recover well enough," Lady MacKay commented. "At least the apple and pear trees. A lot of the cherry trees have died though."

Claray nodded, her hand moving absently down Lovey's back as her gaze took in the overgrown orchard. The apple trees were gray and mossy, with withered leaves. She suspected if the pruning didn't get done before the fruit started to show, the apples would be misshapened and probably over small. But as Lady MacKay said, some pruning should fix that.

The problem was, from what she'd seen during the tour of the gardens and orchard with Kenna and her mother, that there was so much to do. The herb garden still had some herbs growing wild, but really needed to be cleared out and replanted. She couldn't even tell what vegetables used to be in the vegetable garden, though she'd pulled up a baby carrot or two and what might have been a potato. She needed to weed it, and sort out if anything could be saved, but suspected it would just be faster to replant that as well. Now here was more work to be done. And that didn't include the keep itself, which she suspected would be a monstrous undertaking.

She was beginning to feel more than a little overwhelmed at the tasks ahead of her. It wasn't like she had an army of servants to help her. In fact, Claray realized suddenly, she didn't have any servants at all!

And that wasn't all she didn't have. Conall had dragged her off with just the gown on her back, her horse and Lovey.

"Are you all right, **dear**?" Lady MacKay queried gently.

When Claray turned panicked eyes her way, concern immediately filled her expression. "Come," she said, urging her to a small stone wall that ran along the orchards. "Sit down here and take deep breaths."

Claray collapsed onto the wall, and rested her hand on Lovey when he lay his head on her knee. She then tried to take deep breaths, but was a little alarmed to find she couldn't seem to catch her breath at all. It was like someone was choking her and blocking the air.

She heard Kenna ask, "Is she all right?" but it sounded like it was coming from far away.

"What's happening?"

The question was asked in a sharp male voice that Claray was certain was Conall's. It made her redouble her efforts to calm down as she listened to the drone of voices around her. After a moment, she thought she actually might be succeeding, and that was when Conall sat down next to her, drew her into his arms and kissed her.

All that breath Claray had finally drawn into her body was expelled almost at once as she melted into him and sighed into his mouth. Conall's lips firmed out in what she thought was a smile, and then he deepened the kiss briefly, before easing away. He kissed her forehead gently, and then pressed her head to his chest, the words rumbling in his chest under her ear as he assured her, "All will be well. I ken it seems a lot, but everything can all be repaired relatively quickly. All will get done."

Rather than be reassured, Claray moaned at the reminder of what had distressed her and pulled back to eye him with dismay as she asked, "How?"

When he blinked at her in surprise, she pointed out, "I have no servants to help whip this place into shape, no clothes to wear but what I have on, no food to feed you, our guests or anyone else, no medicinals if anyone gets hurt, and I highly doubt there is a single stick o' usable furniture in the keep. We've no linens, no—"

"Breathe," Conall interrupted, and she just caught a glimpse of his alarm at her outburst before he pressed her back to his chest and thumped her back like he was burping a baby. Voice gruff, he assured her again, "'Twill be fine. Yer father was arranging fer yer clothes, medicinals and other things to be packed and sent on a wagon after us with an escort. He expected they'd arrive a week behind us at the latest. And I did bring ye a couple o' spare gowns fer the meantime."

"Ye did?" she asked, pulling back to eye him with surprise.

"Aye. When yer father went to fetch the priest I went into the keep, found a maid and asked her to pack a couple o' yer gowns in a bag and bring 'em down fer me. She did and I took it out and hung it from me horse right away so I would no' forget them in the morning," he explained quietly, and then added, "Ye were in the kitchens with yer cousin Alick at the time, else I'd have suggested ye do it yerself. But I heard the two o' ye in there talking with yer cook about food fer everyone, so just had the maid do it."

"Oh," Claray breathed with wonder at the thoughtfulness.

"In the meantime, me aunt and Kenna have offered to loan ye anything ye need that I did no' think o'." He scowled slightly before admitting, "I asked what I might ha'e forgot, but they just said 'women's things,' so I've no idea what they're on about, but they're happy to supply it, and MacKay is only half a day's ride away, so if ye need something, say so and we'll make the trip."

Claray managed a tremulous smile at the offer.

"As fer linens and such," he said now, "yer da said that fer years ere her death, yer mother had been preparing chests o' goods fer ye to take when ye eventually married me and moved to MacDonald. He had no idea what she'd put in them other than linens and such, but she'd known that things would be hard at first, and had wanted to help as much as she could so he suspects 'twill be useful whatever 'tis."

"Oh," Claray breathed, and felt tears fill her eyes. Her mother was still making her life better, even now she was gone.

Conall brushed a thumb under her eye, to wipe away a tear that had escaped, and added, "He also said he would be sending on yer bed, and the other furniture from yer room and a few other things fer us. So, there will be that at least within the week." He smiled crookedly. "But in the meantime, I decided that with three hundred men and all the wood here, I should set a couple dozen o' the handier soldiers to making trestle tables, and benches and such, so the great hall will no' be empty and we'll all have a place to eat together."

Claray smiled as she felt some more of the panic she'd been experiencing earlier falling away, and then he knocked another problem off the list she'd given him by saying, "As for food, that is what we men are for. I'll take out a hunting party every day if I have to, to fetch back meat enough to feed all. But I doubt daily hunts'll be necessary. These forests have no' been hunted for nearly twenty years except by the occasional passing traveler. They're probably teeming with animals. I suspect we'll only have to hunt every third or fourth day."

Claray managed a smile at that, but was thinking she'd have to raid the garden to find her own meals, or perhaps forage in the forest, and then Conall was suddenly standing and pulling her to her feet.

"Come," he said quietly. "I've something to show ye."

Curious, Claray let him lead her toward the back of the orchards, but then paused and glanced around with a frown. "Where did Lovey and Stubborn Bastard go?"

While the wolf had stuck close to her as she'd toured the gardens and orchards with Lady MacKay and Kenna, Stubborn Bastard had wandered away a bit to eat grass and leaves. Both were gone now though, as were the two MacKay ladies, she realized.

"Me aunt and cousin took them back to the bailey so we could talk," Conall answered, and gave her hand a tug. "Come. Ye'll like me surprise."

Eyebrows rising, Claray started moving again, following him out of the orchard onto an overgrown area around a huge pond that had to be more than two hundred feet long and fifty feet wide. It ran the entire length of the back curtain wall around the castle.

"A pond?" she asked, walking to the edge. Unlike the moat, the water here was surprisingly clear.

"A fish pond," Conall announced. "Me mother preferred fish to meat like you, and we had a natural spring here that would supply fresh water, so me da had this built and filled with tench, pickerel, bream and carp." He stared over the water briefly and then added, "O' course, while he did it partially fer Mother, it came in handy in the winter when food was scarce. Our people never went hungry."

"Do ye think there are still fish living in there?" Claray had barely finished the question when the sound of something slapping the water caught her ear. Glancing toward the sound, she saw a spreading circle on the surface of the pond from where a fish had jumped.

"I'm thinking so," Conall said with a smile.

Grinning, Claray threw her arms around him in a spontaneous hug. He hadn't solved every one of the problems she'd moaned about, but he'd solved a hell of a lot of them. She would find a way to deal with the rest. She'd talk to Lady Mac—Aunt Annabel, she corrected herself. She'd talk to her for some ideas on how to find servants to help with the cleanup and day to day. She'd figure out something, she thought, and pulled back to beam a smile at her husband.

"Ye're a wonderful man fer taking the time to soothe me worries," she told him. "And I'm a lucky woman to have ye to husband."

Conall stared at her silently, his gaze intense, and then he kissed her. It started out slow and sweet, his lips nipping and plucking and sucking at hers, and then his tongue ran along the seam of her lips and pushed between them. Moaning, Claray tried to edge closer, but his hands were between them. His knuckles brushed and rubbed against her breasts, but she was too wrapped up in his kisses to realize he was undoing her dress until he caught her hands and lowered them out of the way.

Claray shivered as the cloth of her gown slid down her arms, and when he released her hands to claim her breasts through her chemise, she tried to put her arms around his neck, but found the cloth caught at her wrists, hampering her. She didn't even think, just pulled her hands free of the material and then clutched at his shoulders as Conall kneaded her breasts and thrust his tongue into her mouth. When Claray moaned in response and pressed closer, her head tilting to a better angle, his hands left her breasts to push her gown off over her hips, sending another shiver through her body as a light breeze caressed her naked legs and arms.

Caught in the web of his kisses, Claray felt his knuckles brush her belly and the muscles there quivered in response. She only realized he had been removing his belt when she heard a soft thud and broke their kiss in surprise to glance down. The belt and sword were now on the ground beside them. He undid the pin at his shoulder then, and his heavy plaid slithered to the ground to join her gown.

Conall started to remove his shirt then, pulling it up and over his head, and Claray started to raise her eyes again, but her gaze got caught on the appendage jutting out from between his legs. It looked much bigger than she remembered it being when she'd seen him bathing in the lake, she thought as he tossed his shirt aside.

Claray glanced up quickly when he caught her hand in his. Conall didn't say anything, just gave her a gentle kiss, his lips brushing fleetingly over hers. Then he straightened and drew her along the edge of the pond to a large low boulder. It wasn't until they got to it that she noticed that it jutted out into the water. There were three small steps hewn into the side that faced land, and several more leading down into the water.

Claray followed when he led her up onto the boulder and then down the steps into the pond. She was surprised to find the water was cool, but not ice cold as it lapped over her ankles, knees, hips. A little gasp slid from her lips when it crested her breasts as she followed him off the last step and Conall turned to her, a smile crossing his lips briefly as he took in the now transparent cloth clinging to the round globes. When he then released her hand to brush his knuckles over one hard nipple pushing at the damp material, Claray gasped and curled her toes into the soft bottom of the pond.

Much to her disappointment though, that's all he did before bending to press a quick kiss to her lips. Then he turned away to dive under the water.

Claray gaped after him briefly with surprise, but then forced her mouth closed and told herself she should be glad. After all, he hadn't ordered her to enjoy his kisses and she didn't want to go to hell, so it was better he hadn't done more than kiss her.

Sighing, because she really would have rather he'd done more, Claray moved further out into the water. It dropped off quickly away from the stairs, but only another foot and a half or two she found when she dove under to reach the bottom. Coming back up a moment later, she treaded water and raised one hand to wipe the liquid off her face, only to gasp with surprise and nearly go under when Conall suddenly surged to the surface in front of her.

"Oh, ye startled me," she gasped, splashing out at him.

Chuckling, Conall caught her hand mid-splash and drew her against his chest for a kiss. A more proper one this time, but she'd barely begun to respond to it when he broke their kiss and began to run his mouth down her throat instead, raising a rash of little tingles there that seemed to flow through her body. When he clasped her waist and lifted her out of the water far enough that he could nuzzle and nip at her breasts, Claray moaned and then shook her head and gasped, "Husband?"

"Hmm?" he murmured, tugging at her nipple through her wet shift.

Biting her lip, she tried to organize her thoughts, but it was impossible with him doing what he was doing. Fortunately, when she didn't say anything, he stopped toying with her nipple and lifted his head to look up at her in question.

"Do ye want me to enjoy the bedding?" Claray blurted the question quickly before she could lose her nerve.

When he stared at her as if she had lost her mind, she moaned in misery and explained, "Father Cameron says only sinners enjoy the bedding and sinners go to hell, but Lady MacKay said as how if ye were giving me pleasure it must be because ye want me to enjoy it, and as I've promised to obey ye I should because that was a vow before God and all. But ye have no' ordered me to enjoy it, so I was wondering did ye want me to? Or should I try no' to enjoy it? To save me soul."

Conall remained still for a moment, bemusement on his face, and then lowered her back into the water and peered at her solemnly. "Wife."

"Aye?" she asked warily.

"I order ye to enjoy me lovin'," he said firmly, and then frowned and added, "If ye're enjoyin' it. Do no' pretend to, but if ye are, then I want ye to." He frowned, not seeming pleased with his own explanation, and then asked, "Do ye understand?"

"Aye, husband," she murmured, quite sure she did. He'd ordered her to enjoy it. She would not go to hell because she was just obeying her husband.

Claray smiled at him, and patted his chest. "Ye may kiss me again if ye like, husband, for I promise to enjoy it."

"Do ye now?" he asked with a faint smile. Then bent to nip at her ear before trailing his lips down her neck.

"Aye," she breathed, squirming against his body in the water. It wasn't the kiss she'd meant, but this was nice too.

"And do ye like this?" he asked, his voice a husky growl as one hand covered her breast underwater and began to knead. "Or this?" His other hand pressed against her bottom as he moved closer to the stairs, so that she rode lower in the water and her groin rubbed against his.

"Oh, aye," she moaned, arching her back and wrapping her legs around his hips so that their bodies rubbed together more firmly.

The action earned her another kiss, this one hot and demanding as he carried her out of the water and up the steps. A moment later he broke their kiss again and laid her in the overgrown grass beside the pond, then dropped to lay on his side next to her. He rested his hand on her chest just below her breasts, opened his mouth, then snapped it closed and glanced back sharply to the spot between her breasts where the baby stoat usually nestled.

"Where's Squeak?" he asked with concern.

Claray smiled slowly, finding his concern for the wee kit adorable when he'd been so displeased at her for rescuing him. Hiding her smile when his gaze shot back to her face, she said, "With yer aunt."

"Aunt Annabel?" he asked with amazement.

"Aye. He got annoyed with being jostled about every time I bent to pull weeds to see what was in the herb and vegetable gardens, so he climbed out o' me gown, ran down me skirt, rushed to yer aunt and climbed up into her gown." She grinned when his eyes went wide, and assured him. "She did no' mind at all. I offered to take him back, but she said he was fine."

Conall gave a disbelieving laugh at that news and Claray grinned and told him, "I like it when ye laugh."

He smiled faintly at her words, and let the hand on her chest cover one breast through the damp cloth of her shift. "What else do ye like?"

"Yer smile, yer face, yer touch," she listed off on a moan as he kneaded the tender flesh his hand was covering.

"I've thought o' ye like this since that day at the river," he admitted in a low growl.

Claray blinked her eyes open to see his gaze moving over her body.

"Yer shift wet and see-through, clinging to yer body. Yer nipples hard and eager, poking the material up," he said. "Ye make me crazy fer wanting ye."

He plucked at one erect nipple through the damp cloth, and growled, "I can see why MacNaughton was so determined to have ye."

"He wanted MacFarlane, no' me," she protested, arching into his touch.

"I begin to think yer wrong about that," Conall growled, and bent to claim her other nipple with his mouth, nipping and sucking it through the damp material. Moaning, Claray slid the fingers of one hand into his hair to cup his head, her back arching to press her breasts up into his dual assault as he fondled and suckled. He then stopped toying with the one breast and let his hand drift down below her hip. Her legs shifted restlessly when it began to skim back up, pushing the hem of her shift before it. Once he had it at her waist, his hand wandered back down, and she cried out when it suddenly dipped between her legs.

Claray gasped, and moaned, her body writhing and head twisting on the ground as his clever fingers caressed her. The sensations he was raising in her stole all of her focus so that she didn't even notice when he stopped sucking at her nipple to watch her face as he pleasured her. But then he pushed a finger into her. Claray's eyes shot open on a cry of excitement, her gaze meeting and caught by his as his thumb continued to caress even as his finger eased in and out. Her body responded without her mind's input, her knees raising and feet planting to push her hips up into each thrust as she gasped nonsensical pleas. And then she couldn't bear it anymore and reached up to pull his head down. She kissed him frantically as he continued to caress her, and then the tension he was building in her suddenly snapped and she broke their kiss on a cry as her back arched and her body trembled and shook.

For a moment, or maybe more, Claray was lost in the sensations washing through her. When she regained some of her sensibilities, Conall was pressing kisses to her eyes, her nose, her neck. Then his mouth covered hers briefly, his tongue stirring her, and she wrapped boneless arms around him and began to kiss him back. When her kisses became as hungry as his, he tore his mouth away and trailed it down her throat again. He found her breasts next, but didn't stay there long before his lips followed an invisible trail down her stomach. Her stomach began jumping in anticipation at once as she recalled their wedding night, and Claray bit her lip and held her breath, almost afraid she was wrong and he wasn't about to—

"Ahhh!" she cried out as his mouth found the spot she'd hoped he was looking for. Dear God in heaven, she loved his tongue, Claray thought wildly as he pleasured her with it. She wanted to dig her nails into his shoulders, but he was too far away so she dug them into the earth at her sides instead. She wanted to wrap her legs around him to urge him on, but was afraid of smothering him, so dug her heels into the ground and thrust her pelvis up instead. And then his tongue pushed into her as if he were kissing her mouth, and Claray came undone for a second time. But this time was stronger than the last and an ululating cry burst from her mouth as she convulsed under the onslaught.

Her body was still spasming and pulsing with her release when Conall shifted up her body and thrust into her. Claray's arms and legs closed around him then, her nails and heels digging in as he withdrew and thrust again and again. Like their wedding night, he quickly brought her passion back to life, and she was suddenly afraid he'd find his release and leave her wanting again as he had then. But even as she had that worry, he raised himself up on his knees, lifted her hips to the angle he wanted with one hand and then began to caress her above where they were joined with the other as he continued to thrust into her.

Conall watched her the whole time, his eyes moving over her jiggling breasts and then to her face as she twisted her head on the ground. Claray had the brief thought that she should be embarrassed, but was too wrapped up in the sensations he was causing in her to care, and then she cried out with her release, and Conall gave one last hard thrust, burying himself deep inside her as his shout of pleasure joined hers.

Breathless and weak, Claray stared up at him as she tried to catch her breath, and after a moment Conall opened his eyes. He released the hold he had on her hip, and dropped to his elbows above her to press a kiss to her lips, and they both froze as a whooshing sound flew past over them. They turned their heads together to stare at the arrow buried in the ground next to them. The end with the fletching was vibrating slightly still, she saw, and then Conall cursed and rolled them both over it and to the edge of the pond, then in.

Claray barely had time to take a deep breath before the water was closing over them. But Conall didn't keep them under long. The cool liquid had hardly closed over her head when he was standing up and dragging her back to the surface.

"Are ye all right, lass?" he asked with concern, holding her by one elbow to keep her from going under as she pushed the hair back from her face. The water was over her head, but just to his neck here.

"Aye," she breathed, managing a smile, and then she glanced around. They were close to the pond wall, but it rose a good foot above the water, so she thought their heads must still be protected so long as they stayed where they were. Certainly, the rest of their bodies were safe from the neck down. The problem was what to do now.

"Me sword's on me belt with our clothes," he muttered, gazing toward the wall of the pond as if wishing he could see through it. Grimacing, he added, "O' course, I can no' fight arrows with a sword anyway. But I'd still feel better having it."

Claray didn't say that she would too, but in truth she would have felt better if he were armed. Just in case whoever shot the arrow came to the pond's edge to try to finish them off.

"Should we shout fer help?" she asked, glancing nervously toward the top of the pond wall. Before he could answer, they both heard their names being shouted.

"Hold on to me side," Conall instructed, and when she clasped his waist, he reached up to grab the top of the wall and surged partway out of the water to look over it. "'Tis Payton and Roderick. I think me uncle and aunt are behind them."

"Thank goodness," Claray sighed as he sank back into the water and began to move them both toward the steps leading out.

Chapter 18

"Ye did no' see who shot at ye?"

Dressing behind the plaid Lady MacKay and Kenna were holding up to give her privacy, Claray smiled wryly at that question. It was only the third time Conall's uncle had asked him that, but she understood. It spoke of the frustration the man was suffering. Something she was experiencing as well, and she hadn't spent the last two decades looking for the culprit who had killed Conall's parents as well as a good portion of his clan, and tried to kill him twenty-two years ago.

"Nay," Conall said wearily. "We heard the arrow whizz past, saw it planted in the ground next to us and rolled into the water. Neither o' us saw anything."

A moment of silence passed and then Payton asked, "Are we thinking 'tis MacNaughton, or the old business?"

Claray froze in the process of doing up the lacings of her gown at that question. She hadn't even considered the possibility of MacNaughton being behind this attack. She hadn't thought of the man at all since leaving MacFarlane.

"There's no way to tell," Conall said finally when everyone was silent. "It could be either."

"Aye," his uncle sighed.

Finished with her lacings, Claray ran her fingers through her hair to try to ensure it wasn't standing up all over the place, and then walked around the plaid and smiled at Aunt Annabel and Kenna, before murmuring, "Thank ye."

"Ye're more than welcome," Lady MacKay said solemnly as they lowered the plaid.

"Aye," Kenna agreed, then balling the material up, she handed it to Claray and added with disgust, "Now go make me cousin put his plaid on. I really ha'e no desire to look on his naked arse again . . . or anything else."

Claray bit back a smile and merely nodded as she took the cloth and moved over to her husband. He and the other men were standing a good twenty feet from where she'd been dressing. They were in a loose circle made up of his uncle, his cousin, Roderick, Hamish, Gilly and Machar. But Conall stood, arms crossed over his chest, in just his shirt, which did not quite cover his dangly bits in front, or the bottom of his arse in back. Claray avoided looking below his waist as she handed him the plaid. She then turned quickly away and walked back to Lady MacKay and Kenna.

"How are you doing, dear?" Conall's aunt asked, rubbing her back soothingly when Claray stopped beside her.

Claray smiled, recognizing the comforting caress as something she often did to Kenna. "I'm fine. We were lucky."

"Aye," Kenna said with a little shudder. "I can hardly believe neither o' ye were shot through with the arrow. I thought ye'd both died when we heard yer screams, they were that pain-filled and anguished."

Claray stiffened, her eyes widening, and then felt herself going hot with a blush as she realized what screams Kenna was referring to. She and Conall had only screamed once each, when they'd both found their pleasure that last time. Good Lord, everyone had come running because of how loud she and Conall had been. Not that she was sorry they'd come. They'd needed their help, but how humiliating would it have been if they'd all come running and found them lying in each other's arms, recovering from the loving?

"Aye. Well, thank goodness they were not shot," Lady MacKay responded.

Claray nodded and glanced to her, eyes widening and her blush no doubt deepening as she noted the amusement in the older woman's eyes. Conall's aunt obviously had a good idea of what had been behind their screams, and that it had nothing to do with the arrow that was shot at them.

"I want guards on Claray."

She turned sharply at that announcement from Conall, and whirled away just as quickly when she saw he was still on his knees, pleating his plaid. His beautiful bare arse was fully on display as he knelt and leaned over the cloth.

"How many?" Hamish asked, and then suggested, "Three?"

Claray's eyebrows rose. Three seemed excessive to her. Surely one or two would do?

"Four," Conall growled, apparently not sharing her opinion. "I want ye to be one o' them, Hamish. There's no one I trust more."

"Thank ye, cousin," Payton said dryly.

"Ye ken I was no' including you in that comment," Conall said with irritation as he finished donning his plaid. "I meant among me men. I trust ye and Roderick like brothers."

"Good," Payton said cheerfully. "Then Roderick can help guard ye and I'll guard wee Claray."

"The hell ye will," Conall growled as he stood and straightened his pleats. "Roddy can help guard Claray and ye'll guard me."

"If ye insist," Payton said with a shrug.

Conall nodded with a grunt, finished with his pleats and then lifted his head sharply. "Wait. I do no' need a guard."

"Aye, ye do," Laird MacKay growled. "Or would ye leave yon lass a widow fer yer pride?"

Claray froze like a doe surrounded by wolves when the men all turned their gazes her way and caught her looking and listening. It wasn't until Payton winked that she had the good sense to quickly whirl away.

"Did ye tell her about the clan members from MacKay?" Payton asked suddenly.

Claray heard Conall curse, and then he was suddenly beside her, clasping her hand and urging her away from his aunt and cousin.

"Wife," he said once he'd drawn her several feet away and stopped to face her. "Ye ken those worries ye had about clothes and servants and such?"

"Aye," she said slowly, wondering what that had to do with MacKay clan members.

"Well, ye'll have servants to help clean up the keep."

"I will?" Claray asked uncertainly.

"Aye. In fact, some o' them have already arrived. 'Tis why I came to find ye earlier in the orchards," he said, and explained, "At least two dozen families, plus another ten single individuals, moved to MacKay for protection after the murders. Their numbers have doubled or mayhap even tripled over the years, and me uncle sent a couple o' soldiers on ahead to MacKay while yer father was fetching the priest to marry us. They were to ride flat out to MacKay and tell those clan members that I was returning and any who wished to join me should pack up and be ready to move. Then as we were riding past MacKay this morning, he sent a couple more to tell them it was time and escort them here to Deagh Fhortan." He grimaced now, and admitted, "I came to find ye in the orchard to tell ye they've arrived, but are waiting on the other side of the moat until the drawbridge is repaired. Unfortunately, ye were upset when I came to tell ye, and then . . ."

He didn't have to say what the "and then" was for why he hadn't told her. She quite vividly recalled what the "and then" had been before the arrow had been loosed on them. The thought made her smile softly for a brief moment, before what he'd said registered and her brain started to pick it over.

These families probably hadn't been castle servants. From what she understood, those had all died in the poisoning. Everyone who ate that night had died. Only the families in their own cottages or farms, who made their own food that night, had survived. But these people were willing to give up whatever life they'd built for themselves at MacKay, to return to their clan's land even though it meant starting over. The thought made her feel awful, and she said as much to Conall.

"It breaks me heart that we've so little to offer them just now. We can no' even give them a roof over their heads."

"Aye, 'twill be tough fer a bit fer all o' us. But we'll all work together to make a good life," he assured her. "And then they'll have their pride, their land and their clan back . . . and that's a lot."

When Claray nodded, he kissed her on the forehead and suggested, "Why do ye no' go explore the keep and see what's what now that the animals are cleared out."

"The animals are cleared out?" she asked with surprise.

"Aye. That was something else I was coming to tell ye when I found ye in the orchards," he admitted with a wry smile. "There was just the one family o' feral pigs, and a few chickens nesting on what remains o' the stairs to the upper floor. The men moved them out into the bailey and are building doors to keep them out."

"Oh."

"Now go on," he urged. "I'm sure me aunt and Kenna are bored standing around here."

Nodding, Claray started to turn away, but then stopped and whirled back to give him a quick kiss, then promptly blushed at the spontaneous action when his eyebrows flew up.

"Wives kiss husbands when they part," she muttered to cover her embarrassment, and headed away, only to have him catch her arm and draw her back.

"That was no' a proper kiss," he announced solemnly, and then commenced to show her his version, which left her breathless and flushed when he released her and walked back to the men.

"WHAT'S THIS?"

Claray tore her gloomy gaze from the moss- and mold-covered interior walls of Deagh Fhortan keep to see that Kenna had moved into a small dark room off the great hall. The younger woman was presently using one foot to sweep aside twenty-two years' worth of detritus that had gathered on the floor. Although why she was bothering, Claray wasn't sure.

"I need a torch," Kenna announced, kneeling now and sounding excited.

Claray turned toward Hamish, but before she could say anything, he barked at the soldier beside him, "Hendrie, find a torch."

The man rushed off at once, and Hamish, Roderick and the fourth soldier, who was apparently named Colban, followed Claray toward Kenna when she headed that way.

"This was the buttery if I recall correctly," Lady MacKay said as she reached the now doorless room just steps ahead of Claray. "And I'm quite sure that trap door you are clearing off leads down into the beer cellar. I can hardly believe the trap door is still intact."

Claray grunted at the comment. She couldn't believe it either. Nearly every other stick of wood in the keep had been eaten away by wood rot—if not wholly, then mostly—thanks to the rain and damp let in by the lack of roof, which had apparently been eaten away by wood rot first, once there was no one around to repair it as needed. All that was left in the keep were three half stairs that the chickens had been roosting on, and perhaps a third of the door into the kitchens. Everything else, including the upper floor, was completely gone. Even the furniture in the great hall had disintegrated or been stolen. Conall's men were going to have a lot of building to do. They would also have to remove the tree that was growing up one wall of the great hall, its roots pushing the stones up and making one heck of a mess.

"With the trap door being in such good shape, the beer cellar may be fine too," Kenna pointed out with excitement as she tugged at the metal ring to open the trap door.

"Let me do it, lass," Roderick offered, slipping past Claray to enter the small room when Kenna couldn't lift the door.

Giving up, Kenna straightened and shifted out of the way for the big man.

They all watched as he bent to grasp the ring and pulled upward. There was a slight hesitation, and then almost a suctioning-type sound as the trap door jerked up. They all crowded a little closer to peer through the square hole left behind. But there was nothing to see. The darkness was absolute.

"We're going to need more than the one torch," Roderick commented.

"Is three enough?" Hendrie asked as the area around Claray suddenly grew much brighter. Turning, she saw the approving look Hamish gave the soldier when he saw that he carried one lit torch and two unlit torches. It made her smile. Hendrie was obviously a slightly older version of Hamish. A man who thought ahead and planned for anything.

Roderick waited patiently as Hendrie lit the other two torches, and then took the last one when he held it out. Her husband's large friend then held it over the square hole to reveal stairs hewn in stone. Glancing up then, Roderick said, "I'll go first. Lady Claray, ye're behind me with Hamish at yer back, then the ladies MacKay, and then Colban and Hendrie."

He was obviously a man used to making decisions. Roderick didn't wait for anyone's approval of his plan, but then started down the stairs with his torch, and Claray quickly followed.

Where everything was covered with debris in the great hall, down here there was just a fine coat of dust that got stirred up a bit by their footsteps. Other than that though, the space looked the same as it had no doubt looked twenty-two years ago. The ceiling, floor and walls—like the stairs—were hewn out of the same limestone that the keep and curtain walls appeared to be built of, and Claray wondered if they hadn't been mined from down here and hauled up to make walls.

"Look at all the beer butts," Kenna breathed with wonder, and Claray turned her attention to the large casks lining the walls as the girl exclaimed, "They're still sealed. Do ye think the beers any good?"

Claray didn't think so, but before she could say as much, Kenna gasped, "Oh, look! Another room!"

When Kenna rushed toward the door, Hamish hurried to beat her there, and then opened the door and led the way in.

"The wine cellar," Claray murmured as she followed Kenna in and glanced over the rows of oak casks.

"Most of them are sealed too," Kenna pointed out. "They might still be good."

"Or poisoned," Roderick rumbled, and told them, "They think the poison was in the beer and wine that night."

While Kenna gasped and immediately backed away from the casks, Claray eyed them silently. She didn't think the sealed casks were probably poisoned. But the ones with seals that were broken might be. She didn't care either way, because she had no intention of taking the risk by drinking anything. Besides, she had another use for the wine. It would solve a problem she'd been fretting over since finally being allowed inside the keep. She needed something to remove the mold and moss from the keep walls. Lye would do the trick. However, they didn't have any, and she didn't wish to wait until they could make it. Besides, the amount they'd have to make would take forever and need a lot of ash. Nay. Using the wine—and undoubtedly in some cases, vinegar that the wine had turned into—would be a much better solution to kill the mold and moss. There was certainly enough here to do it.

"We'd best go back above. The torches will soon go out," Roderick warned, stomping his foot on a bit of burning linen that had fallen from the torch he carried.

Not wanting to try to find her way out of the cellars in the dark, Claray nodded and walked back to where Lady MacKay waited by the door.

"I have been thinking about the moss and mold on the keep walls," Aunt Annabel said as they crossed through the next room to the stairs.

"That the wine in the cellar would take care of it?" Claray suggested.

"Exactly." Lady MacKay beamed at her and they began to chat about how to go about it as they mounted the stairs leading back up to the great hall.

Chapter 19

"THEY'RE HERE! THEY'RE HERE! M'LADY, M'LAIRD SENT ME TO tell ye they're here!"

Claray straightened from weeding the herb garden, and rubbed her lower back as she watched young Dawy race excitedly into the gardens.

"Oy!" someone barked pretty much in her ear, and Claray glanced around in surprise to see Mhairi, one of the clan members who had returned from MacKay. She'd been told the woman was in her mid to late thirties but she looked twice that. The results of a hard life, Claray supposed. But the woman was strong and had worked diligently beside her all day. Now, she was scowling at the fair-haired boy with displeasure and snapped, "Watch where ye're stepping, boy. This is a garden, no' the bailey."

"Sorry," Dawy said, quickly moving back onto the path. "But are ye coming, m'lady? They're here."

"Who's here?" Claray asked patiently, managing not to laugh when the boy's eyes went round with the realization that he hadn't explained.

"Yer wagons from yer da," he told her. "And there's *six* o' them. All piled high with goods and furniture. Me ma near to swooned when she saw 'em."

Aches and pains forgotten, Claray dropped the weeds she'd just pulled up, and hurried out of the garden to make her way toward the front of the castle with young Dawy at her side. She wasn't surprised when Lovey gave up his spot under a tree where he'd been napping to rush to accompany her. Neither was she surprised to see Squeak sitting up on the base of his neck, his little paws clutching at the wolf's fur to keep his seat as he looked around like a little emperor. The stoat didn't like the jostling he suffered when Claray constantly bent over and straightened while weeding the gardens, and had taken to climbing out of her dress and scrambling over to climb onto Lovey to sleep while she worked. Much to her surprise, the wolf was tolerating it.

Shaking her head at the picture they made, Claray glanced over her shoulder in search of Stubborn Bastard and found him right behind her. He wasn't the only one following her. She had a small parade of people trailing after her. Roderick and Hamish were hard on her heels on either side of her horse. She was used to that though; the two men had followed her around every minute of every day this last week. Then came Mhairi, who'd apparently managed to scoot in front of Hendrie and Colban, Claray's other two guards. But behind them trailed the other two dozen women who had been working in the gardens with her. And every one of them looked excited.

The sight made her smile faintly as she turned forward. Then she rounded the corner of the castle, and scanned the bailey. It actually now looked like a bailey and not a forest, she noted with satisfaction.

The last week and a half had wrought a lot of change at Deagh Fhortan. With so many men working on it, the new drawbridge had been finished late on the evening of their arrival. A relief to everyone since it had allowed the returning clan members, and the soldiers who had initially been left outside the wall with the horses, to enter.

It had been a bit of a crowded mess that first night. Unable to sleep in the keep with its mold, moss, debris and the stench from the animals that had lived in it, everyone had been forced to sleep in the bailey among the raised roots of the trees. It hadn't been very comfortable that first night. But with three hundred men and the returning clan members all working together, removing the trees and rebuilding and repairing the castle had gone apace.

Claray and the other women had started their first full day at Deagh Fhortan with splashing the walls and floors of the keep with wine and vinegar from the wine cellar. It had been an effort to kill the moss and mold . . . and hopefully the stench from the animals. While they'd done that the men had first removed the tree inside the keep, and then had used chains and horses to drag the trees out of the ground in the bailey. They'd pulled them out one after the other in quick succession, and stacked them along the wall. As quickly as they'd worked, the men had already had half the trees downed by the time the women finished their work inside and came out at noon.

After a quick repast of oatcakes all around, Claray had led the women out to the orchards behind the keep. They'd spent the afternoon there, pruning the fruit trees in the hopes of improving the harvest when the fruit showed. They hadn't stopped until the sun was setting. Then Claray and the other women had staggered exhaustedly back around to the front of the castle to find all the trees, but for three Conall wanted to keep, gone from the bailey. It had made for a much more comfortable sleep that night, even if it was out under the stars.

The next morning, Claray and the other women had returned to the keep and started scrubbing down the walls and floors to remove the now dead moss, mold and detritus. That had taken the better part of three days, because the women had had to do it three times to return the stone to its original shine. The women had then moved on to starting the same routine over again in the chapel, though it was a much smaller building and had only taken two days to clean properly. After that, they'd marched on to the gardens, to weed and plant herbs and vegetables.

The men had been just as busy. With the trees down, Conall had set half the men to the task of repairing the curtain wall, while another hundred men had been set to the job of preparing the newly downed trees for use: debarking, riving and hewing them into planks, beams or whatever might be needed for repairs. The last fifty men had been set to the task of building the stables with the wood as it was ready to be used.

It had taken nearly three days to build and roof the horse stables and the connected smaller stables for any creatures she collected, as well as an added room for the stable master to live in. Claray had convinced her husband to add it, thinking it a fair trade for any advice or assistance the man might give her while tending the wee creatures. Allistair had been given the job of stable master and had assured her he'd be happy to help. He'd also thanked her mightily for thinking to give him a room when he'd expected to make do with the loft, or rushing back and forth from the barracks. He was one of the as yet unmarried MacDonald soldiers who had worked with her husband.

Once the stables were done, the men who had worked on them had moved into the now clean keep to remove and replace all the wood damaged by wood rot. That had gone quickly as well and now the keep had two huge, thick entrance doors keeping animals out, doors on the kitchens, the pantry, the buttery and the garderobes, and a fine new wood roof with thatching on it that would later be replaced with lead. They had also been working hard on rebuilding the second floor with bedchambers and stairs leading up to it.

Claray knew it wasn't done yet, but now that the wagons had come from her father, she wondered if the floor at least might be done so that they could store her bedroom furniture up there rather than in the great hall. She hoped so; there wasn't enough room for everyone to sleep inside as it was. Half the soldiers were still sleeping in the bailey, and would be until the men finished the keep and could set to work on the barracks roof. She supposed she and the women should start cleaning those buildings next. She would have done already, but food and spices were too important to put off. They would be needed to feed everyone.

"I see Dawy found you," Lady MacKay said with amusement, coming down the keep stairs as Claray paused by the bottom step to eye the wagons just starting over the drawbridge. There were indeed six of them. The men on the wall must have seen them coming down the hill and informed Conall, who had sent Dawy to her.

"Aye." Claray couldn't hold back the grin that spread her lips wide at the thought of having her clothes and things with her. "Did he tell ye they were here too?"

"Aye, I did," Dawy answered for Conall's aunt, reminding her of his presence. "I thought ye was in the keep, so's I went there first looking fer ye, and when I told Lady MacKay why I was hunting ye, she told me where ye was."

"That I did," Lady MacKay agreed with amusement, ruffling the boy's hair.

"Where's Kenna?" Claray asked, her gaze sliding to the wagons again as they trundled across the bailey toward them.

"She was down in the cellars overseeing the removal of the beer butts and wine casks," Lady MacKay told her. "I sent one of the other women down to fetch her ere I came out though, so she should be along soon."

Claray nodded, but mentally struck that chore off her list. They had decided that since they had no idea how the poison had been distributed to the clan twenty-two years ago, it was better to be safe than sorry and get rid of the wooden containers. They needed to purchase more wine and beer anyway to tide them over until they could make their own, and the liquids would come in their own butts and casks that they could then reuse when they were set up to provide for themselves.

That thought made her wonder when Payton and Laird MacKay would return. The two men had ridden out with two dozen men, and a great deal of Conall's coin, to purchase beer, wine, herbs, cheese, flour, vegetables and livestock for the castle. Now Claray just had to worry about pots, pans, skillets, cauldrons, knives, spoons, ladles, a mortar and pestle, etc.

Oh, and a cook, she thought with a frown.

Unfortunately, while most of what was needed in the kitchens was metal and not prone to wood rot, those items had disappeared over the years that the castle was empty and needed to be replaced. The only reason they hadn't been added to the list of things for Payton and Laird MacKay to purchase was because Conall had suggested they wait to see what her mother had packed away for her. There was no sense buying it and possibly ending up with duplicates of different objects. Since her things were supposed to arrive soon, she'd agreed.

"Oh, look! *Six* wagons, Claray! Goodness, I can no' wait to see what's in them."

Claray grinned at that happy cry from Kenna as the other woman rushed down the stairs to join them.

"Do ye ken what all yer da sent?" Kenna asked.

"Nay," Claray said, and then admitted, "Well, aye. Some. Conall said Da was sending me clothes and the furniture from me bedchamber. He also said me mother packed away linens and such to gift me with when I married, but I've no idea what all that includes," she admitted.

Kenna nodded, and then glanced past her and grinned. "Here comes Conall. He's looking cranky."

Claray turned to follow her gaze and bit her lip when she saw her husband's expression. He was looking exasperated and irritated and the way he kept scowling over his shoulder at the four men following him told her why. He was not taking at all well to being guarded, and if the men trailing after him were his own men, she had no doubt he would have ordered them away from him by now.

Unfortunately for him, the four men on his heels were all MacKays. Laird MacKay had ordered Gilly, Machar and two other MacKay soldiers to not let him out of their sight since the near miss with the arrow by the pond. She understood why. It was the same reason she had Roderick, Hamish, Hendrie and Colban following her. They were trying to protect them. But she also understood her husband's annoyance. Or should she say frustration? Because that's what it was. She was extremely frustrated with the situation as well. Not only were they tripping over their own guards all the day long, but sleeping in the great hall every night, surrounded by the entire population of Deagh Fhortan, meant they were never alone. Her husband hadn't bedded her since the pond, and lying beside him night after night, without getting to enjoy his kisses and caresses, was extremely hard. The longer it went on, the harder it got, and the crankier Conall seemed to get.

"Wife."

Claray pulled back from her thoughts and smiled at Conall as he stopped before her. For a moment they just stared at each other, and she swore she could see her own need and frustration swirling in his eyes. Then he sighed wearily, gave his head a little shake and turned toward the wagons that were rolling to a stop in front of the keep.

"Come," he said, catching her elbow to lead her to the back of the first wagon. "Why do ye no' start going through things while I talk to yer father's men and find out why they were delayed."

He waited for her to nod, then turned to walk to where the soldiers who had escorted the wagons were reining in next to the second wagon.

Claray watched him go before turning to survey everything in the first wagon. Her eyes widened when the first thing she spotted were several kitchen items.

"Aunt Annabel," she called excitedly, beginning to drag a large cauldron out of the wagon to see what was behind it.

"Oh, Claray," Lady MacKay exclaimed as she reached her side and saw what she'd found. Pulling out a large pot with one hand and a huge ladle with the other, she showed them to Kenna as her daughter joined them. "This is wonderful. I guess tonight I shall be crossing items off the list I was making of things needed for the kitchen. Actually, I shall be crossing off most of the items. There are things here I hadn't even thought of."

"Is that a grater?" Kenna asked, leaning in to pull out the handmade iron grater.

"Aye," Claray laughed even as tears welled in her eyes at her mother's forethought. Blinking her eyes rapidly, she shook her head. "How did she know we would need all this?"

"Well, she only died four years ago, dear. That was already eighteen years after everyone had fled Deagh Fhortan. I imagine the kitchens and every other room in the castle were ransacked and emptied out within the first couple of years. She obviously thought of that and gifted you with what she thought you might need most. I just wish I had thought of it myself, and I am sorry I did not," she added apologetically. "Perhaps I could have—"

"Nay," Claray interrupted, touching her arm to silence her. Shaking her head firmly she said, "Ye've worked like a dog and slept on the ground this past week to help Conall and I get things settled here. And that after riding night and day to get first to MacFarlane to try to aid us too, then riding back with us at a less-than-relaxed pace. That is a most wondrous gift. Ye've nothing to apologize for."

"Oh, dear girl." Annabel hugged her.

"Ohhhh, Claray!" Kenna suddenly squealed. "This crate is packed with pottery. There are jugs, and bowls and—Oh, I see a pipkin skillet!"

Chuckling, Claray and Conall's aunt broke apart to continue sorting through the wagon. The other women had moved closer to see now and exclaimed over each find with as much excitement as Claray. Even Mhairi managed a smile, something she'd rarely seen the woman do since working with her.

"We should start carting this lot in while ye check the next wagon," Mhairi announced, and Claray hid her amusement at the woman's less than delicate hint that she should move on and get out of the way.

"Aye, thank ye," she said as Mhairi gently nudged her aside to begin retrieving items. The other women immediately joined her and began carting things off to the kitchens as Claray led Kenna and Lady MacKay on to the next wagon. This one held some more items for the kitchens, several fine tapestries to hang from the walls in the great hall, carved wooden chairs and a chess set with the most beautifully carved pieces Claray had ever seen.

The third wagon held everything from Claray's bedchamber at MacFarlane: her bed, mattress, bed-curtains, the table and chairs that had sat by her fire, the small tables that sat on either side of her bed and her three chests of clothes. She wanted to squeal and do a little jig, but contained herself. It was wonderful, but really it was a problem as well since she wasn't sure where she would keep it all until the upper floor was done. Deciding to leave that concern for later, she moved on to the next wagon.

The fourth wagon held pillows, linens, furs, two more mattresses, though there were no beds to go with them, but they could make those.

"Oh, Claray, she sent four lanterns! And look! There is a whole crate o' candles for them too." Pulling one out, she sniffed it and grinned. "I think they're beeswax candles! Those are the best."

Claray swallowed, and sent up a silent prayer of thanks to her mother as she moved to where Kenna was hanging over the side of the wagon, digging through a crate.

The fifth wagon held bolts of material, enough to make gowns, bed-curtains and anything else she might want. It also held things her mother couldn't have set aside for her: fresh food. There was barley, rye, wheat, salt, honey, various herbs and even fresh vegetables that she was sure her father must have ordered put together to be sent to her.

Turning away before she started to weep like a baby, Claray moved on to the last wagon. Much to her surprise as she walked around the back, she found Lovey there, standing on his hind legs, his front paws on the back of the wagon. He'd been with her when Conall had escorted her to the first wagon and she hadn't noticed him wandering away. Curious now, she glanced to its contents and this time did squeal with delight when she saw all the cages holding the furry friends she'd rescued, mended and adopted over the years. At least, the ones that hadn't been released back to the wild: Osbern the three-legged goat, Lowrans the blind wildcat, Grisell the baby cow who couldn't walk when she first saw her and now could but was still quite wobbly on her feet, and of course Brodie the bunny, and her earless little fox.

Claray was about to climb into the wagon to coo at and reassure her little friends when it suddenly started to pull away from her. Startled, she stared after it with amazement, and then turned to

Conall when he said, "He's taking it to the stables. I thought ye'd want to see them settled right away."

"Aye," she agreed, beaming a smile at him for thinking of it.

Nodding, he took her elbow to lead her away, but stopped when Claray suddenly paused to look guiltily back toward the wagons and the people unloading them. She really felt like she should be helping.

Seeming to recognize her problem, Conall glanced toward the eight men who had started following them and said, "Hamish, stay and oversee the unloading. Find some men to help with the heavier items and have them put them where the women say."

Nodding, Hamish moved away at once.

Conall tried to urge her to move then and, when she still hesitated, pointed out, "The women ken where everything should go, and we can help after. It should no' take us long to settle yer wee creatures. But they've been traveling in those cages for a number o' days. 'Tis probably better to get them out and settled in their new home as quickly as possible."

Claray turned back to him, knowing her surprise was showing. She just hadn't expected him to be so thoughtful of the wee beasties. He hadn't seemed pleased when she'd found Brodie, the fox and Squeak and insisted on taking them with her. But then she was beginning to think that was all just for show. Conall certainly behaved with great care around Squeak, making sure he wasn't underfoot or anywhere he might get crushed or injured, and bringing him raw meat at every meal. He also suffered Lovey and Stubborn Bastard following her around with more patience than she'd expected. He didn't let Stubborn Bastard in the keep, but Lovey was allowed in and slept on one side of her while Conall was on the other on the great hall floor. Although that might be because he felt the wolf helped keep her safe.

"Claray?"

"Aye." Offering an apologetic smile, she hurried after him, thinking she would see her little friends settled quickly, and then go back to help unpack. She hoped there was parchment, a pen and ink somewhere in the treasures sent to her. Aunt Annabel had sent to MacKay for that so that they could make lists of what needed doing, but she didn't want to use it all up on her. She did want to write her father a letter of thanks though, for sending everything. It would all go a long way toward making life easier for them, and she wanted him to know how much she appreciated it.

Chapter 20

"Hɪs ears are healing nicely," Conall commented, peering over her shoulder at the fox as Claray smeared salve on the healing wounds.

She murmured in agreement, and then added distractedly, "He should be fine in another couple days. A week from now ye'll no' ken he'd ever been injured."

"Except fer the missing ears," Conall pointed out with amusement.

"Aye, except fer that," she admitted on a soft laugh, and then asked, "Can ye fetch me some linen to rewrap his ears, please, husband?"

Conall shifted away toward the bag of her medicinals. She'd found them stored in among the cages, and had been grateful for her father's forethought. He'd probably realized she'd want to settle the animals first and wouldn't want to search the other five wagons for her bag.

Hearing Conall curse, she glanced around to see that he'd managed to make his way through their guards to get to the bag of medicinals sitting on a shelf by the door, but now he was struggling to make his way back. The seven men had helped them cart the animals in, and then had squeezed inside the smaller stables with them as she guessed they were supposed to do, but there really wasn't room for her, Conall, the animals and all of them. She wasn't at all surprised when her husband lost his patience, and snapped, "Out. All o' ye. There's no' enough room in here to move with ye all inside. Out."

The men exchanged glances and shifted, but no one was leaving, and Roderick pointed out, "We're supposed to be guarding ye."

"Well, then, guard the door. We're safe enough in here with just the two o' us," he insisted. When no one moved, he added quietly, "I'd like a word with me wife. We've no' been alone fer a week."

Claray saw sympathy cross Roderick's face, and then he nodded. "We'll guard the door."

When Gilly and Machar hesitated, exchanging glances, Conall growled, "Ye'll be right outside the door. I think we're safe enough in here with the bunny, calf and goat."

The two men exchanged another glance and then shrugged and nodded to their younger compatriots to lead the way out.

Conall waited by the door until the last man had left, and then closed the door behind them before making his way to Claray to hand her the linen.

"Thank ye," she said, taking it and starting to wrap the cloth around the fox's head. "It was getting hard to breathe in here it was so crowded."

"Aye," Conall muttered, watching her tie off the linen and bend down to set the little fox in his pen. Claray straightened then to watch the fox crawl into the corner of the pen and begin to dig at the straw there. He'd already eaten. Claray had fed all the animals as she'd let them out of their cages. Only then had she checked the fox's ears. She smiled faintly as she realized he was trying to dig a den in the straw, and thought instinct was an amazing thing. He'd been too young when she'd found him to have learned this from his mother.

Conall's hands settled on her shoulders, drawing her back against his chest, and Claray settled there with a small sigh, then said, "Thank ye, fer building the stables for them. I'll worry about them less kenning they're tucked up safe in here."

"Me pleasure," he murmured, nuzzling through her hair to press a kiss to the side of her neck.

"Mmm," Claray murmured, and tilted her head to the side to better expose her neck as the brief caress sent tingles of awareness through her body.

"God's teeth, ye smell good, lass," Conall growled, his hands rubbing up and down her arms as he kissed her neck again and then nibbled at the tender flesh.

Claray opened her mouth to thank him for the compliment, but then gasped as his hands suddenly left her arms to slide around in front and cup her breasts.

"Ye feel good too," he muttered, kneading the suddenly tender flesh and biting her neck lightly, then sucking on the spot briefly before growling, "Give me yer lips, lass."

Claray turned her head back and up, opening to him when he claimed her mouth. His tongue thrust in at once, even as he pushed his hips forward, grinding himself against her bottom through their clothes so that she could feel that he was hard for her. Groaning, she reached back to grasp his hips in response, and kissed him eagerly back. Then gasped and groaned again when one of his hands dropped from her breast to slide between her legs and began to caress her through her skirt even as he pressed her bottom more firmly against his erection.

Breaking their kiss, Claray twisted her head against his shoulder and gasped, "Husband!"

"Aye," he growled, pressing the cloth between the lips of her nether region and caressing her more directly. "I need ye too. I've been goin' mad bein' so close to ye each night and no' bein' able to touch ye. It's been so long."

"Aye," she moaned, shifting her hips into his touch.

"Too long," he added, and then warned, "I fear this is going to be fast and dirty, wife."

"Aye," Claray repeated, unsure what he meant, but not really caring as long as he kept touching her, and then he kissed her quickly, stopped caressing her and began to tug her skirts up. She groaned at the loss of his caresses, and then gasped in surprise when he suddenly bent her over the waist-high fence of the pen.

In the next moment, he startled a surprised cry out of her when he urged her legs further apart and pushed into her.

Conall paused then, his breathing ragged, and Claray swallowed and closed her eyes as he filled her. Then he bent down until his front brushed her back, and clamped his teeth gently onto her shoulder as he began to caress her again.

Claray moaned and grasped the top of the pen as he began to withdraw and then thrust back into her as he touched her. Her body immediately began to struggle, trying to move forward into his caressing fingers and back into his thrusts at the same time. But it couldn't do both, and she ended up doing neither and just bracing herself, taking what he was offering and riding the passion as it got tighter and hotter.

Afraid she would cry out or scream as she had the last time he'd given her pleasure, Claray covered her mouth with one hand to muffle her grunts and moans, and then bit on the side of her hand as her release struck her. She felt her body spasm and tighten around him, milking him, and knew a moment later that he'd found his pleasure too when Conall's teeth bit down harder on her shoulder. Not so hard it was painful, but she definitely felt it as a muffled half groan, half growl came from him.

Panting softly, Claray closed her eyes to enjoy the pleasure rolling through her, and then gasped when he suddenly straightened, pulling her with him. In the next moment, he'd slid from her and turned her to face him, his mouth coming down hard on hers.

Claray was sure he'd found his release, but this wasn't the kiss of a sated man. It was hungry, and demanding, almost rough, and then he urged her to the side and back until she felt the center beam that supported the roof of the stables behind her. Pressing her back against it, he caught her behind one leg, pulled it up over his hip and then dragged her skirt up out of the way in front and thrust into her again.

Gasping into his mouth, Claray wrapped her arms around his neck and held on tightly as her excitement burst back to life as if it had never been sated either. Within moments she was pushing back into his thrusts, and was kissing him back just as demandingly as she fought toward the release she knew was waiting.

This time it came like a small explosion, rocking her mind and leaving her body trembling and weak as he thrust into her one last time and stayed there, his hand tightening almost painfully on her leg as he grunted into her mouth. A moment after that, his grip eased, and then he released her leg and let it drop back to the ground as he broke their kiss.

Conall leaned his forehead against hers for a moment as they caught their breath, and then he stepped away, letting her gown drop back into place.

"Are ye all right, lass? I did no' hurt ye, did I?" he asked now, concern entering his face.

"Nay," she assured him, managing a somewhat embarrassed smile.

He nodded, but then smiled wryly. "Let us hope our bedchamber is ready soon, else I fear we'll be spending a lot o' time in here with yer animals."

When Claray relaxed, her smile becoming more natural, he bent to kiss the tip of her nose.

Conall then took her elbow, stepped to the side, and Claray felt a punching sensation in her shoulder. That was all. There was no real pain at first, just an abrupt, dull pressure. It wasn't until she looked down and to the side and saw the arrow sticking out of her shoulder that the pain struck. Sudden, sharp and vicious it stole the breath from her, leaving her gasping. Raising her gaze to her husband, she saw him turn back in question, and then shock crossed his face.

She thought he shouted something then, but wasn't sure. Darkness was closing in on her vision and her hearing seemed to be fading with it as she lost consciousness.

"CLARAY!" HER NAME WAS A HORRIFIED BELLOW AS CONALL saw the arrow through her shoulder, but despite what he saw, his mind was having trouble accepting it. Everything had been fine just seconds ago. Where the hell had the arrow come from? The question screamed through his mind, and he started to turn in the direction it seemed to have come from, but then saw Claray's eyes close and her face go slack, and leaped toward her instead, to catch her by the upper arms as she fainted.

With his senses suddenly on high alert, the whoosh of another arrow shooting past behind him sounded loud in his ears, but Conall didn't look around. He was too busy trying to hold Claray up and bellowing for their guards. Much to his relief, the men rushed in at once, filling the space around them and exclaiming as they saw what had happened. Conall ignored them, his attention on Claray as he held her up and tried to get a look at her back by peering over her shoulder. His mouth tightened when he saw that—as he'd feared—the arrow had gone right through her and now pinned her to the post.

The crash of the shutters caught his attention and he glanced to them with a frown when the room suddenly went dark. That was why they'd opened the shutters on the window Claray had insisted on being built into the smaller stables. She said the window was to air the small building when she cleaned the pens, but it had come in handy for allowing light in while she'd worked. It had also been the only source of light once he'd closed the door behind the guards after ordering them out. He hadn't even thought to close the shutters then. He hadn't considered that it would allow someone to shoot another arrow at them.

"Claray is pinned to the post and I can no' see," he snapped, and much to his relief someone immediately opened the door. Sighing, he took another look over her shoulder at her back. All he could see was about a half inch of shaft between Claray's back and the post. The arrow tip was buried in the wood.

Straightening, Conall adjusted his hold on her so that he held her securely, but was a bit to the side so that he was as far from the shaft of the arrow as he could get. He then glanced to Roderick. Conall didn't even have to speak; the man nodded and stepped forward to grasp the arrow's end with one hand, then gripped it as close to Claray as he could without actually touching her and snapped the end off just past the fletching. He then helped Conall pull her forward off the arrow.

Once Claray was free, Conall released the breath he hadn't realized he was holding, and immediately scooped her up into his arms.

"Someone grab her medicinals bag," he ordered, but didn't stay to see if anyone did and simply hurried for the door, leaving the men scrambling to follow. Their guards surrounded them the moment he was outside the door, and stayed positioned around them as he hurried toward the keep. Hamish saw them coming and rushed to meet them, reaching them when they were halfway to the keep stairs.

"What happened? Is m'lady all right?" he asked, his concerned gaze moving over Claray as he fell into step next to Conall, forcing Gilly to make way for him.

"Someone shot through the window of the smaller stables, pinning her to the post," Roderick said grimly when Conall didn't answer.

"Did ye see who did it?" he asked at once.

"Nay," Conall growled, and silently kicked himself for not thinking to look out the window the moment he realized what had happened.

"What about the rest o' ye?" Hamish asked, his gaze still on Claray, his expression grim and face pale as he took in the blood soaking into and spreading on Claray's gown.

"Nay. We were outside the door. They were inside alone," Roderick admitted, and Conall could hear the guilt in his voice and knew his friend was regretting agreeing to leave them in the small stables alone.

"What?" Hamish asked with shock. "Ye were no' inside guarding her? Ye were supposed to—"

"I ordered them out," Conall growled, taking the blame he knew was his own. He wasn't surprised at the shocked and angry look

Hamish gave him. He knew this was his fault. Having the men inside with them wouldn't have guaranteed the culprit wouldn't shoot through the window, but he probably wouldn't have bothered since one of the men guarding them would no doubt have been in front of the window rather than Claray. But the men hadn't been there, because he'd ordered them out. Worse yet, he'd planned that all along when he'd suggested she see the animals settled. He'd intended to send the men out and take advantage of a few moments of semiprivacy to have at his wife.

Thanks to their present living arrangements, and the necessity for guards, he hadn't been alone with Claray since the last time someone had shot an arrow at them. He hadn't had a chance to kiss or touch her in a week and a half, and he'd wanted to. Enough that he'd sent their guards out and then pounced on her like an animal there in the pens, taking her with little care or concern.

The worst part was, he'd planned ahead to do it, and had set Hamish to the task of overseeing the unpacking of the wagons so that he could. He'd known his first would argue with him about leaving them alone in the small stables if he'd been there, and had wanted to avoid the argument. So, he'd set the man to a task to keep him busy, and rushed ahead with his plan. Now his wife might die because he couldn't control his own desires.

CLARAY HAD NO IDEA WHERE SHE WAS WHEN SHE WOKE UP. SHE didn't recognize the room she was in, or the dark blue bed-curtains around the bed she was lying in. Frowning, she tried to sit up, and fell back with a soft cry as pain shot through her upper chest.

"Claray?"

That voice, gruff with sleep, made her force her eyes open and turn her head to the side. She stared blankly at the man sitting up in a chair next to the bed, noting the sleepy way he was blinking as worry bloomed on his face. She'd obviously woken him with her cry, she thought, and felt bad about that. Her husband didn't get enough sleep as it was. He was up in the mornings before the sun dawned and straight out to start working, trying to make Deagh Fhortan more habitable for them all. He also worked till late at night, using up torches and rushlights at a ridiculous rate to get things done.

"Wife?" he asked now, squeezing her hand.

Realizing her silence was worrying him, she asked, "Where am I?"

The question made alarm fill his face. "Yer at Deagh Fhortan, lass. Do ye no' recall? We married and—"

"I remember," she interrupted to assure him. "I just do no' recognize this room," she admitted, glancing around. "Or the bed-curtains, or these furs." She ran her hand over the silk-lined fur covering the bed.

"Oh."

That soft puff of sound drew her gaze around to see wry amusement on his face as he took in their surroundings. "'Tis our room. The men finished it the day after yer wagons arrived." Turning his gaze back to her, he added, "And the bed-curtains and fur are from the things yer mother packed away fer ye. But yer in yer own bed, and the other furniture is from yer room as well."

Claray glanced around the room again, this time taking in the familiar table and chairs by the fireplace, her chests pressed up against the wall and the smaller tables on either side of the bed. Recognizing them, she nodded and then asked, "Why am I in bed? And why does me chest hurt?"

"Yer chest hurts?" he asked with alarm.

"Well, I guess 'tis me shoulder," she admitted after taking a moment to pinpoint where the residual pain actually was. It had felt like it shot through her chest, but she supposed it had originated from her shoulder.

Relaxing a little, he nodded. "Do ye no' recall being in yer beastie stables and—"

"I was shot with an arrow," she exclaimed as his words prodded her memory and she recalled the punching sensation and seeing the arrow sticking out of her upper chest.

"Aye," he sighed the word, and then squeezed her hand, and added, "I'm sorry, wife."

She glanced at him with surprise. "Why? Ye did no' shoot me; ye were standing there with me."

"Aye, but if I had no' moved when I did, I would have been the one shot. They were aiming for me," he said solemnly.

Claray frowned at this news as she recalled his kissing her on the nose and then stepping from in front of her just before the arrow struck. Oddly enough the thought that he'd been the target was more alarming to her than the fact that she'd been hurt. Frowning, she asked, "Where are Gilly and Machar and the other two men? Should they no' be here guarding ye?"

"They're in the hall with yer guards," he said, dropping back in the chair and running his hands over his face as if to clear away any remaining traces of sleep. That and the fact that he'd obviously been dozing off in the chair when she woke up made her survey the room again, this time looking for the fireplace and window. The fireplace was no help; there was no sign that a fire had been built in it yet, or for quite a while from the looks of it. There was a jumble of unidentifiable things in it, including old nests from the look of it. It obviously hadn't been cleaned after the men had rebuilt the second floor of the keep, and she wondered if that had been because they'd left it for the women, or because Conall had rushed them out to move the furniture and her in. She couldn't imagine they'd missed it. By her guess, they'd probably used the placement of the stone fireplaces on this level as an indicator of the height the floor should be built at.

Shrugging those thoughts away, she continued looking and found the window. It was more helpful, showing her that the sun was up. She could see it through the window, but it hadn't fully risen and she guessed it was midmorning. It had been afternoon when the wagons had arrived.

"So, I slept through the evening and night?" she asked.

Conall let his hands drop to his lap and shook his head. "Ye've slept fer three days and nights." When dismay filled her face, he explained, "Ye got the fever, lass. Thank God yer da sent a bath with the things in the wagons. The only way we could cool ye down was to fill it with cold water and put ye in it."

"Da sent a bath?" she asked with a happy grin.

For some reason Conall's lips quirked at the question and he turned to gesture over his shoulder at a large brass tub he'd been blocking until he moved in the chair. "It was full o' vegetables and had sacs o' flour and bolts o' cloth all around it in the wagon." Turning back, he asked, "Ye did hear the part about ye being feverish?"

Claray dragged her eyes from the tub to his face, and flushed as she realized he'd also said they'd had to put her in the tub. She was guessing she'd been nude at the time.

Conall nodded, apparently taking her blush as confirmation. "Yer fever broke late last night. I sent me aunt to bed then. She'd been up with me tending ye since I carried ye into the keep." He frowned and then added, "But I promised to wake her if ye woke, so I'd best go let her ken."

Conall stood then and headed for the door, but paused once there and turned back to say, "Yer probably thirsty. I should have thought to—" He shrugged that away, and asked, "Are ye hungry too?"

Claray nodded silently. Her stomach had been gnawing at her since she'd woken up, but it was only now that she knew she hadn't eaten for three days that she recognized what her body was trying to tell her.

"I'll fetch ye some broth," he said solemnly, and then slid out of the room, leaving her alone to examine the chamber she was in. It was quite large. She wondered if the men had managed to finish other rooms too. She hoped so; she'd hate to think she was taking up the only bedchamber in the keep. If Claray had been awake, she would have given it to Kenna and her mother. She'd have to ask her husband when he returned.

Chapter 21

"*D*O YE PREFER THE NAME CONALL OR BRYSON?"

Conall glanced up from the chessboard set up on the bed between them at that question from his wife. Claray was looking better than she had when she'd first awoken. She'd been pale, her eyes dull and hair limp then. Some of that pallor had gone after she'd eaten the broth he'd brought for her. But after the sleep they'd both had afterward, then the sup he'd fed her when they woke up, and the bath he'd helped her with, she was much improved. Her hair was still damp from her bath, but she was also rosy-cheeked and bright-eyed again. She was definitely on the mend, he decided. But it didn't ease any of his guilt over getting her shot in the first place.

"Well?" Claray prompted. "Bryson or Conall?"

Conall stared at her for a moment, wondering how she could bear to even look at him after what he'd put her through, let alone smile as sweetly as she was. Claray had nearly died because of him, but when he'd admitted this was all his fault and apologized while helping her in the bath, she'd waved his words away and assured him she didn't hold him responsible. In fact, she'd taken on some of the responsibility herself, saying she could have protested the men leaving, but hadn't because she'd missed his kisses and touch too and had hoped for what had happened to occur. Claray had blushed while she admitted it . . . everywhere. Her naked body had gone pink in the bathwater, and he'd wanted her all over again. It was only the fact that she was so weak and in obvious pain that had kept him from dragging her from the tub and making love to her again. It was an urge he was still fighting. They were finally alone in their own chamber, something he'd been looking forward to and imagining for that whole week and a half before she'd got shot with the arrow, and he still couldn't love her as he'd fantasized . . . and it was all his own damned fault.

"Well, husband?" Claray prompted.

Conall shook his self-recriminations away and cleared his throat. But rather than answer, he asked, "Which do you like better?"

"I have trouble thinkin' o' ye as Bryson," she admitted apologetically. "Ye seem more a Conall to me."

"Why?" he asked with interest as he moved a pawn on the board.

"Weeell." She drew out the word and then pointed out, "Conall means strong wolf."

"And ye like wolves," he teased.

Claray glanced to where Lovey was asleep on the bed next to them with Squeak curled up on his back, and smiled faintly. "Aye. I do." Turning back to him, she admitted, "But ye also do seem strong to me. *And* as a mercenary ye were known as the Wolf. So, it just seems to suit."

Conall nodded. "And what does Bryson mean?"

"Just son o' Bryce, I think," she said slowly, and then added, "And Bryce means freckled if I recall correctly." Eyeing him solemnly, she pointed out, "Ye do no' have freckles, husband."

Conall chuckled at the words. "Nay, I do no' have freckles."

He watched her make her move, and then considered what his own next move should be as he asked, "How do ye ken so much about names?"

"Allissaid."

"Yer sister?" he asked, glancing up with surprise.

Claray nodded. "She's always blurting out names she's considering giving to the bairns she plans to have with her betrothed when they marry. She then tells me what they mean. Allissaid has a tendency to fret over a lot o' things, and fretting over giving her bairns the right name is one of them. She fears the meaning might influence the bairn's personality. For instance, she'd never name a son Anwir because it means liar or deceit."

"Anwir," Conall murmured. "I knew a Welsh mercenary named Anwir."

Claray pursed her lips at this comment. "I thought she said 'twas an English name, but mayhap I'm wrong."

"Or mayhap she was the one who was wrong and only thought it was English because all English are liars," he suggested.

Claray grinned at the insult to their enemies to the south, and then smiled at him crookedly. "Ye've changed since we came to Deagh Fhortan."

Conall felt his eyebrows raise at that, and asked, "Changed how?"

Claray shrugged slightly, and then winced as the move aggravated her wound. Conall watched her carefully as she closed her eyes and waited for the pain to pass. A moment later, it apparently had, because she let her breath out on a sigh and answered his question.

"When I first met ye, when ye dragged me off from Kerr—"

"When I rescued ye from Kerr," he corrected.

"Aye, that," Claray agreed with a small smile. "Anyway, ye were no' very talkative. Ye mostly grunted or barked orders and I do no' think I saw ye smile once."

Conall wasn't certain how to feel about that description, and he was pretty sure he'd talked more than she was suggesting. Although some of the words that had run through his head may have stayed in his head. He seemed to recall having a lot of them there every time she'd decided to rescue a new beastie. But then she would smile at him sweetly and he'd lose the thread of what he wanted to say. The lass had a powerful smile; it turned her from a pretty gel to a true beauty.

"But ye smile more and laugh now," Claray said, drawing him from his thoughts so that he saw the twinkle in her eye as she added, "And goodness, ye even talk to me."

The corners of Conall's mouth curved up in a reluctant smile at her teasing, but it quickly faded and he ducked his head to peer at the chessboard to avoid her gaze. Mostly because he knew she was right. For the last twenty-two years he'd been a hard shell of a man. The result of losing his parents, his clan and his home, he supposed. Or perhaps a result of all the years he'd spent fighting, first out of anger at the overwhelming losses, and then to earn the coin needed to return his inheritance to its former glory.

But now he was here, and every passing day saw the castle looking more like his childhood home, and the more it did, the more memories it awakened in him.

While the only thing he'd seemed to be able to remember when away from Deagh Fhortan was the tragedy that had forced him to leave, now he was remembering the happy life he'd enjoyed here. Running through the castle laughing with his wolfhound, Aymer, chasing after him. Fishing in the pond with his da, and sometimes even his mother. Playing in the bailey with other clan children. Eating pasties by the fire and telling his mother about his day while she did her mending.

It was softening him. Conall knew that, and he knew it was the worst possible time for him to give in to his feelings. People wanted him dead, both MacNaughton and the faceless, nameless and heartless bastard who had murdered his parents. This was no time to lose the hard shell that had saved his life so many times in battle. A man needed a clear mind to fight his foe, not one distracted with thoughts of whether the fishpond might please his wife. Or who found himself mooning about how she was a hard worker, and so kind-hearted. Or thinking on how her laugh was high and full of joy and made him want to smile. Or daydreaming on how sweet her kisses were, and how good it felt to bury his cock in her warm body. Or wondering whether she might care for him as he'd come to realize he cared for her.

Conall swallowed and reached out to make another move on the chessboard as the memory of her pinned to the post with an arrow through her shoulder filled his head, along with the memory of the horror and fear that had clutched at him then. He'd been desperate to get her to his aunt so she could heal her, and terrified that she wouldn't be able to. That fear had barely begun to ease when Claray had gone feverish on them, and then

Conall had suffered the agonies of hell, worrying that she would yet die on him.

Conall had refused to leave her side for the three days and nights she'd battled for her life. He'd bathed her forehead with cool cloths, dribbled liquids down her throat and even submerged her in the tub filled with cool water, and the whole time he'd sent silent prayer after prayer to the heavens, begging God to let him keep her.

That was when he'd realized that she'd somehow slipped into his heart and made a home there. Because Conall had stayed there in their room with her, uncaring what was going on outside the bedchamber door. Deagh Fhortan had been his only concern these twelve years since gaining his spurs, but with Claray sick and possibly dying, he hadn't cared at all about his childhood home. If it had crumbled around their ears, he could and would build another home for them. He could not build another Claray.

"Ye never did say whether ye prefer Conall, or Bryson, husband," Claray said suddenly, pulling him from his thoughts.

Giving his head a shake, he moved his bishop and then glanced at her before admitting, "I'm more used to Conall and have come to prefer it after being called that fer twenty-two years," he said slowly, and then added, "But Bryson is the name me parents gave me, and I feel I should honor that, so I'm undecided which to go by."

Claray nodded with apparent understanding, and said, "Then I shall just address ye as husband until ye've decided."

Conall was smiling faintly at that decision when she added, "Or mayhap I could use endearments."

Eyes widening slightly, he raised his eyebrows. "Such as?"

Claray seemed to consider the matter briefly, and then shook her head. "I am no' sure. I can no' call ye lovey, 'twould confuse me wolf."

His gaze followed hers to the huge beast whose ears had pricked up and whose head had lifted at her use of his name. Conall silently sent up a prayer of thanks that the endearment lovey was taken and wouldn't be used on him. He couldn't even bear to call the wolf that. It was just too undignified for such a majestic beast, and—he'd like to think—for himself too.

"Let me see," Claray said now, tilting her head up and peering toward the ceiling thoughtfully. "I could call ye me honey sweet."

Conall's eyes widened with horror at the thought of her calling him that in front of the men.

"Or my own heart's root," she added.

Now he grimaced. It was a common endearment, but the root part always made him think of a cock for some reason.

"My sweeting is nice," Claray commented.

"Nay," Conall said quickly, and when she looked at him with surprise, he tried to cover his horror at the thought of being called that, by saying, "I'd rather call ye that and we can no' both use it."

"Oh," she breathed, seeming pleased at the idea of his calling her that.

He made a mental note to use it, and to come up with other endearments to please her. Flower, perhaps. Or petal, to reflect how beautiful and precious he found her.

Her suddenly covering her mouth to stifle a yawn drew his attention, and Conall looked her over carefully, noting that some of the color in her cheeks had faded and she was beginning to droop. She hadn't been awake that long, but she was healing and would need sleep to aid with that, so he grabbed the chessboard and stood up to carry it to the table.

"What are ye doing?" Claray asked with sudden alarm.

"Ye need yer rest," he said, turning to walk back to the bed. "We can finish the game later."

"Oh, but—" Pausing, she bit her lip, and then asked, "Will ye sleep too?"

Conall hesitated briefly, considering all the things he'd neglected these last days, but then his gaze took in her hopeful face, and he decided to stay and rest with her awhile. It was probably for the best anyway. The few winks he'd managed to get in the chair after her fever broke, and before she woke, plus the four hours they'd slept that afternoon, was all the rest he'd had since she'd been wounded. He probably needed to sleep too. So, he patted the wolf's rump to get him to move to the foot of the bed, and then removed his plaid.

Recognizing that he meant to join her, Claray smiled with relief and eased from her sitting position to lie down. Once she was flat on her back, Conall then slid into the bed next to her with his shirt still on.

He would have been more comfortable without the shirt, but had deliberately left it on to remind himself that she was wounded and he shouldn't start in kissing and caressing her like his body wanted him to do. Like it always seemed to want to do.

"Thank ye."

Claray's whisper made him smile, but all he said was a gruff, "Sleep," before closing his own eyes and trying to do the same himself.

CLARAY WOKE UP WITH SUNLIGHT SPLASHING ACROSS HER FACE and a smile on her lips. That smile faded though when she turned her head to find the space next to her empty. Conall had already risen and gone, and even Lovey and Squeak were not there. Blowing her breath out on a sigh, she turned her gaze to the window, trying to guess what time it was.

Midmorning again, Claray thought when she saw the position of the sun. She'd slept late and that irritated her. All she'd seemed to do since waking three days ago was sleep. She'd wake up, Conall would feed her and then they'd talk for a bit, or play a game, and then at the first sign of a yawn, or drooping eyelids, Conall would be urging her to sleep again. She hadn't even been out of her bed in all that time until last night, when she'd insisted she wanted to get up and Conall had carried her to the table and set her in a chair for their shared sup. They'd played Nine Men's Morris afterward and talked, and she'd managed to stay awake for longer than the usual hour or so she'd managed each time before that. Claray wasn't sure how much longer, but guessed by the number of rushlights they'd gone through that it had probably been close to three hours. A sure sign she was healing well, even if she'd slept long afterward.

Another sign that she was healing was that she was sick unto death of being stuck in this room. And she was definitely done with lying about in bed, Claray thought grimly, and pushed the bed linens and furs aside to sit up. She managed the move with little effort. Sitting up in the bed was something she'd done several times a day since waking, and while the first few times had left her shaky and a little breathless with effort, she suspected it was as much from the pain it had caused her wounded shoulder as the weakness the fevers had left her with. This time she felt little more than a twinge from her wound at raising herself to a sitting position, and there was no trembling or weakness at all.

Buoyed by that, Claray slid her feet to the floor, grasped the bedpost and eased to her feet. It took more effort than it would have before taking the arrow in the shoulder, but she managed it. She then simply stood there, grasping the bedpost as she waited for her heart rate to slow, and her legs to stop trembling.

As she waited, Claray glanced around the chamber, trying to plan her moves to use the least amount of effort necessary to dress and leave the room. Weak as she was, she knew the task she'd set herself would be a challenge. But it was one she planned to succeed at. She would get out of this room today. There was too much to do at Deagh Fhortan for her to be a lie-abed. Besides, she was sick of staring at the same four walls. Although she hadn't minded so much when Conall was there with her.

Claray smiled at the thought of her husband. He'd been at her side almost every moment she'd been awake since her injury, feeding her, helping her with her ablutions, playing games and talking. It was the conversations they'd had that she'd enjoyed the most. Especially when he spoke about his hopes for the future of Deagh Fhortan. He was determined to return it to the happy, prosperous castle it had been before his parents' death. From what he had said, his parents had cared greatly for their people, making sure they were clothed, well-fed and happy, and he wanted to do that too.

A smile had curved Claray's lips as she'd listened to his plans. She'd liked that he cared about his people, that he wanted to do right by them. Her parents had been the same, but she knew many supposedly fine lairds and ladies who abused their people, meting out unfair or overharsh punishments, leaving them dressed in little more than rags and, more often than not, with empty bellies. That was no way to treat family, and that's what clan members were, whether by birth or marriage. Sometimes they were family several times removed, but they were still family and deserved their laird and lady's care and concern.

Once the first wave of weakness passed, getting about was not so bad. Being cautious though, Claray was quick about her ablutions, and tried to conserve as much of her energy as she could while brushing her hair and dressing. She bent over as little as possible and stopped to rest when needed.

Still, Claray was quite exhausted by the time she had finished and almost changed her mind and climbed back into bed. But that seemed a great waste after all her efforts. Besides, she really did want to go below and check on what progress had been made since she'd been wounded.

Conall had told her that his aunt Annabel had taken control of things in her absence, at least since she'd regained consciousness and no longer needed constant attention. Apparently, Lady MacKay had gone down the next morning and organized the women into groups, keeping half with her, and assigning half to Kenna. She'd wanted to whitewash the walls before arranging the furniture and goods they'd received, but that task would have to wait until they had the lime to do it. In the meantime, they'd set up the kitchens, and then arranged what furniture they had in the great hall, before heading out to clean the bakehouse even as the men were building a new roof on it.

During that time, Kenna's ladies had finished preparing the cellars for the beer, mead and wine they hoped would soon arrive, and then had headed outside to continue Claray's efforts in the gardens.

Her husband had assured her that the two women were in bedchambers and no longer sleeping on the keep floor. Conall had also told her that he'd assigned men to make furniture and they'd made beds for the mattresses that had arrived in the wagons, as well as trestle tables and benches and such for the great hall. He'd said they weren't fancy, but would do until the few carpenters they had amongst the clan could create more elaborate furniture.

Claray had been pleasantly surprised to learn that three of the MacDonald men who had worked as mercenaries for her husband had actually been trained as carpenters before he'd taken them on. He'd also told her he had other skilled men in his ranks such as stonemasons and blacksmiths, etc., and that their skills had actually saved time and coin in the repairs because they had been able to start the jobs right away rather than wait to find and hire outsiders in the trades. Their skills would continue to be valuable in future too.

Claray had smiled as he talked, glad to see him so relaxed and happy, and thinking that perhaps Deagh Fhortan would live up to its name and they would enjoy some good fortune here after all. Now, she was eager to see all the changes that had been wrought, but she also wanted to help if she could. It didn't sit well with her to know that everyone else was working their fingers to the bone while she was abed. It was to be her home too, and Claray felt she should be helping to fix it up.

She knew she would probably be useless when it came to physical labor for the first day or two, but she wasn't going to regain her strength lying about in bed. And truly, her shoulder was mending nicely, hurting less every day as long as she didn't move it too much. Something she'd discovered while dressing. That had been painful and taxing because there was no way to don a dress without moving both arms. But surely there was something she could do to help out while using only the one hand and arm?

Not liking to think of herself as useless, even if it was temporary, Claray pushed away from the wall where she'd been leaning while regaining her strength, and walked to the door. Knowing that Roderick and Hamish would probably be difficult about her being up and about, she paused to take a deep breath before reaching for the door.

She opened it, all ready to do battle, only to find Roderick and Hamish missing and only Hendrie and Colban in the hall. The two men straightened at once, surprise and concern on their young faces as they took her in. Claray smiled, knowing her chances of getting below stairs had just more than doubled.

Chapter 22

"Have any of the men spotted signs of outsiders camping in the area on their rounds?" Conall asked, noting that several men were riding out of the bailey to start their tours of MacDonald land, even as several others returned. He'd started sending out large groups of men to ride the property from border to border to ensure MacNaughton had not followed them to MacDonald or been behind the attacks. He'd ordered it the day Claray took the arrow.

Not that he thought MacNaughton would try to kill Claray. But then, he was quite sure neither attack had been aimed at her. The first arrow by the pond would have hit him if he hadn't lowered himself toward Claray at just the moment he had. And the same was true of the second arrow in the stables. If he hadn't stepped to the side at the exact moment he had, the arrow would have hit him in the back.

Nay, Claray wasn't the target, and perhaps he was biased, but he really couldn't blame the bastard for trying to make his beautiful wife a widow so he could swoop in to marry her himself. Conall knew he was a lucky bastard, and sent up a silent prayer of thanks to his parents for contracting the marriage to her.

"Nay, they've no' seen even a hint o' anyone camping on MacDonald land," Hamish said, sounding grim and unhappy, and Conall knew the man wished to stop these attacks as much as he did. In truth, he suspected his first held a tendre for his wife and was still angry at him for sending the men out of the small stables and getting Claray injured, but knew he deserved it. He'd let his cock lead him in his decisions and had nearly lost his wife because of it.

"But that does no' mean he hasn't sent a man or two here to get rid o' ye," Roderick pointed out. "They might even be in the bailey itself. With both the MacKay soldiers and yer men too, everyone does no' ken everyone else. They may no' recognize a stranger in their midst. The MacKay men may just assume he's a MacDonald, while yer men are assumin' he's a MacKay."

Conall scowled at the suggestion. He knew all his men, but he did not know every one of his uncle's warriors. Even he might stare right at a MacNaughton soldier and assume he was a MacKay. But he wasn't sure what to do about that, and decided to think up some plan to figure out if that was going on. In the meantime, he changed the subject and asked, "I'm guessin' no one's come forward sayin' they saw anything out o' the ordinary while we were in the small stables?"

Conall had men questioning everyone at Deagh Fhortan on what they'd seen around the time when Claray had been shot. He'd also addressed everyone in the bailey and asked anyone who had seen anything to please step forward and tell either Hamish, Roderick, Gilly or Machar. Unwilling to leave Claray at the time, Conall'd made the request from the bedchamber. He'd had the men gather everyone in the bailey, and then had addressed them from the window. He'd had to shout to be heard, and going below certainly would have been easier, but Conall hadn't been willing to leave Claray. Fortunately, she hadn't even stirred at the noise he'd made.

But it hadn't done any good. No one had spoken up in the days since, so Conall wasn't surprised when Roderick said, "Nay."

However, while he wasn't surprised, he *was* disappointed. He wanted this over with. Conall knew that whether it was MacNaughton, or the old trouble behind these attacks, they weren't going to stop until either he was dead, or the culprit was found. He wasn't worried for himself. He'd lived on the cusp of death for twenty-two years. Claray was another matter entirely.

She'd already been wounded once and he was terrified she might be injured again, or even killed.

Thoughts of Claray had him turning his feet toward the keep. He should return to her before she woke up, he thought. He'd already been away longer than he'd intended. Conall had slipped out that morning, planning only to check the progress on the wall, but learning that the men were almost done replacing the roof on the barracks had made him decide to go inspect that too. It had rained twice this past week. Luckily, both times the rain had been light, and had occurred during the day and not at night. But he wasn't counting on that luck to hold out much longer and would rather get the men who had been sleeping in the bailey into the barracks as quickly as possible.

Fortunately, the roof should be finished by the end of that day, and while he'd been inspecting them, his aunt had led the women into the barracks to start cleaning it. If everything went well, the men should be able to move into it by the sup, he thought as he mounted the steps to the keep.

"For heaven's sake, Hendrie. Put me down. I can walk."

Those words as Conall led the men into the keep drew his startled gaze to the stairs. Hendrie was just stepping off of them with Colban on his heels, and Claray in his arms. Though his wife was obviously not pleased with that fact. While her first request had been made politely, Hendrie's not complying but heading toward the trestle tables with her had her now scowling. There was definite irritation in her voice as she said, "I said I can walk, Hendrie. Put me down now, please."

Much to his relief, Hendrie ignored his wife and continued on to the tables with her. He was setting her on the bench when Conall caught up to them.

Claray turned with exasperation on the man as he straightened, her mouth opening, either to thank him despite her irritation, or to give him hell. But her jaw locked open when she saw Conall standing behind the soldier.

"Hendrie was right to carry ye," he growled, nodding at the man when Hamish's young protégé turned with a start to see

Conall behind him. Turning his full attention back to his wife, he added, "Ye were sorely injured and should no' be out o' bed."

Claray's shoulders sagged as she heaved out a little sigh, but then straightened again almost at once as she argued, "But, husband, I feel ever so much better. And I wanted to see all the changes ye told me about. And, in truth, I'm tired o' being stuck in me room all the time. And I did no' take chances. I was slow and careful getting ready, and walking about our room and up the hall. And there was really no reason fer Hendrie to carry me when we got to the stairs. I was doing fine," she assured him with a glare in Hendrie's direction.

"Begging yer pardon, m'lady," Hendrie put in. "But ye were swaying about like a reed in a strong wind at the top o' the stairs. 'Tis why I thought I'd best carry ye the rest o' the way."

"I was no' doing that," Claray protested, flushing bright pink even as she spoke.

"Aye, ye were," Colban assured her gently when Hendrie glanced his way for support. The young soldier then quickly added, "But yer fever was high there fer a bit while ye were ailing. Mayhap yer a little addled and just do no' recall, or did no' notice."

Claray opened her mouth, closed it again and then frowned and avoided Conall's eyes as she admitted, "I may have been teetering a bit, but I'm sure 'twas no' as bad as Hendrie is suggesting."

"Aye, 'twas," Hendrie and Colban said together, and Conall was hard-pressed not to laugh at her vexed expression.

Ignoring them now, Claray turned back to him and said quietly, "Please, husband. I'd like to sit at table to break me fast and then see everything that's been done. I feel useless lying abed in our room all the time while everyone else works so hard on our home."

Conall softened at her words. He understood completely. He'd never been the greatest at lying about when injured or ill either. Nodding, he waved the men away.

"I'll go see if Cook is about and can fetch some food and drink," Hamish murmured, smiling at Claray before hurrying off toward the door to the kitchens.

Claray looked after the man with surprise, and then turned to Conall to ask, "We ha'e a cook?"

"Aye." Smiling faintly, Conall settled on the bench next to her. "Me aunt recognized one o' the returnin' women as having worked in the kitchens at MacKay. She interviewed her, askin' about her skills, and what she'd done at MacKay, and then asked the woman if she'd be willin' to take on the position as head cook here and oversee the kitchens. They agreed it would be just a temporary thing to see if she liked it and could handle the job. If no', we will replace her as quickly as we can, but if she did a good job and wished to keep the position, it would be hers . . . If ye agreed," he added solemnly.

"Oh," Claray breathed, and then smiled widely. "Aye. That's wonderful." She released a small chuckle and shook her head. "It did no' even occur to me to wonder where the broth and food came from that ye've been bringin' up each day."

"I'm no' surprised. Ye've been mendin' from a serious injury," he said with a shrug, and then glanced around before asking, "What do ye think o' the great hall?"

Claray was silent for a long while as her gaze moved around the large room. He watched as her eyes slid over the clean stone walls with the tapestries hanging on them, gifts from her mother that had been packed onto the wagons. She examined the new, if somewhat plain, trestle tables and benches, and then her gaze moved on to the two large—also plain—chairs by the fire. Each chair had a pretty cushion on its seat, and a small embroidered pillow leaning against its back that the inhabitant could adjust for their comfort. The cushions and pillows were also from the wagons her mother had packed.

"I like it," Claray said finally, and then added in a soft voice, "'Tis starting to look like a home."

"Aye," he agreed, and had to fight the urge to take her hand.

"But," she added with a small frown that brought his gaze sharply to hers, "the floor is so barren. There should be rush mats."

"There will be eventually," he assured her.

His reassurances did not displace her frown though, and she said, "Husband, now we're in a bed in our own chamber, ye may forget what 'tis like to sleep on cold stone at night, but I ha'e no'. I woke up every mornin' feelin' old and sore from the cold leachin' into me bones."

Conall felt his eyebrows draw together at her words as his gaze slid over the stone floor. Right now, the great hall was empty except for where they and their guards sat at the trestle table, but tonight the tables would be broken down and leaned against the walls, and the floor would be covered with bodies as their people tried to get some rest after a long day of hard work. And that, unfortunately, would continue for a while. Once the barracks were done, some of the men would move into it, but they too would be stuck on stone floor until beds could be made for them. The great hall would remain full of sleeping people at night until the MacKay soldiers left and cottages could be built for the families who wished to sleep outside the wall on farms, or in the village that he hoped would eventually be rebuilt.

"Surely our people deserve at least rush mats," Claray said softly. "Or even just rushes strewn about to soften the floor and protect them from the cold stone?"

Conall frowned at her words. He agreed with her wholeheartedly that their people deserved it. The problem was how to do it?

"Ye're absolutely right, sweeting," he agreed. "But how do we manage the task? Half the women are cleanin' the barracks so the soldiers now in the bailey have protection from the rain while they sleep, and the other half are finishin' the work ye started in the gardens. Both tasks are too important to put off for the women to gather rushes."

"Then assign some men to the task," she suggested. "If ye took two dozen men and the wagons me da sent to pile it in, it should no' take long. And I could oversee them meself, show them the best rushes to gather and such."

Her words made his frown deepen. It wasn't that he minded setting men to the task, though he hadn't thought of that himself.

And the truth was, with so many men here, he could manage without two or even three dozen men for an afternoon, but—"I do no' like the idea o' ye leavin' the safety o' the curtain walls."

Her lips twitched with amusement. "Husband, we've had arrows shot at us twice, hittin' me once, both *inside the safety o' the curtain walls*," she pointed out. "Besides, I would ha'e two dozen men with me, and me guard."

"And me," he announced, making up his mind. They would go out that very afternoon and gather enough rushes for the floors of the keep and the barracks. Unfortunately, there was no time right now for the rushes to be woven into mats that could then be sewn together to properly cover the barracks and great hall floors. That project would have to wait until later. But even having the rushes strewn loosely across the floors would insulate the sleeping clan members from the cold stone and give them a bit of cushion too. It would give them all a more comfortable sleep until they were further along in the repairs and rebuilding and could provide them proper accommodations.

Of course, having loose rushes just strewn around the floor would be a bit of a nuisance for the ladies with their long gowns. The material would catch at the rushes and drag them around a bit. But judging by the wide smile Claray was giving him, she didn't care and was willing to put up with the nuisance of it to make their people more comfortable. Another reason to love his wife, he decided. She cared about her people more than her own convenience. He'd met a lady or two over the years who would not have troubled themselves to care. Aye. His parents had chosen well for him.

"WILL YE TELL ME ABOUT YER MOTHER?"

Conall pulled his gaze away from the men hacking down the rushes that had grown along the moat, and glanced to his wife.

Claray was seated on the end of one of the already full wagons and he frowned when he noticed that she seemed to be sorting some of the larger rushes into a separate pile.

"What are ye doin', lass?" he asked, moving back to her side.

"Pickin' out the ones that would make good rushlights," she explained.

Conall's eyebrows rose slightly. "There's no need fer that. Yer mother sent a crate full o' beeswax candles with the things she packed away. We should be good fer light fer quite a while."

"And we'll be good fer light fer longer still if we use rushlights as well," she pointed out with a shrug. "Besides, we have a lot o' fat left over from all the meat yer men have been catchin', cleanin' and cookin' up. It'll take little effort to render it into tallow, soak the rushes in it and make rushlights."

Her words made him smile. Rushlights were generally thought of as fit more for peasants than nobility. Most ladies would not use them, preferring their candles as the status symbol they were. His wife wasn't concerned about status apparently.

"So," she said now, "what was yer mother like?"

"Why?" he asked, rather than answer.

Claray shrugged, not looking up from her work. "Yer aunt Annabel said she was a wonderful woman and mother. I was just curious as to what ye remember and if ye thought so too."

"Aye, I do," Conall admitted, his voice husky as he thought on the memories he had of his childhood before the poisonings. He had more now than he used to. Being here at Deagh Fhortan was stirring them back to life in his head. "She was a verra good mother. I'm sure she had days when she was angry or frustrated by some occurrence or another, but I only ever remember her smilin' and laughin'."

"What else do ye remember?" she asked when he paused, so Conall began to list things off.

"I remember she loved my da and me. I remember quiet nights with the three o' us by the fire. I remember her takin' me swimmin' in the pond. I remember helpin' her pick fruit in the orchard . . ." He paused briefly and then admitted, "She did the actual pickin' and would hand me an apple or pear, and I'd carry it to the basket and set it in, then run back fer the next apple or pear."

Conall smiled at that memory, and then chuckled and added, "And I remember she used to play a game o' chase with me. She'd say she was the ticklin' bandit, and she'd chase me about until she caught me and then she'd cuddle and tickle me until we were both breathless with laughin'."

Claray stopped sorting and smiled at him. "She does sound lovely."

Conall nodded, his gaze wandering back to the men. They hadn't actually had to go far at all to find the rushes. They were growing all along the sides of the moat that surrounded Deagh Fhortan. The only reason they'd even needed to bring the wagons was to carry the rushes back. So, they'd walked out, following the wagons and then following them again each time the men cleared an area, and the wagons moved further along the moat.

"What was yer da like?"

That pulled his attention back to his wife, and Conall watched her work for a moment before answering. "I remember him as strong, and brave, and smart."

"So . . . like you," Claray said with a nod that suggested she wasn't surprised.

Conall stilled at the words, and then smiled at the fact that she saw him that way, but said, "Nay. He was better than me. He loved me mother and me, and loved our people. He worked tirelessly from dawn to dusk and even later, making sure everyone had what they needed."

"Ye do the same," she pointed out solemnly.

"Aye, but he—" Conall frowned and hesitated, before finally saying, "He did no' have a bitter bone in his body."

"And ye do?" she asked, seeming surprised.

Conall's mouth twisted, and he nodded. "I was very angry fer a lot o' years. Bitterly so."

Claray eyed him consideringly, and then shook her head. "Ye do no' seem like that now."

His eyebrows rose slightly, but then he considered her words. Conall supposed the bitterness and anger that had seemed almost to possess him at times when he was younger had mellowed over the years. Perhaps twelve years of warring had helped get it out of his system.

"And do ye no' think that had yer da survived while yer mother and all the others died, he might have been bitter and angry too?"

Conall didn't even have to think over that too hard. His father would have torn Scotland apart to find the one responsible, and make them pay. Aye, he would have been bitter and angry. Sighing, he pushed the thought away and asked, "What were yer ma and da like?"

Claray considered the question briefly, and then said, "Da is a good man. A good father too. He's always fair with us, as well as with the clan members, and he cares about everyone's wellbein'. Like yer da and you, he works long hours to be sure everyone has what they need."

Conall nodded, not at all surprised to hear this. While they'd often been at loggerheads over the years—her father trying to convince him to claim Claray earlier than he was ready to, and he fighting it—he'd never disliked Laird MacFarlane. He'd actually respected him, and was glad he had the care of Claray until he could claim her. He'd liked her mother too the few times they'd met. Claray actually resembled her a great deal, and he knew she would be as beautiful as she aged as her mother had been.

That thought made him ask, "And yer mother? What was she like?"

Claray considered the matter briefly, and smiled. "Actually, I think me mother was a lot like yers, just perhaps not to the same degree. While she was often smilin' and happy, she did no' play chase games and such, but then she had eight children to look after rather than just the one, and was with child quite a lot when we were younger."

"Ye've six brothers and sisters, do ye no'?" he asked.

"Seven," she corrected, and then listed off her siblings and their ages. "Allissaid is nineteen, Annis is seventeen, Arabella is sixteen, Cairstane is fifteen, Cristane is fourteen, Islay is thirteen and Eachann is eleven."

Conall's eyebrows rose slightly, amusement curving his lips. "Aye, yer mother was most like too weary to play chase between havin' all those children."

From that accounting, Claray's mother had been with child every year for five years in a row having Claray's siblings, and only two years between the one before that grouping and the youngest. The three years between Claray and her next oldest sister was the longest rest the woman had got. Although he suspected that rather than a rest, she'd had a miscarriage or stillbirth or two. It was not uncommon.

Conall couldn't imagine what it must have been like to have so many siblings running about the keep. It must have been chaos at times, he thought, but loving chaos. It made him ask, "How many bairns would ye hope to have?"

Claray had gone back to sorting out rushes again, but paused now and looked thoughtful. Finally, she shook her head. "I am no' sure. I would no' mind havin' a lot o' children, but it did seem to wear me mother down havin' them so close together as she did with Annis, Arabella, Cairstane, Cristane and Islay. I think I'd hope fer two or three years between each child." She shrugged. "But I guess I shall just have to be happy with whatever God sees fit to give us."

"Aye," Conall murmured, but he was trying to imagine Claray heavy with child as she carried their bairn, and the idea pleased him. A little girl who looked like her would be nice, or a little boy he could teach to be a good man. Mayhap two of each would even be good, but he didn't want Claray to be heavy with child every year. He'd heard that could wear a woman down and kill her.

Claray's suddenly sliding off the back of the wagon caught his attention, and he raised his eyebrows in question.

"I'm just going to step into the woods for a minute," she muttered. If the words hadn't given him an idea of why, the way she blushed as she said it did, and Conall merely nodded and didn't say anything . . . until Roderick, Hamish, Hendrie and Colban all moved away from the wagon where they'd been standing guard and started to follow her.

"Halt," he said at once, and strode into their midst, his own four-man guard following now. "Ye can no' go with her. She's goin' to tend to personal matters."

"Aye, but do ye think it's wise fer her to be alone?" Roderick asked, and then pointed out, "She's already been injured once."

Conall frowned, his gaze moving to the trees where Claray had disappeared. He really didn't think the attacks had been meant to harm her. On the other hand, MacNaughton could try to kidnap her away from him, he thought suddenly. Mouth tightening, he nodded and strode toward the trees. "Fine. I'll go keep a look out meself. The rest o' ye stay here though."

"That will no' stop an arrow," Hamish pointed out quietly. "She was alone with ye when she took the arrow last time."

Conall paused again, and then cursed, before saying, "All right, we'll follow and spread out and surround her. But do it quietly and do no' let her see ye. Drop to the ground if ye ha'e to if she looks yer way. I'll no' ha'e her embarrassed."

Chapter 23

CLARAY WALKED FURTHER INTO THE WOODS THAN SHE'D hoped to have to, to find some privacy. While the area outside the curtain wall was forested with trees, most were only ten or fifteen years old this close to the wall. They hadn't suddenly sprouted up the very moment Deagh Fhortan was abandoned. The surrounding woods had just slowly crept closer to the castle, spreading out a little further each year.

With the trees being so young, there weren't any nice wide ones she could step around and squat behind, so she walked until she couldn't see the men anymore when she glanced back. Claray thought she'd caught a glimpse of movement close to the ground when she looked back this last time, but it was so quick she wasn't sure what she'd seen. She was fretting over what it might be when she heard bleating. Turning back the way she'd been heading, she scanned the surrounding area, her gaze halting on a sweet little baby deer moving toward her on wobbly legs.

"Ohhh," she almost moaned, enchanted at the sight. It was obviously very young, and not yet used to walking, or perhaps not strong enough. Rather than his legs being directly under him, they were spread out somewhat and he was staggering like a drunken fool.

"Oh, ye sweet thing," Claray cooed when it made its way directly to her and into her skirts. Lifting them several inches to get them out of his way, she watched with amazement as he began to lick and then suckle at her ankle, moving around it as he did, obviously in search of a teat.

"Oh, ye poor dear! Ye're hungry," she said, bending to scoop him up into her arms. The moment she did, he started rooting around on her upper arms and chest, taking material into his mouth and trying to suck milk out of it.

"Where's yer mother?" Claray murmured, giving him a soothing pet as she examined him. He didn't look to be more than a day or two old, but his eyes were dull, and his ears were curling at the tip, a sure indication that he was dehydrated.

Biting her lip, Claray glanced around for any sign of his mother, but suspected the poor doe might have been dinner last night or the night before. Conall had brought her fish for sup last night, but he'd eaten venison and had mentioned the men had returned from the hunt with three bucks and a doe that morning.

Her need to relieve herself forgotten, Claray cuddled the still bleating fawn to her chest and turned to head back the way she'd come. She needed to get it some milk, and quickly. Dehydration was dangerous for one so young.

Not wanting to trip and hurt the fawn, Claray kept her attention divided half on the bleating baby deer, and half on the ground she was covering. She didn't glance up until the shade of the trees suddenly gave way to bright sunlight. She raised her head then, and came to an abrupt halt when she saw Conall and all eight of their guards standing in a half circle in front of her. Not all eight, she realized as Colban stumbled out of the woods beside her and quickly joined the other men.

Her eyes narrowed on them briefly, suspicion rising up within her, and then a shout from the men working to gather rushes caught their attention and all of them looked over to see that a party was halfway down the hill, heading toward the castle. It must have come over the ridge the moment she'd stepped into the trees to be so close already, she thought.

"Me uncle is returned," Conall said, suddenly at her side. Taking her arm, he urged her back toward the wagons loaded with rushes, his gaze sliding over the fawn in her arms as he did. He shook his head, and then smiled crookedly. "It has been so long since ye presented me with a new abandoned or injured beastie ye'd found, I'd begun to think we'd built the small stables fer nothing. I was surprised ye did no' find four or five on our journey home."

Claray smiled faintly at his teasing, but just shook her head. She herself had been a little surprised when she hadn't even *seen* an animal during the journey from MacFarlane to MacDonald. But they'd traveled only during the day and slept at night, allowing them to travel at a canter throughout the day. She'd realized that the drum of over three hundred horses would have been heard from quite a distance and no doubt had sent most animals fleeing in the opposite direction. Aside from which, she'd always been with Conall's aunt and cousin when they stopped at night. Most animals might approach one person for aid, but usually would not risk a group of them.

"Do ye want to wait fer them or take yer deer back to the stables?" Conall asked as they stopped by the closest wagon.

Claray hesitated, and then bit her lip and eyed the approaching party, before murmuring, "This little one needs goat's milk. Yer uncle was going to try to purchase livestock fer us, was he no'?"

"Aye." He looked toward the traveling party, his eyes squinting as he tried to make out what it included.

The two men riding at the front looked to her to be his uncle and cousin. They were followed by several wagons with large casks on them, obviously ale, mead and wine to tide them over for a while. Hopefully, they'd be able to make their own eventually, but until then they'd have to purchase it. There were a lot of wagons with casks. They were followed by wagons filled with what looked to be sacks of flour and perhaps spices, as well as vegetables. But behind the wagons came various animals and a lot of them, herded along by the soldiers who closed them in on the sides and followed, keeping them moving after the wagons. The soldiers on their horses made it hard to see what exactly the animals were though.

"I can no' see what animals he managed to get fer us," Conall admitted after a moment.

"Neither can I," Claray confessed, and then glanced down at the fawn she carried, before deciding, "I'd like to wait fer them to see."

Conall nodded, but caught her by the waist and lifted her up to sit on the back of the wagon where she'd been earlier.

Claray murmured a thank-you, and then turned her attention to petting and soothing the distressed fawn in her arms as they waited. It didn't take as long as she'd feared for the traveling party to reach them. While they took the path down the hill at a slow pace, once on the valley floor they picked up speed and were soon slowing to a halt when Conall walked over to meet them.

His smile when he returned to Claray told her he was pleased with what his uncle and cousin had managed to purchase for them.

"He found everything I asked him to look fer," Conall announced, hopping onto the back of the wagon next to her. "Includin' a couple o' goats with kids. So they'll be producin' milk."

Claray smiled with relief, and then grabbed the side rail with surprise when the wagon rocked as Roderick and Hamish climbed in to sit on one side of the wagon behind them and Gilly and Machar did the same on the other. Hendrie, Colban and the other two young soldiers who had been set to guarding Conall all stood in front of her and Conall, and walked behind the wagon as it began to move.

"The men had just finished fillin' the wagons with rushes when they saw the travelers approachin'," Conall explained, and she peered along the row of four wagons to see that the others were all as full as the one they sat on.

Nodding, she relaxed and turned her gaze back to the fawn. It had stopped bleating and had curled up to sleep in her lap. When Conall's arm dropped around her shoulders, she leaned into his chest and sighed contentedly.

"Me uncle said he brings good tidings," he murmured, pressing a kiss to the top of her head.

"What tidings?" she asked at once.

"I do no' ken. He said he wanted to tell us both at the same time," he admitted a touch wryly.

"Oh," Claray murmured. She supposed he'd been disappointed to have to wait to learn what these tidings were too. Wondering what it could be, she watched the returned traveling party follow them across the new drawbridge and into the bailey.

"MACNAUGHTON IS DEAD."

Claray blinked at that announcement from Conall's uncle and stared at him wide-eyed. She, Conall, his aunt and Kenna were all seated at the trestle tables. Meanwhile, the eight men who made up their combined guards stood behind them, while Ross MacKay and Payton stood facing them on the other side of the table to make that announcement.

It was nearly the sup, more than two hours since they'd crossed the drawbridge with the MacKay men and their warriors and the animals following. But it had taken that long to get everything from the wagons sorted and the animals looked after. Conall's men were even now building fencing to keep the animals from wandering, while others were doing their best to keep the beasts in the area where they would eventually live.

Claray had reluctantly given up the fawn to Allistair to tend, so that she could help Conall go through the provisions his uncle had brought back and decide where they needed to go. Now that was all done, Lady MacKay and Kenna had been fetched from where they were working. Ross MacKay had herded them all to the tables and had insisted they sit before making his announcement.

"Really?" Lady MacKay said finally when no one else spoke.

"Aye." Payton grinned and then his gaze moved to Claray and he explained gently, "He went after yer sister Allissaid."

Claray's eyes widened with alarm. "Is she all right?"

"Aye," he assured her. "Apparently, he dragged her back to Fraoch Eilean and forced her to marry him, but she escaped. Jumped out the window o' the tower, right into Loch Awe. MacNaughton's men searched the shore and pounded the bushes all around, but did no' find her. She stayed in the water and swam all the way to Kilcairn." He shook his head. "I can hardly fathom how she managed it."

"Allissaid was always a good swimmer," Claray said softly.

"She must be," Payton said solemnly.

It was Ross MacKay who finished the tale. "The Campbell gave yer sister shelter when she reached Kilcairn. But somehow, the MacNaughton got wind she was there. He tried to steal her back, and the Campbell took exception. He killed him for his trouble. MacNaughton'll trouble ye no more."

Claray swallowed and managed a smile at this news. But her new uncle wasn't done.

"The Campbell sent news that he'd learned that before Allissaid escaped, MacNaughton had sent men both to MacFarlane and here, to kill Claray and her brother and sisters as they could."

Claray stiffened again, and felt Conall cover her hands where they rested in her lap.

"'Tis fine though," Payton added quickly. "Yer da has men searching the woods surrounding MacFarlane, looking fer the ones sent there, and," he added with a smile, "the Sutherland already took care o' the men sent here."

"The Sutherland?" Conall asked with surprise.

"Aye. They must ha'e camped just across yer southern border on Sutherland land to avoid detection. But they ran afoul o' a patrol o' Sutherland soldiers and were killed in the ensuing battle," Laird MacKay informed them. "The Sutherland himself told us the tale when we stopped there fer the night on our way back here."

"Aye." Payton grinned. "So, ye'll ha'e no more arrows flyin' at ye now and can let go that worry, give up yer guards and concentrate on the future."

"What about the old trouble?" Roderick asked, and there was a moment of silence.

"I'm hopin' it's been so long that whoever was behind that attack is long dead. But we can no' be sure," Ross MacKay said slowly, and then frowned and shook his head and told Conall, "It might be good to keep a couple o' guards on ye, nephew. At least fer a little bit longer. Just to be sure all is well."

Conall nodded solemnly.

CLARAY FINISHED THE MAT SHE WAS WORKING ON, AND SET IT on the small pile growing next to her on the great hall floor. Glancing around at the other women working with her, she noted that they were all making quick work of the task. Soon they could start sewing the mats together to make larger ones to carpet the stone floor. They'd need several to cover the great hall alone, and then they planned to make them for the bedchambers and barracks as well.

Pushing aside the thought of the amount of work yet ahead of them, Claray turned her attention to gathering more rushes. As she began braiding another three-foot-wide and six-foot-long mat, her mind turned to Conall and all that they'd already accomplished. They'd got a lot done with the help of his family. The keep walls were whitewashed, the kitchen organized, the gardens planted and already sprouting. There were now several pens and small buildings for the new animals, the curtain wall was nearly completely repaired and the soldiers had even cleared the area around the castle. Now, while fifty men still worked on the curtain wall, Conall had set a hundred men to clear and plow the old fields where he thought they'd been, so they could start planting.

Claray truly hadn't thought they could get so much done so quickly, and they couldn't have done it all without the help of the MacKays and their soldiers. She smiled faintly as she thought of Conall's aunt and uncle and Kenna. Promising to visit often, the family had left that morning to head back to MacKay. All but Payton. She suspected he and Roderick would remain at Deagh Fhortan until they were sure that Conall's parents' murderer wasn't still around to cause trouble.

"M'lady, I thought ye might like something to drink while yer weavin' the mats."

Claray glanced up from her braiding with surprise, a smile lifting her lips when she saw Mhairi approaching with a mug in hand.

"Thank ye, Mhairi. That would be lovely. I—Ah!" she cried out with surprise as the maid tripped and fell forward, nearly landing in her lap. The woman managed to save herself by grabbing the arm of the chair next to where Claray knelt, but had to drop the drink to do it.

Claray stared down blankly at the cold liquid dripping down her face and chest, soaking into her gown.

"Oh, heavens! Oh, dear Lord, m'lady, I'm ever so sorry," Mhairi moaned, snatching the mug out of her lap and kneeling next to her to try to sop up the mess with her own skirts.

"'Tis fine, Mhairi," Claray assured her, catching the woman's hands to stop her and then getting to her feet. "Do no' fret yerself. Accidents happen. I'll just go change."

"Oh, I am sorry, m'lady," the woman repeated unhappily.

Claray patted her arm and then glanced down to the wolf when he started to rise. "Stay, Lovey. I'll be right back."

The wolf hesitated, but then dropped back to the floor and laid his head on his paws to watch her walk away. Much to her annoyance, Hendrie and Colban didn't stay though. The two men immediately leapt up from the trestle tables where they'd been watching her work, and hurried to take up position on either side of her to escort her across the great hall.

While she no longer had to put up with four men following her everywhere, Conall still wanted two guarding her until they were sure all was well. He had also agreed to keep Roderick and Payton with him as guards for a while too. Claray understood his concern, but felt silly being followed about by the two younger soldiers inside the keep.

"I am only going to change, gentlemen. There's no need to come with me. I'm sure ye can see the door to me bedchamber from here," she said with a touch of irritation.

"But from down here we could no' stop someone from givin' ye a push as ye descend the stairs, could we?" Hendrie asked quietly.

Claray scowled at the suggestion. One, because she hadn't thought of it, and two, because it wasn't nice thinking that someone might want to do that to her. Sighing, she just shook her head and made no more protests as she headed up the stairs to the bedchamber she shared with Conall.

She was caught by surprise when she reached the landing and Hendrie rushed ahead of her. Claray thought he was just going to open the door for her, and he did, but then he held up his hand to keep her from entering, and stepped inside himself. She watched with disbelief as he peered around the empty room, knowing he was looking about to be sure there was no one in there, but she thought it was ridiculous. Claray didn't say so, however. She just shook her head, and then proceeded into the room when he stepped back out and waved her in.

Hendrie pulled the door closed for her once she was inside and Claray started across the room, but found her footsteps slowing before she'd got halfway across. She also began glancing nervously around the chamber. It was empty, and silent and still, yet the hair on the back of her neck was prickling with unease. Which was silly, she told herself firmly. There was no one there. The men's ridiculously overcautious behavior was just making her paranoid. Still, she had that creeping sensation that she often got when she knew someone was watching her, even though there was no one there to do so.

Claray gave herself a little shake to try to chase off the feeling, and then made herself move to the chests of clothes along the wall opposite the door. The one closest to the window held her older gowns, the ones she preferred to work in because she didn't mind them getting soiled or ruined. Opening that chest, she fetched out the pale, yellow gown that lay on top, and then peered out the window and down at the bailey below as she closed the chest.

Spying her husband by the wall, Claray paused to watch him. He was standing talking to Roderick and Payton, and she found herself comparing the three men and smiling to herself as she thought her husband was the fairest of them all. Not that she was biased or anything, she assured herself with amusement, and then made herself turn her back on the pleasant view, and walk to the bed.

High up as she was, Claray wasn't concerned that anyone in the bailey might see her, but that creeping feeling running down the back of her neck still had her on edge, and she looked around the room again as she undid her lacings. Still, there was nothing and no one to see, so she quickly shrugged out of her gown, and reached for the other one even as the first dropped to the floor. In her rush to don it, Claray got a bit tangled in the cloth when she pulled it over her head, and at first stuck her arm out through the neck opening.

Muttering under the gobs of smothering material gathered around her head and face, she tugged the cloth up and her arm down to fix her mistake and then poked around until she found an armhole instead. Claray then did the same with her other hand and shimmied a little to get the cloth to drop down into place, allowing her head to pop out of the neckline. She then tugged the material of the skirt down and scowled when she saw that she'd got the damned thing turned around and had pulled it on backward.

Sighing with exasperation, Claray started to tug on the sleeve of one arm, intending to pull her arms out and turn the gown without having to pull it off altogether. But before she could, pain exploded in her head, followed quickly by unconsciousness.

Chapter 24

"They'll be done with the wall soon."

Conall grunted in agreement as he watched the men work. Three or four of his men had worked as stonemasons for a while before joining him in mercenary work. They were directing the others.

In truth, many of his men had started in different professions before joining his forces. Aside from the stonemasons, he had men who used to be blacksmiths, millers, armorers, plowmen, metalsmiths, carpenters, a baker, a chandler, a cooper and a brewer. One had even been a gongfarmer. Conall hadn't chosen them for what they did; he'd merely approached any man he encountered, or heard of, over the years who was a MacDonald, and had made an offer to them. Join his mercenaries and he would train them in battle, pay them more than they could make at their present jobs, and someday they would reclaim Deagh Fhortan and become a clan again.

Conall had never told any of them that he was Bryson Mac-Donald, but wouldn't have been surprised if they'd suspected. Few he'd approached had refused, although that may have been because so many MacDonald cousins and such already worked for him. Whatever the case, doing that had been something of a pain in the arse. He'd spent a good deal of time training nearly every man in his ranks in battle. It would have been easier to merely hire on warriors who were already fully trained, but Conall had been working toward a goal, gathering as many of the lost and displaced MacDonald clan members as he could.

While it had meant more work for him over the years to train these men, it had paid off well. He now not only had skilled warriors, but he had skilled warriors with other talents and abilities. The stonemasons were overseeing the other soldiers and were ensuring that the curtain wall and inner buildings were repaired properly. The carpenters had overseen the repairs of the roof, building the second floor of the keep and the building of furniture that was needed. The blacksmith had found the old forge and started making the specialized tools needed by the stonemasons and the carpenters, as well as repairing and sharpening weapons.

It had all worked out very well in the end. In fact, while Conall hadn't thought of it when he was taking on these men, doing so had actually saved them money when it came to repairing Deagh Fhortan. He hadn't had to spend the coin on hiring tradesmen to perform the tasks. And that left more money to feed and clothe his people until the fields started to produce, which made the extra hours he'd spent training between mercenary jobs worth it, he decided and then glanced past Roderick when he heard someone shouting. His gaze narrowed when he saw Allistair running toward him from the stables.

"He seems upset," Roderick commented mildly.

"Aye," Conall agreed, and moved forward to meet the man.

"Oh, m'laird," the stable master panted the words as he reached him, then paused to catch his breath before adding unhappily, "'Tis Stubborn Bastard."

Conall felt alarm course through him at the mention of his wife's horse. She loved the great beast, and the man's upset could not be good.

"Tell me," he growled, urging Allistair back toward the stables, aware that Roderick and Payton were following.

IT WAS HER OWN MOAN OF PAIN THAT WOKE CLARAY. SHE PUSHED her eyes open, wincing as the small action increased the agony shattering her skull, but kept them open anyway as she took in her surroundings. Confusion coursed through her as she realized she was in some sort of small, stone building. Or what used to be a small stone building, she supposed, since the thatched roof had mostly caved in to cover the floor around her, and the top three feet of the wall opposite her had crumbled in as well. It was more like a stone pen now with an opening where the door used to be.

Bewildered as to where she was and how she'd got there, Claray turned her head slowly from side to side trying to see everything. She couldn't see behind her, and there wasn't much to see in front and to the sides. Although bits of old roof and wall weren't all that littered the floor. She saw what she thought was an old rusted cooking pot under some of the debris, and the remains of what might have been a bed at one time. The only other identifiable object was the chair she was slumped on, or actually tied to, she realized when she tried to move and found her arms were strapped to the back sides of the chair and her ankles bound to its legs.

That was when her puzzlement turned to alarm. Panicking a little, she jerked at her arms and tried to tug her legs loose, but she was firmly fixed to the chair and wasn't going anywhere without help.

"Oh, yer awake. Good."

Claray jerked her head up and stared at the woman who stepped through the hole where a door had once been.

"Mhairi?" she said with confusion as the woman approached.

"Aye." The servant offered her a serene smile as she stopped before her and looked her over. Then she asked, "Does yer head hurt? It looks like it should. There was an awful lot o' blood from the blow ye took, but I think the bleedin' is finally stoppin'."

Claray blinked at the words, suddenly aware of something warm and sticky along the side of her head and down her neck. A glance down at what she could see of her shoulder revealed the edge of a large stain of blood spreading out from her neck. It made her recall that she'd been dressing when her head had seemed to explode with pain. She also saw that her gown was still on backward, but was oddly relieved by that knowledge.

Turning her gaze back to Mhairi, she asked, "Where are we?"

"One o' the old cottages outside the walls," the woman answered easily. "We're less likely to be interrupted here."

"I see," Claray murmured, but she didn't really, so asked, "Why are we here?"

Mhairi heaved out a sigh at the question, and shook her head with a look of mild disgust. "Because I bungled the job o' eradicatin' the MacDonalds from this earth twenty-two years ago, and ha'e to finish it."

"Twenty-two," Claray whispered slowly, her eyes widening. "Ye're who poisoned Conall's parents and most o' the rest o' the clan all those years ago?"

Mhairi's shoulders drew up proudly as she nodded.

Claray shook her head with bewildered horror. "But—Why?"

"Because they were a blight on the world. An abomination," she spat, pride giving way to fury, and then her shoulders sagged unhappily and she added almost resentfully, "But I did no' get them all as I was meant to. The Devil's spawn got away and has now come back to plague the land again, spreadin' his filth and corruption everywhere. Infectin' even you, a good lass who kenned better than to enjoy the matin' and imperil her soul. And I'm sorry fer that, m'lady. I truly am. I take full responsibility fer it, and I'll see it right."

Claray stared at her blankly as she absorbed her words, and then cleared her throat, and said tentatively, "Mhairi, I ken the church says we should no' enjoy marital relations and—"

"*God does no' suffer man to enjoy the couplin',*" she interrupted, sounding like she was quoting someone. Probably a parish priest, Claray thought, and managed a smile as she nodded.

"Aye," she began. "But—"

"And yet ye enjoyed it, did ye no'?" Mhairi interrupted again, a sly smile curving her lips. "Ye liked him touchin' and puttin' his mouth on ye everywhere and then swivin' ye with his big, hard lance, poundin' ye till ye screamed yer pleasure, forsakin' yer soul."

Claray flushed and swallowed, unsure what to say. All she really wanted to do was slap the murderous bitch. Unfortunately, that wasn't possible tied up as she was.

"Lady Giorsal enjoyed it too," Mhairi announced, saving her from having to respond at all. "She used to squeal like a pig every time her husband poked her. As fer himself, he roared his pleasure with disgustin' fervor. I could barely stand to listen and watch when they escaped out to the fishpond of a night to jape by the water. But I had to bear witness to their sinful ways fer God," she assured her, and then added, "They were evil, and spreadin' their corruption amongst the clan. Soldiers would meet up with the servin' girls in dark corners, both inside and outside the keep, push 'em up against the wall or a tree and have at 'em like the animals they were all becomin'. I could no' let it continue. They were goin' against God," she pointed out.

Claray stared at her blankly. The woman had obviously spied on Conall's parents in their private moments, which she found just disgusting. It sounded like she'd also taken to watching the servants and soldiers too when they tried to find a private spot to indulge themselves. What she'd witnessed wasn't uncommon in castles. There was little privacy afforded any but the laird and lady who had a chamber. The others often sought out dark spots to be together. She didn't bother to point that out to Mhairi though and merely said, "So ye poisoned them."

"Aye." Mhairi grinned again. "Everyone who was at table that night at least, and some who were no'. And it was glorious. So easy. I just slipped it in the wine and ale, and one and all drank it." She smiled, apparently at the memory, and then her smile faded, replaced with a bitter expression. "I put it in their seed's drink too, but the little bastard did no' drink it."

"Conall," Claray murmured, and the woman snorted with disgust.

"His name is Bryson MacDonald, and he should have died that night." She scowled and shook her head. "After watching all at table die, I went up to his room to check on him. I'd put it in his watered-down mead and expected to find him dead too. But when I got to his chamber it was empty, his food and drink still on the table, untouched. I thought he'd wandered out with his dog somewhere as he sometimes did, and then as I started to turn back to the door, I noticed a panel o' the stone wall slightly ajar next to the fireplace. So, I went to the openin' and peered in. Much to me surprise it was a secret passage."

Claray stilled at that. She wasn't surprised to learn there were secret passages in the castle. Most had them. But Conall hadn't mentioned them to her. Still, she suspected this was how she'd been knocked out and removed from their bedchamber without anyone noticing. Mhairi must have crept up through the secret passage, entered the room while she was changing and coshed her over the head, then somehow dragged her into the passage with her and down here to this cottage. Claray was frowning over how the woman had managed that last part when Mhairi continued her tale.

"There are peepholes all along the passage, but most o' them overlook the great hall. Light was splashin' through and highlightin' the young bugger. I could see his horrified little face and knew he'd seen them all die below." She grimaced. "Well, I kenned I'd no' be able to convince him to eat or drink after he'd witnessed that. So, I decided I'd ha'e to wring his nasty little neck to be sure the plague o' putrescent corruption was gone."

Her mouth flattened out with remembered frustration. "He must ha'e heard me when I started in after him. He turned me way, but the light was behind me. I'm sure he could no' see who 'twas. But the little bastard panicked and ran anyway. I followed quick as I could, but he was always a swift one, that boy. Used to keep me runnin' to look after him," she added with resentment, and then shrugged. "By the time I followed him out of the passage and into the bailey, he was ridin' out o' the stables on his pony.

"O' course I gave chase," she assured her. "I took his whore mother's horse and rode out after him. The mare was powerful and should ha'e caught up easily to the pony, but I'd never ridden a horse before. I did no' ken what the hell I was doin' and it was hours ere I caught up to him." Her mouth set with displeasure.

"I grabbed the reins o' his mount out o' his hands and yanked to make him stop and the damned thing reared, topplin' the lad from his mount.

"The boy hit his head as he fell. He was unconscious. So, I jumped off the mare and walked over, intendin' to finally finish him off . . . But then several men rode out o' the woods and surrounded us.

"Well," she said now with an evil smile. "The mare had raced off when I got off her, and I was ever a quick thinker, so I said as how I was seein' the boy safely to his uncle as all was killed back at MacDonald and we took a tumble from his pony. So, they took us up on their horses, pulled his pony behind and took us to their laird, the MacKay."

"And Conall did no' tell them the truth when he woke up?" Claray asked with disbelief.

"From what I understand, he took quite a wollop to his head. Did no' recall the ride back at all," she said with a shrug, and then added, "That's when I kenned I'd done the right thing. God was protectin' me by taking his memory."

Claray suspected it was more likely the head injury on top of the trauma of seeing most of his clan die that had stolen his memory and protected the witch.

"That's why I do no' understand why He let the lad get away from me," Mhairi complained now. "I thought I'd succeeded when I woke up the next morn to the news that everyone, includin' the lad, was dead. I thought the blow to the head must ha'e killed him. And that's what Laird MacKay said happened when I asked." Mhairi smiled faintly. "I was ever so pleased. I thought I'd done God's work and removed the seed o' evil, eradicatin' the blight.

"And, at first, it did seem that me work in His name had done even more good than I'd hoped. Some o' the other bastard MacDonalds who had their own cottages and did no' share the meal had up and fled in fear o' God's wrath when they heard tell o' so many dying. Of those who remained, some were murdered by reivers or other clans, but all fled eventually, either through death or on their own feet. O' course some came to MacKay, and

I kept a close eye on them, killin' any who showed signs o' lustin' and such. Real careful like though," she assured her. "An accident here, an accident there."

Claray closed her eyes briefly as she thought of those poor people, and then Mhairi clucked with disgust and said, "I've passed twenty-two years thinkin' I'd done well, then one fine mornin' the MacKay and his wife rode out with their daughter and a hundred men. No one kenned what was happening except that a messenger had come from the Buchanans."

She sighed unhappily. "And then two soldiers returned. They were exhausted, they were. Had ridden night and day to bring us the news that Bryson MacDonald yet lived. That he'd survived that night and had been smuggled out to Sinclair to live under a different name to keep him safe until he was an adult and could claim Deagh Fhortan and rebuild it to its former glory. They said all MacDonalds who wished to join him should pack up and be ready to go when we got word that they were passin' MacKay."

"Well," she said grimly. "I kenned then that I had to come finish me work. God would no' look kindly on me did I no' complete it. So, I packed up me things and left with the others when two more soldiers arrived to tell us 'twas time to go. And here we are," she said with a pleasant smile. "I'll kill ye, and then him, and then me work'll be done.

"At least, I think 'twill be done," Mhairi added with an uncertain frown. "I do wonder if I should no' kill the remaining MacDonalds too with another dose o' poison to the wine and ale just to be sure I'm really finished." She pondered that briefly, and then muttered, "I'll have to think on that. I've still a little time. So long as I do it ere anyone learns the two o' ye are dead, it should work fine."

Claray stared at her with bewilderment. "But ye're a MacDonald too. How could ye kill yer entire clan like this?"

"I'm no' a MacDonald," she snapped, suddenly furious again. "I was a Douglas. I just married a MacDonald. I thought him a fine man at the time, hardworkin' and kind. But the bastard was as evil as everyone else here. Makin' me enjoy the beddin' and imperilin' me immortal soul," she said with disgust. "Riddin' the earth o' him and all the other carnal animals here was the only way to redeem meself and me son in God's eyes."

"Yer son?" Claray asked with surprise.

"Aye. I was with child when I started the purge o' MacDonalds. I did no' ken until a little after. At first, I thought to kill the bairn the moment he was born, but I could no' do it. I've raised him good and proper since though, puttin' the fear o' God in him. Between that and finishin' me work here I hope to save both our souls."

Claray sank back in the chair with a small sigh as she thought of the hell this woman must have put her son through with her "putting the fear o' God in him." What would that include from a woman who was running about murdering unsuspecting MacDonalds who were unfortunate enough to choose MacKay for their temporary home and who she deemed sinners? Claray was also more than a little distressed to recognize part of herself in the woman. She had worried for her soul because she'd enjoyed the bedding too. But where she'd accepted that it must be all right because she'd vowed to obey Conall and he'd ordered her to enjoy it, this woman had . . . well, she'd lost her mind as far as Claray could tell. Mhairi believed that enjoying the bedding was a sin that would see her soul in hell, but that killing so many innocent people would redeem her. It was madness.

"Now," Mhairi muttered, straightening to approach her, knife in hand. "Sadly, because I did no' eradicate the blight as I'd originally thought, he's managed to infect ye with his corruption and lustful ways. And I'm sorry fer that lass. I truly am. But ye've surely suffered enough, and 'tis time I put ye out o' yer misery."

Claray's eyes widened with horror when the woman raised the knife overhead. When Mhairi started to plunge it downward, she instinctively threw her weight to the side, trying to get out of the way.

Chapter 25

"Nightshade?" Conall echoed with dismay.

"Aye," Allistair said miserably. "I'm sorry, m'laird. I do no' ken how it got into Stubborn Bastard's stall. I mean, someone *must* ha'e put it in there, but I ha'e been here all day and I do no' ken how it was put in without me seein'. And I do no' ken how long 'twas in with him ere I noticed."

Conall waved that away and asked the question he thought more important at the moment. "Did he eat any o' it?"

Allistair peered into the stall and shook his head sadly. "I do no' ken."

Conall wanted to ask if there was anything the man did ken, but bit back his temper, and stared at Stubborn Bastard unhappily.

"Nightshade'll kill a horse as sure as it does people," Roderick said in a solemn rumble.

"Aye," Payton agreed. "And I'm thinkin' Claray would be fair distraught if she lost her horse."

Conall ran a hand wearily through his hair, knowing everything they said was true.

"Do ye think we should tell Lady Claray?" Allistair asked reluctantly. "I mean, we do no' even ken if he ate any. Mayhap he did no', and 'twill be fine," he said hopefully.

"Mayhap," Conall muttered, hoping that would be the case. He was not eager to be the bearer of these particular tidings to Claray. She loved the big, dumb horse, and would most like blame him for having the beast moved to a stall and out of the way of the men working. He'd insisted on it after Stubborn Bastard had taken a bite out of one of the men's arses when he'd got in the way of the horse following Claray. She hadn't been pleased at his being locked up in a stall, but had understood. That understanding would go out the window though if the great beast died.

"Christ!" he muttered with disgust. "Nightshade. Why the hell would anyone want to kill the horse?"

"Ye mean aside from the poor bastard he bit?" Roderick asked dryly.

Conall grimaced at the words.

"M'laird?" Allistair queried. "Do we ha'e to tell her?"

"I'm thinkin' ye probably should."

Conall turned sharply at those apologetic words to see Hamish standing at the entrance to the stables, his concerned gaze on Stubborn Bastard. Obviously, he'd been standing there long enough to understand what was happening.

After a hesitation, Conall shook his head. "There's no sense upsettin' her when it may no' be necessary."

"Aye. He may no' have even eaten any of the nightshade," Allistair pointed out with a desperation Conall understood. The stable master adored Claray for both her skill with animals, and for insisting they build a room onto the stables for him to sleep in. She was a goddess in the stable master's eyes and he did not want to disappoint her any more than Conall did.

"But what if he did eat it?" Hamish asked, and pointed out, "If so, Lady Claray may ken a remedy fer the poison. If she does, and ye did no' tell her about this, and Stubborn Bastard dies . . ." He shook his head. "I suspect she'll never forgive ye."

"He has a point," Roderick said solemnly.

Conall cursed at the words and closed his eyes briefly at the thought of her reaction if the beast died. It would not be good, he thought grimly.

"I'll tell her," Allistair said, his shoulders straightening. "I'm the one responsible fer his care, and I'm the one who was here when nightshade was put in his stall. I'll tell her, and ask does she ken a remedy."

"Nay." Conall shook his head wearily. "I'll tell me wife meself."

He strode out of the stables, unsurprised when Roderick and Payton followed. Conall crossed the bailey at a quick clip to keep anyone from stopping him with questions or worries. The sooner he got this done, the better. If the horse had eaten some of the nightshade, and there *was* a remedy, it did seem that the more swiftly it was administered, the better. Besides, to his mind, it was always best to get unpleasant tasks done quickly, and this *was* going to be unpleasant. Not because he thought Claray would rail at him or even blame him, but because she would be upset and worried and—

Good God, what if she cried? Conall thought with horror. He'd never seen his wife cry, not properly anyway. A tear or two had leaked from her eye in the gardens their first night here, but that had been from stress and anxiety over the large job ahead of them, not from grief or true upset. It would break his heart to see her having a proper cry now. But she loved that horse, so the chances were good that he was about to. The idea was almost enough to make him turn around and walk the other way, but he straightened his shoulders and carried on manfully, making it all the way to the keep without being stopped, and much too quickly for his liking.

Ashamed of his own cowardice, he jogged up the steps to the keep and entered, his gaze searching the great hall as he started across it. There were several women weaving rush mats in the open area in front of the fireplace, and the wolf was there lying next to a stack of mats near the clear area where Claray had been earlier. But she was gone. So were Hendrie and Colban though. Even as he noted that, the wolf raised his head and glanced toward the top of the stairs. Conall followed his gaze, and spotted Hendrie and Colban standing outside of his bedchamber door.

Turning to Payton and Roderick, he muttered, "Claray must be in our chamber. Ye may as well sit down and ha'e a drink while ye wait. I suspect there's no cure for nightshade and I'll be havin' to comfort her. That could take a while."

"Oh, aye," Payton said, his tone solemn, but eyes twinkling with amusement. "Comfortin' a lass can take hours."

Ignoring that, Conall turned to head to the stairs. He saw the wolf stand up and stretch, but ignored it and jogged up the steps to the landing.

"Claray?" he asked as he approached the door.

"Aye. Inside, m'laird," Hendrie answered. "Mhairi spilled some mead on her, and Lady Claray came up to change."

Nodding, Conall opened the door and started in, only to pause in confusion when he saw the room was empty.

"I thought ye said she was in here?" he growled, glancing over his shoulder.

"She is," Hendrie assured him, and then stepped up to the door and looked in. Amazement immediately covered his face. "She was here, m'laird. We walked her up, checked the room and then left to let her change. She's no' come out," he assured him, his wide eyes moving over the room with bewilderment, and then stopping on the window. Horror mounting on his face, the man suddenly hurried to the window and leaned out to peer down.

For one moment, Conall thought his heart had stopped as he realized that the man was thinking his wife had either fallen or jumped out of the window. But then the man straightened and turned back with a completely flummoxed expression, and muttered, "I do no' understand it. She never came out."

"Blood."

Conall turned sharply to Colban as he said the word with dismay. The other soldier had followed Hendrie into the room and now stood pointing at the bed. Conall walked to the bed at once to examine the stain on the white fur covering. It was almost in the middle of the bed, mostly just a few droplets and one larger irregular circle of it.

"There's some on the floor here too," Hendrie said grimly, and Conall walked around to peer, first at the discarded, damp gown on the floor, and then at the droplets leading away from the bed and toward . . . the wall? He stared at it silently for a minute, and then suddenly spun on his heel and headed out of the room.

"Do we follow him or wait here?" he heard Colban ask anxiously, and Conall paused at the door to look back.

"Ye wait here and hold anyone who enters," he ordered, and started to turn away, but then paused to add, "But be warned, the door is no' the only entrance."

Conall didn't explain further, he simply walked out and pulled the door closed. He wasn't surprised to find the wolf there with Squeak on his back. The animal had probably assumed he would stay in the room with Claray and had intended to join them. Conall almost told the wolf to go back to the great hall, but when he glanced down and saw that Roderick and Payton were gone, probably in the kitchen or buttery, fetching food or drink or both, he had a sudden thought that changed his mind.

"Come," he growled, patting his leg. He led the wolf to the next room up the hall. It was the room his aunt and uncle had occupied before heading back to MacKay. Payton was now using the room while Roderick was in the next room up the hall. Conall felt a little guilty for intruding on his friend's room when he wasn't there, but pushed the worry aside as he opened the door. He stepped in and held the door open for the wolf, then closed it behind them both.

There were secret passages in the stone outer walls. One used to be in his old room, which was where this new room had been built. He assumed there was one in the master chamber as well, where his parents had slept, but he'd never explored in there to find it as a child, and had no idea how that one was opened. He did know how to open this one though.

Walking to the side of the fireplace, he ran his fingers over the stones there and then pushed and turned one. Conall stepped back as the wall began to open and then scowled as he peered into the darkness. He hadn't thought to grab a candle or— His gaze landed on a rushlight in a holder on the table next to the bed.

Conall hurried over to grab it, and then walked out to the hall to light it from a candle in a sconce there. He then held his hand before the rushlight to keep it from going out as he hurried back into the room his cousin was using. The wolf was standing in the entrance to the passage, his nose up and sniffing, and Conall felt his hopes rise.

"Do ye smell Claray?" he asked, crossing the room to stand next to the wolf. "Find yer lady. Find Claray."

Conall wasn't sure whether the wolf would recognize his wife's name, so was relieved when the beast slid into the dark passage and set off. Hoping the animal was tracking Claray's scent and not just exploring, Conall followed quickly, pulling the panel closed behind him.

CLARAY GRUNTED IN PAIN AS HER MOVEMENT SENT THE CHAIR she was tied to toppling over sideways. It left her helpless on the ground, still bound to the chair and unable to get out of the way when Mhairi followed and started to slash out at her. Unable to do anything else, Claray closed her eyes and waited for the pain to strike. It came as something of a surprise when—rather than feel the pain she expected—she heard Mhairi bark, "Let me go!"

She was even more startled to hear a man's angry voice next. "What the hell are ye doin'?"

Blinking her eyes open, Claray lifted her head off the ground to peer wildly around and thought she'd weep with joy when she saw that Hamish was there and had caught the woman by the wrist before she could stab her.

"I'm riddin' Deagh Fhortan o' its evil!" Mhairi shrieked, and began to struggle. "Let me go! 'Tis what God wants!"

Hamish wrestled with her briefly, but when she got her hand loose and slashed his arm, he growled and slammed her into the wall. Claray winced as she heard the crack of the woman's head hitting the stone. Eyes wide, she watched Mhairi crumple to the ground in a lifeless heap, and then Claray let her head fall back to the dirt and closed her eyes on a sigh of relief at the knowledge that she was saved.

"Claray? Are ye all right?"

Blinking her eyes open, she managed a smile for the man who had rescued her. In the next moment though, she was wincing in pain and closing her eyes when the bindings dug painfully into her side, hip and outer leg as he shifted the chair back to its upright position. It landed on all four legs with a bump that she felt throughout her entire body.

"Are ye all right?"

Claray opened her eyes again to find Hamish kneeling in the dirt before her, his expression full of concern as he gazed into her face. Managing a smile, she nodded weakly. "Aye. Thank God ye found us, Hamish. Mhairi is mad. She's the one who poisoned Conall's parents and the others, and she was going to kill me too."

"Whist, loving," Hamish soothed, palming her cheek gently. "Yer safe now I'm here. She can no' hurt ye. I plan to save ye, body and soul."

Claray stared at him blankly. "What?"

"WHERE TO NOW, WOLF?" CONALL ASKED IN A QUIET VOICE. They had reached the final exit of the passage. There had been three or four along the way besides the ones on the upper floor that led into the bedrooms. Each had a peephole that he'd been able to peer through to see what lay beyond. The first exit after the bedchambers had come after descending a set of steep stairs. It had opened into the pantry. The second had opened into the chapel. There had been another set of stairs leading downward again before a third opening, a trap door that had opened just outside the curtain wall. This fourth exit, however, appeared to be the last and had opened out into a small, empty cave with steps leading up to another trap door.

Conall had pushed it open and led the wolf out into a tiny area surrounded by bushes. After leading the way through those, he'd scanned the forest around them and then asked his question of his companion. Or companions, he supposed as his gaze slid over Squeak, who was now standing on the wolf's neck with both paws on the top of his head as he looked around, sniffing the air just as the wolf was now doing.

When Lovey turned and started to lope to the north, Conall followed silently, his gaze searching the forest around them and the ground for any signs that Claray and whoever had taken her may have passed this way. But he couldn't see a damned thing that would back up the possibility. He'd have to depend on the wolf to lead him to his wife, and hoped he was right in doing so.

Chapter 26

"*I* DO NO' UNDERSTAND, HAMISH? WHY ARE YE TOUCHIN' ME like that?" Claray asked with confusion, and then deciding she wasn't really as interested in the answer as she was in being set free, she requested, "Please untie me."

"Hush." He pressed his fingers to her lips and shook his head. "'Tis fine. All will be well. I ken ye did no' want to enjoy the bedding."

Claray jerked her head back sharply, alarm and embarrassment coursing through her. "What?"

"I heard ye talkin' to Lady MacKay on the journey here," he explained. "I ken ye were worried that yer husband's pleasurin' ye would land yer soul in hell. And I heard the stupid bitch try to tell ye that if he gave ye pleasure he must want ye to enjoy it and so ye should because ye'd vowed to obey him." His mouth tightened. "I worried about ye then bein' so led astray by the bitch. I truly did."

Claray swallowed. "Hamish, I—"

"Let me finish, lass. I do no' blame ye fer anything," he assured her. "Do ye remember on our first day here, when Conall went to find ye after we got the feral pigs out o' the keep? Ye were in the gardens with the bitch and her daughter."

"Aye," Claray said with confusion. "What o' it?"

"Well, when the ladies returned without ye, I thought I'd best go check and be sure he was no actin' the animal he is," he explained. "But ye were no' in the gardens, or the orchard either. Ye were in the water when I got to the edge o' the trees, and I arrived just in time to hear him order ye to enjoy his touch. I ken the whorish way ye acted then was no' yer fault," he assured her. "Ye'd vowed to obey him, so o' course ye had to obey, or at least pretend to enjoy it when he put his filthy hands and mouth on ye."

"Oh, God, ye watched us?" she asked with horror.

"Aye, and I saw all the filthy things he did to ye," he said, but while his tone of voice was solemn, his eyes were not, and his free hand was rubbing his groin. "I tried to kill him then, to free ye, but he moved and me arrow sailed right over him, and then he rolled ye into the water and a hue and cry arose."

Claray stared at him silently for a minute, her mind bouncing around like a trapped bird inside her skull, and then whispered, "It was you who shot me in the stables."

"Aye. I'm sorry, lass," he said apologetically. "I was aiming fer Conall, but he moved again." Annoyance crossed his face, and he added, "He treated ye sorely, bendin' ye over the pen and japing ye like a bitch in heat, then up against the post like a harlot. I kenned ye probably found it unbearable and I meant to end him. I never meant to hit you."

Claray stared at him with disbelief, wondering how he could think that would make it better. She had no desire to see Conall dead. She loved him.

That was a thought that caught her by surprise. Claray had liked Conall from the start, admired his sense of honor and determination to look after his people. She also appreciated all he had done for her, rescuing her from Kerr, carrying her before him on his mount while she slept, no matter that he was exhausted. He'd also been most patient with her rescuing animals at every turn on the way home to MacFarlane when she'd known he hadn't wanted her to. He was a good man—he worked day and night here to build a home for them all, and he'd tended to her when she was injured and ill with such gentleness and kindness. And then there was his loving.

Aye, at first Claray had worried that her soul might be in peril because of the pleasure he gave her, but she'd come to terms with that. It was just too beautiful and intimate to be something God would begrudge them. Surely, if He hadn't wanted them to enjoy each other like that, He wouldn't have made it possible for people *to* enjoy it as they did. At least that was her reasoning. Perhaps it was just a justification to allow her to continue to enjoy her marital bed without guilt, but since she found it impossible not to, she was happy to accept that justification.

Whatever the case, with all that she admired, respected and enjoyed about her husband, Claray supposed it would be surprising if she did not love him. Conall was a man worth loving, and she simply could not bear the thought of this man ending his life.

Realizing that Hamish was talking again and that she'd missed part of it, Claray concentrated on what he was saying again, in case there was something she could use to save herself and Conall.

"—and I told her that, so I'm no' sure why she decided to kill ye anyway," he added with grim resentment.

"Told who what?" Claray asked uncertainly.

"Me mother," he said with exasperation. "I told her that he'd ordered ye to enjoy it. That's why I do no' ken why she's so determined to see ye dead."

"Yer mother?" Claray asked with bewilderment, and then followed his gaze to the unconscious woman lying against the wall. Eyes widening with dismay, she asked, "Mhairi is yer mother?"

"Aye," he admitted with disgust, and then glanced back to her. "She's mad. Always has been. Used to brag to me on how she'd cleaned out the den o' inequity that Bean and Giorsal MacDonald had wrought here. She thought she'd killed the son too, but obviously she mucked that up like she mucks up everything." He turned a sneer on the woman and muttered, "She was no' a good mother."

Claray bit her lip, unsure what to say. She couldn't imagine the childhood he must have suffered through. But that didn't excuse his actions now. Conall's own childhood had been a horror thanks to this man's mother, and he wasn't going around trying to kill others. Well, other than his mercenary work, she acknowledged, and then pushed that thought away and concentrated on getting herself out of this mess. The man kept saying he was saving her, perhaps she could use that to her advantage.

"Thank ye, Hamish," she said now, and when he turned back to her, she managed a small smile and assured him, "I appreciate that ye're tryin' to save me soul. Now, do ye think ye could untie me, please? I should like to leave here."

"Soon," he assured her, running his hand down her cheek. "I ken yer scared, but I'm goin' to help ye."

"It would help me if ye untied me," she pointed out.

"Aye, but like I said, I need to talk to ye first."

Claray's teeth ground together, but she held on to her patience. "About what?" she asked. "If 'tis about yer mother knockin' me out and draggin' me here, I'll explain to Conall that ye were no' involved. He's a good man. He'll no' hold ye responsible."

Hamish smiled sadly. "Lass, I'm the one who coshed ye over the head and brought ye here, and I'm sorry fer that, but I could no' take the risk o' ye refusin' to come with me or cryin' out. And 'tis fer yer own good anyway."

Claray swallowed the fear trying to clog her throat, but held her tongue. She wasn't surprised by his words. She'd been hoping his mother had been behind it, but even as she had, some part of her mind had recognized that Mhairi MacDonald could not have carried her out to a cottage outside the wall.

"Besides," Hamish continued, "Conall's no' a good man, lass. He's forced ye to enjoy the beddin', and we both ken that's wrong. But 'tis fine," he continued before she could respond to that, although she had no idea what she could say anyway. "I plan to tend to that fer ye. I'm lookin' out fer ye."

"How do ye plan to tend to it?" Claray asked, quite sure she didn't want to hear the answer.

"I'm gonna kill him."

Exactly what she hadn't wanted to hear, Claray thought on an inward sigh. Hamish was obviously as mad as his mother. She supposed she shouldn't be surprised what with her raising him and feeding him all her bitter theories on what God expected and wanted.

"See," Hamish went on, "that way, ye'll be free and we can wed."

Claray stiffened at that. This was not something she'd expected.

"And I promise I'll never imperil yer soul by makin' ye enjoy the beddin'," he vowed, his hand moving to her knee and beginning to squeeze. "In fact, I'll be sure ye do no' enjoy it, so yer soul is safe."

Hamish squeezed harder with every word he spoke. But Claray refused to show that he was hurting her. She'd heard some of the women talking, and from what she understood, Hamish had some unusual tastes when it came to the bedding. Pain excited him, and the last thing she wanted to do was excite him. So, Claray bit her tongue and didn't react, until she felt the bones grind in her knee and couldn't bear it anymore, and finally gave in and cried out in pain.

"There," he said soothingly, releasing her leg the moment she cried out. "See. With me yer path to heaven'll be a sure thing. Fer 'tis surer ye'll get to heaven through pain and sufferin' like His own Son did than pleasure. I'll be a much better husband to ye, Claray, and a better laird to our people too."

Claray thought she'd rather roast in hell than marry the man. She couldn't believe he'd think she'd agree to marry someone promising her a lifetime of pain. Much as she loved God, if that's what He expected of her to get into heaven, she would say, "Thank ye, nay." But in her heart, Claray didn't think that was what He wanted at all. Not if madmen and their mothers thought it was the only route, and that was what she was dealing with. A madman and his mother.

"How do ye plan to kill him?" she asked quietly, trying to sort out how much time she had to escape and warn Conall.

"Soon as he gets here, and that should be soon," Hamish muttered, straightening suddenly. "I had mother spill the mead on ye so ye'd go up to change, and I put nightshade in Stubborn Bastard's stall so he'd have to seek ye out to talk to ye about—"

"Ye poisoned Stubborn Bastard?" she interrupted with alarm.

"Nay," he snapped with irritation at the interruption, and then grimaced and said, "Well, mayhap." Scowling he said, "All I did was put the nightshade in his stall. If the stupid beast ate it, there's naught I can do about it. Besides, 'twas necessary," he assured her. "I needed to get yer husband alone, and the only way I could think to get him away from Roderick and Payton was to have him follow the path yer bleedin' wound made when I carried ye out through the secret passage. That's why I had to hit ye so hard. 'Twas part o' me plan. Ye needed to bleed freely so he'd ha'e a trail to follow. I'm sure he'd no' want the others kennin' about the secret passage. He'll usher them out o' the room and come after ye alone. Then I can kill him, we can marry and all will be well."

Claray felt her heart sink as he described his plan. Mostly, because she was very much afraid it might work. Conall probably wouldn't want anyone else to know about the secret passage. He hadn't even told her about it and she was his wife. Which meant he probably would follow the trail of blood alone. That in itself wouldn't worry her too much, but he trusted Hamish and, seeing him here, Conall's first thought might be that he'd got here first to rescue her just as she'd first thought. It might make him slow to realize the situation and give Hamish just a few seconds' advantage. That might be enough to get him killed, Claray realized. She really didn't want Conall killed.

WHEN THE WOLF STOPPED SUDDENLY, CONALL WAS AT FIRST afraid that he'd lost the scent. But when he moved up beside Lovey and saw the ramshackle old cottage in the clearing they stood on the edge of, his heart started to pound. He knew instinctively that this was where Claray was.

Reaching down, Conall put a hand on the wolf to be sure Lovey didn't charge forward and give away their position, then glanced down with surprise when he felt Squeak's little claws moving up his hand. The wee stoat was scrambling up his arm to his shoulder. Leaving him there, he murmured, "Stay," to Lovey, and started into the clearing.

He was perhaps ten feet away when he heard voices coming from inside. Although *inside* was a relative term when it came to the building. There was no roof or door, and the stones on one of the two walls he could see from where he stood were missing from about two-thirds of the way up. That's where Conall went, easing up to the shortened wall to peer over it.

"Why?" he heard Claray ask, though he couldn't see her. All he could see was the back of a man's head and shoulders, and the half wall opposite the one he stood outside of. While this one was missing its top one-third, the opposite wall was half gone from the looks of it. If the man weren't facing it, he would have considered walking around and creeping in that way to take him by surprise.

"Hamish?" Claray said grimly when he didn't answer her question. "Why?"

Conall's gaze sharpened on the back of the man. He hadn't recognized him until his wife spoke the man's name. Now his gaze narrowed on his first with confusion as he tried to sort out why he was here with Claray. He didn't have to wait long for his answer.

"I told ye why. To save ye from eternal damnation," Hamish answered simply.

"Aye, but Conall—"

"Bryson," Hamish corrected. "He's Bryson MacDonald, and while I always just assumed me mother was mad when she ranted on about his parents' behavior, now that I've seen how he treats ye, I begin to see her point. It's no' right, Claray."

"But he trusts ye, Hamish. He told me so himself. He said ye'd been his first fer a good five years. How can ye just—?"

"And I trusted him," Hamish interrupted. "But he lied to me all these years, lettin' me think his name was Conall. He lied to ye too," he added solemnly. "Lettin' ye think he was dead and ye'd never marry. Seein' how he's treated ye since the weddin', it might ha'e been kinder if that had been the case," he added grimly.

There was a moment of silence and then Claray said defiantly, "Well, I'll no' marry ye. So, I guess ye'll have to kill me too."

"O' course ye'll marry me," Hamish said with a certainty that was either the most condescending thing Conall had ever heard, or the most arrogant. "'Tis the easiest way fer me to claim Deagh Fhortan and the position o' clan chief without a lot o' bother."

Claray issued a snort of disgust. "So, there's the truth. Yer just like MacNaughton, wantin' to marry me to gain property and power. Only, while he wants MacFarlane, ye want to rule MacDonald and claim Deagh Fhortan."

"Aye, and why no'? Me father was the younger brother o' Conall's father. I'm the next in line once he's dead."

Conall stiffened in shock at that. The only sibling his father'd had was a bastard half brother who had died along with everyone else during the poisoning. His uncle had told him that. He'd also told him that the man's wife had been Conall's own caretaker for a short while after marrying him. She'd been in charge o' seeing he was bathed, dressed and fed, and had kept an eye on him when his parents were busy or away. Conall didn't remember either of them, the half brother or his wife. Those memories had left him after that night, and were among a few that hadn't yet returned. But while his uncle had told him that the woman had got him away from Deagh Fhortan after the murders and brought him to MacKay, he hadn't mentioned her having a son. However, if Hamish was the son of his bastard uncle, Conall supposed the man might have a claim to Deagh Fhortan if he himself were dead.

Claray's clucking with irritation drew his attention back to the conversation taking place in the small, crumbling cottage.

"Wonderful. Here I thought ye as mad as yer mother, and turns out yer just greedy," she said with disgust. "And 'tis that greed that'll see ye found out. Do ye kill us and try to claim Deagh Fhortan as yer own, ye're the first one they'll suspect, because ye'll be the only one to benefit," Claray pointed out. "Conall's uncle Ross'll figure it out and see ye dead."

"I told ye, I'll no' kill ye. Just him. I'm marryin' you," Hamish muttered.

"And I told ye I'll no marry ye," she responded tartly, and then warned, "If ye kill Conall as ye plan, and then drag me before a priest, I'll refuse. And then I'll tell one and all that ye murdered me husband. I'll see ye hang fer it."

Cursing under his breath at her foolish bravery in threatening the man like that, Conall moved around the building, a frown curving his lips when he saw Lovey creeping around the back corner of the cottage. Wondering what he was up to, Conall quietly unsheathed his sword and stepped into the hole that had once been a doorway.

Hamish had been standing with his side to the doorway when Conall had started around the building. He'd expected him to be there still, but instead he'd moved. Hamish was standing behind Claray, who was tied to a chair. He was leaning over her and peering down the top of her gown even as he pressed his sgian dubh to her throat.

"Ye might want to rethink that, lass," he growled.

"Why?" Claray asked with a complete lack of fear. "Because ye'll kill me? I'd rather be dead than ha'e ye fer a husband, Hamish. Call me a sinner all ye like, but I love me husband's lovin', just as I love him. Ye're nothin' to me but a hedge-born cumberworld."

"Why ye dirty puterelle," Hamish snarled, grabbing her by the hair and yanking her head back, the knife digging into her throat so that blood began to drip over the edge and run down her neck. "I'll—"

"Ye'll release me wife," Conall growled, stepping further into the room.

Hamish's head came up, and Claray tried to raise her head too, to look at him, but stopped as the knife sank deeper into her flesh.

"Well, if 'tisn't Bryson MacDonald," Hamish said bitterly, releasing Claray's hair to switch the sgian dubh from his right hand to his left, but keeping it at her throat. He then withdrew his own sword. Now armed with two weapons, he said, "Drop yer sword or I'll slice her throat open right now."

Conall didn't even hesitate, he dropped the sword at once. He even held up his hands to show him they were empty before propping them on his hips, placing his right hand close to his own sgian dubh. "Let her go, Hamish. 'Tis me ye want. Claray has naught to do with this."

"Oh, aye, she does. She'll either marry me or die," Hamish assured him as he released Claray and walked around her toward him. "Mayhap after I kill ye, I'll swive her a time or two. She seems to like japin', and I'm told I'm good at it, so I might yet convince her."

Claray snorted at the claim. "No' if what the lasses say is true. They say ye've a prick like a string bean and can no' get it hard without hurtin' a lass first. Pathetic," she pronounced.

Hamish struck out at her so quickly he took them both by surprise. Or perhaps he was the only one, Conall thought grimly when Claray took the blow with equanimity, simply turning her head slowly back from where his blow had turned it to the side. She licked away the blood that ran from the corner of her split lip before asking dryly, "Did that excite ye?"

Conall saw Hamish's hand tighten around the sgian dubh, knew he was going to hit her again, and couldn't bear it. He started forward, only to pause when Hamish whirled back and raised his sword, poking him in the stomach with it.

"I was plannin' on killin' ye quickly as a kindness fer setting Deagh Fhortan to rights fer me," Hamish growled. "But now I'm thinkin' I'd rather kill ye slowly. Mayhap I'll even leave ye alive long enough to watch me rape yer woman before I finish ye both off. That," he added grimly, turning to glower at Claray, "would excite me, I think."

Conall started reaching for his sgian dubh the minute the man turned his head. His fingers had just closed around it when Squeak suddenly launched himself off of his shoulder and leapt the few feet to the other man. He landed in the center of his face, slid down and clamped his sharp little teeth down on Hamish's lip to catch himself, or perhaps just because the man had hit his Claray.

Whatever the case, Hamish roared in pain and instinctively dropped his sword to reach for the wee stoat, to pull it off.

Conall quickly bent to snatch up his own sword and then thrust it into the man as he brought it back up. Much to his relief, Hamish's hand squeezed into a fist inches from Squeak, leaving him unharmed as his eyes, widening with confusion, found Conall. It looked as if he was bewildered as to how he'd ended up getting stabbed when only a moment ago he'd held all the cards. Then he dropped to his knees.

"Squeak," Claray cried with alarm, and the wee stoat reacted at once, launching himself sideways into Claray's lap just before Hamish fell forward, flat on his face.

Chapter 27

CLARAY GLANCED FROM SQUEAK TO CONALL AS HER HUSBAND kicked aside Hamish's weapons and bent to roll him over. She grimaced when she saw the man's wound. Conall had jabbed the sword in from below, driving it up under his ribs, and probably piercing his heart. But when the man had dropped to his knees, the sword had still been inside him and still held by Conall. It had ripped up through his chest before it was pulled out. If the sword hadn't pierced his heart with the first blow, the gaping chest wound he'd ended up with would have killed him.

Straightening, Conall moved to her now.

"Are ye all right, love?" he asked, kneeling before her to begin untying her legs.

"Aye," she breathed, managing a smile.

"Yer bleeding," he growled, his gaze sliding up to her neck and then back to the ropes he was trying to undo. Finally, he gave up trying to untie her and simply sliced through the ropes around one leg with his sgian dubh.

"'Tis fine," Claray assured him when he didn't immediately move to the other leg to remove the rope there, but reached up to tip her head back instead so that he could look at her neck.

"Ye'll ha'e a scar to remember this day," Conall growled as he examined the wound. Scowling, he met her gaze and added, "Ye ne'er should ha'e angered him. What if he'd killed ye outright? I could no' live without ye, lass. I love ye."

Claray's eyes widened, tears springing to film them at the claim, and then movement behind him caught her eye. Shifting her gaze past her husband, she saw with horror that Mhairi had regained consciousness. She was now rushing at them with her sgian dubh in hand and raised, ready to plunge it into Conall's back. Claray had barely opened her mouth to scream a warning when she heard a growl from behind her and a gray streak flew overhead, crashing into the woman.

"Lovey!" she cried with concern as Mhairi struck out at the wolf with the knife, just before his teeth closed on her throat and they both crashed to the ground.

Conall was moving at once to help the beast, his body blocking her view as he knelt over the pair.

"Is he all right?" she asked anxiously.

Conall didn't answer, except for a curse as he quickly began to cut a strip of plaid off of his great kilt. That was answer enough, and Claray immediately started tugging at her arms, but they were still bound tight to the chair. His freeing one leg had done nothing for her arms.

Cursing now herself, she glanced to Conall and asked, "How badly is he hurt?"

Conall finished what he'd been doing, which turned out to be his binding the wound on Lovey's side, she saw as he now turned quickly to help her.

Claray's gaze slid over the wolf and woman as her husband began to cut her free of the chair. Mhairi was alive, but not for long judging by the gurgling sound that was emitting from her every time she breathed. Lovey had torn her throat open, and blood was pouring from the wound, she noted, but her only concern was Lovey. The wolf was lying on his side, panting shallowly, the plaid around his chest already darkening with blood.

Conall cut the last of the ropes away from her and tried to examine her neck, but she pushed his hands away and lunged out of the chair to go to Lovey. But there was nothing she could do there without her medicinals.

"We need to get him back to the keep," Claray said anxiously, running a soothing hand down the wolf's back.

"I need to bind yer neck first, love," Conall said grimly.

"When we get back," Claray said impatiently, and tried to scoop up the wolf into her arms.

Cursing, Conall pressed a second strip of plaid into her hands that he'd apparently cut from his great kilt and then urged her out of the way. Bending to pick up up Lovey, he ordered, "Bind yer neck. Yer losin' a lot of blood."

Claray peered down, surprised to see that there was a great deal of blood soaking into the top of her pale-yellow gown. She hadn't realized that Hamish had cut her so deeply. Frowning, she quickly wrapped the plaid around her throat and tied it off as tightly as she could without choking herself, and then followed when Conall started out of the hovel. But she glanced back nervously at the door.

"Mayhap we should make sure Mhairi is dead first," she muttered, hesitating to leave.

Conall paused and turned back, his gaze sliding to the unmoving woman. "Why was she here? What had she to do with this?"

"She's Hamish's mother," Claray breathed, feeling suddenly weary. "She's the one who poisoned yer parents and the rest o' the clan when ye were a boy. She was mad and thought she was carrying out God's will."

Claray turned back to her husband to see myriad emotions cross his face before it settled into a cold mask. He shifted and for a minute she thought he might go back and finish the woman, but then his gaze dropped to the plaid around her throat, and he turned away. "I'll send men out fer them when we get back. We need to get ye to the keep so I can tend yer wound."

Claray followed him out of the cottage without protest. She would have felt better making sure the woman was dead, but Lovey needed tending. She wouldn't risk his dying because she'd delayed. Besides, she was beginning to feel a bit woozy. Blood loss, she knew. She didn't think her neck was bleeding badly enough to cause it. But it wasn't the first wound she'd taken that day and her head wound had bled freely.

Taking deep breaths to try to clear the fog starting to descend on her thoughts, Claray concentrated on placing her feet one before the other and little else until her husband suddenly called out next to her, his shout startling her.

Lifting her head, Claray saw that they had come out of the woods and were walking along the edge of the moat. It was the warriors on the wall her husband had called out to. Now men were shouting back and there was a lot of rushing about on the wall. Riders would be sent out to get them she knew, and murmured, "Thank goodness," before losing consciousness.

CLARAY WOKE WITH A POUNDING HEADACHE. GRIMACING, SHE opened her eyes and then closed them again when the pounding immediately increased. They'd been open long enough, though, for her to see the fur spread over her and recognize that she was in the bedchamber she shared with her husband. Safe, tucked up in bed. That was enough to know for now.

"Here, love. Drink."

Claray recognized Conall's voice and opened her eyes again as his arm snaked under her shoulders so that he could lift her up and press a drink to her lips. She drank dutifully, finding that once she'd started, she didn't want to stop. She was terribly thirsty. But Conall only let her sip a bit of the cool water, before pulling the drink away.

"Let it settle fer a minute, love, and we'll try some more," he said before she could protest, and when Claray relaxed, asked, "How are yer head and yer throat?"

"Me head's pounding, and me throat's a little tender," she admitted in a whisper.

"Aye. Allistair said as that was probably how 'twould be. Between yer head wound and yer throat, ye lost a lot o' blood. It looked like there was more on yer gown than could be left in yer body."

Claray grimaced at the claim, and then gulped down more water when he tipped the mug to her lips again. But this time when he took it away, she swallowed and asked, "Allistair tended me?"

"Aye. Ye and both yer wolf and Stubborn Bastard too," Conall told her, and the words had her eyes widening with remembered alarm.

"Are they—?"

"Both are fine. Stubborn Bastard is recovering nicely in his stall, and yer wolf is right beside ye," he pointed out with amusement.

Claray glanced to her other side to see Lovey tucked up under the furs next to her. She blinked at the sight, and then narrowed her eyes when Lovey opened one of his and eyed her briefly before closing it again. Her gaze slid to Squeak, curled up asleep on the pillow next to her, and then she looked to her husband. He'd let the wolf lay on top of the furs on the bed a time or two while she was recovering from the arrow wound, but once she'd started feeling better, he'd insisted the beast sleep on a rush mat next to the bed. Now apparently, he was not only allowed on it, but in it.

"He saved us both and took a ferocious wound doing so," Conall said quietly. "Allistair was afraid we'd lose him. But once he'd pulled through the night, he decided he'd be all right. He deserves the bed."

The words made her beam at him, and Claray blurted, "I love ye, husband."

The words just slipped out. She hadn't planned on saying them, but they were true for all that, and much to her relief, Conall pressed a kiss to her forehead and then pulled back to meet her gaze and said, "I love ye too, wife."

Claray was just relaxing, her smile widening, when he added, "But do ye ever taunt a madman with a knife to yer throat again, I swear I'll take ye over me knee and paddle ye till ye can no' sit fer a week."

Scowling, Claray tried to turn her head away, but he caught her face and added grimly, "I thought I'd die when he was sawin' at yer throat. I could no' bear it again."

Claray felt guilty then, but told him, "I did no' realize he'd cut so deep. It did no' hurt."

"Yer blood was up," he said with understanding. "I've suffered many a wound in battle that did no' hurt right away. But that just means ye ha'e to be even more cautious."

Claray nodded, but—reminded of Hamish and his mother—now asked, "Did ye send the men to collect them? Were they still there?"

"Aye," he said on a sigh, and then shook his head. "I did no' recognize her as me nursemaid."

"It has been twenty-two years," she pointed out gently. "She was only fourteen when ye last saw her, barely more than a child."

"A child who killed more people in one sitting than I ha'e in all me years in battle," he said bitterly, and then asked, "Did she say how she poisoned them?"

"It was in the wine and ale as yer uncle suspected," Claray admitted.

Conall nodded. "And she thought she was carrying out God's will, ye said?"

Claray hesitated, and then sighed and explained, "She was very confused. The church says we should no' enjoy the beddin', that only sinners do. Yet her husband, much like yerself, apparently troubled himself to be sure she did enjoy it. I fear it plagued her and made her fear fer her soul. And then, I gather she witnessed yer parents . . . er . . . enjoyin' themselves by the pond," she said delicately, and then rushed on, "And others around the keep as well, and felt sure the only way to redeem herself fer her own enjoyment o' it, was to . . ."

"Kill 'em all," Conall said dryly when she paused to search for a way to say it.

"Aye," she breathed regretfully.

Conall was silent for a minute, and then asked, "Are you troubled by me making ye enjoy it?"

Claray flushed, but admitted honestly, "I was at first. But I've resigned meself to it."

"Resigned yerself?" he asked with concern. "Should I stop—?"

"Nay!" Claray interrupted quickly, and then scowled. "Do no' you dare stop. I love the pleasure ye give me, and if 'tis wrong, then I'll happily serve me time in hell fer it."

"Ye will, will ye?" he asked with a faint smile.

Claray nodded, and then added, "But I do no' think the church is right about this. I love ye, and the loving is an expression of that. 'Tis beautiful and precious." Pausing, she smiled slightly, and added, "Besides, ye ordered me to enjoy it, and Father Cameron did make me vow to obey ye. I can hardly be punished fer keeping vows the church made me make."

The concern easing from his face, Conall chuckled and hugged her close. "I do love ye, Claray. Yer beautiful, and clever, and sure to drive me mad and scare me witless at times. But I'd have it no other way."

"Neither would I, husband," Claray murmured, hugging him back. "Neither would I."

Read on for a sneak peek at

Immortal Rising

Coming Summer 2022

Chapter 1

"How many?"

That question from Lucian Argeneau made Stephanie open her eyes. She'd closed them to concentrate on the many voices sounding in her head, but now glanced around at Lucian and the group of rogue hunters awaiting her answer. It was predawn on a warm fall evening, the sun sending streaks of orange and vermillion out to pierce the night sky ahead of its arrival. But it was still pitch black in the copse of maples they stood in. Even so, she didn't have trouble making out the twelve people ranged around her, or the overgrown yard of the somewhat rundown seventies-style bungalow on the other side of the trees.

The benefits of night vision, Stephanie thought grimly, and ground her teeth as she tried to block the flow of thoughts and memories pouring through her head from the men and women around her, as well as the people in the house, and pretty much everyone else within a mile radius of her. Not that she was sure it was a mile. It could be that she was picking up the thoughts and memories of people as far away as two or ten miles for all she knew . . . So many voices in her head.

"Stephanie? How many?" Lucian repeated, sounding impatient now.

"There are thirty-two rogues in the house," she responded calmly, unconcerned by the grumpy man's irritation. "And one more somewhere behind the house."

"Behind it like in the backyard?" Mirabeau asked, moving closer to her side.

Stephanie glanced at the tall woman with fuchsia-tipped hair, and shook her head. "Farther away. Past the woods behind the backyard."

"Probably just a neighbor on the next street then," Lucian said dismissively, and turned away to begin giving his orders to the others.

Stephanie scowled at his back, but waited until he finished with his orders before saying, "I don't think it's just a neighbor, Lucian. The feeling I get is the person is—"

"Your feelings do not matter. Whoever it is, is not someone we need worry about now," Lucian interrupted. "We will check it out after we take care of this nest."

"But—" Stephanie began in protest, only for him to cut her off again.

"Stay here until we clear the house."

Stephanie turned to where Mirabeau had been a moment ago, intending to enlist her aid in getting Lucian to listen, but the other woman was gone. She'd already melted into the dark trees to head around the property to the spot where she was to take up position before the group closed in on the house.

All of them were now gone, Stephanie realized as she turned back to where Lucian had been, only to find empty space. She was alone in the woods.

Stephanie threw her hands up with an exasperated huff and then lodged her fists on her hips and surveyed the situation. Despite the darkness and trees, she could make out several different hunters moving through the woods around the house, finding their spots. After having worked with them for several years, she knew the routine. They'd basically surround the property, and then approach at a signal from Lucian, closing in like a net drawn tight around the house. Each person had their orders. Some would guard windows or sliding doors while others would charge through the back and front doors, the idea being that no one inside should evade capture once the house was breached.

Stephanie watched the group maneuver, but her mind was elsewhere. She could hear that other voice from beyond the woods behind the house. The owner was responding to a beeping sound, going into a small room to check—

"Cameras!" Stephanie barked the warning as the thought entered her mind, and then scanned the front of the house for the security cameras. She couldn't see them, but knew they were there. Fortunately, either Lucian could see them or he was just trusting her, because he immediately barked an order and the slow approach was abandoned in favor of a much swifter one.

Stephanie watched as Lucian led the rogue hunters Decker and Bricker through the front door. There was no sudden shrieking or sounds of chaos. The rogues in the house were all either already asleep or settling down to sleep at this hour. It was why the hunters struck at dawn, so that they could catch the whole nest and not miss any inhabitants who might be out and about during the evening.

It was also always easier to take them by surprise, Stephanie thought, and then closed her eyes and focused on that lone voice again. She'd known about the cameras because this person had been checking them and had seen the hunters closing in on the house. He wasn't just a neighbor. He was connected somehow to this house. She'd gotten that feeling earlier, but hadn't been sure how exactly he was connected to it and the people inside. Now she tried to sort through the person's thoughts for an answer.

Stephanie sifted through the multitude of voices in her head until she zeroed in on the one she wanted again. The individual was in something of a controlled panic now, if there even was such a thing. His thoughts were urgent, but he had planned for this raid, knew exactly what he had to do, and was doing it. He was gathering the things important to him and preparing to flee the area. He'd have to set up somewhere else. It was inconvenient, but not unexpected. It was always best to know your enemies, and he had plans in place. There were—

"Bombs!" Stephanie shrieked, her eyes shooting open as she began to move. Running for the house, she yelled, "Bombs! Get out! Get out! Get out!"

She spotted Mirabeau at one of the side windows, with Tiny at the next one over, and felt a moment's relief as they, along with the others who had remained outside, began to back warily away from the house. But only a moment's worth. Three men had entered through the front door, and three men had no doubt entered the back as well. More importantly, Decker—her brother-in-law—was one of those men at the front. If anything happened to him, her sister, Dani, would—

A relieved sob slipped from her lips when she saw Decker coming back out through the front door with Bricker on his heels. Her brother-in-law was looking toward her with a combination of confusion and question. Obviously, they'd heard her shouted warning from inside the house, but weren't sure what to make of it.

Stephanie opened her mouth to tell him and everyone else that the house was about to explode, but the words never left her lips. Like lightning before thunder, the blast hit her first. Stephanie experienced a jolting sensation like nothing she'd heretofore known. She imagined it was similar to how it would feel to be hit by a freight train.

Since it was the blast wind that picked her up and threw her backward, the fact that there was suddenly no oxygen for her lungs was a bit confusing. Stephanie had no time to ponder that, and was sailing through the air before her ears picked up the boom of the explosion.

She landed hard on her back in the overgrown grass, and found herself briefly staring up at the brightening sky before she could find the wherewithal to move. But then Stephanie gathered herself enough to stumble to her feet again. She was vaguely aware that she was swaying as she scanned what she could see of the yard and the people in it. Most of the hunters in her view seemed only mildly injured. There were a few moans and cries of pain from those who had suffered broken bones, or head wounds, but more were on their feet and checking the injured than were down.

Mirabeau and Tiny were among those up and about, helping the others. Decker, she saw, was crouched over Lucian. Obviously, the head of the North American council and unofficial leader of the rogue hunters hadn't got out of the house before the explosion, but she presumed he'd been close enough to the door to be tossed out by the blast. Judging by the smoke wafting off him, he'd also caught fire, if only briefly, which suggested the bombs had been incendiary in nature.

Stephanie waited until she saw Lucian move before turning her gaze toward the woods in back of the house again. This time she didn't have to work hard to hear the thoughts of the lone man. He was a calm mind amid the pained and upset hunters in the yard, and the chaos and agony of the panicked rogues trapped in the now-burning house. He was glued to the camera monitors, his focus now on her as he wondered how she had known there were bombs.

Her brain not yet firing on all cylinders after the shaking it had taken, Stephanie burst into a run toward the back of the property. Her only thought was to catch the bastard before he made his escape.

The woods behind the house were much deeper than those at the front, but there was something of a path through it. Just a dirt trail wide enough for a person to slip through the densely growing trees. Stephanie took it at a dead run, using all the speed her body could give her. It made the trip much faster than it would have been for a mortal, so fast that she was caught a little by surprise when she suddenly burst out of the woods into a clearing around a second house.

This yard was no better kept than the other. What had probably been a beautifully manicured lawn at one time was now overgrown with waist-high grass and weeds. Stephanie slowed as she approached, her gaze sliding over the light shining from the windows of the dilapidated old Victorian two-story house as she neared the dark wood door. It was solid, without a window to see inside. She was reaching for the door handle when the chaotic thoughts from the scene she'd just left faded enough for her to catch the thoughts of the man inside. He knew she was there. He was waiting.

Stephanie released the handle and retreated a couple steps as she reached around her back for the gun tucked into the waistband of her jeans. It was loaded with darts full of a drug that had been developed specifically for rogue hunters to use. It was the only thing that could take down a rogue immortal with any certainty.

"Steph?"

She jerked around in surprise to see Mirabeau sprinting out of the woods and hurrying toward her. The fact that she'd left the scene of the explosion rather than staying to help with the wounded had obviously not gone unnoticed. Neither was the fact that she now had her gun out. Mirabeau's expression was both surprised and concerned as she focused on the weapon. Which was completely understandable, Stephanie supposed. She usually left the actual capturing of rogues to the others. Her presence at these hunts was generally to tell them how many rogues they had to deal with and where they were. She also helped with the questioning after, pulling the answers Lucian was looking for from the captured rogues' minds like plucking cat hair off a sweater. But, despite her years of training alongside the hunters, she was always kept back from the actual takedowns.

"What—?" Mirabeau was halfway across the overgrown yard when she began to ask her question. The one word was all the woman managed to get out though before her gaze suddenly shifted past her. Mirabeau's eyes went wide with alarm a heartbeat before she suddenly stumbled and fell.

Stephanie instinctively started to move toward the other woman, but then just as quickly whirled back to the house. The door was now open, and a man stood in the doorway, tall, blond and attractive. He had a gun aimed at her, and even as she recognized it as one the hunters used, one like the one she was holding, he pulled the trigger. She felt a sharp pain in her chest, and glanced down at the dart piercing the edge of her left breast just over her heart, then she too fell as a warm wave rushed through her and every muscle in her body suddenly abandoned her. Stephanie didn't lose consciousness though, nor feeling, and would have winced if she could have as she slammed to the ground and her head bounced off the hard-packed dirt path.

She came to rest on her side with her eyes closed, but her mind still functioning. Stephanie heard movement and tried to open her eyes, but didn't seem to be able to manage that. All she could do was listen to the sounds he made as he approached. He must have squatted next to her, or bent over to reach her, but whatever the case, she felt his hand on her shoulder and then was turned onto her back.

"You knew about the bombs. How did you know about the bombs?" her attacker muttered as he took the gun from her lax fingers and then tugged at her clothing, no doubt to check for any more weapons. "And how did you know there was a house back here? Or that I was in it?"

Stephanie didn't even bother to try to answer. Not that she thought he expected her to. She suspected he was muttering to himself, and might not know she was even conscious. She shouldn't be, and wasn't exactly sure why she was. Like the gun he held, the dart had been easily recognizable as rogue hunter paraphernalia. That dart should have knocked her out. Yet she hadn't lost consciousness and could feel a tingling in her fingers and toes that suggested the drug was already wearing off. This was unexpected.

"Steph."

She was so startled that he'd used her name that her eyes shot open, and for a moment Stephanie was sufficiently distracted by the fact that they actually would open, that she forgot what he'd said.

"That's what she called you, Steph."

Stephanie peered at him to see that he was looking off toward Mirabeau and not at her. Even as she noted that, he turned his gaze back to her. His eyes immediately widened when he saw hers were open.

"You shouldn't be awake," he said, sounding nonplussed. "The dose in that dart would have knocked an immortal out cold for at least twenty minutes."

Stephanie wanted to tell him to go to hell, but unlike her eyes, her mouth still wasn't working. She wasn't able to move her jaws, and her tongue was a useless thing in her mouth. Then he was suddenly leaning over her, his fingers forcing their way inside her mouth and pressing on her palate behind her canine teeth. Disgusted and furious, Stephanie tried to bite him then, but her mouth still wouldn't work.

"You have metallic tinted eyes like immortals, but no fangs," he muttered, retracting his fingers and eyeing her with fascination. "And if the drug from the dart is wearing off this quickly, you obviously have a stronger constitution than immortals. What are you?"

Unable to punch him in the face or claw his eyes out as she would have liked to do, Stephanie just glared back at him.

"This is fascinating. Perhaps I should take you with me," he murmured thoughtfully, and glanced toward the open door to the house behind him as if considering the logistics of doing so.

"Beau? Steph?"

Stephanie instinctively tried to turn her head toward that shout in the distance, but unlike her eyelids, her neck muscles didn't suddenly start working and she was unable to.

"Damn," her attacker muttered with what sounded like frustration.

Shifting her gaze back to him, she saw him look briefly toward the woods and scowl in the direction the shout had come from. He then shook his head and stood. "It looks like I'll have to leave you behind. But I sincerely hope we meet again, Steph whoever-you-are. I should like to get you on my table and find out what makes you tick."

A cold smile of relish crossed his face at the thought, and then he turned and moved unhurriedly into the house and closed the door.

Stephanie stared at the oak panel, almost afraid it might open again and he'd return for her after all. While her first response to this man had been fury and disgust, the emptiness in his eyes and that smile of his as he'd announced his desire to get her "on his table and find out what made her tick" had wiped out both emotions and sent an icy flood of fear through her veins. She was more than relieved to hear a curse sound much closer just before Tiny raced into view as he rushed to Mirabeau's prone body.

"What the hell happened to them?"

Stephanie recognized Decker's voice before she saw him speeding toward her.

"Steph? What happened?" Decker repeated when he dropped to his knees at her side and saw that her eyes were open. Apparently, finding her lack of response alarming, he reached toward her and then hesitated. She read the worry in his mind that he had no idea what her injuries were and didn't wish to aggravate them or hurt her.

"Mirabeau has a dart in her neck," Tiny growled, sounding seriously pissed.

"A dart?" Decker glanced toward the other man with amazement. "What kind of dart?"

"One of ours from the looks of it," the big man said grimly, and she saw him pluck the dart from Mirabeau's neck and examine it briefly before tossing it aside. Tiny peered down at his life mate briefly, and then looked toward her and Decker. "Steph must have been shot too, look for the dart."

Decker turned back to Stephanie and she saw his eyes travel over her body before shifting to the ground around her. When he suddenly cursed and reached for something in the grass beside her, she knew it must be the dart before he picked it up to examine it more closely, moving it into her view. It must have been dislodged from her chest when she'd fallen, she thought.

"Damn. It is one of ours," Decker growled before slipping it into his pocket. He cast a quick, wary gaze toward the house, scanning the windows and door and then turned his attention back to Stephanie. His expression was troubled as his gaze narrowed on her open eyes again and she didn't have to be a mind reader to know he was concerned as to why they were open, and what that meant.

"Her eyes are open!"

Stephanie shifted her gaze over Decker's shoulder at that surprised exclamation to see that Tiny had scooped up Mirabeau and carried her over to join them.

"Yeah," Decker said unhappily. "But she can't seem to move or speak."

"The effects of the dart must be wearing off then," Tiny said, sounding relieved as he peered down at Mirabeau, limp in his arms. "That means Beau should wake up soon too."

Decker grunted what sounded like agreement, but the way he was looking at her made Stephanie think he didn't really believe that. But then she could hardly blame him. She doubted more than five or six minutes had passed since she'd been shot and it certainly hadn't been twenty minutes since the explosion and her racing back here. With his life mate unconscious in his arms, Tiny was too upset to have taken note of that. However, she wasn't Decker's life mate, so his upset wasn't as extreme as Tiny's. Oh, she could hear his thoughts and knew he was worried about her. Even if she hadn't been able to hear his thoughts, she would have known he was worried about her. While Decker was legally her brother-in-law, in truth he'd become much more than that over the last nearly thirteen years since he'd rescued her and Dani from Leonius Livius, the no-fanger rogue who had turned them. Decker had become like a real brother to her, as well as a friend, and even a father figure at times. But that wasn't the same as a life mate, and Decker was still able to think much more clearly than Tiny at the moment.

"Take Beau back to the vehicles and send as many hunters as are able to help search the house," Decker said suddenly.

Tiny hesitated, his worried gaze sliding to the house. "I don't like the idea of leaving you alone here when there's someone running around with a dart gun. Besides, wouldn't it be smarter to check out the house right away? What if whoever shot Stephanie and Beau gets away before we can search the house?"

"What if whoever shot the girls gives us the slip and comes out and beheads the women while we're searching the house? Or what if they shoot us and behead all of us before anyone thinks to follow?" Decker countered, standing up now and turning to face the house, his gun at the ready. "Go. Quickly. I'll guard Stephanie and watch the house until help arrives."

Tiny didn't bother to respond to that. Decker's pointing out that they could all be shot and beheaded was enough to have the man moving at once. Stephanie watched him go until he was out of her line of vision, and then shifted her gaze to Decker. The tingling in her extremities had been moving inward as the minutes passed. From her fingers to her hands and wrists and beyond, and from her toes to her feet, ankles and calves. Her jaw was also now tingling, as was the tip of her tongue. Stephanie tried to move her fingers, and this time was able to do it. The same was true of her toes. She couldn't talk yet, though, but should soon be able to.

"Can you blink?"

Stephanie shifted her gaze back to Decker and then closed and opened her eyes.

The sight made him nod grimly, but he cast another wary glance toward the house before looking at her again and asking, "Did you see who shot you? Blink once for yes, twice for no."

Stephanie blinked once.

"Was it a hunter?" he asked next.

She wasn't surprised by the question. She and Mirabeau had been shot with hunter darts, and the man had used a hunter's gun. It wasn't surprising Decker would worry they had a rogue who was also a hunter. Stephanie also wasn't surprised by his relief when she blinked twice to tell him that wasn't the case. But his relief was short lived as he then began to worry about how the rogue had got their hands on a hunter's weapon. While she read that in his thoughts, he didn't bring it up, but instead asked, "Did you recognize the person who shot you?"

Stephanie hesitated. She hadn't recognized the man, but his thoughts had told her who he was. She couldn't convey that with a yes or no, though.

"Is there more than one?" Decker asked when she was slow to answer. He barely waited for her to blink twice before shifting his gaze back to the house for another wary look. It made her wish she could tell him there was no need for him to keep checking the house. The man was gone. His thoughts were getting fainter in her head as he moved away from the vicinity. He was on foot, taking a trail through the woods on the other side of this house to somewhere where a vehicle waited, stashed there for just such an event.

"So, one person," Decker murmured and then glanced down at her again to ask, "Male or female?"

That made her raise her eyebrows, which caught her by surprise. The drug was wearing off quickly if she could raise her eyebrows. She was pretty sure she hadn't been able to do that when he'd first got here.

Realizing the mistake he'd made, and that she couldn't answer his question with a yes or no, Decker asked instead, "Male?"

Stephanie blinked once for yes, but a lot of her concentration was on her mouth now. Her tongue was tingling like crazy, like she'd had novocaine and it was wearing off. Most of her jaw and face were tingling madly now too. She tried moving her tongue in her mouth and was surprised to find she could. Stephanie tried her jaw next and was relieved to find she was able to move that too.

Decker had turned to look at the house again, but now peered back at her to ask, "Did this guy—"

"Dressler," Stephanie managed to spit out, although the word was somewhat garbled and with little air behind it.

Apparently able to understand her despite that, Decker was staring at her with horror when the sounds of people crashing through the woods sounded. The other hunters were coming. Too bad they were too late.